THE BENTEEN CHRONICLES, VOLUME ONE

RISING LION ASCENDING MOON

A Novel

NEAL ARMSTRONG

HEART & LIFE
PUBLISHERS

Rising Lion, Ascending Moon

©2025 Neal Armstrong

All rights reserved. No part of this book may be reproduced or used in any manner without the prior written permission of the copyright owner, except for the use of brief quotations in a book review.

Edited by Sam Severn
Proofreader: Donna Huisjen
Cover art by Frank Gutbrod
Layout by Robert Dolsen
Interior graphics by Neal Armstrong
Author Photograph by Jackie Armstrong
Published by Kevin Miles
Audiobook Production: Domesticated Man Studio Productions, LLC

Paperback ISBN: 9798218640309
Ebook ISBN: 9798218640316
Library of Congress Number: 2025905311

HEART & LIFE
PUBLISHERS

Grand Rapids, Michigan

Acknowledgments

What a minefield are the processes of acknowledgments. People and forces deserve their due, but the danger is that some are inadvertently missed. I will attempt my best recollections.

I am deeply indebted to *An Indian Winter* by Russel Freedman to accurately inform my rendering of Mandan life on the Upper Missouri in the late 1820s. This book made me feel as if I were there, and I tried to create that same feeling for the reader. I also absorbed much practical knowledge of the period from books like Stanley Vestal's *Jim Bridger: Mountain Man* and a multitude of searches online for historical data—more than I care to count. This fascination with the bold and courageous has followed me for decades and informed this story with at least some modicum of historical accuracy.

I am also forever grateful to those long souls who listened or read my early manuscripts. They were nearly as hardy as the characters of which I wrote. Those early renderings were awful, but my friends persevered as I absorbed their hope. My Friday morning men's group listened to me repeatedly and encouraged me to continue, and my wife, Jackie, after numerous refinements, listened to at least four read-throughs and hung on my words. She has never flagged in her belief that we had found some gold and has been indispensable on this crazy ride.

I have also used the services of about six beta readers who looked for holes in the story, and their feedback was more than heartening. I will not list them here, but they know who they are and will receive an early copy as soon as it's available. You guys were awesome!

Kudos to my developmental and line editor, Sam Severn, from Nashville. Sam taught me to deepen the interiority of my characters and make them more relatable. Sam, you're a gem.

Much thanks must go to my faithful formatter, Bob Dolsen, for his unrelenting work to get the type, layout, and internal art lined up. He was a trooper. I am also tremendously grateful for the services of our amazing cover designer, Frank Gutbrod, who designed a cover so masterfully it almost makes me weep.

I would also like to give a huge "shout out" to Lynn Garreau and Matt Larghi from Domesticated Man Productions for their patience and mentorship in the sound studio as we laid down the audio tracks. Their professionalism and kindness were a wonder to me and I am deeply grateful.

I am also humbled by numerous financial patrons who believed in me and contributed generously.

But perhaps the weightiest contribution to any success this book might achieve is due in large measure to my dear friend Kevin Miles, the proprietor of Heart & Life Publishing. Kevin has graciously donated his time and expertise to seeing this project through, and, frankly, without him I wouldn't have had a clue. He's done this for others multiple times and seems to thrive on the details of it all. Kevin is making a dream come true, and I haven't the words. But I will try. I owe you big time, buddy. Thank you to the moon and back.

-Neal

1

OCTOBER 1827 — KENTUCKY

EZRA BENTEEN AWOKE, his throat raw. He groaned, his voice a whisper. "Ya got too much green wood there, boy," Papa'd warned him last evening. He clambered quickly down the crude loft ladder from his bed, his practiced feet and hands deftly grabbing the rungs in the darkness. Truth be told, he'd chosen poor wood, for he needed the distraction it brought. Every night was a siege on his bed. For the last eight years he had dreaded the terror of the dark—when night had come and he could no longer stave off sleep. He would slip into the abyss where demons lay, hissing their dark sermons of self-recrimination and shame. "Where's your sister?" and "Who you gonna kill next?" He would nod off for a bit and it'd all begin again, and he'd wake in the early morning before all the others, jolted from sleep by images of his little sister crying his name, his own body soaked with sweat and his heart thumping ferociously. Tending the fire was a mercy to him, a leap back into the sane material world, such as it was.

In minutes, he'd rekindled the fire and loaded it with dry oak. Last us the rest of the night, he thought. Gingerly, he made his way back upstairs, sat on the edge of the bed for a while, and then quietly walked to the wall and pried loose a piece of chinking between the logs. He stared south through the gap, across the meadow, lit hard by a nearly full moon. There, three big bucks jousted each other, groaning, shoving-jabbing each other with ivory lances. In minutes two were gone and the winner paused and looked about triumphantly, his skin draped tightly over a sleek muscled frame, his shadow cast long. He moved slowly toward a large oak near the tree line and began his feed on fat fall acorns.

Finally stifling a yawn, Ezra shuffled to the wall and replaced the chink. Bracing himself for the predictable next few hours, he settled back into bed, anxious for the first rays of dawn … and the refuge that only light can bring.

Boots scraped across the frosted porch floor just after dawn. A hard knock rattled the door. Ezra stirred in the loft as a voice sang out, calling his father's name: "Abe ... we need Esther. Johnny's got the croup and can barely breathe. Mary didn't think it'd wait 'til mornin."

Abraham Benteen unbarred the door, and Reuben Sykes spilled in. Sykes coughed twice and wiped his mouth. Abe looked him up and down, shocked, even in the dimly-lit room. Reuben was drawn, hollow-eyed, exhausted. He sank onto a stool and sighed, his voice quavering. Abe gently rose and stroked his old friend's shoulder—a man he'd once sworn knew no fear, one he'd seen rush the Brits when nearly all his companions had been swept into the next world. But on this day, Reuben was a broken-handled axe, and his courage had leeched away. He slowly warmed his shaking hands by the fireplace as Esther poured him stale coffee.

She immediately busied herself gathering her medicine bag, a strange assortment of tinctures and powders she'd harvested from the woods, and Abe trotted to the lean-to behind the cabin and saddled Esther's horse. He returned stiff and ill at ease. His eyes darted from Reuben to Esther and back again. He sat with them both and commenced to prime her two pistols. Finally, he cleared his throat. "Listen ... both of ya," he said, his voice calm yet grave, "I seen horse tracks ... maybe eight men ... poachin' game off'n our land and the neighbors.' Men like that can be ... unpredictable." He gripped Esther's hand. "I'm comin' with," he said.

"No, you're not," she said sharply. "Davis'll be here tomorrow to pick up the hogs."

"Well ... Ezra can deal with him," Abe said.

"We're not making our boy responsible for dealing with that man. He's barely sixteen, and Davis is oily as they come. You need to be here, Abe. Reuben's tough as iron. Be as safe with him as you. You told me so yourself."

"Huhmm ...," he sighed. Abe glanced at Reuben. "You're gonna hafta care for Esther, Reuben. Are you up for it?"

"I'm feeling' stronger already just bein' here, Abe. I'll get her back to ya. Got my word on it. You know how we feel about her," Sykes said.

"I do," said Abe.

"Reuben," said Esther, "have some stew. I need to speak with my husband." She grasped Abe's hand firmly and they walked outside. She leaned in close. "I don't fear those men you spoke of ... but I do fear what you're doing to our boy. Get this thing cared for by the time I get back, Abe, 'cause your war with

Ezra has to stop. It's not bringing Abbie back ... and it's killin' him and me. He lays in that loft at night and twists and moans like a fevered 'coon 'cause a you, and I won't abide it a day longer. I'm done, Abe. Him and me ... we'll leave ... go live with my parents. A White woman might not do that ... but I don't fear it. You've never touched us, but you beat us just the same. Your bitterness is a consumption ... squeezing the breath from us. We can't breathe, husband. I can't breathe!"

Next morning, Abe and Ezra sat on the porch waiting for Esther to return. A rifle cracked in the distance and Abe said, "It's old man Ellis huntin' deer. Been takin' one ever couple days a' late." Ezra didn't tell him, but he'd heard everything his mama had said the morning before, and he'd slept fitfully as usual. But last night was even worse. When his parents fought—and it was usually over him—it made his guts churn.

Later that morning, Esther failed to show, and by noon Abe's eyes had dread in them. He muttered bitterly, "I shoulda' gone with her," and, come early afternoon, both men had nearly lost their minds. They spread out, sprinting and stumbling through cornfields, faces slit from the leaves, jumping over rail fences—nausea deep in their bellies.

"Esther! ... Mama!" Their hound Willie ran on ahead and they followed, gasping for air, their legs outrunning their lungs.

Willie squalled hard and dropped over a ridge about a mile from the cabin and went crazy. Abe followed and stumbled down behind him. He yelled up at his boy, "Don't come down here!" But it was too late. There was Esther, dress above her waist, her scalp lifted and her fingers chopped off, a ball through her chest. Abe hurriedly covered her as Ezra spit up, and their legs fell away beneath them. A large dead man with yellow teeth and thick, dirty nails lay beside her, a cavernous hole where his eye had been and powder burns on his cheek. Reuben's mare lay nearby, saddleless, a mortal wound through her guts.

Reuben was nowhere to be found.

They sat there and couldn't talk. And then they started sobbing and groaning. "No, goddammit...nooo! noooo! noooo! Oh, Gaaawwwd ... Oooooooh Gaaaaawwwd!"

In time Abe rose to his feet and whispered to his son, his voice flat and unfamiliar. "Get Ginnie and two blankets. Hurry now." Ezra ran up the ridge and returned quickly. Abe wrapped her tenderly and lifted the bundle on the horse. In two hours, with not a word spoken, they'd laid her under. The boy was numb.

His feet and hands tingled.

"Ain't talking over your mama right now, boy," Abe said. "We gotta hurry … I need ya! You hearin' me?" Ezra fumbled with the bridle of his horse, his eyes glassy. "Goddammit! Listen to me! We got dogs ta hunt," Abe said. "We're gonna butcher ever' last one of them sons-of-bitches. Get your rifle and pistols. Put an edge on your hawks and saddle the gray. I'll grab food. We ain't letting this trail go cold!"

They moved hard for two days, almost losing the trail twice when a hard rain nearly wiped it clean, and finding it again where the killers followed a creek bed and trailed upstream for nearly a mile before jumping the bank on the north side. But Abe studied it all out. By noon he'd found the trail, and they followed it 'til the sun got hot again. And then, losing daylight, they lit torches and pressed hard.

Finally, later that early evening, Abe rose in his saddle and put his fingers to his lips, whispering, "Smoke. It's them." They hobbled the horses and snuffed the flames.

In a bit, they heard voices and crept toward them. In minutes they had crested a ridge, and then, there they were. Ezra'd never forget what they looked like. Seven of them—dirty, rough animals about a fire, drinking coffee; two limping and moaning; one holding a bloody rag to his face; others draining a jug and slicing strips from a spitted deer. They'd put much time into their double-backs and the dragging of limbs behind their horses, sweeping their sign, but this day, they'd gambled badly against the wrong man and his son. The trackers were two seething badgers whose den had been raped, and they'd come for payment.

"Loose the horses and lead 'em to the creek," Abe whispered. "You get back here, and we're puttin' all them shit-eaters down. All of 'em. Wake up, boy!" he said.

"I hear ya," Ezra said. But it wasn't true. His brain raced like a wounded dog and he'd no mind for any of this. These were just bad men around a dying fire, not knowing what darkness was coming for them. But, he told himself, Mama'd gotten no better than these inbreds were about to.

They hid inside a big hollow sycamore for a while, waiting for the camp to go silent. The waiting was hell. Ezra's teeth chattered in the crisp fall night as the cold crept into his bones. He pulled his hat tight over his skull and watched numbly on as his breath fogged the moon.

Abe signed to move and in moments the two stood inside the ring of men. Abe pointed to two men nearest his son, sweeping his hand over the rest. They'd be his. They gripped their hawks tightly and stepped forward.

Abe moved like a ghost, quiet as an owl on the glide in the dead of night, slitting the throats of three men furthest from the fire—an unfeeling iron phantom clamping a hand over each mouth as he worked toward his son. But the last man was waking the two closest to Ezra, so Ezra moved quickly.

Steeling himself, he got his first man right away, plunging his hatchet in his head like an ax in a green melon—the blood spattering his face like warm thin soup. The second was just like the first, but the man rattled hard and stirred the others, so Abe gathered speed. His fourth man reached for his knife, and then Abe saw fingers and a scalp with a ribbon dangling from a cord around the man's neck, a wound on his face. Abe buried a knife slowly in his chest and screamed like a bobcat, "She cut ya good ... didn't she?! I'm scalpin' ya and cuttin' off your head. Givin' it to the wolves, ya dirty son-of-a-bitch!"

They were so busy with the six that the seventh ran into the dark, heading for the river. "Shhhhhh," Abe whispered, finger to his lips. They listened as he crashed through the saplings, and then all went strangely still. Abe took advantage of the lull. He went man to man, scoring each scalp with his skinner, yanking them up 'til they broke free. It sounded like corks popping from fresh jugs, and Ezra winced and retched. He saw stars and steadied himself as Abe hacked off the man's head and threw it into the trees.

"Give me a hand with this, boy. Need to cut off their britches so's the wolves get at 'em." Ezra froze. Abe said again, "Give me a hand here!"

"No, sir. I'm done," Ezra said.

"What'd you say, boy?" Abe snarled, drool dripping from his chin.

"You heard me. I'm done!" He glared at his father like a treed panther, mad as hell, tasting sour bile.

"Screw you, boy. I ain't forgettin' this. Ya gonna piss yourself?!"

Ezra's vision closed in. His head pounded. He yelled at his father, "Stop it!"

Shoving his son aside, Abe turned to the first man and hacked off fingers until all of them were cut up. Ezra bent to puke. Abe grabbed his shoulder hard to straighten him, but his son knocked his hand away. Abe's voice hissed.

"Don't spit for these men. What we done here was too good for 'em! I oughta burn 'em all! Ever' damn one of 'em!"

Ezra looked about and saw men naked and all cut up like butchered hogs—meat with boots on.

"Papa," Ezra said, his eyes glaring past the gore, his body quivering with rage.

"Whaaaat ... ?"

"You'll not be touching me like that again."

They found the last man the next morning. He'd obviously tripped and fallen headlong into a ravine, snapping his neck against a boulder. He was about Ezra's age. Papa's face softened for a moment and right away went hard again. "Foxes and 'coons'll take care of him soon enough." He glanced back at the kid and said all low and spook-like, "Ya sorry bastard hung around with the wrong people."

They spun their horses and headed back home.

2

THE NEXT SEVERAL MONTHS were an unbroken cord of grief, rage, and disconsolation—a necklace made of vipers. And there seemed no end to it. Abe's mourning was virulent and bone-deep. He groaned bitterly during the night, rising bolt upright in bed, face crazed and drenched in sweat, staring absently at his feet and screaming, "Esther, Esther!" and collapsing to repeat the process, over and over again.

Ezra attempted to sleep but often woke up screaming himself, the faces of his victims crying out his name or rising from the dead and traipsing after him like craven beggars, pleading for a second chance. Sometimes he saw little Abbie, covered in worms, crying out, her tone angry but pleading. "Where are ya, brother? Where are you?"

He'd hoped this was the worst of it all, but then Papa's drinking began. Abe guzzled more mash than Ezra thought possible, and when the family stash had been thoroughly plundered, bartered for more from the McDougal cabin ten miles upriver, 'til they finally cut him off. He even went so far as to cut down and burn Esther's honeysuckle vines that she'd often said reminded her of the smell of prayers. "Lots of damn good they done her. I'll have no talk of her prayers in this cabin!"

So for weeks the death-defying cycle continued, with Abe trekking into the wilderness with his rifle and returning every several days with fresh meat lashed to his mare. But he ate only small snatches of food and grew gaunt and disheveled, hollow-eyed. He talked feverishly to himself, ranting indecipherably, trailing off to whispers, palavering with spirits. Ezra consoled himself that his father had at least the presence of mind to load his weapons and provide for himself and his son, but those illusions came to a shattering end one day when he entered the forest to hunt for his father, and there, within a mile of the cabin, found eighteen deer, four black bear, and innumerable turkey and game birds lying dead, rotting, and undressed. He needed no more convincing. His father had spiraled into madness, and the slaughtered animals were its sickening proof. What recourse did he have?

His mind raced wildly, desperately seeking a plan to save them both. He'd little choice but find an answer of sorts. Perhaps he'd bind Abe during his night terrors and speak strongly to him in the morning when he was more to himself. But that thought grieved him, and involving his Uncle James or the neighbors seemed ill-advised. He wouldn't shame his father before them. Not yet. Not 'til there was no other way.

At times he wondered if he should save his papa at all. Most times he hated him and could do little to please the man who seemed hell-bent on despising him, for Papa had never forgiven him for Abbie's death. But Papa was the only blood he had left. No, he'd stay with his father until it was no longer possible to do so, or until Papa killed him, but he'd not go down without a fight.

Mama'd believed that one day the "real" Abe would return to them both—the man who loved his family more than the jug he'd crawled into after the death of his daughter. She'd modeled a fiercely stubborn perseverance and taken little shit from him that had not been answered back. "Someday ...," she said, "someday Abe Benteen's returning to us both. You just wait and see."

So fevering for solutions, and feeling nearly as mad as his father, Ezra awoke one morning to hear the faint shuffling of hooves in the brush. Wiping sleep from his eyes, he looked up in time to see Papa coming down the ridgeline, Ginnie in tow, an old white-muzzled fat doe draped across her withers. His spine stiffened as his father drew near. Something felt wrong. His mind whirled as the gaunt figure approached—dreading this wraith-man, like a child expecting a beating. In brief moments it all became clear. It was Papa's face. His eyes were blood-red. Rivulets of clean streaked his filthy gaunt cheeks, and the hardened and blank stare had given way to a gaze soft and clear. "We gotta talk," he whispered.

They covered the distance to the cabin, and Papa pulled chairs from inside and placed them under Esther's great oak. He stared off, gathered himself, and began.

"Somethin' happened in them trees, boy."

Abe paused, his voice cracking and low, laboring. "They's a bad storm last night up on the ridge. Did ya ... did ya hear it?"

"Nope. Didn't hear a thing."

"Really?"

"Nothin'."

Abe trembled and his face went white. "Well, lightning struck the old cherry and blew 'er apart right in front of me. Drove a big splinter through both cheeks ... like a spear a' sorts." His voice shook. "And then I heard me a Voice ... sweet as I ever heard. Took my legs clean out from under me. I—." He choked back tears. "I grabbed me that splinter ... and yanked, but she was stuck in bone. Woke up this morning, splinter was ... was gone. Got no words ... Done dark things, boy. And I dragged ya into all of it. I'm so sorry, son. Please forgive me for what I ..." He ceased, struggling, gathering air. "And son, there's mo—."

"Yeah," said Ezra cooly.

"I laid in them woods for hours, I think. Not sure. Couldn't a' stood if I'd a' wanted. Like warm, sweet fire been pour't in me. Like hot molasses went right through me and soaked the ground. And when I woke, I felt all clean inside. Thought about them men we killed and I swear ... didn't hate 'em no more. Can't even 'member their faces ... You believe that?" He went mute again and cried until Ezra thought he must surely leave out of respect for his grief, but then he suddenly stopped and lengthened himself—his voice gathering force.

"And somethin' else: we ain't stayin' in this bottom, son. Sellin' all this and movin' west. We all loved it here. I loved it 'cause your mother did. But she's gone now. My God ... how I ..." His chest rose and fell. "Trip to St. Louis'll be good medicine for us, son. Too many memories here." He began to speak of new beginnings, gazing off into the distance toward the shattered cherry up on the north ridge. Peace shined from him.

Ezra gazed wide-eyed at his father, stunned at his odd declarations, hoping against hope that it was all true—that the hard and unpleasant man he knew as his father had died last night in a hail of lightning bolts and splinters. But all he really knew was that his sinewy frame uncoiled for the first time in months, and a long-forgotten inner warmth flushed his face and washed the length of his body. Perhaps tonight his dreams would begin to uncoil themselves just a bit. God, he hoped so.

3

THE LAST THREE MONTHS had passed quickly since Papa's "change." Abe rode to see Esther's Delaware parents, and they were nearly broken by the news. He stayed on with them for a month until they'd rallied some. In truth, he needed them as much as they needed him.

Ezra's mind slowly began to uncoil itself from the trauma of the last months but was triggered easily. The simple violence of shooting and dressing game was often enough to bring a round of fresh horrifying dreams. He said nothing to his father, but Abe knew, for his son talked in his sleep, and Abe, more than most, knew what violence could do to a man.

Abe sold the homestead at a slight loss to Uncle James, repaired tack, and they set out for the Mississippi and the port of St. Louis. Ezra often sensed his papa's deep sadness, but it was not the animal rage of previous days. Abe was a new man with a different spirit, and yet Ezra never had reason to doubt his strength.

They encountered foul men during the trip westward, and Papa was still a bull. "Pull that piece and one of yas ain't goin' home!" he'd warned two men who'd tried to rob them. But in the main, Abe's smoldering rage had been nearly replaced with childlike wonder, an intense curiosity about nearly everything, and a zest for life that most felt instantly upon meeting him. And for the first time in eight years, Ezra felt flickers of safety with him.

Ezra grieved as well, but quietly for Papa's sake. His relationship with his mother had been complicated, and he thought often of her as they journeyed. She'd been an extraordinary woman. Educated at the mission school, she'd loved books and was rifle-quick with a quote when it suited her. Physically striking, with splendid facial features, broad shoulders, and superbly athletic, Esther'd bested both him and Papa repeatedly in her stickball games—bloodying both their noses, chipping his tooth, and breaking Papa's thumb last fall, all without apology. In truth, they played with her reluctantly—out of man-pride.

She'd helped form a brooding and ferocious young man who'd found himself in countless fights with local boys over his Indian mother. Once he'd tied into a large drunk who spoke poorly of her, and at thirteen he'd beaten the man unconscious and had to be dragged off. He'd become a wounded bear, and Abe's moods and shaming had clinched it all tight, like a nail bent over on a freshly-shod horse. And when he pondered her, his thoughts were all mixed together like a bag of dyed porcupine quills. She was a beautiful soul, but dangerous as hell. And she'd permit no neutral opinion of her.

But he did think of her often, and the impact she'd made. Most of the neighbors, still smarting from the Indian wars, had been won over by her selflessness and tenacity. She'd refused to respond poorly to any of them, gradually wearing them down, and on the day of her death had been returning from nursing a sick child upriver. And so, the community was enraged at her murder. The entire valley would have hunted down and crushed her killers—with or without Abe's help. He knew it. The fools had sealed their fate the moment they'd touched her. The neighbors had shown their respect for her the only way left to them. They'd gathered up the murderers' weapons and horses, sold them, and divided the proceeds to Abe and the widow of Reuben Sykes, who strangely enough was never found.

His father, sometimes when he was drunk and had forgotten his feud with his boy, had compared him to his mother, and that seemed glorious to him. He reveled in his own natural athleticism, for it was the one good trait left to him that he found hard to deny. Abe had once told him, "You move fierce ... like your mama." And since he'd not heard words of affirmation for years, he had held on to those when he'd felt like smashing Papa, for they seemed to humanize him somehow in those long days before his encounter with the cherry tree.

St. Louis had been unlike anything Ezra had ever known. The streets smelled of oxen shit, wet mud, whiskey and smoke, and cheap prostitute perfume. It bristled with folks of every stripe and variation—merchants and Mexicans, Irish and Indians, trappers and traders, whores and wheelwrights. And those were merely the leading edge of an innumerable company of the great hopeful.

Sights and smells flooded Ezra's senses like bandages ripped from the blind, and the two held on for dear life, for it seemed it all might steal their breath away. The entire city oozed with color and adventure and enthusiasm for all things West.

Down one street, prostitutes hawked their wares to the lonely, and Abe caught his son gawking, open-mouthed at the "ladies" in their plunging bodices, their breasts nearly popping free. "Ya catchin' flies, son?" Ezra's face flushed, but Papa grinned mischievously.

"Ya wanna spend money on a whore?" Abe asked. Ezra's face grew even darker.

"Let me tell ya somethin'," said Abe.

"Yes, sir."

"Truth is," said Abe, "ain't one of them girls ever dreamt of growin' up an' bein' a whore. Maybe their man died and they was starvin,' or they was treated poorly as kids. Some got kids to fee—."

"Ya mean th—?" Ezra blurted.

"I mean … most of 'em don't wanna lie on their back to feed themselves. So, don't judge 'em not knowing their story, boy… Now ya sure ya don't wanna spend money on a whore?"

"No, Papa!"

"Well … I do! I wanna make myself a fortune and come back here and buy a couple of these girls out. And I'm gonna set 'em up in some sort of respectable business so's they can take care of themselves proper-like. That's how to spend money on a whore—the onliest way. It's a damn ugly business, son. Ain't no one comin' out purty."

And then, there were the mountain men. Rough, uncouth—some surprisingly literate. Many were buckskin clad and all fiercely independent, rawboned and knuckley—some with unspoken pasts; others filthy inebriates and brawlers—and all stank. Yet they carried themselves proudly, as if they possessed a lofty secret the civilized were unaware of. The two frequently listened to their scary tales of Indians, beaver, and the exquisitely beautiful country filled with game and the lethal grizzly bear.

One drunken "orator" brashly claimed, "High price of beaver'll make a man a fine livin' if'n he can stay alive and keep his hair from hanging on an Injun lance!" And the part about the "fine living" was true. The stylish in Europe craved hats made from the abundant animal, and the lure of adventure and a lucrative end had drawn the daring and colorful in its wake, like foam trailing a wheel boat heading north up the Missouri.

One night, Ezra and Abe sat again, drinking in stories from a band of heavily-liquored beaver catchers, and during a lull Abe launched a bold assault on the bleary-eyed roughnecks. "Me and the boy wanna join up!"

A long awkward silence followed, as the men stared at them, obviously stunned and amused at their audacity. One man cried out, "Well ... who the hell—"

"Let 'em talk!" bellowed another. "Got hisself a pair, alright."

Quickly, a red-haired man, their apparent leader, with a thick-barreled chest and bullish neck, spoke. "Well now ... you fellows look like farmers to me. How do ya intend to contribute?" He cocked his right eyebrow and bore holes in Abe with his eyes, as if he'd been this way before.

"We were farmers ... good ones," said Abe sharply. "But the boy here's been doing a man's work since he was six. And I served in the last war. I tracked and scouted and skirmished some. And I done things—things I wish I could take back...

"But me and the boy come out west to start us a new life. And we ain't 'fraid of much. I'd fight any of ya here says we can't keep up. We just need some learnin' ... is all. And this boy's the image of his mama, and she had more grit than any man in this room. I'm telling ya plain ... he'll pull the weight of any three of ya if ya show him how to keep his hair!"

At once, all their watery eyes fastened on Ezra, and sensing the moment, he glared fiercely at them 'til he could maintain his bluff not a moment longer. And then his stern gaze softened into an impish grin, and like a giant door swung on tiny hinges, the men woke from their whiskey haze and roared deep belly laughs back at him. The red-haired man composed himself and motioned for quiet. "I believe ya, farmer ... and your boy seems fierce. We'll take you on. What's your name?"

"Name's Benteen. Abe Benteen. This is my boy, Ezra." Quickly, the faces of the veterans softened, and more whiskey poured, and as the two rose to leave, the captain and his troop stood to shake hands with them.

That night Ezra's mind raced wildly and sleep was hard to find. He pondered how quickly their fortunes had turned. Abe's bold question had begun it all, and he'd won over the men with his own spontaneous performance. He took a measure of curious satisfaction in this unknown yet growing ability to think on his feet and was pleased his father had witnessed it. And on top of it all his father had actually bragged on him to the men, and it was foreign and sweet and embarrassing all at once, like he couldn't possibly deserve it—like it was some great trick. But his heart said otherwise, for it was the fullest it had been in months. And he felt strangely home, somehow. Maybe tonight, there'd be no nightmares, and he'd not piss himself. Wouldn't that be something?

4

THE LAST TWO WEEKS had been full ones, and Ezra began to have the occasional night of unbroken sleep. And then there was the matter of pissing himself when he slept. He hadn't quite studied it out, but the foul and embarrassing practice had nearly stopped.

Cap'n schooled them on the required tools and the best choices for animals and weapons. They sold Abe's prized stud and bought two heavy-barreled fifty-three caliber rifles and lead, powder, and bullet molds. Abe spent a lot of money on the rifles and told his son, "We ain't going cheap, boy. Might be our edge … if we get in a fix." Abe had one of the rifle's barrels shortened by nearly three inches and the stock by an inch, and when Ezra questioned him, Abe grinned curiously, saying, "Someday, you're gonna need a little smaller piece." And that was that. No amount of coaxing could wring another word from him.

Each picked out thick woolen capotes and winter footgear, along with coffee and sugar and tobacco. Abe also purchased several greased leather bags brimming with pemmican, the nutritionally dense mixture of fat, powdered buffalo meat, and wild berries. "Could save our lives if game grows scarce," Abe said one day. "Might get rough, son. Gotta be ready. Rifles and food … be like gold where we're going, I 'spect." They finished off their supplies with eighteen beaver traps, some fine skinning knives and fresh whetstones. All'd be heaped onto their two horses and three mules. Ezra thought it hard to believe the entire load might be necessary, but they'd be gone from civilization for a long time. Papa nearly forgot the canvas wedge tent and laughed sheepishly that, "Keepin' dry ain't all that important." He was embarrassed by the omission for he was nothing if not prepared, but giddy as a boy on a fishing trip. Ezra could see it in his eyes, and it amused him. Much to his surprise he caught himself beginning to like his father again.

Derrick McKay, their captain, led the procession out of St. Louis on June 14, 1828. He rode a short-coupled, chiseled, strawberry-roan mare with blond tail and mane and cut quite the figure. He was barrel-chested and handsome, though noticeably bow-legged, and sported ham-like hands and a large diagonal scar just above his left eye. Ezra looked him up and down and thought him the most freckled man he'd ever seen.

The men were slow arriving. They'd celebrated hard the night before the big push-off, well aware that strong drink and women would be behind them for some time. Most clung to their horses like sailors in heavy seas and said little but what was demanded of them.

McKay rode behind his men, noticeably amused at their stoic demeanors and muffled groans, rifle rocking on the worn pommel of his saddle, the forearm of his piece worn hollow from the many miles it had balanced there. He was the picture of quiet confidence, of firsthand knowledge of what lay ahead. The two new members were often visited by the grand man, who rode casually up and down the line, the rippling muscles of his mount a near perfect match to his own.

Occasionally, he asked how they were doing and offered bits of counsel on the tribes they would encounter in the ensuing months. "I'll teach ya, boys," he told them. They were assured that some would be friendly and that he'd school them in protocol and tribal custom as the need arose.

He spoke much about the abundance of game and the great herds of shaggy buffalo that sometimes clogged their pathways for days at a time, making travel difficult, if not impossible. His colorful words and transported stares mesmerized them. Both men's hearts burned, clinging to his stories, longing to see the wonders firsthand, to watch the Indians hunting from horseback, running beside their dangerous quarry, sometimes lost in clouds of dust, and eventually emerging again as the dust cleared, the butchering already taking place—the organs greedily gobbled down raw and blood dribbling from their bronzed chins.

But perhaps the most intriguing tales were those of the "grizzer" bears, as the Cap'n called them; giant reckless beasts with massive claws and shoulders so powerful they could break the neck of a bull buffalo with a single swipe. McKay's eyes widened as he fumbled in his pocket, retrieving a giant claw of nearly four inches. He handed it to Ezra carefully, plodding artfully as though he relished this part of the story.

"This son-of-a-bitch nearly sent me under, son. Got his teeth marks in my ass, by Gawd. The men saved me, but not 'til he took nine heavy ball. Bastard fell on me and took all of 'em to roll him off. Got me a bad fever in my ass from that boar, but a Crow medicine man saved my life with some hellish awful-smellin' poultice. Smelled like wolf shit." He grinned and paused, pensive, a faraway look in his eyes.

"The Crow ... now them's good folks to know. Might steal your horses though," he said, laughing, slowly glassing the horizon like a predator looking for food. "And that, friends, is why we trap in bands. The West's a handsome woman with a fickle temper. She'll pleasure ya at night and butcher ya in the mornin' if ya don't show her respect. Got her own ways, my green friends. So learn 'em, 'cause the simple die quickly where we're headed.

"And another thing: treat the Black Hairs right. And don't never show 'em fear. They'll smell it! They's warriors since childhood—taught to fight and ride since they could touch a horse's belly. And they're hardened to pain and hunger. They honor savvy and balls. And always—and I mean always—remember this, for it's the highest of all truths on the upper river: watch your hair!"

Ezra gathered the horses, packed the mules, and saddled the mare. He drove numbly forward, face expressionless, roiling in the shock of the last twenty-four hours. He gathered himself to plot his next few trance-like steps.

He and Papa had departed from McKay and his men two days earlier, when all in the party except the "Easterners" and a few others had fallen violently ill after gorging on fresh beaver. He'd nearly begun to eat when Abe gripped him and told him to refuse, shouting to the rest, "Somethin' ain't right with the beaver, men! There's death in the pots!" The men laughed, but Capn's' face was troubled.

"Good God! What a ya sayin', man?" said Cap'n. Abe thrust his hand in the air, fingers to his lips, and closed his eyes. Every man fastened on him.

"Don't eat this beaver, men. Me and the boy won't. The All Seein' One's warned ya." An uncomfortable silence followed, 'til finally nervous laughter broke it. Most began to eat but a few abstained, including the captain. Shortly, McKay tamped his pipe and motioned for Abe to join him for a walk. They strolled for nearly two hours and Cap'n heard of Abe's ease with the Unseen, his experiences in the war, and the tragic murdering of his wife back East. Cap'n was intensely curious, plying Abe with question after question. In time Abe interrupted him. "I need to talk to you ... about the boy."

"Go ahead."

"Well, he's ... he's different," Abe said.

"I see it."

"Thing is, Cap'n, folks that don't know him see only he's a powerful scrapper. His mama and I wounded him bad. He fights quick without thinkin.' Got a rage inside, and I, uh ... I fear it'll get him killed out here lest he learns to lean into his head more."

"It could," said Cap'n.

"But he's smart as a mountain cur," Abe said. "Boy don't fight 'cause he likes beatin' on folks. Most of the time he's just defendin' someone. Got him a big heart. I need someone ta teach him to slow down a mite. Someone he respects more than just me. Truth is, he may listen to you more than me. Him and me ... well it's ... let's just say we got unfinished business. Esther said ..." His voice cracked, "said he was gonna be somethin' special. That we had to keep him 'live long enough so's he could see it."

"Well, I'm in for it, Abe. We'll help him find it, you and me."

They returned to camp about midnight, content that each understood the other a bit more, and slid under robes by a dying fire. Their slumber would be brief, though. The Angel of Death's weaker brother was about to pay a call.

At about 2 a.m. the moaning began, and within the hour nearly the whole camp sang the same pitiful tune. One by one, the men crawled outside the camp, heaved violently and then stooped to defecate. It all happened so quickly, and their weakness and fever were so fierce, that most had not the strength or time to drop their pants.

Hardened men shit themselves, wallowed in the dirt like spine-shot dogs, and whimpered as those waiting for the rattle of death. McKay, unfazed himself by the pestilence, moved from man to man seeking to help but soon found there was little he could do. He'd seen men poisoned before, but after emptying themselves they usually got better quite quickly. But as the morning dawned and sunlight lit the campsite, the scene was anything but heartening. Men lay in their filth, shirts stained with puke, a few retching up blood. The stench of it all rose in putrid clouds, stinging the nostrils of anything drawing breath, and the healthy retched outside their tents from the vapors. Those with enough strength called out for Abe to pray for them. And so, he knelt from man to man, calling out to his God for each one, and finished his rounds in the late morning. Men with desperate, terror-filled eyes had grown eerily calm under his hand.

In time, he sat exhausted around the main cooking fire and spoke quietly to the few who had heeded his warning. "Dump that beaver in the river ... and scour the pots ... and boil 'em out twice. Are ya listenin'?" And then his voice faded and he crumpled like softened doeskin and fell instantly asleep, not to awaken for hours. Much power had passed through him.

Later that evening, he rose from his stupor, sat upright, and glanced about. The moaning had begun to lessen some, and Cap'n passed from man to man, delivering water to those who could hold it down. Ezra watched as the infirm responded to McKay and Papa as sick children to their mothers, and he sensed a growing awe of his father, particularly among those whose faces no longer contorted in agony.

The next several days witnessed a slow recovery among the men, and all began to take water, with the exception of one young Virginian who grew steadily weaker and lapsed into a coma. On the third day, a shout rang out that he'd passed. Abe calmly arose, laid his food carefully down, and strode purposefully toward the boy, his face an odd display of grief and smoldering rage. All the rest watched on.

Kneeling beside the poor boy, he felt his neck for a pulse, but found none. He closed his eyes and gestured for quiet. In moments he nodded curiously and smiled, as if he'd received an answer to some unspoken questions, and then he did the most curious thing—an action so odd the camp would talk of it for weeks. He opened his eyes, balled his right fist, and delivered three furious blows to the young man's chest, each harder than the one before it. Almost immediately, the young man coughed, grabbed his chest, and sat upright.

"Get this man water now! Now!" he shouted. Then that strange man calmly rose to his feet, massaged his bruised knuckles, and shuffled back to his spot as some were heard whispering among themselves, "What just happened?"

The recovery of the trappers was painfully slow, but four days after hell had come to call, the men began to sip broth that the healthy had prepared, and the strong soon became the only hope of the weak, for they drew water and prepared their food. The singular movement the ill were forced to accomplish daily were their crawls outside the camp to relieve themselves, and this nearly did in the weakest. And though they dreaded it, they'd little choice and soldiered on like the hardened ones they remembered themselves to be.

Abe and Ezra made daily hunting forays and returned with elk and the occasional buffalo cow. They were quickly astonished at their tameness and found the hunting embarrassingly easy. The beasts were so unaccustomed to humans they seemed to lack the usual wariness of the animals they'd hunted back east. "Ever dream of huntin' like this, boy?" Papa said. "Ain't this somethin? Makes Kentucky look thin."

Ezra had never seen his father so happy and content, yet Papa still missed

Mama terribly. Ezra caught him occasionally weeping when he thought he was alone, and sometimes he talked in his sleep, groaning for his wife. Yet he was a painful contradiction for he seemed to have been born for the land and the time, and so Ezra studied him carefully, intent on learning the ways he seemed to suck effortlessly from the land and his God.

Ezra was envious, but it gave him hope. If Papa could change so much, then what about him? Could he be liberated of the shame that seemed to dog him nearly every day, and the sense that he would always terribly fail those who trusted in him? Shivering, he pulled his jacket about his ears, his hat tight to his skull. This place'll teach me more than I ever dreamed, he supposed. Perhaps he was the luckiest of all young men, and his thoughts raced to experiences to come, especially meeting the Black Hairs, as McKay called them.

Late one cold bleak and gray afternoon, the captain motioned Abe for a walk. McKay lit his pipe as the two made toward a cluster of willows. His gait was stiff, shoulders drawn high, a telling nervy cant to his voice.

"We're supposed to meet the Mandan in about a week, Abe. But the men ain't ready. And uh … I'm about to ask a terrible thing of you and your boy, not havin' our experience and all. Would… Hell, I'll just say it. Could you and Ezra head out early and meet the Mandan? Always kept my word to them people. We trade for horses and food and often overwinter with 'em. They're good people. Four Bears is an ally and like a brother to me. Treats my word as gospel." He paused and his face grew even more taut.

"What else, Cap'n?" Abe asked.

"Well … I'm fearin' he'll send braves to find us and weaken his village. Sioux and Ree been hard on his heels. Abe, you find the Mandan and tell 'em what's happened here. Tell 'em we're on our way. Tell 'em we've many trade goods and look forward to a grand reunion—a great time sittin' on the roofs of their earthen lodges.

"Tell 'em we'll watch the children play, and our men and theirs'll bet on footraces and eat fat buffalo and guzzle down corn and squash soup. And you tell 'em the Cap'n misses his old friend Mato-Tope and his great nation. Will you do that for me?"

Touched at the captain's passion, but moved with mischief, Abe turned away and asked coldly, "What's in it for me, McKay?" Instantly, an awkward silence hung between them, and Abe felt McKay's powerful hand grip his shoulder.

Abe spun to meet him and exploded into laughter, showering them both. McKay lost his grip and did the same, and for a bit each man savored the laughter and relief of the other. It had been a god-awful twelve days, and both men's sinews had drawn tight. Abe grew serious and clutched McKay's massive paw. "Be honored, Cap'n."

The Benteens headed out onto the prairie for the next several days with four of the company pack mules, hunting buffalo for the recovering sick. By the end of the second day, they'd dressed out five fat cows and loaded the mules and their personal mounts with as much meat as they could carry. By noon on the third, they arrived back at camp and began to slice the meat into thin strips, hanging it from rope to dry.

The captain was relieved at the provisions. The troop now had adequate food, and he urged the two to leave the following morning. "Get your asses gone ... 'fore the weather snares ya!" The autumn mornings had grown crisp, and early snowfalls on the upper Missouri were not unheard of, he told them. He spoke again of his fear that the Mandan were already growing concerned and repeated that he wished to spare his old friend Mato-Tope the grief of worry.

He sketched a map for them, estimating that they were about four normal days riding—three if pressing hard—from the Mandan village. "We should be 'bout two weeks behind ya if the men recover as I think ... and the weather stays fair."

Soon they settled in for the evening and, after a smoke and a bit of rum, lay by the fire, pulled their robes about them, and fell fast asleep.

The next morning was bittersweet, and there was a bite in the wind. Tack was checked, horses and mules saddled and packed, and goodbyes spoken quickly. Men not given to much emotion wiped tears from their eyes when shaking Abe's hand. Others strong enough rose to their feet and embraced him, apologized for not having heeded his warning, and thanked him for his prayers that most felt had saved their lives.

They all grew especially still as one man came walking weakly forward with a buckskin package. It was the young Virginian. "Tell him the story, Timmons! Go on," his companions urged.

"On our last overwinter with the Mandan," said Timmons, "during them early spring thaws, we found the bones of a giant beast with massive tusks a-poppin' out a wash. We took them tusks and divided 'em piecemeal-like 'mongst ourselves. But we made something for ya. We'd like you to have it in … in appreciation for all ya done for us, sir."

His voice broke as he handed the package to Abe. Abe gripped the man's hand tightly and slowly unwrapped the buckskin covering. He struggled for speech as his eyes fastened on a finely carved ivory medallion, scrimshawed in India ink with the words, "Abe Benteen. A prince among men. Saved our LIVES."

Abe's voice caught, his eyes watering. Timmons leaned into him and whispered in his ear, "Think you busted my breast bone." Abe grinned.

"You're alive … ain't ya?"

"Yes sir," he chuckled. "Reckon it was a good trade. Mister Benteen, we'll all miss ya … somethin' fierce."

Abe's body softened as he scanned the faces of the men around him, and his eyes brimmed with fresh feeling. He saluted them, swiveled in his saddle, and shouted, "We'll see you all at the Mandan village, very soon!" And with that, the Benteen clan leaned forward in their saddles and trotted northward into the vast unknown.

The sun reached high overhead as the morning faded into noon, and the grass lengthened and swayed as the afternoon breeze began its play. The endless prairie bent under its sway like a vast uncharted sea, waves breaking and roiling and casting its mystic trance on the two riders, now two tiny ant-like specks under a magnificent cerulean canopy.

They trotted forward, stiffened with pride, for they of all people were now honored carriers of important news to a mysterious people. Periodically, they crested a ridge or stopped to rest their mounts and mules on the high points along their route. Abe reached often beneath his jacket and retrieved the brass spyglass he had acquired in St. Louis. He scanned the horizon carefully and spoke of what he saw. "Good Lord, boy. Must be what Eden looked like, I swear. Your mama would a'—." He bit his lip as tears coursed his wind-burnt cheeks. Ezra eased his horse close and placed an arm on Abe's shoulder. His father shook.

"Yep, Papa. Mama woulda love this—all of it … I miss her too."

Abe wiped his eyes and continued his scan. Mostly he witnessed the presence of the ubiquitous buffalo or the evidence they had been there—huge swaths of torn and well-worn paths, as though the ground itself had been shorn of vegetation by some great machine. Occasionally, he caught snatches of cruel nature, wolves bearing down on the sick or the young and tearing them to bits.

But Abe's real intent of the glassing had more to do with spying other humans before they themselves were seen. McKay had said an encounter with hostiles was unlikely, but not impossible. He'd advised them to at least be aware of their surroundings, for the staggering beauty of the land could easily lull a man into carelessness. "Enjoy the trip, Abe, but don't get bewitched," McKay had counseled. "This country can leave teeth marks in your ass."

On the afternoon of the second day, Abe began his usual scan of the horizon and instantly froze. "Ezra, they's riders. Maybe twenty of 'em. Far out. Eight … ten miles. Driving a score a' horses. Moving hard northwest. 'Spect a raidin' party. Seem to be in a hurry to put distance 'hind 'em. Think they're too far away to see us—movin' too fast to care. Not heading where we came from, anyways. Cap'n and his men'll be safe … I think."

They camped that night and told stories of Mama and her wildness, and how she wanted them to read some, and how they resisted her so—and how she quoted the Bible to them and even bits of Shakespeare. And then the next day she'd beat them both bloody in the clearing back behind the cabin with her hickory racket and tend their wounds afterward. They talked and laughed and cried, and Abe sobbed so hard, and then laughed at the very next story Ezra told 'til tears ran down both their cheeks. And then they wiped them and started all over again. It'd been a marvelous thing, perhaps just what they needed. But that night, he heard his father's muffled cries again, like a child not wanting his parents to hear.

And lying flat under a quarter-mooned sky, a saddle for a pillow and racking his brain for answers, Ezra became a mother comforting a fevered child, keenly aware that only time offered hope. Damn those men! Goddamn them all over again!

The next day passed without incident, but the weather changed quickly. The azure skies waxed the color of old lead, and the temperature dropped twenty degrees in less than an hour. They donned thick capotes and heavy mittens and stuffed moccasins with buffalo wool as the next hours spun into miles. Both men peered longingly across the landscape for water and shelter for the evening. And then the snow began—in truth, more of a sideways-driving sleet and freezing rain that stung their faces and coated the saddles and rifles with liquid glass.

Abe halted, staring into the distance, his back to Ezra. He hung his head and wept, and Ezra gave him room. Finally, he came alongside and pressed his father's shoulder softly. "I know you miss her, Papa." Abe paused, unable to speak for long minutes.

"Ain't 'bout your mama, son," he sobbed. "This is about us ... you and me. Don't you see? I've wronged you, boy. My God, I've kicked you like a dog. I want you to know that ... that Abbie's death weren't your fault. It was me, son. It was all me. Oh my God! It was aaaaall me." He sobbed and sobbed, his voice muffled. "Will you—"

"Don't Papa. Please. I ..."

Abe's face fell and he grew silent. Finally he whispered, his voice quavering, "I understand, son. We got time." Ezra'd not seen his father this shaken since he'd spoken of lightning knocking him to the ground.

At last, they spied a depression on the horizon and a dark dotting of trees two hours distant. The animals had moved steadily all day with only brief respites, and both men and beasts were weakened. The sun, and then the cold wind, had sucked moisture from them all and would force rest soon. So onward the train plodded, the men no longer awed by beauty but driven by instinct and necessity. And after what seemed an interminable stretch, Abe shouldered his glass and smiled. "See water, boy. Horses'll smell it soon enough. Don't give 'em their heads, though. More spent than they know."

The weary troop continued their northern trek for several miles until, as predicted, Abe's horse caught the scent of water. Soon all the animals grew impatient with the pace and began their controlled acceleration. Papa held his gelding in check and the rest followed reluctantly, especially the mules.

A half mile from the creek bottom and arms exhausted from restraining his mount, Papa relaxed his reins and shouted, "Let Satan bite the ass! Hold on!" In moments the animals forgot their fatigue and stretched out like thoroughbreds, all decorum lost—both men holding on for dear life. Abe turned to see Ezra struggling to maintain his seat and shouted over the din of the mules and the driving wind, "Don't fight 'em, boy! Let 'em go!" His face crackled. "This is life, son! Ain't it!?"

Ezra saw his father, pulsating in the moment, unwilling to fear the unknown or let chaos dim his joy. He was the freest man Ezra had ever seen, and it made him oddly angry. Papa's zest was infectious and inexplicable. He determined to talk about his father's "secret" soon.

That night, they ate like hungry fox kits. Ezra hobbled his charges and turned them loose to graze by the creek. They pawed the fresh snow, greedily yanking large hanks of green grass from the shallow bottom floor. Later that night he'd picket them before he clambered under his robe.

Papa lit his clay pipe and blew a smoke ring at Ezra. The latter waved it away, annoyed.

"Ain't up for jestin' tonight, sir. I'm bone-tired and morning's coming," he yawned, "and my robe's shoutin' my name ... hard."

Papa's eyes twinkled. "Well then, go picket those animals, old man. Maybe soon we'll talk more about what happened to me in them woods. I'm turning in, too. Not feelin' good. Ate 'nough for two."

The cold roused Ezra just after daybreak. He spied his father still sleeping. "Papa, wake up," he whispered, but there was no response. "Papa ... wake up!" He yawned and smiled and grabbed a small, egg-shaped stone and hurled it at his father's back with force. It thudded ominously.

His face drained white. He stumbled to his feet, threw his robe aside, and leapt the few steps to his father. "My God! It's happenin' again! No, no, no!" Abe's face was gray and cold, dried blood crusting his parted lips and nostrils. Ezra gasped and his legs buckled. He collapsed on the snowy ground, face buried in his hands, stunned, numb, nauseated.

He sat there pinioned—how long he did not know—lost in the fog of it all 'til his burning butt jolted him from his trance and forced him to rise. With knife and hawk and bleeding nails, he dug a place in a thicket three feet deep and laid his father in it, covering it with rocks from the creek bottom. He carefully laid the sod back in place. He'd done his best to honor

Papa. His voice broke as he recited Psalm 23.

The words caught in his throat and mocked him. What had happened? My God ... what had happened? Something inside his father had broken in the night and he'd no chance for goodbyes. Chasing rage, fresh pain and panic caught in his chest. Waves of nausea swept over him. Both of his parents were gone. He tasted supper coming back up.

He fumbled in Papa's saddlebags, retrieving a flask of whiskey McKay had given his father. He swirled it in his mouth and swallowed it all. And then he took a second draft, staring at his feet in the snow, and searched his gut for the next step. Rational thought was gone and his face flushed—dread washing over him in great prickly surges. *What am I gonna do? What would Papa do? My God, what's happenin' to me?* Fear ripped through him and throttled his breath. He felt his heart about to explode and then he spoke out loud, startling himself with the strength of his voice. "Don't do this! Don't you do it. Your parents raised ya strong. You stop this feeling sorry for yourself now ... 'fore it kills ya. You listen to 'em, now. You hear me?"

His breathing slowed, tears still streaming. And then like a tap on the shoulder, in minutes it came to him. He knew his father's ways. Papa would do the next thing, and then the next, and then the next. That's what Papa would do. A little at a time. Brick by brick.

He began to breathe.

Wiping his face with snow, he scanned the horizon for the animals and was relieved to find them only forty yards to his north. "Oh God, yes ...!"

He tacked them up, broke ice for them to drink, and rolled and secured his robe behind his saddle. He filled his canteen, reprimed his pistols, and gathered Papa's things. Dipping his face twice in the icy creek, he grabbed a handful of jerked buffalo and cinched the belt of his woolen capote. He swung up on Papa's big gray, the saddle creaking loudly—he'd never noticed it before—and stared in the direction of his father's well-hidden grave. Tears broke over him. "My God, Papa. I'll never see you again! Where's your God in all of this?"

He glowered and raged for long minutes, swore bitterly at the heavens again, and went silent. He sat on his horse for an hour, tethered by grief and the irreparable finality of it all. And eventually looking northward, he cast one final glance behind him, tears streaming, and shouted, "I love you, Papa! You are a prince among men. I'll never forget you! And well ... well, tell Mama I miss her somethin' awful! And tell Abbie ... I'm so, so sorry."

He dug his heels into the flanks of the big gelding, and the small party plodded out onto the prairie again.

The haze of shock cleared just enough to reconnoiter the struggle that lay before him. As the sun rose, his thoughts raced wildly. He and Papa had calculated last evening to be nearly sixty miles from Mih-Tutta-Hang-Kusch, the Mandan village. A solid fifteen hours of straight riding, provided there was no reason to stop. And of course, there'd be reasons, especially to rest and water the animals. But what concerned him at present was the bitter cold and driving wind. His face stung and went numb. He rubbed it curiously and felt nothing. His ears were numbing as well, and he pulled his hood over them. He reckoned the temperature to be near zero and falling. Far too cold for late fall.

Soon the wind drove a light, stinging snow again that cut his eyes like sand. What good was McKay's map if he couldn't see more than a couple hundred yards? "Jesus ... !"

Occasionally, the sun broke the gloom, but in the early afternoon, the temperature dropped still more, and the wind and fine snow grew fiercer, so he called a halt, dismounted to check and comfort his animals, and was shocked to find one of the mules gone. Somehow, the lead line had come loose, and the mule had drifted off with nearly half of his beaver traps and the tent. "Dammit! ... 'Spect some Injun's getting a fine mule." He stroked the remaining animals and remounted. He could see nothing and halted, hoping for a break.

In an hour, the sun did peek through the clouds, and he was stunned at what lay about him. His small company lay embedded in a vast sea of buffalo—tens of thousands, heads forward with rumps to the wind, encrusted in white fine grit. *Papa would have loved this.*

He winced, for he needed Papa's eyes now more than ever, but that was gone. He was gone. He'd had so little time with his "new" father, and the loss grieved and angered him—grieved him to the bone. And he'd never granted his father the absolution he craved. Their unfinished business sickened him. He'd wished to punish Papa and he'd acted terribly small, and now there was no way to repair any of it. Perhaps his father had felt the same when his mother had failed to come home, and he'd never made amends with her. He swore again. "Damn! None of this shoulda happened. Hafta figure it out myself ... now."

He gingerly rode into the wind through the sea of massive bodies, and oddly, the sheltering beasts paid him very little mind. It seemed that riding into the wind kept the leading edge of the great shaggies from scenting him and his animals, or perhaps the fierceness of the gale so dissipated his scent that it was no longer detectable. He soon dismissed his speculations and settled into the saddle, lulled by the occasional grunt of the bulls.

The sun came out late in the afternoon, and eventually he parted ways with the herd and the wind settled some. Then the light snow ceased, and the temperature dropped even more. They desperately needed to find water soon, and he needed to stretch his legs and get blood flowing to his extremities—if he were to keep them, for they were growing more and more numb by the moment. He halted to dismount, but his left leg had gone to sleep and his feet were nearly numb, and when he lighted on the frozen ground he collapsed like a drunk. The big gelding, spooked by his fall, ran the length of a bowshot, trailing the other animals with him as he stopped to paw the frozen grass. He looked back comically at his fallen master and resumed his search for food.

Tears welled up as bitter words choked him, and he screeched out, "Papa! Are you seeing me? Mama? ... God?!" And then he thought to himself once again, *What would Papa do?* And the answer came: *Papa'd laugh. He'd warm his feet, stir his blood, and retrieve his horses, believing all the time there was a purpose and lesson in it. Even the hard parts.*

So, he righted himself—laughter seemed impossible—and walked 'til his feet regained feeling. He retrieved his animals and resumed the search for water, hoping it might save the lives of them all, especially if they were forced to travel all night. None of them would survive unless they kept on the move, but if they kept walking, they just might arrive at the village tomorrow. And he hoped to travel by moonlight for the next ten hours, for the moon had been like a second sun last night.

On the little company plodded, frozen grass crunching beneath them, beating out a crackling rhythm like a walking metronome, five pairs of eyes darting longingly for distant signs of trees and creek bottoms or small rivers. And then the mules began to bray loudly, over and over again, a plea for help and attention. Ezra shouted for them to stop, and the sound of his voice soothed them for a bit, but not long. And then the whole song began again.

He soon thought of his father, of how he might have found humor in the mules, and he chuckled at their attempts to communicate. "I'm holdin' court with mules. Papa, you'd a loved this." Tears dripped from his chin and froze on his capote.

His sinewy frame quivered and exploded with laughter. "What the—?" He gathered his thoughts, muttering to himself, "Ya damn fool ... Papa'd laugh at those mules right now. Honor him with it." He forced out a blood-curdling whoop chased down instantly by a heaping scoop of crushing shame. "I must be moon-crazy, Papa gone ... and all." He groaned and sobbed, crystals forming on his lashes.

But soon, the sun traced its arc toward the western horizon, and the young rider consoled himself with the brilliant moon rising high in the cloudless sky. He needed it to search for water and was even more confident now in his decision not to stop. If they could survive the night, the morning sun just might save them all. He began to shiver, and it troubled him, for McKay said a man must stay warm to keep a clear head.

He dismounted the gelding and stroked the rearward animals. They seemed well, though weary, and stood in place for several minutes. The mules took comfort in that he had paid them some heed, and one of them leaned into him and licked his face. The warm tongue felt good. It was not human affection, but he'd take it. He kissed the nose and drew the big head into his shoulder.

He rubbed the hindquarters of both horses but lingered more on his own mount. He stroked his ears and whispered gratitude to Old Tom, and grabbing his reins, began to lead the procession on foot. His concern that the mules might betray the party's presence to wolves was quickly dismissed when distant wolves began their howls, and the mules quieted immediately. The possibility of death by freezing or wolf attack would keep the ornery animals quiet and moving all night long. He smiled, for he surely loved these mules. They were amazing animals—incredibly surefooted and had remarkable stamina. Doggedly stubborn. They, unlike horses, would never drive themselves to the point of death. They'd simply stop or lie down first. But tonight would call them to violate their first instincts, for stopping could kill them, and he believed them shrewd enough to know.

And now the moon shone brilliantly, a massive mottled white orb perched on the black, the sky a glittering mass of flickering splendor—jewels tethered on soft satin. Ezra marveled at the beauty as his ears caught the eerie howl of the distant predators and the unceasing crunch of animals' hooves on ice-covered grass. And then he fell to the ground, pain shooting from his left ankle, clean up to his ass. He lay still for a moment before spying the hole that had snared him. Twisting himself and examining his ankle, and finding it too tender to walk, his heart sank. *What am I gonna do now? I'll freeze!*

He calmed himself for a few moments, undid his foot packs, and stuffed them and his mittens with more wool. *I'll not go wobbly!* He gingerly remounted, loosened his robe from behind his saddle, draped it over himself, and wedged it tightly around him, covering his feet. He'd exhausted his options. *I could be dead by dawn.* It'd be six hours to daylight, and only the Great Sovereign, as his father called him, knew how all would play out in the next few hours. Ezra prayed. It was a foreign tongue that Mama had used often, and he almost never—but if he ever needed help, it'd be now.

He noticed that the fatigue of the last thirteen hours had taken its toll. The horses began to stumble occasionally, and Ezra too was beginning to flag. And despite his bundling, the cold was creeping in as the night dragged on.

In time, the horses seemed to have found a trail of sorts, and he let them follow it. He soon found his head bobbing and caught himself drifting off to sleep. No longer trusting his wits, he jammed his mittened hands into several voids in the pommel of the saddle, hoping to weld himself inextricably to it in case he lost consciousness. In moments he was gone, only to catch himself again and stiffen back upright, his swollen ankle eliciting a reliable wince on each occasion. He began to dream of his mother—*What ya mean I'm gonna be a warrior?*—and then awakened. But as the night wore on and his body grew colder, he became drowsier and finally quit awakening at all.

Still, on the party trudged, mile after mile after mile, following a well-worn path to who knew where, heeding the instincts of survival and loyalty. And even the stubborn mules, moving more slowly now, plodded on like the legions of ancient Rome after some infernal pyrrhic victory. And the big gelding, locked in a struggle for life itself, and borne along by the strongest of all instincts—the will to live—shuffled doggedly forward, dragging them all in his wake.

5

THE MORNING SUN hinted its rise as dawn broke slowly, and soon the small party was spotted by village sentries. Leaderless for the last five hours, the pitiful packtrain, hairy faces and eyelashes encrusted with hoarfrost and ice, eyes glazed opaque with exhaustion, continued their dogged march into the center of the great village, Mih-Tutta-Hang-Kusch. There the gray gelding was halted by two men who gently pulled its ashen rider from his saddle, carrying him into a round earthen lodge in the center of all the others.

Soon the entire village was alive, its inhabitants pouring out of their lodges in the caustic morning cold, snow crunching under soft moccasins, their breath speared by the first rays of dawn. Clutching their robes about them and whispering excitedly, they jostled for place to see "him." The elders acquired the best view, while still others climbed the roofs of the adjacent lodges and peered down.

The two men who'd taken charge of the proceedings motioned for two women who set about laying several large buffalo robes on the earthen floor hair-side up, one upon the other. They stripped the young man naked and laid him in the center of the piled robes. Then they removed their own clothes and wedged him between their warm copper bodies. Immediately the men covered the three with two thick robes that had lain against the wall and motioned all others away.

That day young and old spoke excitedly of Ezra as his supplies were stored away. His animals were cared for quickly and with great respect, although some questioned whether they might survive at all. One man immediately volunteered to water and feed them and place them inside his own warm lodge until they'd recovered, while another promised to care for the mules in the same manner.

So, the great wait began. Would the young man survive? The village was divided. Some said they'd never seen one be so gray, and yet live. Others, that this must be a man of great measure and his animals of special courage to survive in such weather. The elders counseled the people to stop their speculation and to wait patiently for answers, that the Lord of Life would make all known soon. And so, all waited to see what would be.

    Time dragged slowly that day and into the evening, but daily village life continued on much as it had before the "gray one" had arrived. Men left the palisade and headed onto the prairie to scout for game. Women transformed tanned hides and buffalo robes into clothing and artistic wearables, while craftsmen heat-shrank wet bull-buffalo skin into war shields, and the old told stories and taught lessons to the young. Some of the young men crafted weapons for hunting and played competitive games to harden and sharpen their fighting skills, and the most fortunate made love to their wives. Most went about their lives as usual, and yet behind it all lay a burning query: What has happened to the young man? As smoke curled from the top of each lodge that night, many anxiously waited to see what the next morning might bring.

    So, at dawn, they spilled from their lodges, robes wrapped tightly about them, their fists balled tight, wiping sleep from their eyes. Men pulled their thick woolen capotes tight as teeth chattered in brittle air. Women huddled tight to their men, and children to their mothers, and the breath of hundreds hung like morning river-fog in the dense stillness.

    Again, villagers jockeyed for position. Young, strong warriors made way for the gray hairs, who were stacked like firewood around the entry of the lodge. In moments, the hide-door covering was lifted and young women who'd climbed the roof of the adjacent earthen lodge peered down into the opening, hoping for the best of views.

    Abruptly, the medicine man lifted the robes to reveal the three naked ones. The women immediately awakened, drenched in sweat, and pulled dresses over their work-hardened bodies. Watchers paused as all grew oddly still until finally one of the gray hairs muttered in his native tongue, "Well ... is he to walk on Mother Earth again?"

    Several of the young women giggled and pointed at the naked man. Others shushed them. And then, it happened. A camp dog wound its way through the myriad of legs and began to lick the lips of the naked man, who reflexively brushed him away, eyes still closed.

    "He walks again on Mother Earth!" the old man shouted. Immediately shocked from slumber, Ezra opened his eyes and peered down his naked torso and across his man-parts into the faces of the Mandan, shouting loudly while covering his privates with both hands, "HEEEEEEY!"

    Those closest let out great whoops and shouts. The young women poked and whispered to each other as two dignified men lifted Ezra to his feet and handed him his clothes. All was pandemonium as camp dogs added their barks and howls, and Ezra stood dumb and naked before them, gathering his wits, naked save for his left hand covering his privates, and weakly raising his right.

The people grew still. "I'm Ezra. McKay's coming soo—" At McKay's name, the people erupted again in deafening shouts and whoops and shrills. Finally, the chief stepped forward, embraced him, and handed him his shirt. He drew it over his shoulders, wobbled, and promptly fainted dead away.

He slept for the remainder of the day, but he did dream. He saw men cut up, and he saw Mama and his father laugh once more, and Abbie was with them all, running by the river and catching fireflies. And then he dreamt of Mama lying over the ridge and the ugly man lying beside her, until in the early morning he lay in a great hollow world, numb to the chatter that filled the lodges and the fierce speculation as to the meaning of his coming. But his arrival and near-resurrection had filled them with wonder, and numerous ones dropped by the lodge to inquire of his health. Some of the young women spoke lustfully of the well-built stranger, while some young braves downplayed the importance of their new guest's arrival.

The word spread that a great feast would be called to celebrate the strange one—very soon.

Early in the afternoon, Ezra awoke and dressed himself. The ankle was still swollen but a bit better. He opened the lodge covering just as the village chief began his entry, and the two awkwardly collided, knocking the chief backward on his butt.

He reached for the man's hand, pulled him to his feet, gesturing apologetically. The chief glared sternly back and then laughed. He quickly pulled Ezra inside the lodge and motioned for him to sit. He muttered to one of his wives, who wrapped herself in a smallish robe and left hurriedly.

Shortly, she returned with a young woman in tow who plopped down beside them. The woman's face was dirty and her hair matted. She stared straight ahead, her eyes fierce and face sullen, an angry rash on her left cheek.

The chief slowly slid a long pipe from a quilled bag and lit it. He drafted carefully and handed the pipe to Ezra, who trapped the smoke and attempted to blow a ring. The chief stared into the fire, silent, a slight smile curling his lips as Ezra fumbled awkwardly. The younger woman introduced herself as Dog-Eater and the chief as Mato-Tope, or Four Bears, the war chief among his people. Her English was good.

Ezra's heart pounded as he told Dog-Eater the reason for his mission. He stared at the woman and swallowed hard. "Tell him ... tell him McKay is coming."

"Who's McKay ... and who are you?" she inquired.

"I ... am Ezra. I'm a friend of his." She translated to Four Bears. He smiled and rubbed his hands excitedly.

"He wants to know why McKay is not with you," she said.

"Tell him McKay's men are sick, but are healing. They'll be here in ten days, he hopes." Ezra paused and searched his memory. "Tell him McKay has a message for him. Tell him he's anxious to feast and bet on foot races with his old friend. That he wishes to sit on the top of Four Bears' lodge and watch the children play ... and to stuff himself with buffalo haunch and squash soup. Tell him McKay misses his old friend and his great nation. Can you 'member all that?"

"I have a memory like a kicked dog," she said. When she had relayed it all, the chief's face brightened at the news of the captain's safety. An odd silence held for the span of what must have been nearly a minute. Finally, the chief broke the quiet with a pitiful, guttural cry, followed oddly by a joyful shout. He spoke again as Dog-Eater translated: "He says his heart was sad when he thought the captain and his men had been taken. But he is happy again and thanks the Great Spirit that his White friends will come soon.

"He says these White men are good; that they are missed much here; that soon feasting and games and trading will happen again. He says good times are coming, that McKay and his men will stop the raids of the Sioux and the Arikara, and the village will feel safe again. He says ... he believes you are the man of the dream."

Ezra's eyes grew wide and Four Bears smiled. The chief grew still, staring into the smoke and speaking slowly, pausing often as though he were delivering a message that could not be hurried. The chief said, "Many of our people wonder why you were treated like a prized war pony, and I have chosen not to tell them until now. We have always been good to the Whites ... and they have been our friends. But you have been treated as one of our own, returning from battle. And now I tell you why." He paused, this time even longer, blew a second nearly perfect ring, and laid the pipe carefully beside him onto a reed mat, as if it were a good friend.

"Two moons ago, our holy man had a dream ... a dream of a dead White man who tumbled into camp, tied to his horse. Our holy man said we must do all in our power to bring him back to life; that First Man told him that he is a 'powerful one' and we must teach him our ways; that he will love our people and become a great man. And that is why my people have saved you, and two of our women covered your gray body with their own. In two suns, I will call a great feast where I will tell all this to the people. There you and your animals will be celebrated for your courage. Many will want to touch you. Others will give you choice pieces of meat and corn. Young strong men will be jealous and will give you stern looks, and pretty women will bat eyes at you.

"And this is my counsel to you, young one: Show respect to all and walk humbly. Ask many questions and eat whatever is offered, for these are the ways of the Mandan. If you do this, you will do well here."

And then Mato-Tope rose to his feet, cradled his splendid pipe in the crook of his left arm, and left.

Ezra spent the rest of the day pondering the words of Four Bears. It all seemed too much to take in. He was a young man without parents and a home—not nearly convinced of the prophecy of his mother. *I done nothin' great ... 'cept survivin' the way here ... and maybe that was just dumb luck.*

In the afternoon he limped about the village and found himself captivated by its sights and smells and laughter. Enroute, an old man smeared his ankle with a greasy salve and said strange words over him, and occasionally he was offered food or water or a piece of freshly roasted fat. He gestured warmly, received the gifts, and ate 'til he was sick. But still the food came, and so on and on he ate, 'til he ducked behind a lodge and dumped his belly. Finding his legs and wiping his mouth, he raised his head to find a small crowd gathered round, smiling broadly. Others laughed and poked each other, as though a great joke had just been played. He paused and gathered his wits and forced a smile. Immediately a loud cry erupted from the crowd as some pressed close and patted him. An old woman offered him a gourd of water, and he swirled it in his mouth and spat it into the air, playing the clown. Again, the people howled with laughter as he played their game.

He spied young women staring his way and took note of several sullen young men glaring at him. He remembered Papa's words about his physical prowess and felt their power rise up in him. "You move like a panther, boy." They would be won over. One way or another.

The day passed quickly, and the next saw the offers of food lessen a bit as the people showed him mercy for the previous one. The little children followed him about, babbling excitedly, clinging to him like a camp pet.

One little boy grabbed him by the hand and led him to a spot at the north end of the encampment just beyond the palisade walls where groups of youngsters had assembled with bows and arrows. He was quickly astonished at how well the little ones shot. One of the older boys offered his bow for him to try. He looked it over, judged it too delicate, and handed it back. The boy ran to the edge of the clearing, grabbed a larger bow and longer arrows, and ran back. "For me?" The boy nodded. Ezra sized up the weapon. It was a badly dinged, sorely-used piece, but sound. He flexed it several times, nocked one of the battered arrows, and sent the shaft aloft out onto the prairie. The arrow arched upward nearly out of sight, sticking in the short grass nearly two-hundred paces distant. *Lordy ... that was something!*

He limped childlike after it as his young friends followed close behind, shouting and whooping their approval, giggling at the wonder on his face. The arrow had transported him, and they noted his pleasure, proudly. He pulled the old missile from the soil and studied its construction. *If only it could speak.* Its blood-stained feathers were badly worn and nearly gone, and he imagined it had killed buffalo or an elk or two, or perhaps an enemy. But it mattered little. Today it had given him powerful pleasure and had afforded him standing with his new friends. And something deep within drew him to it. The sweeping arc of the arrow piercing the sky had bitten him hard—like the first moist kiss of a beautiful woman.

Ezra spent the rest of the day observing the ways of the village. Some of the people were somewhat fair-skinned and of lighter hair, and he ached to know why. The Cap'n had said the French had traded with the Mandan for over a century and that maybe their seed had mingled. Others in St. Louis speculated that perhaps they'd inter-bred with Viking explorers. In months to come, he'd find very little resolution to any of it.

And by day's end he found his ankle pain fading and the swelling nearly gone.

The people had shown him kindness that surpassed his expectations, and his time with the young boys had pricked the delicate scab of loneliness he felt over the loss of his parents. He wept quietly behind a lodge. Composing himself, he turned toward the village and spied a young woman staring furtively in his direction. He pretended not to notice but, to his own surprise, abruptly stared and walked right at her. "Hey! You!" She smiled and ducked inside her lodge. He'd not meant to embarrass her, but only to prove his mettle to himself. Women seemed a powerful mystery to him and scared him some, for most seemed fragile and very unlike his mother, and that very fragility gave him pause. He'd no experience with it.

But this had been a beautiful woman, and looked strong, and her obvious interest excited him. There had been few young women back home that he'd found attractive, and the farm work had kept him more than occupied. And then there'd been the issue of his temper, for it'd frightened most away and had been a point of considerable concern to their fathers. In truth, he'd not gotten close to any of them.

Ezra struggled to see in the dim light of the lodge and was surprised to find Dog-Eater and the holy man sitting by the fire. The medicine man beckoned him to sit between them, and immediately a conversation began.

"He says tonight will be a great feast in your honor," she said. "He says the war chief will tell the people who you are, and the people must show you kindness and teach you their ways. He says you are to learn the Mandan ways and ask many questions, and always speak the truth. He says, 'Do you understand?'"

Ezra nodded, smiling faintly. "He says tonight young women will flash hot eyes at you," she said. "But you must master yourself." The medicine man spoke again, and Dog-Eater grew agitated and raised her voice at him. The conversation ceased for a moment, but soon her face grew resigned and her words tumbled free, "He says I must go with you to the feast and speak the White man's words to you. I don't wish to, but you're a great one, he says. I'm to meet you here when the sun has hidden itself!"

She rose quickly and was gone.

At sundown, she returned. She'd groomed herself, scrubbing her face 'til her cheeks had taken on a rosy, wind-burnt coppery hue. Even her rash was fading, and her altered appearance puzzled him. She grabbed two winter robes from the shadows and gave him one.

They made their way quickly to the center of the village. Villagers had already assembled, accompanied by bonfires and the beating of several large rawhide drums. Soon the singing began, and as the fires crackled, people of all ages gathered round expectantly, some gnawing freshly roasted buffalo ribs and laughing.

Camp dogs scurried between legs searching for warm, discarded bones. Yip ... yip ... yip. Warriors strode proudly about, wrapped in finely painted robes chronicling their battle exploits. Moccasins crunched snow as gray hairs stood especially close to the fire, and all showed them deference.

In time, the chief appeared and stood on a thick log, placing him shoulders above even the tallest. He waved his hands, and the people slowly grew still. Dog-Eater leaned into Ezra and spoke into his ear. Her words and breath seemed softer than before.

"My people ... tonight we will dance and sing and eat until the fire has died and bellies are tight. Young men will court young women and some will choose wives. Others with bad hearts will make peace with their neighbors, and the young will play and watch us all conduct ourselves. Tonight ... the Lord of Life watches over us like sentries watch over our walls. Soon, Captain McKay wi—." At McKay's name, the people grew loud. The chief smiled, paused and waved his arms a second time. Again, the crowd fell silent.

"But tonight, we honor a new guest. Three suns ago he rode into our village as a dead man ... and his animals as little better. Few have ridden his path and lived. Our women poured their warmth into him, and we all waited to see what would happen.

"But he returned from the land of shadows and has spent the last two days resting and enjoying our people. I am proud of our people for their kindness to him. Many have asked, 'Why has he been treated like one of us?' It is a good question ...

"Two moons ago, our holy man had a dream that troubled him. He told me of it, but I told no one. He saw a frozen White man lashed to his horse, riding into our village in a time of deep cold. He said we were to do all in our power to bring him back to Mother Earth.

"The Lord of Life said he was a powerful one who would become a great man. He said we were to teach him our ways that he would excel even our finest, and that he would marry one of our own." The chief motioned for Ezra to come forward and stand beside him. Ezra clutched the arm of Dog-Eater, guiding her onto the log with him. Dog-Eater began to translate his speech:

"This year's been a year of sadness for me. I've avenged the murder of my mother ... and buried my father. You woulda loved him. I came to know your Captain McKay and was with him when his men grew sick and nearly died. He sent me to ya ... to let ya know he was still alive, that he'd be coming soon.

"But on my way the cold grew bad, and I hurt myself. I tied myself to my animals, and they brought me here. And then you treated me as one of your own and brought me back to life. I am powerful grateful. I hope to honor ya as you've honored me ... I'm Ezra ..." He paused, took a deep breath, and scanned the faces. "But I have a request. Dog-Eater seems—" At once, Dog-Eater's face grew troubled, and her talk ceased. The chief glared sternly at both as Dog-Eater balked and then ever so reluctantly continued. Ezra spoke again. "Dog-Eater seems sad, and I don't know why, but she's treated me well and will be with me much 'til I learn your tongue. I ask that you gladden her heart a little ... for my sake. Her face makes me sad."

When he'd finished, an awkward silence fell over the people and whispering began. Ezra glanced at the chief and Dog-Eater but found himself unable to read them, except for what might only be described as pure terror on Dog-Eater's face—as if a death sentence had just been handed her.

Finally, the chief spoke. "Our young friend has asked a bold and good thing. Dog-Eater came here six moons ago when our men raided her village. Her man fought bravely but was killed. She was brought here to live as a slave among us and she has worked hard, and we have treated her badly. She is bitter ... and I do not blame her.

"Today ... it is time today to treat her as one of us. She has no man to care for her. So, men, I ask you to give her food! And you women ... please treat her as your sister! Today, Dog-Eater has become one of us!" A hush fell over the crowd.

And then, ever so slowly, Dog-Eater's head lifted. She scanned the crowd, her eyes wide with wonder. And then she did the unthinkable. She beamed—the first actual smile that any Mandan had ever seen on her face—and grabbed the arm of her deliverer. Ezra's heart leapt. He put his arm about her waist and pulled her close, and the people shouted.

He'd just witnessed a remarkable thing. He'd asked boldly, and an abused slave had been freed and adopted. Dog-Eater's face waxed pretty and she cried before them all. She was glorious!

Ezra pulled his robe higher and nestled into the brown musky wool, and the fibers tickled his nose. He breathed deeply and grinned. Courage had knocked on the door of uncertainty, he had opened it, and his body crackled with life. The air tasted like Papa's pipe and sweet apple pie. Do you see this, Mama? Papa?!

The two passed through the throng, interrupted by admirers offering steaming pieces of food to both. Ezra and his word-maker ate 'til their bellies pained them, and finally he grabbed her hand, and both ran beyond the crowd and threw up. They stood weakly upright, wiped their mouths, and exchanged knowing glances—like two soldiers who'd watched each other's back. They laughed 'til their bellies hurt again but seemed powerless to stop. She embraced him fiercely and wept.

In time, recovering, he grabbed her hand, and they shuffled slowly back to the fires, wrapped deeply in their wooly robes, their faces ruddy from the ferocious cold, keenly aware each had experienced a great thing. They'd been deeply honored by the people and their leadership, and both had a growing sense that they'd found home.

The singing, drumming, and feasting continued long into the night, lit by roaring fires and the nearly full moon. Ezra began to think that perhaps he was the luckiest of young men, despite the recent losses of his parents. Joy mingled with his pain. His eyes moistened. How proud they would have been of him now. "But I'm so lonely," he groaned.

His heart pounded as he considered the prophecy of the medicine man. Would he truly marry one of the young women here? And what might she be like? The thought spun him up hard. His mother had spoiled him for all but the most exceptional of choices. She had been a beautiful woman of remarkable qualities, exceedingly tough of mind and body but guided by extraordinary generosity and largeness of heart, and the prospect of searching for a woman like that made his heart hammer wildly. He mused briefly on his encounter with the young woman earlier in the day, his blood running hot at the mere memory—pounding in his temples and sweating his palms.

The raucous feast continued as the moon vectored the sky. The singing and drumming grew less fierce; the gray hairs began to stumble, and even the young, proud warriors, dressed in finery and encased in splendid painted robes carved from the backs of shaggy beasts, began to slow. And finally, one by one, the people left the center of the village and shuffled to their lodges, just as dawn began to break. Lodge fires were stoked as weary celebrants clambered under thick robes and fell asleep. But village sentries maintained a sharp eye, for they dare not sleep. Their enemies surely didn't.

6

THE DAYS THAT FOLLOWED were a feast of experiences, and Ezra reveled in them all. His obvious enjoyment and curiosity were an amusement to the people. He found himself ensnared by the inner workings of village life and inquired of some young warriors about their painted robes. Initially reluctant to talk, they were soon overcome by pride in their garments.

Dog-Eater translated their replies and seemed pleased to accompany Ezra. The other men showed her kindness, and after one particularly rich exchange with a young man, he ducked quickly into his lodge and returned with a leather bag of jerked buffalo for her. She smiled and quietly thanked him. Ezra's heart warmed, and he winked at her. She'd be cared for until she had a new husband. *These are good people.*

The warriors explained the meanings and symbols of their battle robes. The robes told the stories of their exploits in battle and successful raiding and chronicled a record of their "counting coup" on their enemies. The coup fascinated him. It involved the touching of an enemy with a stick or the hand and then returning safely to one's friends; this was the highest honor, preferred above a kill or a scalp. It was the most daring and audacious thing he'd ever heard, and he vowed someday to see it—or even do it, if the occasion presented itself. Someday.

One young warrior invited him to his lodge for something "special," and he took Dog-Eater with him. The young man offered her some pemmican and then asked her to leave. She nodded and was gone. It was then that Ezra saw a beautiful, lightly smoked buffalo robe on a sapling frame, hanging perpendicular to the floor of the lodge. The blonde and orange highlights along the spine and shoulders were striking. It seemed the finest he'd yet seen.

His eyes adjusting to the dimmer light, he noticed the faint black outlines on the robe of human figures, horses, weapons, and scenes of great chaotic triumph. He was about to witness the actual painting of a young warrior's most glorious acts. The moment was sacred, he suspected.

He cast his eyes about and saw three small brass pots suspended over a tiny warming fire and a number of bone brushes and sharpened sticks on a small log close by. The young man dipped a spongy bone brush into the first pot of warm hide-glue paint, meticulously wiping the excess onto the edge of the pot and skillfully placing the end of the brush in the center of one of the outlined horses. He pressed forcefully, deep into the fibers, and worked outward to the outline of the animal.

The muted yellow made for a stunning image, and Ezra nodded his approval. Soon the man picked up another bone brush, dipped it into a second pot, and began a second horse, this time a gorgeous red ocher. Ezra groaned his admiration, much to the artist's delight, who dipped his brush a second time and handed the brush to Ezra. "Oh, I couldn't," he said. But noting the man's disappointment, he accepted the brush, took a deep breath, and steadied himself. He slowly touched the brush to the unfinished horse and meticulously worked the paint deep into the soft leather.

Ezra dipped the brush again and then, concentrating with all his might, painstakingly completed the image, handing the brush back to the artist. He forced a smile, his legs trembling. He'd been given a great honor, helping to record the sacred story of another man's life on the most beautiful of canvasses, keenly aware he could have ruined it all.

The man smiled broadly and pointed at the image just completed. He was deeply pleased. He offered the brush again, but this time Ezra refused. He'd been both honored and initiated in spectacular fashion, and the rite had spent him. *Ain't temptin' fate a second time.*

It soon became obvious to both that it couldn't be completed in a single day, for the warrior had been brave and his exploits many. So, when the sun began its fade and the paints were nearly gone, the man washed out his pots and motioned for Ezra to sit. Within moments a slight, pretty woman entered the lodge and began preparing food, a brass pot of buffalo stew mixed with corn and wild turnips.

Ezra studied his new friend. He was a fine-looking red man, with the most prominent of cheekbones, a boldly formed nose, and dark and piercing eyes. He pinched the young woman's bottom while they hunkered about the fire, and she slapped his hand away, giggling, busying herself with quillwork at a distance as both men smiled at each other.

McKay had forewarned Ezra of the Indian practice of offering wives to guests, for some believed power was transferred through intercourse. "They might offer you women, son … if they count you worthy." And most believed the shaman's prophecy. *This can't be happening. Oh God! Papa?*

Her fingers brushed his ear.

Moments later, an awful clamor pierced the stillness from outside the walls of the lodge. The two men arose and ran out the entrance to find the village in chaos.

7

In minutes, Mato Tope stood on the high log in the center of the village, motioning for stillness. Ezra looked for Dog-Eater and caught her sprinting toward him. She leaned in, chattering excitedly, "He says two of our men were scalped by Sioux while hunting buffalo. The others have returned to say the Sioux are many and are coming, that we must prepare to defend our old ones and our children. He says three men have returned from the south. They say McKay and his men are only one day away, pressing hard to get here."

At this last bit of news, the troubled faces of the people brightened and shouts pierced the confusion. Even the helpless and weak seemed heartened. The chief resumed: "Our enemies would gore us like the bull, but they have forgotten we are the People of the First Man. We have killed the bull with arrows and lances for many winters, as did our elders. We will slaughter these proud bulls like we were hungry … and our children starving. Our young men will kill these bad hearts, and we will dance around the village fires with their hair on our long poles.

"So, pray to the Lord of Life and watch his deliverance. He will crush the evil spirit Ochkih-Hadda who brings the Sioux against us, and our young White friend will see how the Mandan conduct themselves with courage. Very soon, our White brothers will be here to help us, and they will dance and feast with us after the battle. Be brave, my people. Our warriors have killed many bulls!"

The people's mood changed almost immediately following the chief's passionate oration, and now the formerly fearful moved with purposeful urgency. Men of all ages shouldered smoothbores, checked flints, and filled shooting bags with fresh powder and ball. Others strung and flexed war bows and straightened arrows. Still more painted their faces, chanted strange words, and hugged their wives as others ran to the palisade walls to wait for the Whites.

The entire village had been mobilized within minutes, and while Ezra'd heard stories of war from his father, nothing had prepared him for what he'd just seen. Even many of the women in the lodges had armed themselves with their husbands' lances and spare firearms—a few with old horse pistols, moving with a confidence borne of experience, fed by fresh hope.

He stared on, open-mouthed at the people, undone over how life had trained them to live in such a state of practical vigilance, awed to see them bearing up with such courage. *My Lord!*

In the center of the village, a small group of painted braves assembled on war ponies conferred with the chief. The conversation was clipped and solemn, and quickly the three riders left, trailing three ponies behind them, riding south and hard. Dog-Eater informed her charge that the men would act as scouts and return soon with word of McKay and his men.

In the meantime, women brought food to the men on the walls, and children played close to their lodges and mothers. Mothers willed fresh strength into their faces as the young ones played on. But today was different from yesterday. Today they were watched over especially closely.

The temperature had risen noticeably, the recent early cold snap had abated, and the village grounds were smeared with a thin layer of greasy mud, its residents sliding noticeably as they walked. Many ran to their lodges and exchanged muddy moccasins for dry fresh ones smeared with a thick layer of white waxy buffalo tallow. Others peered anxiously over the walls in the direction of their White friends, whose long rifles and deadly aims were the envy of the village, prompting a few of the young men to trade up to three horses for a single rifled weapon, when it could be found.

So the inevitable wait set in as the cloudy sky cleared and the sun broke brilliantly. Ezra scanned the palisade walls for a better view of the Mandans manning their posts, and they were a terrifying sight. Some sported tattooed faces, now partially obscured by red vermillion and black war paint. Their thick rawhide shields, dense enough to turn arrows and in some cases even lead ball, and brightly emblazoned with spirit animals, stood close by their bearers.

Some sang as others chanted, and all seemed to suck strength from the sound of it all. Ezra found himself almost overcome by the sheer spectacle, balanced on the lip of raw unforeseeable outcome. *I've come far in seven months.*

He'd never dreamed of a life this pungent and deadly. He took a deep breath and shivered.

The afternoon vigil dragged painfully on as wives brought bags of pemmican to their husbands. They scanned the horizon for movement. For anything. And then the cry came from a sentry. Someone threw the man a brass-looking glass as he began a frenzied account of what he saw: "Crow ... many ponies and riders ... riding hard. Very large group of ponies ... Men chasing them. Maybe Sioux?"

At the news, a great cry let out. The Crow were friendly and arch enemies of the Sioux, and their presence and war prowess would be invaluable. At their furious speed they would arrive within the hour. Most considered this good news, until another cry sang from the wall. A second spyglass was handed to another man.

"It is McKay. He and his men are riding like pack wolves. They will be here before the Crow!" Pandemonium erupted, for the news was almost too much to bear. Warriors danced and women shrilled. Dog-Eater sprinted to Ezra to translate and spilled the words into him. He embraced her and ran to his lodge, grabbed his rifle and pistols, and returned quickly to the walls. There he found a spot on the catwalk and peered into the distance, and then he saw them—tiny fly-like specks in the distance. *God ... they're here!* In minutes the trappers, all thirty-one of them, spilled through the gates of the palisade. Their pained and drawn faces said it all. They'd ridden their mounts nearly to death to rescue their friends. The Mandan shouted and hugged them like long-lost family returned from the dead.

But their horses demanded immediate attention. They were a pathetic lot—covered in salt-foam and mud, their eyes wide and bloodshot, nostrils flared and furiously sucking air. Some bled from their muzzles. They were terrified—ridden beyond their limits, and several that had carried two men fell to the ground, seizured, and died where they lay.

The Mandan launched a desperate effort to save the rest. They ran to their lodges and returned in minutes with bowls of softened cornmeal moistened with water. Others brought dark cakes of sugar and forced it into the mouths of those farthest gone. Ezra found dark sugar in his own pack and ran into the fray along with the others.

Riders stripped saddles and weapons from their mounts, while those not needed on the walls began walking the animals. Some Mandan, sensing several horses about to lie down, unsheathed their knives and poked the rumps of the most vulnerable to prevent them, knowing they would never rise again if they were to lie in such a horrid state.

The chief quickly found the captain and embraced him. Immediately sign language flowed and relieved laughter broke out. Women brought food and fresh water to the exhausted men, and they gobbled it down reflexively, fiercely. Within minutes, light returned to their faces and men grabbed and checked their weapons, re-primed their pans, and felt for their knives and 'hawks. Some made their way to the walls and found places for their rifles.

A sentry shouted, and the gate opened once again. Nearly seventy mounted Crow and a herd of sixty trading ponies breached. They stumbled numbly forward, their horses burdened down, their faces pinched tight with exhaustion and rage and the bitterness of flight. Again, the villagers brought them food and cared for their animals as the chief and others greeted them, and the two parties engaged in rapid-fire signs.

Once more a sentry cried out, and five mounted Indians entered the palisade. Ezra looked about for Dog-Eater. "McKay lost several horses on their way here. They died from the run, and that's why several of them were riding double when they arrived," she said. "The Crow were coming to trade ponies for corn and supplies when they were ambushed by the Sioux nearly a day ago. Seven of their men were killed and some of their horses were lost. They're 'spitting fire,' as you Whites would say! One of the men killed was a great man and a leader among their people, and they want blood and scalps for all of this.

"The five men who just entered are from the local Hidatsa village. They're allies of our people and enemies of the Sioux. They're afraid the bad ones will bypass our village and attack theirs, but our chief has told them we'll surely help them if they're attacked. They're pleased with the chief's words."

Ezra helped where he could, watering horses at the river and walking out spent mounts. He was amazed how the mood of the people had shifted dramatically within the last hour. The addition of the trappers and battle-proven Crow had bolstered the hopes of even the most faint-hearted.

The chief began immediate discussions with McKay and the Crow. They concluded that the Sioux, despite their superior numbers, no longer held the upper hand, that their horses were done in. It was highly unlikely they'd attempt an attack on the village. Some wondered why they'd continued their pursuit well beyond the range of good sense in such bad weather, for they were a savvy people. Perhaps, some said, "The evil spirit 'Ochkih-Hadda' was leading them to their deaths." It all seemed foolish and out of character. "The Sioux are bold,"

Cap'n said, "but not stupid."

The chief warned that their Hidatsa friends were in the gravest danger. Many of their men had gone hunting, and those remaining were not enough to defend their walls. So they agreed they'd not allow a massacre of their allies. Fifteen White rifles and forty Crow with smoothbores would blunt and quickly halt the attack, and the Sioux leadership would not risk the humiliation of too many dead braves.

And then there was the weather. If it turned cold again, the Sioux would be in desperate shape. Their weakened horses needed food, and the only source was the cottonwood bark at the Mandan winter camps or stored corn in the Hidatsa lodges. The bark, however, would not regenerate exhausted animals. It was largely a subsistence source.

The Mandan, on the other hand, had enough corn to recover the White and Crow animals quickly, enabling them to conduct harassing and deadly raids on the retreating Sioux desperate to return home. The next several days would reveal the strategy of their enemy, but most agreed the Sioux were doomed. They'd need audacity and the greatest of luck to recover themselves.

That night sentries were posted on the walls, and plans were made to rescue the Hidatsa if they were attacked. Forty Crow and half of the well-armed Whites would ride to their aid on fresh Mandan ponies that had not borne the weight of riders over the last harrowing twenty-four hours.

The Crow, despite their fatigue, craved battle. The loss of their esteemed one, Crazy Bear, had galled them. Their warriors whetted scalping knives by the light of cooking fires.

Ezra hunted about for McKay, and both men caught each other's eye at nearly the same moment. McKay embraced him with such force that the young man nearly cried out. "You did it, boy! Ya made it! Couriers said you came in alone, nearly dead. Where's Abe? Is he here yet?"

Ezra's face fell. "He's ... gone, Cap'n. On the way here ... just didn't wake up one mornin'. Buried him in a thicket." He began to sob. "Hardest thing I ever done." Cap'n's face went white. "Thomas led me and the mules over the last sixty miles. Tied myself to him. Thought I was going under for sure. Folks here nursed me to life. I created quite a commotion ... I reckon. And you were right, Cap'n. These people here are fine." Ezra wiped his eyes. "God ... it's good to see you again, sir."

"My Lord ... I can't believe he's gone!" Cap'n said. "I just can't believe it. We all loved that man. Just don't make no sense. Felt like my bro ... " His voice trailed off. "Damn this! I feel—!"

"Ain't no one's fault," said Ezra. "Just life, is all. Did what he loved. He wouldn't a' had it any other way. Lived life holdin' nothin' back. I reckon we honor him best by not grievin' too long. I suppose that sounds strange. I'm struggling too, sir."

Cap'n wiped his eyes and stared off. When he returned to himself, his voice was low and quiet, almost a muffled groan. "Yeah ... they do shine. Me and the men love it here. Mandans is traders of the first order, but they're fair, and our men'll marry some of 'em. We trade and celebrate with 'em and never worry about our goods. And their women can be pretty. Ya noticed?"

"I have," said Ezra. "Was bold with one the other day. Saw her staring at me and walked right at her. It was ... somethin'. I could stuff everything I know 'bout women in my powder horn, but I mean to learn."

"I'll teach ya, boy. But the men know more 'an me. I'll say this: any man that'd bear up under what you have these last number of months has a lot of sand. You'll go far, son. I see it."

The Cap'n turned away, his chest rising and falling—a stifled groan leaking from tight lips.

8

SCOUTS WERE SENT OUTSIDE the walls on fresh Mandan ponies to monitor their foe and, as expected, soon discovered that the Sioux were totally bled. Ezra asked Cap'n about going with them but finally decided against it. "I wouldn't ask, boy. They got too much on 'em right now ... and you ain't proven. But I'd volunteer for a raid if it comes to it. They'll need ever man they can. Why so anxious?"

"These people been good to me, Cap'n. I figure I owe 'em somethin'."

"Ever' man here owes 'em somethin'," Cap'n said. "They're everythin' I said they was, ain't they?"

"They are."

The Sioux had moved to the cottonwood groves for fire and shelter, and some were spotted coaxing their horses to nibble on their own food as they watered them from the creek. The horses were weakened and gaunt. Three of them were slaughtered for food and consumed on the spot, and the scouts sensed fear in the camp. Their horses would offer little help for retreat, and none for combat. But the fresh meat began to brighten the eyes of the discouraged, and words of strategy and recrimination began to flow among them.

Some angry warriors brooded and exploded with shouts, pointing at a large, powerfully-built man in their midst, as others looked on nervously. Soon the big man rose to his feet, fierce eyes betraying his anger, and spoke in flat steely tones to his accusers. Shortly, the angry ones drooped their shoulders and dropped their eyes, seemingly ashamed of their own impudence. The man spoke for several minutes and pointed through the trees. The Mandan scouts took notice and steered their shaggy-haired ponies back toward the village. The big man had pointed in the direction of the Hidatsa.

Back at the village, Crow and Whites listened to their report. Most believed the Sioux would be heading to the Hidatsa village, for the scouts told of the haggard condition of men and animals and how they'd need food and fresh horses for their homeward trek. And the Sioux had few options left but to overwhelm the undermanned village with superior numbers, kill some, and steal fresh horses and supplies. Fueling their desperation was the plunging temperature. One of the Crow who'd accompanied the scouts shouted out angrily. Dog-Eater was summoned to translate his fevered words.

"He says the war party is led by Crow-Killer. Says the big man has killed many Crow and shown great contempt for the Crow nation, that he must die and his scalp hang from a Crow lance. He says now is the time, and his people are no longer afraid of this man. Says Crow-Killer's medicine is leaving him, that he will die very soon—that he feels it in his belly."

When the scout had finished his report his comrades screamed their fury. The macabre sound chilled Ezra's blood, conjuring up memories of his own rage months before when he and his father had executed those men. Now he was sure he was about to witness the highest and most brutal of adventures. MacKay's voice rang out, "Ya goin' with the rescue party, boy?"

"Yessir! I am."

"Boy?"

"Yeah, Cap'n?"

"Don't get out on the skinny branches. Watch the Injuns. They know when to fight like wildcats … and when to use their heads. I'm standin' in for your papa."

"Yes sir."

"Well then … let wisdom and fury lead ya."

"I will, sir. And Cap'n … ?"

"Yeah?"

"I appreciate it. Feels good to have a man like you givin' me counsel. I got no one."

They'd depart at nightfall on fresh horses, swing wide of the Sioux to conceal their movement, and hopefully wait undetected within the village to deliver withering fire to the first wave of attackers. The next hour was filled with gathering weapons and saddling fresh ponies. Men pulled on thick woolen capotes and mittens as the evening air grew bitter, and flakes like badger paws clung to shoulders and hoods and mittens.

The deteriorating weather made the Sioux attack even more imminent, but if they could arrive well ahead of the unmounted Sioux the soft downy mix would quickly cover any trace of their arrival and presence.

Soon the gates swung wide and fifty-five well-armed men rode in a wide arc away from the cottonwoods and headed on a trot toward the Hidatsa village. Twelve miles away, the Sioux began their slow, laborious walk to the same destination as the snow began to pile up. The Sioux were locked in a life-or-death struggle. A few began their death song, the big man glared at them, and they went mute. But their faces raged.

Several miles away and closing hard on the Hidatsa, Ezra thanked his Creator for a thick woolen capote, a hardy pony, and his place in it all. He'd heavily armored himself with a sound rifle and two belted pistols, a tomahawk, and his papa's treasured belt knife. He'd use them all if it came to it. His stomach churned, pondering the outcome of the coming clash. He pulled his capote hood tight and cinched his wide leather belt. His stomach dropped as reality quickly bit him. *What if I have more bad dreams of men I'm 'bout to kill?*

His senses screamed, staring into the void of churning snow, spearing flakes on his tongue, and asking himself the question: was this all really happening? And what might the Sioux be thinking as they struggled to the same destination? The contrast between the two companies was stark. One was well-equipped, well-fed, and confident; the other hungry, cold, weak, and desperate.

But desperation could turn a weak man into a lion, he knew, at least for a short time. He'd seen it first-hand. He'd once witnessed a cornered panther kill three hounds and maul a man before Papa put it down, and it was dead-tired when it did it. And the Sioux still possessed superior numbers—perhaps as many as two hundred, the scouts had estimated, though probably not all had engaged the trek to the village. But even a force of one hundred and fifty desperate souls could hit like a prairie cyclone if their adversaries were not ready for them.

Within two hours, the men arrived at the village gates, and the troop was welcomed in. Relief loosened the faces of the Hidatsa, as their chief and warriors walked their guests through the layout of the village. The leaders divided the incoming forces on the wall, sprinkled among the Hidatsa. It was agreed that any part of the wall especially beleaguered would cry out so reinforcements could be mustered. It was also strongly conjectured that the Sioux would of necessity be bringing crude cottonwood ladders to breach the walls, and the bearers of those ladders must be shot immediately. Others thought there might be an attempt to set the walls on fire and that those braves needed to be dispatched before all others.

So, five sentries stood on the walls as they usually did, while all others huddled below out of sight of the enemy. The snow had erased all sign of their arrival. And soon the wait began as women brought hot food from their lodges and fed their newly arrived militia.

At four-thirty a.m. the snow stopped, and the moon lit up the darkness. At five a.m. a single sentry toppled from his perch into the village proper, an arrow through his throat. And so, the attack began. Men dropped hissing food in the snow and scrambled up the catwalk with weapons to find crude ladders propped against the walls and attackers already beginning to breach.

Then pistols, smoothbores, and rifles flashed lightning-like in the near dawn, and nearly thirty Sioux were badly mauled in the first assault, tumbling backward into the snow. Another wave began just seconds later, before reloading was possible. Arrows from the Sioux killed several and wounded more than a few, but this time knives and bows from the Crow and Hidatsa were employed as ladders were pushed backward under the withering fire of the native archers.

As Whites reloaded and waited for just enough light to hit targets at distance, a final wave reappeared, led by Crow-Killer and carrying fresh ladders. "Comin' again!" a man shouted. And then groans and screams from the walls pierced the bitter air until the White rifles were employed, sweeping scythe-like and halting the third and final assault.

Ezra employed his rifle and pistols and buried his hatchet in the skull of one tall man attempting to breach. In moments the badly stung Sioux ran for their lives, leaving behind their dead and wounded, and the Crow and the trappers quickly mounted their ponies and pursued them, the Crow shrieking their war cries after them as the first rays of dawn revealed the gore staining and melting the snow just beyond the walls.

In minutes the men had surrounded the nearest group of almost seventy warriors and discharged their rifles and smoothbores into the lot. When the smoke cleared, only forty remained on their feet, including the big man, Crow-Killer. Several Crow rushed him, hoping to count coup or strike him down, but despite his exhaustion he killed four quickly and grinned defiantly at the rest. Quickly the battle lulled as all watched to see what might happen next.

And then, without warning, Ezra went white-hot. Groaning like a wild animal robbed of cubs, he leapt from his horse and exploded through the crowd straight at the big man, who swung his war club back at him. He ducked beneath its arc as the blades sliced his capote and twisted mid-air to slap the man's cheek so hard the blow spun him a quarter turn.

The warrior stood stunned, lance still in hand, blood pouring from his shattered eardrum. The young Kentuckian, cheered on by the Crow now, and shocked by his own audacity, backed up nearly six paces and glared. Warmth soaked his shirt and he struggled to breathe. Adrenalin flooded him.

But the sting of the coup had enraged the warrior and, eyes narrowing to slits, he picked his target and hurled his lance harder than he ever had. And then, Ezra did what none had ever done before, or ever seen. He dodged the lance—and caught it! Immediately the Crow, smelling humiliation to come, screamed with delight, some mocking the towering warrior, his own eyes wide in disbelief. Ezra taunted him, moving ever closer, and for the first time in his life a look of doom appeared on the man's face.

Ezra mocked and teased him with feigned throws, all the while edging closer, until at last he drove the long blade past the shield and through the chest of the brute and out his back. The great defiant stood on his feet for some seconds, spitting blood and fighting gravity, until the Crow, as one, surrounded him and drove him to the ground with war clubs and smoothbore butts. Their shrieks and howls echoed all the vanquished Crow souls that had perished because of the man with the black medicine. But today, his medicine was gone.

But it was not over. One of the Crow pointed at the scalp of the big man and then to Ezra, but he shook his head and pointed to all of them. It belongs to you, he signed. One of the men made expansive cuts on the scalp and took it all, including the ears and face and even the eagle feather woven into the crown. He held it aloft, and again a second bout of shrieking madness pierced the early morning cold, making Ezra shudder.

Immediately the Crow descended upon the body, disfiguring it in every possible way. The hands, feet, and head were severed and the rest left to feed the wolves. The dead man's weapons were quickly gathered and offered up to Ezra as a gift to the new "lion man," as some began to call him. They wrapped them quickly in a buffalo skin, lashing the bundle to his pony, and proceeded one by one to scalp the piles of Sioux who had fallen around the fort, gathering up their weapons as they went.

Many of the remaining Sioux had begun the long, painful trek back to the cottonwood groves, hoping at least to warm themselves before singing their death songs, while some of the Crow, not yet sated, ran some down and slaughtered them from their ponies with smoothbore and bow and warclub. Ezra gathered himself, mounted his pony, and slowly followed after them. But not for want of war. He was done, numb, exhausted.

The dead stretched nearly a mile. The rest were left to limp back to their companions, no longer capable of mounting a charge, and certainly no longer a viable threat to any of the villages or their people. Tomorrow, the Mandan and Crow would determine what to do with the survivors. They were a pathetic lot—freezing, dispirited, and wounded terribly—a proud horse people with broken horses and no way to regather themselves.

In the aftermath of the battle, the facts were clear. The Whites had suffered one slightly wounded man and devastated the Sioux with their accurate fire. The Hidatsa had lost three men, and three more wounded, including one woman who had dispatched her attacker. Even the Hidatsa sentry, arrowed through the throat, had survived.

The Crow had lost a total of seven men, including the four who had attempted to count coup on Crow-Killer, and two more were seriously wounded. But the numbers for the Sioux were staggering. Nearly one-hundred forty had perished in the bungled assault on the Hidatsa village and the retreat back to the cottonwoods. Most concluded that it had been a glorious victory and a particularly well-coordinated response to the Sioux aggression.

In time, the victors would celebrate around roaring fires, and scalps would be tied to long poles and men would dance around those fires, while the Sioux would stay close to their own fires, slaughter more of their horses for food, and lick their wounds. They would listen dejectedly to the songs of their victors and rue the day they'd failed to turn away from a bewitching fool.

Ezra sat numbly on his Mandan pony among hard and bloody men. What he'd seen was carved into his brain. He'd never forget the maniacal screams and bloodlust of the Crow, for it reminded him too much of the execution of his mother's murderers and of his own father's madness. Nor could he ever forget the brotherhood of the brave souls bound together in defense of their wives and children, or his fight with Crow-Killer, and the near ease with which he had dispatched the legendary fighter.

But his own success mystified him. It all seemed like a dream of sorts. He ran his tongue over his chipped tooth, sucking blood from a smashed lip and remembering his mother's blow that had wounded it years ago. In seconds he cried out, sobbing, some of her ways clearer to him at last. "Oh Mama ... I understand now. Maybe you knew all along."

So, there he sat, wrapped in his woolen capote, spattered with blood atop the wiry little paint, pondering the prophecy of the holy man. A "powerful one," the man had called him. "One who would excel all the rest and marry a Mandan woman." Maybe it was true. Perhaps tonight was a proof of it all.

But now all was swimming. Adrenalin had worn thin, and he gasped for breath as his vision closed about him. He slumped forward and slipped noiselessly from his horse into the deep powder, like silk cloth sliding from the edge of a polished table.

9

Within hours, Ezra and the rest had entered the village, triumphant and exhausted. The leaders of the groups talked with the Mandan chief and McKay, who'd stayed behind to protect the people. The casualty count was taken with overwhelming consensus that the campaign had been a rousing success.

The decision was made to forestall the victory celebration and scalp dance until after a good night's sleep. The Mandan mounts, warriors in their own right and weary from the day, were taken into lodges and picketed with the rest.

Upon Ezra's return, it was discovered that Crow-Killer's club blade had punctured his back and collapsed his lung. The medicine man and McKay worked feverishly to save the young man's life, and the wound was quickly staunched with feather down stuffed into the hole. However, a deep slash nearly six inches long called for immediate attention.

McKay flushed the wound, liquored his patient senseless, and stitched it as best he could. Ezra groaned, his store of stoicism robbed by pain. "Oh God, Cap'n. I ain't drunk enough! Make it quick! Quiiiick!!"

Warm food was offered to those who had fought, and Crow and trapper alike spread their robes in the Mandan dwellings. Women woke through the night and tended warming fires as weary fighters spoke in low tones about the great fight with the Sioux and the young man who'd fought like an animal.

Puffing his pipe, McKay pondered the stories and stared into the coals. Tomorrow he'd talk with the "lion man," as some of the Crow now called him. When Ezra had rested, he'd hear firsthand what had driven him to act so rashly. It was becoming clear that the Benteen clan were a great mystery, unlike any he'd ever known.

Ezra slept poorly, but there were no nightmares—only the feeling that a heavy hammer had been taken to him and that he had swung an even heavier one. The wielding of it just hours ago had nearly killed him, and he took stock. It seemed to him that a man paid a heavy price for killing another. If this proved to be his calling, would he grow hard and unfeeling as his father had been? Would he find refuge in a jug to still the memories, to blur the faces of the men he had silenced forever? Killing was a curious thing. It stole from a man all that he was, robbed his memories before they were formed, and stole his seed before it was even planted, and he was unsure any man should ever have that sort of power. But last night's killings had seemed different from those of the men he and Papa had killed. That had seemed pointless and pure vengeance, and he had been forced into it. But last night he had gone on an adventure; and as brutal as it was, he had clawed to save his friends, and there had seemed some strange satisfaction in it all.

He lay in a whiskey haze for hours, staring at the ceiling of the lodge as its owners made crude amorous sounds during the night, as if he weren't even there, and he was too sore and spent to see the humor in any of it. Dawn could not come soon enough.

Exhausted bodies lay still 'til the sun rose high overhead the next morning. Eventually, camp dogs began prowling and whining, anxious for bones and scraps. Women arose to tend food, and soon the smell of stew pots began their magic, and hungry warriors, bruised but happy, eyes bloodshot from too much danger and too much exertion, began the pleasures of too much food. It'd be a day of glorious excess. Men would tell their battle stories and the recounting of coup and scalps snatched from the dead. The gray hairs, women and children—would lionize their men and celebrate the exploits of the Crow, Mandan, Hidatsa, and Whites, and there'd be hours of preparation for the great feast to be held when the sun went down.

Older boys dragged cottonwood branches to the center court, constructing three large piles nearly one hundred feet apart. They were crudely aligned, allowing for a spacious dance area and spots to cook and observe.

A small group of Crow warriors arrived at noon to visit Ezra. They dropped off a fresh capote to replace his bloodstained rag and flooded him with all sorts of gifts. They did not stay long. Later, McKay and some of the trappers dropped by and paid their respects as well. Their stay was brief. They told him they were making a litter for him so he might attend the celebration in style, just in case he needed it. Ezra winced and forced a smile. "Ain't sure I'm up to this, Cap'n."

"I'll be back for you, boy," Cap'n said. "I 'spect the Mandan and Crow wanna show you off tonight. I'll bring whiskey by and we'll take the edge offa' your misery 'fore we go. You'll be alright, son. We got ya!"

Ezra spied Dog-Eater slinking his way. She grinned coyly and spoke deep into his ear, "Little brother ... the Crow are saying many big stories about you. They say you counted coup on Crow-Killer with a slap that broke his ear—that it cracked like a rifle. Others say you caught his lance and drove him through. Is it true? Well ... is it?"

He smiled weakly, hesitant, 'til she balled her small fist and hit him smartly in the leg.

"Oww! Yeah, it's true. I killed 'im, and gave his scalp to 'em. Don't know whether my coup counts or not. He hurt me bad. But yea ... I gave them the scalp. Got no use for it."

"I know," she said. "They're preparing it for the dance this evening. Your gift to them was very generous. Don't be surprised if they offer you gifts and speak much about you. Some are calling you the 'lion man.' Some say you are not a man at all—that you are an old one returned from the shadow world. They say you made Crow-Killer look like a child." His face flushed.

"Had to be done," he said. "Had a smile on his face ... like he liked it all. I reckon he was like the man who killed my mama. Gave his scalp away for all he'd done to 'em. They earned it." Dog-Eater looked squarely into his eyes and began to weep.

"What's wrong?" he asked. She hesitated for a moment, struggle on her face.

"The Lord of Life must love me very much, my friend. Men provide for me. Women treat me as their equal. You've changed everything. I see the holy man's prophecies are true. My heart is full ... for you are my best friend ..." Her voice broke and she looked away. Ezra smiled, touched her face, and gently turned it to him.

"I'm beginnin' to believe too, Little Dove," he said, "but I'm the proud one. Proud of the woman you've become—your place of honor here among your new people. I'm not forgettin' ya."

They gazed into the flame, saying nothing—fearful to mar what only presence could speak.

The men had eaten and were walking around in the village, some assisting in the preparations for later that day, enjoying the sun after the previous day's bitter cold. Crow donned warm clothes and walked spent ponies around the village. Others led mounts to the river and watered them there. But Ezra remained about the fire, accompanied by two older women preparing a pot of stew. The two talked freely—the others couldn't speak or understand English well. By now it was difficult to hide the special bond between them.

Dog-Eater spoke again. "You called me Little Dove. Why?"

He replied matter-of-factly, "It fit ya when I first met you. 'Dog-Eater' seemed harsh and you were rough and ..."

"And what?" she probed.

"Well ... you weren't very pretty," he said. She nodded. "But that changed and your face turned soft and pretty. There's a kindness 'bout you now. 'Dog-Eater' don't suit ya. 'Nother name you'd like?"

She stared off a bit and, clenching his arm tightly, laughed. "It's a good name. I like it." She grew still, sidled up very close, and whispered in his ear. Her warm lips felt good. "I've something to tell you, little brother. Do you wish to hear?"

"Of course."

"Well ... two good men in this village have their eye on me. I'm a fat doe chased by hungry hunters. They seem to be wherever I go and it all seems ... too much. They may see you as my closest kin. Perhaps the chief. I'm confused."

Ezra scratched his chin slowly, teasing the time 'til she popped his thigh again. His wound was screaming, and he mustered strength not to scold her. "Alright. This is how ya do it. Look for the bravest, the best hunter, the most generous ... and the kindest, and the one most respected by the old and the wise. And don't consider an angry man or one who treats the weak poorly. And one more thing: don't ya choose a man with plans to have more than one wife. He's gotta know how you feel 'bout that. You choose a man like that, and you'll do well."

Her eyes grew large. "How does one so young speak so old?" He rolled his eyes and grinned.

"Suppose it's my parents' talk—" He caught himself. He rose to his feet, head swimming, and struggled to maintain his footing. She steadied him and he tousled her hair. And then, wrapping his robe about him, he exited the lodge and took a deep breath of cold, bracing air. His shoulder throbbed. *I need me some whiskey ... and I need it now!* He made his way to the captain.

"How ya feelin'?" McKay asked.

"Like I been mule-kicked. Feel my heart beatin' in my shoulder. I feel ornery ... like I wanna punch somethin'. Take you up on some of that 'medicine' of yours."

"Well, lad ... sit down and let ole Doc Cappy look at ya. Lift up your shirt ... Stitches look good an' tight ... and there ain't no festerin'. Gonna flush it again though." McKay uncorked the bottle.

"Shiiiiiiiit! Ya done?"

"Yeah! But ya know, we gotta care for your insides. I'll drink with ya ... so's ya don't feel so lonely." And in a quarter hour both men were feeling no pain and Ezra refused the stretcher. He'd attempt navigating the night with Captain and his men, standing upright under his own power. "A buffalo steak might fortify me some," he told his escort.

Beaten paths had formed in the village from the gathering activity and the walking out of the Crow ponies. Extra firewood had been piled close by unlit pyres, and six Mandan headed out onto the prairie looking for more game. Soon three returned, reporting that they'd found several hundred buffalo only a few miles from the encampment. Immediately, a group of nearly thirty armed men and sixty women headed for the herd with the intent of killing and retrieving enough to last the night.

Within hours they returned with their horses and drags sagging with freshly butchered cows. The village pulsed with life. Tonight would be a magnificent affair, thought the people, and camp dogs would feast on the warm bones of the freshly slaughtered life-givers. Creator was good.

Late in the day, large hide drums were positioned in the center of the village opposite the firewood pyres. And then fires were lit and drummers began hypnotic chants. Some sliced choice cuts of fresh buffalo laden with fat, throwing pieces onto large beds of willow boughs for the people to choose from. Still others, mostly older children, fashioned sharpened sticks to distribute along with the meat, and those preparations would continue throughout the night as more meat was consumed and sticks were lost to heat.

The sun fell and soon rosy hues of dusk were swallowed by the black as the village assumed a surreal look. Hissing fires slowly settled into superb coal beds for cooking, and these cast an orange-pink glow upon the snow-capped lodges and palisade walls.

People of all ages began their move toward the fires and the mountainous piles of meat. Ezra watched the best cuts being offered first to the fighters, followed by the elders. Some, having skewered their pieces, propped their meat on rocks that had been placed throughout the beds, and soon the sizzling of fat and the smell drifting throughout the commons drew even the frail and infirm from their lodges to engage the full-blown life of it all.

Ezra scanned the Crow and pulled his woolen cap tightly over his ears. He'd never seen them outside of duress, but today they seemed truly and utterly happy, their taut faces relaxed and pleasant, loose. The anxiety of the last two harrowing days had been leeched away by the great victory over their enemies, and their exhaustion remedied by a long warm sleep in the Mandan lodges. Their great nemesis had been humiliated, slaughtered and scalped, and his defeat would be noted forever in their tribal winter count. He took deep satisfaction at having helped alleviate their pain and braced himself for possible Crow speeches about his part in it all. In fact, he rather dreaded the possibility. Praise made him uncomfortable—sometimes made him look for a place to hide.

He spied a tall Crow striding his way. Little Dove, seeing the man, trotted to Ezra. The Crow waited for her, resting a buffalo robe on his hip, carefully clenched to his side. "He's White Wolf," she said, "a war chief among his people. He says the Crow will always have a place in their land for you. That you may hunt and trap and trade in his land freely, and you may take many wives from among their people. He says you are the fiercest man he has ever seen— that you fight like the badger ... and have very big medicine. He wants to give you a gift from himself. It means a great deal to him, he says, but he wants you to have it."

Ezra's face went warm. He nodded, pausing as the tall man shifted the roll from his hip into his outstretched hands. And then he carefully unfurled the roll, revealing two items of the highest quality. The first was the robe itself, an exquisitely tanned and supple cow with magnificent blond, wooly shoulders. The tall one spoke again. "My wife made this for me. She is the finest robe maker in our village, and I've not yet painted it. It's yours. Inside the robe is my best sinewed war bow and lion-skin quiver and arrows. I've never made another like it. The arrows are still dark with Sioux blood."

Ezra's face flushed a second time. His mind galloped, struggling for just the right words. He offered his hand. "I'm honored. I'll learn the bow and treat it well. And I've a new friend in this village who'll help me paint this fine robe. Let your woman know it pleases me. Your generosity embarrasses me." The tall man gave a puzzled look, embraced him, and as quickly as he had come spun on his heels and disappeared into the crowd.

Soon other Crow began to make their appearances. They donned their supple robes crafted by their skillful women and strutted like proud bulls. Their tall frames and long hair—some touching the ground—set them apart, and Ezra found it difficult to look away.

As night wore on and the great heaps of meat shrank, Mandan, Crow, and Hidatsa stretched their bellies, drank broth, and danced so hard they stopped numerous times to refuel and rest. And then they danced again. Finally, the Crow retreated into their host lodges and returned with long poles, the scalps of their enemies tethered to the tops. Before speaking, Four Bears ascended the log in the midst of the village, motioning for silence. He called for Dog-Eater to join him. Directly, she began the translation for both Crow and Whites.

"My friends ... tonight is a time of great joy. So, eat 'til your belly is tight and give the choicest pieces to the warriors, for they are our honored ones. Yesterday, our enemy the Sioux were cut down by strong men here before you. White rifles cut through bad ones like cornstalks.

"The Hidatsa stood their ground as a cornered bull ... and fought with great courage. One wounded Hidatsa women killed her attacker with a rock." At this, the people erupted in howls of delight. "And she is here with us tonight." Again, they cheered. When a few moments had passed, the chief motioned for quiet.

"Yesterday was a fine day. Our White friends would call it a 'shining' day ... and we will mark it on the winter count of our people so that someday our children will know what happened here—that we acted with great courage. Tonight, we honor all who fought and we dance the scalp dance with them. They were chased here by the fierce ones, but their swift ponies brought them to us just in time. And yesterday they slaughtered many Sioux and deserve to dance and honor their dead.

"Now ... some have asked me about the death of Crow-Killer, and you have all heard many stories ... Many days ago, our White friend, Ezra, stumbled into our village during a night of great cold. He was gray, and our women smothered him with their warmth 'til he returned to Mother Earth again.

"Days later, you all learned that his coming had been foretold by our holy man—that he was an unusual one destined for a special path, that he had big medicine. We've all watched him learn our ways for nearly two moons. He has treated us with great respect and has asked for nothing from us. We have grown very fond of him.

"Yesterday he volunteered his rifle and rode on a borrowed pony to defend our Hidatsa friends. There he killed many from the wall and rode down Crow-Killer and a band of nearly seventy Sioux. He sat on his pony, I have been told, while that proud one killed four more Crow and insulted us all.

"Those who were there tell me a big story. They say the young man rushed the big man like a lion and struck his face so hard blood ran from his ear. Never had anyone counted coup on Crow-Killer and lived.

"And then ... then our young friend turned and taunted the big man. All say that in his rage Crow-Killer hurled his lance, swift as a rifle ball ... and that our White friend caught it. And then he taunted and lanced the big man through. Many witnesses have told me the same, and they all speak as one. The Whites, the Mandan, the Hidatsa, the Crow. None of all these fighting men had ever seen such a thing. I have never heard of such a thing. You be the judge, my people. Is he the one of the shaman's dreams?

"I have one more thing to say before we feast and our young men dance. Our daughter Dog-Eater has become a dear and honored member of our tribe and makes talk plain. You have honored her, as the young White man and I have asked. And this shall never end. But from this time, she shall no longer be called Dog-Eater. She has a new name that better suits her. She will be known as Little Dove and has become like a daughter to me. That is all I have to say."

And with that, Four Bears gripped the arm of his new daughter and they stepped from the log. Her eyes filled with tears as she pondered the change in her status over the last two moons. Her White friend's medicine changed the fortunes of his friends and enemies, and she was glad he had come. He had warmed her heart and changed her fortunes, yet part of him puzzled her no end. He still seemed quite unconvinced of his power.

Those sporting scalps on poles began their dance around the three fires. Others, still cooking meat, snatched the cuts of meat quickly from rocks and embers, before the area became a place of frenzied activity. Some of the Whites had planned to dance with scalps as well, but, not having consulted with the chief, thought the better of it. Soon many Crow, a few Mandan, and several Hidatsa formed a long line led by White Wolf, who hoisted the scalp of Crow-Killer on a fourteen-foot pole. It was a macabre display. The dead man's scalp, face and ears attached, lit amber by fire and swinging eerily side to side, seemed as a ghost floating above them all.

Soon, fresh Mandan men manned the big buffalo rawhide drums, and the drumming, singing, and shrieks began in earnest. Ezra studied the patterns of the dancers. This was no spontaneous activity. These men had danced since childhood, and their smooth, animalistic patterns provoked him. He yearned to ape them and was confident of his athleticism, for the physical had always come easily for him. But this movement to music seemed awkward, like swinging a hammer with the opposite hand. So he'd make friends with a man who could show him how to dance, and they'd escape to the cottonwood groves where his awkward attempts would be hidden. There he'd gain some mastery.

But he took little joy in this particular dance, for he'd never acquired or developed a taste for the practice of scalping. In part, it horrified him. His father's use of it had made him spew, yet he understood its purpose. Some believed the soul resided in the hair and that the disfiguring of the body made it unfit for the afterlife. The threat of scalping might deter a less-than-earnest enemy, and it could win a man prestige, but he'd find another way. Still, he'd honor his friends who had no such scruples.

At the height of the frenzy, Ezra looked about the camp. Young and old alike bundled tightly in thick robes, some grasping still steaming buffalo meat, chins glistening with warm grease. Wet dancers shed buckskin shirts as steam rose from sweat-drenched bodies, oblivious to the cold.

White Wolf occasionally lowered the pole, and numerous Crow rubbed the scalps, screaming ecstatically, caught up in some unseen world of struggle and triumph. Occasionally, new dancers took the place of the old, hoisting the poles skyward like great, grisly battle flags. The dance area bristled with brutal sensuality, and one could nearly smell the blood and hear the groans of the fallen.

In time, the Crow and Mandan waved to the Whites to join them. McKay looked to the chief, and he grinned and nodded. McKay's fighters joined the circle of scalp dancers, awkwardly mimicking the warriors' movements. The invitation was an honoring of the Whites, for they'd cut down nearly forty Sioux and stopped the last deadly assault on the Hidatsa. They'd earned the right to dance, even if they danced poorly, and they certainly did. Mercifully, some Crow dancers came alongside and offered to teach them.

At long last the two camps tired, and most sat to rest, ending the awkward foray of the Whites. The gray hairs were amused by them, but the Cap'n was chagrined. The trappers began to poke fun and mock each other, and the Crow howled with laughter; most of the village, captured by the self-deprecation of the Whites, joined in the laughter until eyes filled with tears and people held their bellies. Ezra witnessed again the powerful place of humor in the culture of these people. A White man here had better learn not to take himself too seriously, for he'd soon find himself out of place. *I'll not be that man,* he vowed.

10

EZRA SOUGHT OUT CAP'N. "Sit down, son. Ain't a single thing you might say that'd insult me. Pride's all leaked out." He leaned his head back, laughing 'til he lost all composure, clawing for air, his face a light purple. He calmed himself and almost immediately roared again 'til finally he paused, his finger in the air. "My God, that felt good! Like a purty girl just lanced a boil on my ass. Last weeks 'a been hard. Some men fell back after you and your papa left us, and then … then the Mandan found us and told us you'd made it through.

"Ya know, I found hope in that, boy. Drove ourselves nearly to death to get here 'fore the Sioux did. Leadin' men's a lonely business. Can't let 'em know you're as afraid as they are.

"Tonight's the first time in a while I've felt anythin' but dread. I've not laughed in a … a long time. Laughter's medicine, ya know. My mother used to quote that to me. Got you a Bible, Lion Man?"

Ezra paused. "Got Mama's. Hid it from Papa when he was burnin' all her stuff. It probably saved the life a' me and Papa." His face grew pensive, a faint smile curling his lips. "Mama played stickball with Papa an' me like she was warring with us. Brought it from her people. She bloodied our noses and broke Papa's thumb. Chipped my tooth. She was somethin,' Cap'n, but she beat us up bad … and I hated her. Ways never made a lick of sense to me—at all, 'til yesterday.

"And then one day, Papa told me her secret. Said she felt it her job to toughen us up. He said, 'Time to let her know you ain't needin' her trainin' no more, but don't hurt her too bad,' so I hit her hard and dropped her … and you know somethin'? … She never cried out. Not once. Tears in her eyes, and she never flinched. Couldn't walk for a week. And that was that. Not sure I'd a' ever rushed that Sioux without her beatin'. Suppose she saved my life, Cap'n."

Cap'n grew quiet, his brow pinched in long silence. "You're in for the time of your life here, boy. You'll find a woman. I see 'em eyeing ya. Think you're everything they want. Ya know they seen ya naked?" he laughed.

"Folks here know you got plenty a' courage and a good heart. Them things are prized out here. Ride out on the prairie between storms this winter ... and prove your worth as a hunter to 'em. I heard me the prophecy, boy. All these people believe it. Got a strong feeling it's wound tight 'round your parents' prayers. Your daddy told me about you months back. Said, 'The Great Sovereign has plans for that one.' I trust your Papa, son. My ... I miss him."

"Me too, Cap'n." His voice wobbled. He shifted his weight, staring at the ground. "So, what about the Sioux in the cottonwoods, sir? I'm done with killin', and hell ... they ain't much of a threat now, eatin' their own horses and all."

Cap'n nodded. "If it were up to me," he said, "I'd say we load 'em all up with provisions and warm clothes and let 'em walk home. I reckon they'll tell their people that Crow-Killer got 'em all killed by pressin' the Crow the way he did. And ya damn well better believe the survivors hate him for it, for they's embarrassed they didn't oppose him. And Injuns don't follow bad leaders long. You can bet they're ashamed of themselves. Like he had some sorta spell over 'em. I never seen Injuns act like that.

"I know there's bad blood between these tribes, but the Crow and all the rest better think real hard. Wipin' out the Sioux might be plumb stupid. Retaliation might ... it might just bring the devil here. Seems to me some unexpected mercy'd go a long way in healing this thing. Gonna use what standing I have and spend it all in the next council."

Cap'n left. Ezra looked about the fires, noting the gray hairs heading to their own lodges with tired and contented faces. But as the crowd thinned and the festive spirit faded, hundreds of eyes were trained on him. Young and old, child and warrior, and those no longer occupied by dance and satisfied with food began to stare.

Ezra's head shrank into his shoulders. He scanned for the quickest way to the lodge. Suddenly, Little Dove leaned in from behind and spoke tenderly in his ear, "Don't hide, little brother. These are the eyes of great affection and wonder. The entire village is talking about you. Even the jealous men have been won over, and the young women burn for you. You must accept the respect of all and act with great care in the matter of the hot mares."

The village awakened late again the next morning. Stirring quickly, a delegation of Crow and Hidatsa, along with McKay, made their way to the chief's lodge. The issue of the remaining Sioux had to be dealt with, for most agreed their enemy would die soon, and many Crow seemed anxious to grease their path to the next world. But White Wolf cautioned the warriors to consider his counsel. "Brothers, your blood runs hot to kill the Sioux, and if you choose to fight, they'll be dead before the sun stands overhead. They have been our enemies for many years, and this would seem a fine chance.

"But consider my counsel. The Sioux are a vast tribe, with many more warriors than our own. If we kill them all, others will rise up and destroy us and our wives and children. They will not rest until we are all driven from this land.

"This is what I say: the Sioux will soon freeze and die. If we treat them as brothers ... feed and clothe and lead them home, we may save our people. Their survivors are furious with Crow-Killer and will tell of his foolishness to his people. I say that if we kill them, we have teased the great bear ... and we and our children and our wives will choke on our own blood for years. These are my words."

When he had finished, several hot-heads arose, and their leader spoke fiercely: "White Wolf is a good man ... but today his counsel is not good. The Sioux we see today will live to fight again. Then we will wish we had killed them all. I have no more to say!"

Several others rose and spoke as the first, but then a great commotion arose among the rest, and voices shouted back and forth. In time, the angry men calmed, and White Wolf resumed. "My people, these are hard things, too. You wish to torture and kill the Sioux, for that is what they would do to us. But we must remember the good of our people and lay our anger aside. What will we do, my brave friends?"

It was decided that all needed time to deliberate, but decide they must. Soon. In hours—not days, for the remaining Sioux would die quickly, and the peace overture would soon be past. All broke from the meeting and were seen talking and brooding, some angrily but others showing great restraint toward the angry ones. Little Dove left the meeting shortly after and relayed the affair to Ezra. He was disturbed at the uncertainty of the proceedings. Later that day, the council was called again, and this time the Crow delegates summoned him and Captain McKay.

McKay's words mirrored those of White Wolf. "Me and my men'll help you take the Sioux home. We'll do whatever ya need." And then he sat down. One of the hot bloods asked to hear from Ezra. He rose slowly, his legs quivering, breath coming fast, and addressed the Crow directly, "I'm a young man. But in my few years I've already shed much blood. I'm a warrior, I reckon. But I ain't had much choice. Early this year, bad Whites murdered my mother. My father and I tracked 'em to their camp and killed 'em all, and it made my heart sick. Later, the rage of my father burned his heart black 'til the Master of Life gave him another one. When it was dark ... he brought darkness to those around him.

"Two days ago, we fought the Sioux and nearly wiped 'em away. Today, they sit in the cottonwoods eatin' their horses and cursin' Crow-Killer and wishin' they were home with their people.

"My Crow brothers ... you've asked to hear my heart, so I'll tell you. If you show mercy to these enemies of yours, it may purchase kindness for your people. I'm done with killin' these men. I'll not help you kill the Sioux in the cottonwoods. I'm done, I tell ya. I see no point in it." He leaned against the lodge wall and stared straight ahead, his face expressionless, legs solid again. His words hung like sweet, strong smoke. For long moments no one said a word. But then the mood of the room began to shift, and the whisperings began.

In minutes the leader of the opposition spoke, quietly at first. "I understand your words, Lion Man. I think White Wolf was right. You have taught me. I'll no longer fight his counsel, and I will help the Sioux return to their village. And I say this: if any of the young men try to kill the Sioux, I will beat them myself!"

In time the lodge emptied, and Ezra sat by the council fire all alone as the tension lifted from his tight shoulders. He grew loose and sleepy, staring into the embers, the shock of his speech seeming to him the stuff of dreams. *How had he found those words?* He closed his eyes and thanked the Creator for his gift of persuasion. It felt too weighty and powerful—ill-fitting for his years. A present of sorts. *I understand none of this.* Seven months earlier he'd never have envisioned life in this wild and dangerous place. Nor could he have imagined rubbing shoulders with the most wonderful and terrible of peoples. His eyes grew moist at the unfolding mystery of it all.

He'd been so absorbed in thought that he failed to sense the presence on his left. A small, strong hand gripped his upper arm as a voice spoke gently in his ear. Her lips brushed him, and the warm breath stirred unfamiliar feelings. "Strong words, little brother," she whispered. "Wise talk from one so young. The Crow were won over by you. Do you know that? I heard them. They say your words are as powerful as your hands. If you asked them for their ponies, they'd give them all to you. They'll be your friends forever ... Do you see this?"

He hesitated, staring into the coals, avoiding her question—unnerved by the strangeness of all that was happening—of who he was becoming. She spoke again, this time more forcefully: "Do you believe this?"

"Yes ... I believe it, but I'm unworthy of all this." She grew quiet, straining for just the right words.

"I think I understand. I was a slave ... and treated like dung by the village. I hated them for killing my husband. But everything changed, and today I'm the chief's daughter. Today I have standing, and handsome men follow me everywhere. Some days I feel I'm dreaming and that this must not be; that I am unworthy of it all and should lower my head and no longer accept my new place. But I think ... I think that is the slave talking. And I am no slave.

"And you are not like the rest, Ezra. You're the 'dream man' ... and you've been made this way. My good friend must not run from himself. We need you!" When she had finished, her voice grew soft and sad.

"The two men I told you about are talking to the chief about me. Both are good men, and I think either would treat me well. I am hoping Yellow Elk will win over my new father. He's handsome and seems kind and generous. I think I would like him as my husband, but—" Ezra waited.

"But what?" He pressed gently. He touched her arm, and her frame stiffened. She fought back tears.

"My heart's torn by another. I fear I cannot heal."

"Do I know this man?" he asked.

"Yes. You know him quite well ... but it cannot be. He must marry—" She sobbed quietly, rising to her feet. He stood up and embraced her hard. His heart pounded and his tongue froze in place.

"I must go, little brother," she said, breaking free and bursting out the lodge entrance. He groaned in the dimly lit room, now aware of feelings he'd hidden from himself for some time. In moments he was on the prairie, running and running and running 'til his legs gave way and his stitches bled.

He'd just been clubbed a second time, and he'd no defense for any of it.

The village moved quickly to rescue the Sioux. Most agreed it in their best interest to assist the Crow, and some of the Hidatsa threw in their lot as well. An old Sioux man who'd lived in the village for years volunteered to speak with the Sioux, and a delegation made their way to the cottonwoods that very afternoon.

The battered and dying Sioux, understandably wary, slowly overcame their suspicion when thick packets of food, robes, and warm clothing passed among them. Those too sick to stand the cold any longer made their way back to the village and slept in the warm lodges of their benefactors. There, Mandan and

Crow men slept in shifts to guard them, while others planned provisions for the journey of the Sioux back to their homes.

Some of the sick and wounded were judged unable to travel. It was determined that the stronger be ferried back on Crow and Mandan ponies, with the others to arrive in a second caravan later on, or perhaps to walk home in the spring. Those left behind might also serve as hostages if the Sioux responded poorly to the Crow and Mandan and Hidatsa emissaries. But it made little difference. Those who had recommended leniency had risked much. If the Crow and the rest were cut down, those who had advocated such a course might never be forgiven. They had crossed a deep river, and there was no going back.

The early winter receded a bit, and plans were laid for the trip. All Sioux capable of travel were placed on their borrowed mounts. They and the Crow and Mandan began their historic trek on a day when the temperature and sun had risen auspiciously. Was it a sign?

With fresh mounts, warmly clad men hugged wives and mounted up. Each horse carried bags of corn for their own provision, and other riderless ponies carried even more. The drawn and hardened faces of the Sioux, now softened by food and the kindness of their victors, seemed no longer convinced of imminent destruction. They, too, settled onto their mounts, and Ezra saw looks of gratitude and even faint smiles on the faces of more than a few.

If the weather held, the journey there and back would be accomplished in about three weeks. He was glad he'd not be accompanying them, for he longed to stay put for the winter, eat his fill, and recover from his wounds. But he was grieved over his last meeting with Little Dove. They'd left much unsaid. Maybe things that needed to be said, but there was no point in it all now. Both knew the prophecy of his marrying a Mandan woman, so the matter was settled.

Little Dove had made herself scarce, except for occasions when her translations were essential, and when Ezra did see her, she quickly averted her eyes and walked away. Her avoidance seemed cruel to him, though necessary, and he respected her for it, but truth be told he missed her desperately—the perfect curve of her neck, her dark eyes, the soft lips brushing his face and her breathing warm words into his ear. He missed it all so much his eyes watered and his stomach fell away. Thinking about her made him feel gut-shot, as if rough salt had been crammed into his stitches.

But he'd move on. He knew Papa would counsel him to take the next step, and then the next, and then the next, until one day, as Papa would have said, the pain would fade and he could breathe again. But at present his heart hurt like a fist to the throat. So, he'd sleep all day and wake late and talk to Captain about the great hole in his chest. He'd seen grief drive a man mad, and he would not take that road. Instead, he rose early the next morning, driven by the need to talk. McKay offered him hot, strong coffee that burnt his tongue and sharpened his wits, and he spilled his story so abruptly that the man urged him to stop several times to catch it all. "Slow down, boy. Ain't goin' nowhere."

"Been bit hard … ain't ya, son? Truth is, she's a good one. The men all seen it … and they're jealous. But you got yourself a situation now. If you're to follow the prophecy I 'spect ya need to let her go. She's adopted into this tribe, and I don't know what that means. Ya might be messin' with the Divine if you take matters into your own hand, and I wouldn't risk it. And I hafta share this with you, son.

"Talk is that Yellow Elk's gatherin' horses to buy her from the chief … and he's damn close. So best brace yourself, boy, and make yourself scarce for a couple a' days. Don't torture yourself with the spectacle of it all here. Listen to me! If it were me, I'd take that geldin' a' yours and your new bow, and I'd go camp in the cottonwoods for a week. And I'd learn to shoot that damn thing. You shoot it 'til your shoulders ache—'til your fingers blister and bleed. Work the bow, son. Let it hurt you so bad ya can't feel the pain back here. Get, boy! Get the hell outta here!"

11

EZRA PACKED ROBES, rifle and bow, and pemmican to last the week and stopped to pick up the gray and thank its caretaker. He offered the man the knife of Crow-Killer, but he'd take nothing for the horse's care. And then the man made the sign language, but he couldn't make it out, and his eyes watered as he fought to master himself. *God, I love these ...*

He swung onto the saddle. He'd forgotten how large his old friend was compared to the Indian ponies, and the saddle felt foreign under him. Leaving the gates, he wondered whether the people were talking or had guessed his reason for leaving. But it mattered little. Distancing from the village would allow him to grieve unfettered. Cap'n's counsel was sound, but it hurt like hell leaving—or at least leaving like this.

The gray day mirrored his soul as he made for the grove, but then the sun shot through, piercing the clouds with brilliant narrow shafts, strafing the prairie and shattering the pewter skies. His mount lifted his head and perked his ears. "Thomas ... you and me need to get away for a bit and forget what's back there. I'll rub ya down and feed ya and remind ya I've not forgotten you. You saved my life, old man. You were Papa's favorite. Ya know that?"

He led his mount to the creek, and the gray drank for some time. Thomas lifted his head and nuzzled into the crook of his arm and stayed for longer than he ever had. Ezra leaned into him and sobbed. Old Thomas had been everything a man needed from a horse, and more. And now he was giving more than could ever be repaid, and it made Ezra weep.

He gathered wood and prepped the camp. He needed the physicality of his surroundings—needed to distract himself in the bracing air with the smells of roasting game and strong coffee. And he yearned to master his new weapon, to take Old Tom for a lope out on the prairie, to search for game tracks. If it were possible to assuage his grief, this land held promise. The huge expanse made him feel small—and it felt good to know that there were things bigger than his pain. *Where's Papa's whiskey?* He was glad he'd tucked it away. He'd little experience with spirits but had witnessed men dulling their pain with them. And maybe this might be just the time.

He searched his pack and spied the bow case and quiver of arrows. Sliding the bow from its case, he fingered its length. Even the sinew backing, often rough and fibrous on such pieces, was the smoothest he'd ever seen, and the sinew string was masterfully woven. Such a weapon, he thought, with such fine accoutrements could garner a fine price, and his Crow benefactor might never craft a weapon this fine again. His generosity was humbling. *This is fine ... for sure.*

He built a fire, laid in wood, and placed the weapon by the fire to warm it. In minutes, he slipped the string onto the nock and pulled it gently to warm the fibers in the brisk air. He gingerly tested it at half draw and then a few more times at full draw to the chest. It was stiff and potent, to be sure. One that would accomplish his mission out here this week. It could send a well-placed arrow clean through a cow and out the other side. It would challenge his strength and blister his hands and be just what Cap'n ordered.

He built a crude target of cornstalks he'd gathered at the village and wrapped them tightly with rawhide cordage until he had a piece nearly two feet square, which he set before a downed, rotten log just beyond his campfire. And, backing up five paces, he notched one of the arrows, pulled the string smoothly to his chest, and released the shaft. Whaaap! The power of the bow astonished him. The arrow buried deep into the bundle, nearly toppling it over. He whistled at its smoothness, "Whoooweee!" For a bit, he cared little about accuracy but allowed his fingers and shoulders to sense and feel the movements. His fingers grew tender quickly, as he shut his eyes and shot the target again and again, this time allowing the bow to find its own place in the loose cradle of his hand. He was surprised that even with his eyes closed, his shots were finding their mark. But it wasn't long before his fingers went numb, and he was done. He held it and squeezed it tightly. "I'll master you, bow. And I'll call you Esther ... 'cause you're strong as Mama."

He stoked the fire, resaddled the gray, and soon determined that a canter on the prairie looking for game seemed in order. So out they went, gently riding east, occasionally stopping and glassing for game. They rode for the next hour, until he spied several dark masses a mile or so away. It was a small group of buffalo, perhaps a dozen. Not enough to alert the village but enough to warrant a hunt the next day. He looked westward back to his camp nearly ten miles distant and spied the sun slow-trotting over the sill of the world.

They began an easy lope back home. Tomorrow he'd rise and distance himself even further from the pain of the village. He'd ride east and find a great shaggy to slaughter.

Two days after Ezra had left the village, Yellow Elk presented his horses to Little Dove's father, and the arrangement was done. Yellow Elk was a fine man, and most in the village were happy, though some whispered about Ezra. Some believed that he had left that he might not witness the marriage; others had noticed that Little Dove had seemed distant and sad. But most believed Yellow Elk had chosen a fine woman of noble character and that she would give him strong and good babies.

On the day Yellow Elk took her to his family's lodge, the new couple seemed happy. Yellow Elk beamed, his white teeth gleaming from a wide and handsome tanned face. Little Dove's face shone as well, for somehow she'd made peace with her fate and would grow to love Yellow Elk. But inside she cried a little, vowing that no one must ever know.

Ezra slept fitfully, his sleep interrupted by dreams of stolen things, and when the sun arose, he hunkered under his robes and fell asleep for several more hours, until he stirred midmorning, stoked the fire, and made coffee. His feelings sat on his skin, and thoughts of missing family and Little Dove flooded him. *What if she is the one ... and I just let her go?* He swore. Self-pity rushed him and he groaned, shut his eyes, and took a deep breath.

Soon the smell and sound of sizzling meat and strong coffee washed over him, and he felt hungrier than expected. He ate almost wolf-like, licking warm grease from dirty, blistered fingers.

Uncasing his bow, he warmed it, releasing several shafts to limber the weapon and his shoulders. This morning's session would be different from yesterday's. Today, he fixed his eye on the center of the target, drew the string to his chest, relaxed his fingers quietly, and watched the arrow fly. The first buried to the feathers, rocking the target backward several inches.

"Did ya see that, Thomas? Did ya, boy? Ain't that somethin'? Go right through a cow." The gray whinnied and strained on his picket.

Ezra followed the first shaft with the balance of the quiver, each time concentrating on a tiny spot and relaxing his fingers. The relative ease he felt at the accuracy of these early attempts surprised him. It was not Mandan accuracy, but he'd take it. And when he got better, he'd shoot better. *Need me a teacher.* He gathered the arrows, backed further away and let more shafts fly. Again, most of the arrows embedded in a span the size of a man's torso. He shot multiple rounds at nearly fifteen paces and, in spite of his clumsiness, was quite proud of himself. His somber face hinted a smile.

Recalling the captain's counsel, he spent himself. He rubbed his fingers with fat and warmed them until the feeling returned. They were raw. He dipped them in whiskey and drank a second cup of coffee. In time, memories of Little Dove stung him and forced him to rise. He saddled Tom, pulled on his capote and mittens, and was off. The gray loped east, settling into a slow smooth trot. Occasionally, they stopped to glass the distance and, after nearly two hours, spotted the small herd of the previous day, grazing near a stand of willows. The wind at their backs, the two swung wide in a large arc of nearly a mile to avoid being scented and quickly closed the distance from the east.

Ezra strung his bow and raised the brass spyglass to his cheek. There were eight cows, two calves, and a mammoth bull that watched over them all. His chest tightened. A bull like this could gore and kill them both, and he could never justify the wounding of loyal old Tom. The danger quickened his nerves. His skin prickled.

He remounted and swung below and downwind of the unsuspecting prey, stopping frequently to glass before continuing his approach from behind them. Two hundred yards out, he stopped one final time, glassed again, and discerned no visible sign of apprehension. He leaned forward to conceal his form, nocked an arrow, and walked slowly forward. Soon he found himself on the perimeter of the herd, about sixty paces from the closest cow and calf.

He sensed a shift and stopped Tom. He turned his head slowly and found the entire group looking his way. His temples pounded. He couldn't move. If they didn't detect man-scent, they might not bolt, and the bull might not charge. He determined to freeze until they relaxed, but soon the bull began circling, hoping to gain wind of him. And then it all turned.

The bull snorted and charged ferociously from thirty paces. Ezra reacted and whirled the frightened gelding at the last moment, just missing the battering ram of shoulder and lethal horns. Tom exploded forward, desperately seeking to save them both. But a horn caught a front leg, and in seconds they were both down, the big bull savaging the gray over and over again, snapping his shoulders and ripping open his belly with his black, rough horns as Ezra frantically struggled to clear himself of the saddle.

He came to himself, scanning the ground for his bow and pistol, but found neither. The bull stood motionless, breathing hard, eyes blood-red with fury, glaring and snorting at only eight paces, contemplating another charge at the last danger left standing. The two locked eyes, both now enraged at the other, until the larger flipped his tail, snorted, and trotted off.

Ezra's knees buckled. The swiftness of the attack had stunned him, and he was left breathless, shaking, hollow. He'd made decisions that should only have been considered by an experienced plains hunter, and he was not. Not by a long-shot. "Oh, my God, Thomas's a-dyin' and it shouldn't a happened!" He walked toward Tom on quivering legs. The battering had been a lethal one. Tom lay at odd broken angles, his front legs destroyed—his belly ripped open.

"Thomas … I'm so sorry, old man. It's all my fault. I hope … I hope you forgive me. I'm not certain I … Oh, God, what have I done? What have I done to you?" He slid up behind Tom's shoulder, gathered the animal's wheezing muzzle close to his own, and kissed it, sobbing.

"I'm sorry. I'm sorry, I'm sor—" Trembling, he turned away and slid his skinning knife across Tom's throat, feeling his battle mate shudder as spurting blood drenched them both. It was all over in a minute.

He turned his head and heaved 'til nothing more came up. In time he came to himself, stripping Tom of saddle and tack. He found his bow and pistol and began his trek back to the cottonwoods. It'd be a long walk carrying such a load, nearly five hours, and he could ill afford to get caught out on the prairie overnight. The thought of sharing the darkness with wolves, one pistol, and no fire drove him forward at a slow trot.

"That will not happen! Ain't addin' more stupid to this day. You dumbass. Damn my pride in all this!" he sobbed. When he'd walked a mile, he spotted movement on the horizon and brought the spyglass to his cheek. It was a White man coming at a trot in his direction. Long minutes later the figure greeted him. It was McKay.

"Ezra, … that you? It's me. For Christ's sake, man! What's happened to ya?"

"Been outfought by a big bull 'bout a mile back west. Gored my horse … nearly got me. Had to put Old Tom—" Ezra's voice cracked. "Tom's gone, Cap'n, and I got 'im killed. Damn my pride. Who'm I to think I could hunt buffalo like the Crow? I'm—"

"You stop it … right now!" said the older man. "If ever a White man could hunt buffalo like the Injuns, I 'spect it's you. You'll learn it. Just got a bit ahead of yourself is all, and we all … hell, we all get ahead of ourselves. The hardest part's forgivin' ourselves. Ya hearing me, son?"

Ezra shook his head and the tears flowed. He sobbed out how much he'd loved his horse, and how foolish he felt—how he'd just killed his father's horse and that felt like hell to him. The captain stepped forward and embraced him for a bit, as his father might have done. The captain pointed at Ezra and laughed. "Swing up 'hind me! You can dip in the creek and wash the blood off ya. I'll get the fire goin' and head back to the village and get you some clean duds and a fresh capote. We'll burn that damn thing a' yours!"

Cap'n dropped off his charge and headed back to the village. Ezra plunged beneath the water and scrubbed himself clean of blood. The water numbed him, and when he could stand not a moment more, he sprang from the creek, his lithe frame beet red, and sprinted toward the fire. There he wound his arms windmill-like, forcing blood into his extremities and feeling every inch alive. He snaked closer, seeking every fragment of warmth—millimeters from scorching himself—and smelled the sick stench of singed hair.

He threw another big branch onto the fire, and the green wood hissed and spewed embers about him. He wrapped himself in a thick woolen blanket and screamed into the darkness, "Aaaawwwwww!" and then he wept—hard. Really hard. *Am I crazy? Am I?* He danced around the fire naked, for a moment fancying himself a Crow returned from battle, but he could only think of the day's mauling. He'd returned from battle alright, but he'd been battered horribly, and a good friend had died. He was no conquering hero.

Wolves howled in the distance.

Within the hour, the captain had returned with fresh clothes and a new mount. Ezra dressed quickly and greeted him enthusiastically. The two men sat down around the fire, and McKay pulled a small flask of whiskey from his capote and passed it to him. "Don't mean to corrupt ya, boy. I've jumped in cold streams before. It makes me swear and laugh … all at the same time. Never talked to the Mandan about it, but I suspect they know. Injuns're the toughest people I know. Their grit in the cold's a wonder. The ignorant think 'em dirty as hell … but it ain't true! I seen 'em knock holes in the ice to bathe.

"Son, I brought you back a present from the Crow. I told a few ya lost Old Tom and that ya needed to borrow a horse. They insisted you take this one. My God … he's handsome. They traded for him from the Nez Perce. Three-year-old black appaloosa with a White 'medicine hat' and white spots all over his ass. Wait'll ya see 'em in the light. He'll melt your eyes."

"Should I accept that, Cap'n?"

"Ya ain't got much choice without offendin' 'em. I tried paying 'em for it and they nearly struck me. Wanted you to know in plain talk ... that this was their gift to you. I say, take it ... and enjoy their generosity. 'Spect it'll follow you the rest of your days ... whether ya like it or not. And another thing: they say this is the fastest horse they've ever seen. I only ask ya let me ride him once."

"Yes, sir!"

"And son ... I need to tell you what you already know."

"Yeah ... She's gone, ain't she?"

"Yep. Yesterday. Yellow Elk took her to his mama's lodge. Ain't no goin' back."

"I miss her breath in my ear, Cap'n. She was a brave little thing. We'd grown close."

"I know," said Cap'n. "Losin' a woman's a pain can't be wrapped up. Lost mine some years back on the Missouri coming up here. Leah came with me on a keelboat. We snagged on a log and I never found her. Never forgiven myself for any of it. She was somethin', son. Red hair and white creamy skin ... and fiery. Injuns never quite knew how to handle her, but they loved her heat. If I'd not been around ... I swear she woulda married some war chief. It fit her. Gawd, how I miss her!"

His eyes misted, he stared off and for a moment seemed lost. "But I got me a good life here with these men and the Injuns in this place. This here's the marrow of the world, son, and I'll be damned if I let the pain of her loss keep me from this life now. She'd forbid it for sure."

"Cap'n," Ezra said, "sometimes I wish ... I mean ... I wish the people we know were all those of little consequence. Then when they leave us we wouldn't mourn their passin' much ... if at all."

"You wouldn't wanna live in a world like that," Cap'n said. "No color to it. Like ... like food without spice, or plain lookin' women. That's how I see it. Woman like my Leah made every day a splash a' red. Wouldn't ever trade that away."

"I know. Hard to hear, is all."

"Brought some tobacco. Sound good?" asked Cap'n, a boyish smile stretching his face.

"Well, I never tried suckin' it in, but I'll give it a good thump. Can I have me some more whiskey?" The captain tamped his pipe and handed it to Ezra. Shortly the smoke bit his lungs, and he hacked and hacked.

"Can't take it deep in like that 'til your body warms to it, boy. You sucked before I could stop ya. Feeling poorly?" queried Cap'n.

"Yes, sir. It's comin up."

"Well ... turn away!" McKay tilted his head and roared. "I'm sorry, boy. Just that every time one of you virgins takes his first draft or swallows a chaw, the same thing happens and most of 'em ignore my warning. Let it go, son. It's coming up anyways." Ezra's face paled and he spewed, and Cap'n leaned his head back and howled 'til tears came to his eyes. When Ezra recovered, they both laughed wildly—so hard they wore each other down to whimpers.

"Lord. I've not laughed this hard since Papa and I traveled from Kentucky to St. Louis," Ezra said. "That man provoked me. Never saw a man so full of life. I miss him, and you makin' me laugh reminds me a' him. He woulda loved all this ... and the Mandan would a' worshiped him."

"No doubt they woulda," said Cap'n.

"But you got some of his qualities, Cap'n. Your plainspokenness is just like him."

"My God, you do me a great honor," Cap'n said, "but I tell ya ... you got his seed in you. I'll do what I can to school ya and watch it grow. Here's what I think, boy: follow your callin' and learn all you can from the Mandan. Give yourself to their ways. And another thing I oughta say, and it feels kinda tender after what happened to your Thomas today. The thing is, courage ain't your problem. But courage'll get your spine broke or your scalp lifted out here ... real quick, 'less it's tempered with judgment. So, lean into your head a bit more in the days to come ... and watch these Injuns. They're savvy at knowing when to act and when not ta. You got all the raw parts.

"And this is just as important. When your heart heals some, open it to another woman. The village is full of women that watch you constantly. I seen it. Some fine as your new horse." Cap'n's voice grew wistful, "I envy ya. My time with a good woman may be gone for good, but you're prime beaver. So, study, boy. And if ya get stuck, seek me out. Shinin' times are a coming. I feel it.

"Now, where's your papa's whiskey?"

The two slept hard that night, the whiskey and conversation having blunted any chance of an early rising, the midmorning sun finally waking them; after coffee, the two parted ways.

The captain's last counsel to Ezra was to stay several more days at the camp so his re-emergence would not so easily be traced to Little Dove's wedding. It seemed good counsel. He decided to spend time practicing his bow on less dangerous animals in the grove—perhaps a rabbit or a deer.

The next morning, he studied the horse and judged the captain's account accurate in every way. The horse was splendid, with a deep and powerful chest and a chiseled, muscley rump, the blanket of white splotches on the ebony butt rivaled only by the pure white mask of hair over the inky black head and white-tipped ears. He crept slowly toward it, talking soothingly as he closed the gap between them, at last running his hand along the powerful spine. But the caution had been unnecessary. The big stud seemed at ease with his new owner.

He slid his palm over the neck and down the legs of the finest horse flesh he'd ever seen; checking for the most minute of flaws, he found nothing. He closed his eyes and sighed, for this was the most exquisite of gifts, dwarfing even those of White Wolf. He'd no words, but he remembered those of Little Dove: "Creator must love me very much for bringing you to me."

Now he understood how she must have felt, and his heart brimmed with gratitude. Only yesterday, his poor decision had cost the life of Old Tom, the most loyal of friends. And he'd whipped himself hard for that one. But today, the Unseen had given him a second chance.

He wept ... again.

12

Three rabbits and two days later, Ezra re-entered the village and picketed his horse directly outside the lodge of his host. He'd thought it through. *I'll show I'm my own man—that my heart's strong. Ain't no other way.* Little Dove deserved it, and the entire village would be observing him for a while. He had to act nobly … 'til he felt noble.

Shortly, several Crow gathered round to stroke his animal. It was clear they were happy the animal was his. He stroked the stud and crossed his hands over his heart to sign his gratitude, and they slapped his shoulders and laughed. *These people feel like kin.*

He walked into the lodge and the women acknowledged him. The greeting, however, seemed somewhat practiced, as if they were assessing him. He smiled and sat by the fire, as one of them led his horse inside and picketed it with two others.

Friends dropped by, some with food. Others sat by him and stared into the fire, saying nothing. He knew he'd been missed. No words were necessary.

The next morning he rose with purpose. He hoped to see Yellow Elk and his new wife and perhaps smile at them, for that very act would be healing, and he craved it. He'd not seek them, but neither would he avoid them. This morning, for the first time in weeks, he felt a measure of strength. He made his way to the trappers' quarters and stepped inside. "Cap'n. Need me a new translator, and someone who'll teach me Mandan and maybe even Crow. Know anybody?"

"Well …" said Cap'n, "there's an old man here who grew up Sioux, but's been here for years. Knows English to boot. The men are very fond of him. Name's Black Otter. Jeffreys can bring ya to 'im. Gets along well with him. Jeffreys … take Ezra to see the old man."

Jeffreys slipped a blanket over his shoulders. They stepped outside into a bitterly cold morning as snow crunched acorn-like beneath them. He led Ezra to a lodge on the outskirts of the village and, entering the lodge, motioned for Ezra to follow. When their eyes had adjusted, Jeffreys and Ezra sat by the old man and said nothing for some time. Finally, the gray hair pulled a pipe from a soft quilled bag, lit it, and drafted. He halted and passed the pipe to Ezra, who attempted unsuccessfully to blow a ring. Black Otter looked on, a faint smile on his craggy face. The old man spoke in slow measured tones: "My friend say you want to speak Mandan and Crow. Is this true?"

"Yes."

"Why?"

"Because I wish to learn Mandan and Crow ways, and I no longer have someone to make talk for me."

"What will you pay me?"

"Whatever ya think is fair."

"Would you pay me a fine Nez Perce stallion?" The old man stared into the fire, stoic. Ezra hesitated, weighing his answer carefully.

"Yes, if you must have it!" Again, a long, awkward silence. The old man's eyes twinkled, stifling a smile.

"I don't want your horse, young one. I'll teach you talk ... even Sioux if you'd like. I'll teach you our ways and cause you to flower like squash blossoms. It'll be my honor. You can pay me in fresh game. I am Black Otter."

In the days to come, Ezra encountered Little Dove and Yellow Elk, and the chance meetings went well. The closed door of marriage in fact brought unexpected release. Ezra's heart no longer dreaded seeing her walking about, smiling lovingly at her new man. She seemed genuinely happy, and, in time, the thought of her new life made him happy as well. She'd endured much and had come far, and life had seemed to reward her for her courage.

As December came, the early false winter hardened into its usual form, and all wondered about the delegation of the Crow. If they weren't seen soon, the tribal leaders spoke of sending scouts after them. Some whispered the worst: "Perhaps they've all been tortured and killed." Some said, "And thrown over a buffalo jump." Still more speculated that perhaps a great snow had halted their progress home and that the scouts would discover this to be so. Some, including Ezra, began to feel the pressure of their earlier decision.

The elders took counsel and decided that, on the morrow, two well-provisioned scouts would begin the journey toward the Sioux with gifts to smooth their passage. However, on the morning of their proposed departure a sentry shouted, and the palisade gates swung open, to the astonishment of all. White Wolf led his men and the riderless horses the Sioux had formerly sat. They appeared thinner and weary, but overall quite fit, given the distances and the weather.

The village elders gathered about him, and for the span of ten minutes White Wolf spoke broken Mandan, until Black Otter was called for. The elders and the chief gathered close. White Wolf reported that the return had gone well, with very little incident. The Sioux leadership had listened to the stories of their warriors and of how Crow-Killer had acted the fool. Some of the young warriors craved revenge, until the older ones who'd returned spoke their minds. "Crow-Killer," they said, "had become proud and arrogant" and was responsible for the wasted lives of too many fighters.

The Sioux elders had thanked the Crow for caring for and returning their men. Some had even given gifts to White Wolf and his leading men. But now a company of forty Sioux with horses to transport their wounded back to their village lay a mile outside the village, waiting for permission to enter. The chief mounted his log in the center of the village and called for all to listen.

"My people," he began, "many days ago, some of our men and nearly all the Crow left on a fateful journey. We decided to care well for our enemy and send them back to their own people. Our brave Crow friends and some of our own warriors risked their lives to do this thing.

"Our returning warriors tell us many good things. They say our people were well treated and slept in warm Sioux lodges for several days and that the returning Sioux told the others what happened here—how Crow-Killer had led his warriors to their deaths. They say their people were very angry at that arrogant man and burned down his lodge and gave his wives and horses to others; say that only a very special man could count coup on Crow-Killer and kill him. So, they have come here now to get their wounded ones ... and to meet this man.

"And now, I think it good we invite them in and feed them well and let them sleep in our lodges. This they did for our people and the Crow. We are far more here than they, and our warriors are fierce. I do not fear their presence here.

"In the past, we have killed each other and mingled our blood with theirs. But today I am tired of blood. Today I counsel that we forget our feud, if only for a little while, and treat the Sioux as brothers. But I say this: If anyone here cannot control their anger, tell me now. I will not spill more Sioux blood because of a Mandan with a black heart. What do you say, my people? ... What do you say?" The people grew silent until, as one, they spoke. Within the hour, the

Sioux had filled the village and brought their extra horses within the palisade walls.

Ezra had listened carefully to Black Otter but understood little. He pieced together most of it when the Sioux entered the village, and he soon, quite by accident, found himself standing next to Yellow Elk and Little Dove. He greeted the two and asked his old translator what had been said. She whispered to Yellow Elk, who nodded kindly.

"The delegation went well, little brother," she said. "The Crow and our people were well treated and slept in the lodges of our enemies. The returning Sioux spoke with fierce anger about the arrogance of Crow-Killer and how his pride had led to so many deaths. They were humbled by the kindness shown to their returning ones and to those still healing here.

"So, they came to sleep in our lodges for a little while and take their people back with them. But this thing you must know. They heard how you killed their fiercest one, and they fear you. And know this, old friend … they came also to meet you!" Her dark eyes danced as she repeated, "They came to meet you!"

Ezra's face flushed. He grabbed the hand of Yellow Elk, blurting out to them both, "You're a handsome pair, and I hope you have many babies."

Yellow Elk embraced him, and Ezra, embarrassed by his tumbling words but happier than he had been in some time, spun awkwardly and strode away, light as fresh snow. "My God, I'm free!"

The next several hours were frenetic. Older children gathered wood for large fires in the village proper. Meanwhile, Sioux chiefs made counsel with the Mandan, Crow, and Hidatsa in the largest lodge in the center of the village. For hours the pipe passed around the smoking circle, as Black Otter made talk for all. When his voice grew hoarse, the important ones convened a break, and women brought in steaming brass pots full of corn, beans, and finely minced buffalo and wild turnips.

Hungry travelers smiled and dipped broth with horn spoons, and a few ate too quickly, amusing the rest with their squeals. Even the somewhat wary Sioux laughed, and any tensions that might have been, faded. One of the Sioux chiefs asked for Ezra, and Four Bears sent for him. The uncertainty of the invitation and his placement with the rest made Ezra queasy. Blood drummed in his ears. His chest felt hollow. *What am I doing here?*

Shortly the Sioux chief began to speak, referring to the other chief in question: "He says his name is Broken Horn ... that he is a war chief for the Lakota. He says today is a day like he has never known, that the Sioux have made war with the Mandan and Hidatsa and Crow for many winters. Even so ... his people have sometimes come to this spot to trade meat and hides for corn and horses. He says he does not understand what has happened to his people in recent days.

"Two moons ago, a powerful war leader from his people acted a fool and led his braves against the Crow and the Two Villages. His arrogance led to the deaths of many of his people. But many days ago, the Crow and the Two Villages returned his wounded men, well fed and warmly clothed, and continue to care for their wounded here.

"He says he came here to honor this kindness and bring a gift of fine ponies for your people, that they have brought meat and robes made by their women, and hope to trade for corn and beans and return with their men in several days ... if the weather holds. He says he knows they are at our mercy, but they are brave men and not afraid to die. He asks to eat with us and sleep in our lodges while his horses rest, and then they shall leave.

"He says your kindness has stirred them. Some of his people say it is a great trick—that their enemies cannot be trusted. Others say they are tired of war and crave peace. He says only that he does not desire war—that the Mandan have a great trade village and that they would do well to not fear our reprisals and trade with them each fall."

Broken Horn took over speaking. "Crow-Killer had once been a great warrior. None who fought him ever returned home or counted coup on him. But he became a black heart, and I am glad he is gone. We burnt his lodge and gave his property to our poor.

"Many women today have no men to hunt for them, and many children have no fathers to teach them. This is the work of Crow-Killer. My heart hurts that I did not oppose him. But I have heard that one of your own did. I have heard the story of that great fight, and of the White man who fights like a ghost. Today, I would hear him."

The room grew eerily still, as Broken Horn beckoned the young man to stand. Ezra rose to his feet, frantically gathering his thoughts. His voice cracked. "My name is Ezra. I've only been in this country for three moons now. My time here has been good, and the Mandan have become my family.

"One winter ago, my Lenape mother was murdered, and I helped kill those men. And that began my learning war. And then I lost my father on my journey here, and the Mandan, the Hidatsa, and even the Crow have become my family. So, when your people attacked the Crow and the Hidatsa, I thought it right to help my new people and found myself angry at the pride of the one you call Crow-Killer. I counted coup on 'im ... and killed him with his lance. I took no pleasure in it, but he was a bad one ... and had to die." Ezra sat down with a sigh as heads bobbed about the room. Thoughts flooded him. Where had this calm talk come from? *My legs shake but I sound like an old chief. How?*

Broken Horn stood and spoke with growing force: "The young one has spoken well. When I was young, I hungered to prove myself in battle with my enemies ... and I loved blood too much. But as I have grown older, some young men think I have grown weak because I talk peace. But young men have not yet lost their fathers or brothers or cousins. They have not had their wives slaughtered or captured ... and made the slaves of their enemies.

"I have seen all of these things. The words of this young one are my words as well. He may sleep in my lodge, for my people fear his medicine and will never touch him. I hope someday he will visit our people.

"Today, I give him my war shield. May it protect him and provide him safe passage through our land. These are my thoughts!"

13

At dusk, Ezra entered Four Bear's lodge. He was warmly greeted by the war chief and his wife, Brown Woman, and soon they were eating the most succulent goose stew Ezra had ever tasted. Four Bears studied his face, smiling.

"Do you like goose?" he asked.

"Yes. Where'd the sweet come from?" Ezra asked.

"I trade for honey from a young boy in our village," said Four Bears. "He has no fear of the bees, and when his face is swollen, I know he has new honey. Who puts honey in their stew?" he chuckled. "It's my gift to you. Do you know who I am?"

"Yes, father."

"But do you know why I am called Four Bears?"

"I do not."

"Aaah … It's a good story. Would you like to hear it?"

"Of course." The young man's eyes darted about the lodge. Three horses stood picketed, and a bundle of plush winter robes lay beyond them in the shadows. Reed mats lay about the fire, and a war bow with two quivers of arrows hung by it. A war robe festooned with painted martial images and pieces of bone and copper buttons hung from a post. A fancy chief's trade gun leaned against another, and a painted red wooden knife hung in the man's hair. He wore a knee-length elk skin shirt covered in coup stripes.

The chief's face grew lively. "I was once in battle with the Assiniboine. There, my friends said I fought with the fury of four bears, and that became my name. Do you know why I've invited you here to tell you this?"

"No," said Ezra.

Four Bears rubbed his chin and paused, smiling softly, gazing upward. "When my brother was lanced by an Arikara—you Whites call them Rees—I walked into his village and killed that man with his own lance. And I told everyone there, 'Come to my lodge and fight me. None of my people will stop you.' So, now do you know why you are here?"

"No, sir," said Ezra. Four Bears began to laugh.

"Of course, you don't. You've not yet grasped your path ... or your strength. So, I tell you—few will stand before you. This has been my path. Know that I respect few men in battle, but one is sharing goose with me. You are chosen by First Man for a strange way. It's a great mystery we don't understand ...you and I. Do we?"

"No father. It's just that ... that all that's happened seems ... it seems too much. I feel like I'm drownin' sometimes." Four Bears re-lit his pipe, his eyes curious and kind. He closed them, his face placid. He spoke nothing for long minutes, finally rising to his feet and pulling Ezra to his own.

"Go now, my son. Think on these hard things, but not too long. It will unfold before you, as it has for me. And, young one ... find a woman. There's a special one here in this village. You will find her ... soon enough. It will be a fine hunt for you."

The young Kentuckian hurried into the darkness, his brain ablaze. The thought of a woman made his blood hot, and while it might take time, he was filled with promise that threatened to burst his chest. Four Bears had lit the flame of hope and fanned it white hot.

December grew bitter after the Lakota had left for home. Many of the Mandan moved from their summer lodges to the cottonwood groves, erecting their hide lodges for the balance of the winter. The cottonwood bark provided fodder for their ponies, and many seemed to find the shelter of the trees preferable to their earthen homes. Ezra moved as well and lived with the medicine man and his family. They hobbled their horses in the grove and stayed inside as much as possible, the temperature plunging on some occasions to nearly thirty below zero.

On the coldest days, Ezra led his horse back to the village to Black Otter's lodge, picketing him inside and spoiling him with rich Mandan corn, but not too much, for he was told it could make a horse sick. He wasn't convinced the Appaloosa could endure the cold or the meager provisions of the tough Indian ponies, and he vowed to not lose another fine animal without cause. When he asked about the village to purchase corn, he found none who would sell. Instead, baskets appeared mysteriously outside Black Otter's lodge every morning, until he found it necessary to tell the old man he needed no more. And then, as mysteriously as it had come, the daily corn stopped.

Ezra visited the old man almost daily as their language lessons progressed. When the gray hair asked which language he'd like to learn first, Ezra was direct. "Mandan. I wanna learn Mandan."

"You've chosen wisely. You'll have need of the Mandan talk if you're to speak to the pretty ones here. I have seen them when you're around. They wish to make talk with you." Ezra grinned sheepishly, avoiding the old man's eyes, but his heart leapt.

Black Otter continued, "I'm an old man, and my woman left me many years ago. A great sickness swept through the village that made people's faces rot, and took her away, too. We had large hearts for each other for many winters, and she taught me how to treat a woman well. If you'd like, I could teach you about Mandan women, you know. If you find the right one, you've found the white buffalo. They'll bring medicine into your lodge," he said, placing his hand on his chest, "and keep your heart good. Hear me on this."

"Perhaps you'll teach me more than how to make the talk, then," Ezra said, "'cause I'm very lonely. I'm only eighteen winters, but I long to find a good woman, and I need wisdom."

"Ahhh ... the village has many good ones," said the old man, "but a small number of the very best. There are a handful here as handsome as your horse ... with wise and strong hearts. But I think you've a special path to travel. You must have a very strong one to travel with, or your path will crush her.

"Many of the silly ones here want to bed you, but do not falter. When you've found the right one and paid her father, then you may do what young people do. You'll stay wise if you do not sleep with your woman until she is handed over to you. If you choose this path, your mind will stay clear. That is what I believe in these matters, but this is not the Mandan way. Do as you wish."

Toward the end of December, McKay entered Black Otter's lodge during one of the nearly daily language sessions, and the two embraced as a father might his son. "Tomorrow's Christmas, son. Ya oughta come by. Jeffreys is gonna read the Christmas story, and some of the men are gonna give presents to each other. Least that's the rumor. We've invited a few of the villagers. Some of 'em heard the story before and seem spelled by it. Puts us White men to shame.

"Won't start 'til mid-afternoon with singin' and food and such, and a bit of rum and whiskey for warmth, of course." McKay's green eyes flickered. "And one of our men used to work in a French bakery in St. Louis. He's traded for sugar, and we spirited some yeast and flour into our packs back there. Got no butter, but bear grease'll make a passable substitute.

"So, come. The men'd love to see ya. Ain't a one of 'em forgot what you did two months back. Liable to rub ya for luck. Oh, and Black Otter ... we'd like you to come, too. The men got a special 'ffection for ya. They'd be disappointed if ya didn't show yourself."

It was settled then. Ezra and his teacher had plans for Christmas.

After the captain left and Ezra had returned from watering his horse, he left his teacher for the day. He strode through the village breathing deeply the icy air and the earthy smells of food and animals and feeling terribly alive.

The entire village had been blanketed with a thick layer of snow during the night—the shape of all things now rounded by the downy, frozen soft. Ezra, nerves afire and captured by the wonder of it all, failed to see the opening of the lodge cover directly to his right. A young woman exited the lodge, leading a blue roan mare with four white socks directly in front of him. A woolen capote draped about her shapely form as she strode purposefully out the palisade gate toward the river. He gave her little thought 'til she stopped abruptly, whirled about as though she had forgotten something, and headed directly back toward him. He attempted to see her face, but the setting sun was at her back and he caught only the fleeting whites of her eyes. Reaching him, she halted, spoke a few words he couldn't understand, and handed him the lead line. Within seconds she re-emerged from the lodge with another horse in tow, and an axe for breaking ice. This time she grabbed the lead of his animal and gestured her gratitude. Ezra signed an offer to carry her axe, and she nodded. Both trudged through the gate in the deep powder.

The time of the last breaking had been some hours earlier, and the ice was thick and demanded he stop a while to rest his burning shoulders. The woman reached for the axe and began to swing away. She arched the heavy tool expertly, shocking him with her power. And then she spent herself and handed the axe back at him. The two repeated the process for the next hour, seeming to find some humor in it, grinning at each other's heaving and exhausted attempts to reach water.

At last, when both were nearly spent, the blade bit broke through the final layer, showering them both with icy shards, and they laughed at the silliness of it all. He'd been unable to clearly see his new friend's face, but now amber shafts of twilight broke across her as she faced west. Warm, she peeled back her hood, revealing the most exquisite dark eyes, high cheek bones, a beautifully formed jaw, milk-white teeth, and a faded scar just above her left eyebrow. *She's beautiful! And strong as a bull!* His heart thundered like that of a fast pony galloping across hard ground. He caught himself—slowed himself, fearful of spooking her with an unfettered enthusiasm that threatened to swallow him alive.

The horses drank their fill as the young woman held the lines of both animals. Ezra grabbed her axe and shouldered it, and they walked quietly up the grade to the encampment. He felt feather light. How had he not noticed this one before now? Perhaps somehow, she'd been lost in the remarkable events of the last two months—or that his growing affection for Little Dove had blinded him to her presence. But he was not blind now.

That evening he slept well, more convinced than ever that Creator was good and life held promise. The older women in his lodge seemed amused at his dumb grin. They signed to him, but he couldn't understand. They giggled and he wondered if they'd seen him with the young woman and whether people were already talking. In the morning he'd go see his teacher and ask him about her. He could see it all play out in his mind. Black Otter's eyes would flash, his grin creasing his crinkly face as he'd give Ezra a great going over, enjoying every minute of it. But he reasoned that it'd be worth it all to know more about last evening's mysterious stranger.

In the morning, Ezra pulled on his winter moccasins, stuffed them with wool, and ate breakfast. The morning was especially cold, and the women stoked the cooking fires hotter than usual. They had stuffed every chink, and soon the temperature became quite comfortable.

He made goodbyes and headed to the palisade for his lessons. He'd begun to piece together words and phrases, even a few in Crow, and his sincere and sometimes humorous renderings made his Mandan friends bend with laughter.

Black Otter was in fine form, his eyes already a-twinkle and a curious set to his lips. "How's my young friend today? Did you sleep well? Sometimes when a young man breaks ice, he sleeps like the dead. And sometimes … sometimes when he breaks ice with a pretty woman, he may never walk Mother Earth again. How'd you sleep?" Black Otter grew silent, his face strained and belly taut under his elk-skin shirt, heroically stifling a laugh.

"My shoulders ache," said Ezra, "and as you seem to already know ... I slept like a heavy stone last night. I'm tired but happy. I'm good, old one. Very good. Last night I broke ice with a pretty woman who swung the axe like a man. I wanna know more about her. Who is she?"

"Aaah ... that one. The ice breaker. Yes, she is a strong one. Some think too strong. But she's a good heart. Is that who we are making words about?" Black Otter began to shake as his eyes watered.

"Yes. You know it's her, and I need some answers!" Ezra's voice rose, annoyed.

"You do not need answers, young friend," said the old man. "You want them. What you need is wisdom. But I will answer you nevertheless. Her name is Moon ... and she's the medicine man's niece. Her father is a respected one here. I know him well and know he will not give his daughter to just anyone.

"If you choose this path, it will not be easy, for Moon is a special one, and all know it. All the warriors here desire her ... but are puzzled by her. The other girls her age no longer play games with her because she has bruised them so badly. Lately, she has learned to play more ... gently. Even the boys quit their play with her some winters back. She broke arms and kept our bone-setter busy. She—"

"She actually broke bones?"

"Yes. Several times."

Ezra's eyes widened. "She's stronger than them?"

"Not any longer. The boys have grown past her. But she shoots and rides as well as any of them."

Ezra's brow furrowed. "Are you joking with me, grandfather?"

The old man shut his eyes and went mute. He gathered himself, furrowing his brow, choosing his words precisely, a surgeon selecting his tools. "The village loves her kindness," said the old man, "but some fear her strength. She is ... unusual."

"Is someone courting her?" asked Ezra.

"No. Her father fears she will live with him forever and die a lonely gray hair. Be aware, my son."

Ezra and Black Otter left for the trapper's party, but not before the old man had changed into a fine shirt and wrapped himself in a plush robe. As they strode the length of the village, Ezra turned eyes toward Moon's lodge, hoping to catch another glimpse of his mysterious companion. Tonight, he'd spend considerable energy calming his imaginations. He owed the Cap'n as much.

In time they stood in the midst of the lodge, the central fire stoked higher than usual, and the captain greeted them. Some of the men had made Christmas decorations. A small, crude table had been placed by the central fire pit with the most appealing item of all—a wonderfully crafted cake, three tiers high, covered in icing made of trade sugar, bear grease, and molasses. Apart from the woman of last night's encounter, Ezra thought this the most magnificent and lovely thing he'd seen in months. It reminded him of the colors of St. Louis and the creations from his mother's clay oven. And it all made his eyes swim.

Some men unwrapped a few jugs, as the captain set two containers of spirits on the table by the cake. "Tonight, men," he said, "we're here to celebrate Christmas—to have a fine old time. There are Mandan and several Crow with us. Black Otter is here with his young student, Ezra, and our friend'll make words for us, if he would be so kind."

Black Otter grinned and the Cap'n went on. "Jeffreys'll read the Christmas story for us shortly from the Good Book, and when he's done some of you men who brought presents can give them away. Many of ya are savin' some for the girls down at the cottonwood camp. Can't say I blame ya.

"We all know this's been a tough year. We made it this far 'cause of Ezra and his father and our friends here. I need not tell ya ... I'm not a religious man. But I'm powerful grateful we made it here, and we didn't lose a one of us. Tonight ... tonight we'll acknowledge the Great One and his Son for takin' mighty fine care of us. And boys ... when we're done with the readin' and all, we'll feast and drink the little bit of spirits we have, and carve up that cake like starvin' hogs. Tonight, we're the most blessed of men."

And for the next seven hours, Crow and Mandan and a few Hidatsa plied the captain on the mysteries of the baby and the incarnation. Others stuffed their bellies with corn, beans, and fat buffalo seared in hump fat. And then, of course, there was the cake.

That marvelous ...glorious ... cake.

14

It was January, the season some Indians call the time of "popping trees," the cold so deep that cottonwoods explode like gunfire. Ezra sometimes heard them in the middle of the night when the sun had gone and the temperature had plunged. *My God, this is a wild place!*—the "marrow of the world," the captain called it. And Cap'n was right. Ezra was coming to believe he could not live anywhere else. It was certain a man could not live half-heartedly here, for he'd soon die. It demanded everything a man could muster, and sometimes more. He remembered one of McKay's early speeches about the West, likening it to a beautiful and dangerous woman who'd pleasure you one moment and kill you the next, and he believed it now more than ever.

He ruminated on the words of Black Otter regarding Moon, but his friend's description of the young woman scared him not a lick. The best he could figure, she seemed a great deal like his mother, with a big heart and full of fire. And he'd no desire for a tepid, weak sort.

In the following days, he missed Moon and grew curious and in time discovered she had been tending her ailing mother at her lodge in the village. Her sisters had been watering the horses for the last two weeks.

On his way to see Black Otter one day, he spied her stepping outside for firewood. He offered to help her, and she nodded. She led the way into the lodge, his eyes struggling to adjust in the dimly lit room. He placed the wood on the hard-packed earthen floor, and his eyes scanned the interior of the lodge. It was a prosperous home. Two fine ponies stood picketed at one end of the lodge.

He'd barely noticed their exceptional quality before—with sinewy, muscular, finely formed heads and square muzzles and padded with long winter hair.

The lodge itself was well provisioned with baskets of corn and winter-kill robes. To one side of the room hung an exploit robe painted with the story of its owner. A war shield, a lance, and two trade guns hung from the main supports near the center of the lodge. The center firepit was bordered by stone, and an imposing fellow in his upper thirties sat near it. Moon sat tending her mother, who lay covered in thick robes, her head propped up by a large, buffalo-hair-filled pillow. Moon spooned warm stew into her mouth.

Ezra attempted a few words of greeting he had memorized from Black Otter, then tried an apology for his intrusion, but hadn't the vocabulary. The man motioned for him to sit across from him. All sat round the fire for some time in silence. Occasionally, the parties exchanged awkward smiles, and soon Ezra settled into the rhythm of the Mandan way. He was becoming used to this way of communicating—the comfort of quiet, with few words exchanged, but he was determined to try. Pointing to the ponies, he swept his hand toward Moon and the axe lying close to the fire. The man smiled, nodding. Ezra pointed to the woman lying prostrate, tilting his head in question. The man responded with a slight nod, "She ... better."

"Good, good!" Ezra blurted out nervously.

Directly the man stood, shook Ezra's hand, and gestured to Moon. She wrapped her capote about herself and grabbed the horses' lead lines. Soon, the two were headed to the river. Walking together through the palisade gate, he saw people watching them. Ezra felt a strange calm as they walked, frequently stealing a side glance at her form and face. Hanks of straight, ebony hair had escaped the hood, framing her oval face for the second time in his recollection. High cheekbones, a strong jaw, and flawless skin and dimples framed the most piercingly intelligent eyes he had ever seen. She was a sight—the most intriguing figure his eyes had ever lit upon, and his heart beat fast and hard. His mittened hands grew sweaty.

Arriving at the river, both gave their horses their heads. The animals froze as though tied to some invisible stake. His experience with animals, especially during recent months, had taught him that they were creatures not merely of instinct but at times of remarkable intelligence. They seemed to memorize patterns and recall the faintest of cues, and today they did not disappoint. They knew to wait on the water and it amused him, and he longed to communicate his observations. He'd probe.

"Can you speak the White man's words?" Ezra asked. A long silence. Moon turned and faced him.

"I can make the White man's talk. Black Otter's my friend. He's taught me many things."

"The gray hair has taught you?"

"Yes. He's taught my father also ... but I know more."

"Why didn't you talk the last time we met?"

"It's not my way. I was waiting for you to try."

"Why?" he said. She hesitated for some time before continuing, "I ...

"I waited to see ... if you have courage." Ezra's eyes widened.

"So ... you think I lack courage?" he asked.

"No. Your fight with Crow-Killer will be painted on the winter count of our people. I think you fear no man."

Ezra's brow furrowed. "Then what do you mean, 'if you have courage'?" Again, Moon paused, leaning slightly forward.

"Brave warriors have hunted me many times. But they all run away. Are you hunting me?" Her eyes bore into him, her face a strange palette of curiosity and rising anger.

"I think so. Is there a reason I shouldn't?"

"Have you talked to Black Otter about me?" Her voice rose a measure as she shrunk into her hood.

"Yes, I've talked to him. He told me about you. Please hear me."

"What?"

"I'm not afraid of you. I'm not afraid."

"Why must I believe you?" Tears welled.

"Because I see a great kindness in you."

"And?" What does th—"

"And I see the strength of the woman who birthed me. She scared men, but not my father. He was strong like her ... in a different way. And my mother carried the kindest of hearts. Black Otter told me you were kind."

She turned to face him now. "Do you have more words to make?" she asked.

"No. Can I stop by your lodge more often ... to visit your family?"

"Don't you wish to see me?" she probed.

"If you're there ... I'll see ya."

In time the cold seeped into them, and the swinging of the heavy axe seemed good again. Moon swung ferociously as Ezra looked on fondly, and after the last cut and the watering of the horses the two weary cutters retrieved their animals and made for the village. But the grade upward felt different somehow. Though they had toiled harder than before, they seemed not to notice. This time, their full hearts carried their weary bodies home.

It was nearing the end of January and the temperature became deadly. Several ponies nestled along the river died one morning, and McKay reported that the mercury had dropped clear into the stem of his thermometer. "Forty-five below," he grunted, stamping his feet on the frozen ground.

Some who'd sought shelter in the winter camps herded their ponies to the village and picketed them in the lodges until the bitterness broke.The gray hairs and the sick stayed indoors, but, amazingly, life continued on. Ezra's respect for the hardiness of the people grew as he watched them thrive in such weather. They were prudent but bold, and when the temperature had risen twenty degrees men began to hunt again, and children laughed and swept down the bank onto the frozen river on buffalo rib sleds, enjoying themselves immensely, their laughter echoing across the river and beyond.

One day, after a week of mild warming, a small hunting party left the warmth of the village to venture out onto the plains and returned some hours later, reporting that a herd of several hundred buffalo had been found an hour north of the main village. Within the hour, nearly fifty Mandan and Hidatsa, twenty Crow, and thirteen Whites mounted up and set out in pursuit. Some of the Mandan brought smoothbore trade guns along with their bows, for experience had taught some that the bitter cold occasionally shattered a bow at the most inopportune time—that only the sinewed bows could be fully counted upon.

Ezra loaded up his trade gun, pistols, and as much warm clothing as his body could carry. One of the Crow offered a hunting pony to him, and he reluctantly agreed. He was not yet willing to risk his own horse in such an endeavor and was uncertain the stallion had been trained to hunt buffalo anyway. The Indian horses, however, had been taught to run alongside the dangerous beasts, evading the aggressive horns, and could be steered with pressure from the rider's knee, leaving the hands free to handle weapons. He was humbled, for to be offered another's horse was a great honor. A single well-schooled animal represented countless hours of training and provided food, clothing, prestige, and shelter for a family. Its owner had gambled much.

A few miles out, the party spotted the herd and began their approach downwind. The buffalo seemed unaware of the hunters until the group was within three hundred yards, and then they began milling about. In time, two massive bulls grew wary, and soon the entire herd was on the run.

The hunters, led by the Mandan and including Hidatsa who'd joined in, closed the distance. Ezra watched, open-mouthed, as mounted braves rode directly alongside the stampeding buffalo, firing their smoothbores at point-blank range. The sharp pounding and clatter of hooves on frozen ground, the cracking of smoothbores, and the breath of terrified animals fleeing for their lives hung mist-like in the brittle air. Then a heavy snow began to fall and softened the forms of men and beasts and slaughter, and his breath caught in his chest—the scene nearly undoing him with its raw, unbridled beauty.

On four occasions, he witnessed the nimble mounts adroitly sidestepping murderous charges from furious cows and a few giant older bulls. One horse and rider went down in the confusion as a massive bull went for the horse, who, defying all odds, miraculously fled to safety. Another rider deftly scooped up the downed man, his trade gun splintered on the ground, and spirited him to safety. There he regained his mount and resumed his hunt. It was a magnificent display of horsemanship and courage. *I'll never farm again!* This was the purest form of adventure, and Ezra's heart stretched to grasp it, an extravagant gift seeming too good to be true. He could scarcely believe his eyes.

As the party raced on, the hunters left a trail of dead and dying buffalo behind them, and soon the Whites began their quest for winter meat. Ezra closed the distance on a cow and her calf and, swooping down, realized danger too late. The cow, feeling her calf threatened, swerved and bore down on him. His mount cleared itself, but the cow's horns battered his leg calf. He grimaced, his moccasin filling quickly with warm blood. Maneuvering closer again, but more gingerly than before, he delivered a killing blow and mercifully horse-pistoled her calf seconds later.

He wiggled his toes. "It ain't broke," he shouted to McKay. "I'm trying, sir!" he groaned. He reloaded, killing another three cows and one more calf, each time taking care to stay beyond the range of those deadly black horns. The danger and speed and ferocity of it all was jarring. He leaned across his horse and puked.

Within the span of an hour, stretching over three miles, the prairie was littered with the carcasses of nearly two hundred animals. In the distance, he spied a train of women, older children, and pack animals headed toward them. It seemed as though the entire Mandan and Hidatsa villages were sending help to butcher and retrieve the game. "Gotta get em back 'fore nightfall ... or they'll freeze and be a devil to cut up!" shouted Jeffries.

And then, to Ezra's amazement and total delight, he watched some of the Indian hunters pull the still warm hearts from their kills and eat them raw before him, the warm blood dripping from their chins. One offered him a piece and, and thinking it rude to refuse, he joined them. "Good! "Very good!" They laughed heartily, mocking the blood dripping from his face. He craved a mirror so he might see himself, but he supposed that its absense, if he looked anything like his companions, it was a fine thing. The blood was salty and the flesh tender, and it seemed the best food he had ever swallowed. He laughed at himself.

He hobbled to his mount and recounted his steps. Locating his first kill, he dismounted next to it. He clumsily removed the heart, bit off a large piece from his own kill, and gobbled it down. A few close by came to his side and slapped his back affectionately. One brave dipped his fingers in the blood of Ezra's animal and smeared two streaks across the bridge of the White man's nose.

A small group of nearby Crow found their kills, identifying them by the color of their arrows. Ezra watched the Crow cut the hide down the spine, unlike the Hidatsa and the Mandan. Crow women, Cap'n had told him, unable to flip the heavy animals free of their hides, had learned to cut the skin down the spine, freeing it from the animal one half at a time. Later, they sewed the skin together with sinew and painted the seam. "That's where the red stripe comes from, son," said Cap'n.

Shortly the butcherers arrived on the scene, leading pack horses trailed by large travois, the sapling frameworks on which the monstrous amount of meat would be piled. Soon, at least eighty women, he judged, began their arduous work of gutting, skinning, and butchering the animals. Most of those slain were cows, along with a small number of calves and some young bulls. The older children were employed too, under the supervision of their elders, and their knives separated tendon from bone, but a bit more slowly than their mentors.

He'd killed four cows and two calves and badly lacerated his left leg, all in under an hour. Mustering crude language skills, he rode among the people and offered three of his cows and one calf to whomever might want them. He'd break the right horn of all he'd shot, and those could be distributed at will. The men and the butcherers nodded as he trotted to the one kill he intended to take home.

Sitting on his borrowed pony, he marveled at the remarkable efficiency of the people, gingerly massaging his calf, and turned in time to see Moon sliding off her horse and striding boldly his way. She carried two knives and, saying nothing, began the butchering of his animal. He dismounted and limped toward her, leaving crimson prints in the snow. She frowned and waved him off.

"I'll look at your leg when we're done here. You've not been careful enough … You're a crazy one." She grinned and pointed at his animal. "Watch the Mandan way, White man. Perhaps next time, you'll be alone with no one to help you." Her voice grew stern. "Mandan women are the finest butcherers on Mother Earth."

"Then show me," Ezra said, stifling a smile. He studied her as she deftly cut, separating shoulders and loin and hide. Again, he offered his assistance, and again she refused. But this time her voice had grown soft.

"What do you intend to do with your kill? Do you have more than this?"

"I'm sharin' this cow with three others and your family. I killed four cows and two calves. I'll give 'em away 'cept for the calf. I'm keepin' 'im."

"It's good to give much away," she said. "Generosity means much among my people. But why give meat to my family? Food is always plentiful in our lodge. Do you need to prove yourself as a hunter to my father?"

"I'll prove myself as a hunter to your people—not just your father. Got plans to be the best hunter in your village. But I can't separate meat from bone … like you do." His solemn tone had softened, a slight smile curling his lips.

"Are you mocking me?" She tilted her head playfully.

"I'm not mockin' you. I'm dancin'. Don't ya feel the dance, pretty lady?"

"I don't understand this thing of 'dancing'," she said.

"Moon … both of us are dancin' right now," he said. "We dance when we cut the ice together. We've been dancin' for a while now … you and me. I'm not afraid to follow your blade. Are you afraid of my dance?" She turned away, wiping her eyes, and resumed her knife work, blood on her cheeks.

"I am afraid of this dance, as you call it," she said, "but if you continue to water the horses with me … and visit my family, I think I'd like to learn it …"

Ezra's heart thumped and he fought to still himself. He closed the two steps between them slowly, grabbed her bloody hands, and vigorously massaged them, her blood staining his own as he looked into her eyes and smiled.

Her black eyes dilated, open and unguarded, her face visibly relaxing and her shoulders uncoiling. She was beginning to trust him, and he could feel it. He'd walk softly and let this wild pony come to him.

15

FEBRUARY OPENED with a brief warming spell on the upper Missouri, and the mercury rose into the thirties during the days when the sun shone. Many in the village, and the Hidatsa as well, acted as though spring had come. Some men walked about shirtless, their naked upper bodies draped by merely a robe and with one shoulder uncovered, tattoos exposed to the world. Children played at games, and some women played a game of ball, the object of which seemed to be keeping the ball in the air as long as possible, using only one's legs.

Ezra watched Moon teaching the younger girls, impressed at her skill. He studied her form as she moved, noting her every curve and liking everything he saw. She was not a large woman—five-feet-three and one-hundred-thirty pounds, but she moved with deceptive speed and restrained power. She called her girls to gather around.

"My friends ... the Lord of Life has given us a beautiful day to play and stretch our bodies. And we have a fearless warrior who watches us, I think ... with great curiosity and amusement. I hear from many that he fears nothing—certainly not a group of young women. Would you like him to play with us?"

The girls giggled and motioned that Ezra join them. Moving toward them, one of them kicked the ball his way, too hard for the range. It smashed the side of his face, watering his eyes. The girls gasped, waiting for his reaction. He groaned and clutched his face, "Oooowww..." and fell dramatically on his butt. Immediately the whispers began. Some scolded the kicker, but Ezra sat a bit longer, pointed directly at the girl, and nodded his approval. The girls immediately cheered him then, several smirking flirtatiously. They were not more than thirteen, though for the moment they acted much older. He'd won them over in the opening salvo and had worked them masterfully.

For the next little while, Moon schooled her students—all of them. She was superb. A pure marvel to watch. She cut quite the figure in her long-sleeved elk-skin dress, leather leggings, winter moccasins, and a blue woolen cap. She shed her coat, and he scanned her sleek body once again. Strong but feminine—powerful but sleek. *This what you saw, Papa?*

As the day wore on, the girls began to leave, and the lessons became more intense. In time, more and more of the attention focused on Ezra, and the remaining girls stopped to watch. The teacher kept the ball suspended in the air, at will, seemingly indefinitely. In total control. He was stunned at her athleticism. *She moves like you, Mama.*

Then she finished, tossed the leather ball to him, and motioned him to do the same. Her dark eyes flickered mischievously. Without hesitation, he kept the ball aloft for longer than any had expected and then fell awkwardly forward, the ball rolling from him.

The girls went silent. "He's angry," some whispered. He slowly crept forward, grasped the ball in his teeth, and rose to his feet. Flicking it upward with a flip of his head, he caught it deftly in the crook of his left knee and cradled it easily for long moments, setting it down on the ground when he was ready with the greatest of care. He smiled at his new friends and grinned hard at his teacher. She smiled back, faintly.

When the girls had left, the two made their pilgrimage to the river with their horses, and he brought his own horse with him. During a lull, Moon ran her hands along the spine and the legs of the splendid animal.

"I find no flaws in this horse, White man. How?"

"Don't know. Sure there's somethin', but I can't find it either." He paused. "Did you enjoy teachin' today? I watched ya. You're very good."

"And?" she asked.

"Ya mean … how you tried to embarrass me?" He paused once more, a smile tugging his lips. "And did you see? It didn't work … 'cause you're better than me … and I don't care. You're strong and I love it. Won't ask ya to be less."

"Are we dancing again, White man?"

"Yes, darlin' … We've been dancin' all day."

March slowly came into view, and Ezra found himself spending more time with Moon and her family. Her mother was growing stronger and making slow rounds through the village. It was clear that her family had all grown quite fond of him.

He busied himself greasing horse tack and learning as much talk as he and Black Otter could find time for. He discovered he had facility for language and asked his teacher to help him with some Crow, for most of the Crow who'd overwintered in the village would be leaving soon, and he hoped to speak with some of them before they left for their homes to the west.

One day he asked Moon if she'd join him for a ride. He wished to try his new horse and scout for game. "I'd like that," she said, but counseled him to speak with her father about it. So before he might stop himself, he strode straight into Black Bull's lodge and sat down by him. "Sir, I'm takin' my horse out ta test him and scout for meat. I'd like your daughter to ride along. Can she?"

Black Bull was mute for a bit and instead invited Ezra to dip a spoon into the pot. He lit his pipe and handed it to the young man, who drafted and blew a ring upward. "Moon is a fine woman. Do you see that?"

"I do, Father. I'll care well for her."

"I know. I watch you. You're a good man. You've shown much courage to be so close to my daughter."

"I suppose, but I've never been afraid of Moon. I'll never fear her."

"Yes ... that one," the man said. "A strong she-bear full of sweet inside. My people love her ... but she's confused them. I think you've helped her find her path. She's made her mother and me fear for her future. Since you've come, we no longer fear."

"Good! She's made me happy, but I can't stop my talk much longer. My words are about to jump outta me."

"I see it." Black Bull grasped his hand and grinned. "Make the words soon. Her mother thinks she is ready." Ezra's heart pounded. "Tomorrow you'll take my two finest buffalo ponies," said Black Bull, "and I'll give you a bow I've made for my daughter in secret. Take yours as well. Nothing pleases her more than shooting with one who loves the bow as she does.

"She loves to shoot far out onto the prairie ... to lose the arrows in the sun. We've done this many times together, her and I. But these things have caused her some confusion here. Do them with her, and she will love you for it. She wants only to follow her path and journey with one who loves her. And return with more meat. I need to know you can hunt."

Ezra found her in the lodge of her uncle. Those villagers who had made their winter homes down by the river had begun moving before the river ice broke up and the bottoms began their seasonal flooding, so he loaded his horse and began the journey with the rest. He and Moon walked the grade 'til he thought he would burst. "I spoke with your father."

"Yes?" she prodded. He continued walking. She asked again, this time more earnestly.

"And?"

"About what?" he asked. Her eyes narrowed, and he went on, "He …

"He said 'yes,' but that you're a stubborn bull—that I should be ready."

"Are we dancing again?" asked Moon, rolling her eyes.

"You're learnin', pretty one."

"You think I'm pretty, then?"

"No. I think you're … beautiful." Her face flushed. She looked away.

"I don't know what to say."

"Don't need no answer. I love to see you like this."

"And how is that?"

"Undone."

They left early the next morning on the two borrowed horses. Her horse pulled a large travois. His was laden with weapons and robes. It was obvious to the watchers that this was a hunting expedition, but it was also clear that something mysterious had passed between them during the winter months. A father'd not loan his prized ponies to just a daughter's passing fancy, and no one in the village perceived Ezra as "just" anything, anyhow. Many had been talking for some time about the possible pairing of Ezra and Moon. One of the Crow warriors, a man of considerable reputation, had expressed strong interest in her in recent days, but even he'd faded, like all the rest. She'd been glad when he'd left for his home, for he was just one more rebuke, and she vowed no more of it.

But then Ezra had come along and pursued her in his dogged but relaxed manner. His ways had given her time to breathe and his perseverance had proven he was not afraid. Nearly all had come to the same conclusion. Even Little Dove thought the match a good one and rejoiced in the path of her old friend.

The small party headed west, in the direction of the Crow. One of Moon's camp dogs followed along behind them. He was wolf-like and stood taller than most of the dogs at the village. Ezra recognized him as one who'd trailed him about the village since his arrival, but had never come close.

As they traveled on and the sun rose high overhead, they stopped to glass the horizon. They pulled jerked buffalo from beneath their capotes, and the warm sun on their faces and the pungent meat stirred them. Ezra groaned as he chewed. Moon said, "I think the Lord of Life loves me, and today I sense it more than I ever have. I have things to say."

"I'm listening."

She continued, "I feel this because of you, Ezra. You're Creator's gift to me and my best friend and ..."

"And what?"

"There's something in the creek bottom ... over there. Do you see it?" she asked.

Ezra glassed hard. "There's a group of nearly ten elk. Even more deer down there. You up for a stalk?"

"I'm always ready, White man."

"Moon, I got something for ya. Your father sent ya a gift. Best see it now." He reached inside the coiled robe and drew out the bow case with its arrows and quiver. "Your father wanted you to have this. Said he made it just for you—that it was very important you have it. His eyes danced when he talked 'bout you and the bow."

She slid it from its case and ran her hands along its length, gasping. It was a fine piece of Osage, the back expertly sinewed. It was clear her father had spent much time crafting the gift, for he'd assessed her draw and poundage perfectly, and it was compact enough to shoot from horseback, should she want. But it was no weak bow. He'd made her a killing piece, and her heart leapt at his confidence in her.

"Look at this, Ezra. Isn't it beautiful? It's almost as handsome as you."

"You think I'm handsome, huh?"

"If ... if a lion can be handsome."

"We can't hunt, Ezra. This bow's untested. We'll find somewhere to shoot our weapons and make sure of our arrows. Yes?"

"Of course."

They retraced their steps until they found a beautiful plain bordered by another creek bottom and willow grove. They strung their bows and hobbled the animals. Moon flexed her bow. It was stiff but smooth, the work of a fine craftsman who understood its intended user. She reached for an arrow. "No one makes an arrow finer than the Mandans. Did you know that? Your Crow arrows are good, but not like my father's. Let's unbridle them and let them run." She winked. She arched her bow and let go for distance. For several seconds the arrow was lost from view, but then it re-emerged as it fell earthward, its iron point clinking at nearly two-hundred paces in the stony ground.

Again, she let go, and then again and again and again, until she had spent her quiver. From where they were, she appeared to have grouped them uniformly together. She stood, triumphant, her face stretched tight. She cried out, "It's time for you to shoot your bow, Ezra. Do not spare me! I'll know if you do."

He slid the first arrow onto the string and, noting the grouping of the previous shots, let go his first shaft. It arched into the blue and slipped beyond her farthest by nearly twenty paces, but that was to be expected. His was a potent man's bow. He unleashed the next five, and four more eclipsed hers by nearly as much, with one settling in amongst her own.

He scanned her face for disappointment but happily found none, for she was eminently pleased that both had shot further than most. They continued for some time until she'd broken in her weapon and developed a feel for it.

In time, they found a rotten piece of soft cottonwood. He aimed at the crook in the log, standing at nearly fifteen paces, and buried three arrows in a space the size of a man's head. Grinning broadly, he gestured for Moon. She stepped forward and delivered four shafts in rapid succession, the first of which went wildly astray. But she quickly corrected until the last two nearly touched one another.

Not to be outdone, Ezra unleashed several more, nearly touching her last two. They locked eyes and laughed, and she lay her bow down and bounded the few steps to her friend, embracing him in tears—squeezing him tightly like a cougar its prey.

"My heart is full, Ezra! So full!"

"So is mine, and, Moonie … My God. We're out here … together. Seems like a dream!"

He gave her a lingering kiss, and they embraced for long moments. She closed her eyes and relaxed in his arms, her face canted upward toward him, sun spilling across her smooth skin. He gazed at her, instantly captive to her long lashes and dimples, until, not knowing what should come next, he kissed her smooth forehead and relaxed his grip. She stood still but opened her eyes and smoothed his lips with her finger. *I can't believe this is happening,* he thought. A shiver ran his length.

They shot quiver after quiver full of arrows for the next several hours—Moon calmly teaching and correcting him. He began to feel the form, and his arrows flew truer 'til he was hitting melon-sized objects consistently.

Losing track of time, eventually they looked about them, keenly aware that good daylight had passed, and made camp. Moon watered the horses while Ezra built the evening fire, and in time the horses had been staked, a pot of coffee hung over the fire, and elk sizzled on a spit. They crept closer to the fire as the sun slipped away and wolves began their howls in the distance. Her dog sidled up her leg and slid against her. Unfazed by the heat, he licked her fingers as she stroked him. She pulled a bit of elk from the fire and gave it to him. He swallowed it greedily and sank even closer, seemingly satisfied for the time being.

Ezra moved nearer to her, pouring himself a cup of steaming coffee. Her dog growled. "He's alright, boy," she said, stroking his neck. He offered a taste to her, and she turned away. "I've no tongue for the black water," she admitted. Both rubbed tender fingers with warm fat and leaned toward the fire. Charged air hung between them as they pondered their next words carefully. Finally, Ezra broke the silence, "Got words to say, Moon. I—"

"I know your words," she said. "I know them before you speak them. But I ask one thing: let's make them after our hunt tomorrow. I cannot tell you why, but you'll know the reason soon. Will you do this for me?"

"I'd do anything you ask, Moonie, but won't sleep good. I'm 'bout to bust. I'll be a poor hunter tomorrow."

"I feel safe with you," she said. "I've never known anyone like you."

"Feel the same," he said, squeezing her hand.

16

THE REST OF THE EVENING was bittersweet. Both chafed at having left so much unsaid. When they'd killed their hunger and checked the horses, they retired. Both slept badly.

They fell back to sleep in the early morning, not waking again until midmorning sun startled them. Ezra rose hurriedly and placed coffee on the fire. As Moon stirred, he brushed her cheek with his hand and wished her good morning. Gazing at the softness of her copper skin, the curves of her neck, the sweep of her jaw, and her long lashes, he suddenly felt an overpowering desire to kiss her—to hold nothing back. He was stunned and distracted by his hunting partner.

"Get up, Moon," he said brusquely. "Got real coffee this morning. It'll make hair grow on your face. I like me a woman with lots of hair on her face."

"The black water tastes like buffalo piss!" she said, face scrunched. "I think he stumbled over me in the darkness. I'll try some."

"Must a' been the one that laid on me," he groaned.

They splashed their faces in the icy water and downed two pots of strong coffee. He pulled a bit more pemmican from his pouch and fed the dog. Both pulled their bows from their cases, laying them by the fire.

Ezra was the first to speak. "I feel strange. My hands are numb. Ears a-ringin'."

"Me too," she said. "My heart's beating hard. I feel sick."

Desperate, he sprinted out onto the plains, his powerful legs churning like a quick pony, holding nothing back, before collapsing back at the fire. She, frantically seeking relief, ran wildly in ever-widening circles about the camp, 'til she dragged herself back and dropped beside him. And in the confusion, they fell into each other arms, holding on tightly until the buzzing and numbness had left them. Soon it was late morning, and they were both very much awake.

Judging the camp a good spot, they left their travois and supplies on site and rode west again, hoping the game had not left. Halting on a ridge, Ezra glassed the area of the previous day. He glanced at her, a wide, contented smile creasing his face. "More than yesterday, Moon. I say we circle downwind. Approach from the south." They lit off their mounts and hobbled them and grabbed their bows. High grass would cover their approach but still required they close in low to the ground.

The next two hours were tedious. They moved inexorably forward, occasionally rising just high enough to glass the herd and determine whether they'd been spotted. Finally, they were close enough that the spyglass was no longer necessary, and the wind favored their final approach. Moon was on all fours before him, crawling forward so slowly he wanted to push her. Distracted by her rump, he watched her cat-like stalk. "Oh ... my!" he whispered.

She glared back at him. "What?"

"Nothing."

"Well, be quiet!"

"Yes ..."

Within a quarter hour, they'd reached the end of their cover and come to the edge of the grove. The grass had been shorn by prey, and the cover was sparse. He pointed toward a large willow forty yards from the nearest elk, and they began slow-crawling in the grass, now less than two feet tall. They reached the tree and lay there resting for some time, facedown. Finally, he cupped her back and whispered, "Let's get to our knees and wait for 'em to come past the tree. Good?"

"Good," she said. She grabbed his hand and whispered, "Tonight, we'll eat fresh elk. We'll take two cows from our mother." They sat motionless for two hours, backs against the willow, 'til she touched him. Pursing her lips, she pointed beyond the tree. He strained with all his strength 'til finally he heard it—the swish of grass, the twigs cracking close. They nocked their arrows and waited, bows in the ready position, waiting some more.

Within minutes, they glimpsed movement on their flanks and caught the flash of brassy rumps from two mature cows less than twelve paces away. Ezra motioned that Moon shoot first. He'd unload at the first sound of her bowstring. So, in seconds she released and struck clean through the heart of the first as he pierced the lungs of the other a split second later.

Both sat, hearts hammering, listening to the scattering of other animals. Some ran out onto the prairie, confused, while others remained blissfully unaware. Again, they nocked their arrows, and shortly a fat doe appeared on their left, oblivious to their presence. He motioned for her to shoot, but she waved him on. He passed a shaft completely through the animal, just behind the foreleg. The doe stood stunned for nearly a minute, shuddered, and collapsed to the ground, dead.

Moon grabbed Ezra's hand again, squeezing it forcefully. She froze, gazing to his left. A monster bull elk had crashed just beyond them and stood unmoving, gazing back toward the creek, broadside. He slid another arrow onto his string and buried it to the fletching behind the left shoulder. The brute spun and trotted slowly away, as both sat waiting for his thud.

But it never came. Ten minutes more and no crash. And then another half-hour for good measure, both hoping the bull had gently lain down and bled out. Finally, Moon pinched Ezra's arm and rose to her feet. Ever so gently, one soft moccasin in front of the other, feeling for the slightest twig, they moved until the two cows and the doe were found. But the bull was still somewhere ahead. They followed the blood trail for several hundred yards, until she caught him leaning against a large willow, breathing hard. She motioned to Ezra. He leaned in close and whispered in her ear, "Take him."

She crept so close he was certain she'd be scented but then deftly launched an arrow through the heart of the old master. The bull looked about, stumbled drunk-like, and collapsed in three steps. She turned to Ezra and ran toward him.

"You've given me the best of gifts. My heart has never been this light." She kissed him.

"Ya don't owe me nothin'. I'll get the horses and cut us a second sled. Start the butcherin'. You're faster than me, ya know," he said.

Within the hour he'd returned with the horses and the travois. In four hours, all of the animals had been skinned and quartered and loaded onto the two travois. Ezra estimated that they had nearly seven-hundred pounds of meat and was glad they'd built a second travois. Now they could both walk alongside their animals and talk for the next several miles 'til they reached camp. But the truth was, they were exhausted. It had been a rigorous day, and they'd slept poorly. It'd be a fine thing to clean up in the creek and warm themselves by the fire. They'd watch the sunset paint the prairie and make powerful talk. There they'd enjoy the company of good friends and lovers of the hunt and the bow.

They arrived in their camp as the sun waxed red and lowered, and then rolled over and vanished—the only evidence it had ever been there the salmon belly of the clouds. Ezra rekindled the fire until it hissed and popped. He gathered a trade blanket and sprinted into the darkness toward the creek. Minutes later, he burst from the trees, clothed in the blanket and shouting like a man on strong rum. "I just washed up in the creek, and I'm about to scream. My God, what a day! I might just jump over these horses, Moon. I feel like a bull! I'm … I'm gonna howl!"

She stood, amused, and then grabbed her own blanket and sprinted to the creek. She returned and stood by him. When her teeth quit chattering, she began to laugh. "My people are very strong. We've bathed like this for more winters than we've recorded, but I think ... I think we've forgotten the joy of it. It's good to see it through your eyes. Some of my people feel as you do. Even the old sometimes feel young." She paused and her eyes grew moist. "Ezra ... you make me laugh." He sidled closer to her and drew her close. She melted, leaning into him.

"Would you like to make talk ... from last night?" she invited.

His heart pounded in his breast—the wings of a frightened bird in a small cage. He grabbed two robes and they wrapped themselves in the thick winter wool, the blazing fire painting the under-canopy of the branches like cathedral spires over them.

"Last night you didn't want to talk, and I don't know why," he said. "You said you couldn't talk 'til after we'd hunted and that you'd give the reason. Tell me why."

She began slowly. "Among my people, a man proves his worth through bravery and courage and generosity. Men fight their enemies and hunt dangerous prey to feed their families. And this is the way of a good man. But some good people—not all—think it strange that a woman hunt and kill as a man who enjoys these things.

"I couldn't make talk with you last night 'til you saw me hunt the elk. But I saw today you are not afraid of my strength. Now I see ... you're my best friend, forever. My father made the bow stiff so you might see my strength, I think."

Ezra swallowed hard. "I spoke with your father before we left, Moon. I told him I had words to make with you. Words that ain't been said yet. He knows we'll talk while we're together ... and he's glad we're here." She sighed and her eyes filled afresh.

"When I first met you," he said, "I thought you the most curious thing I'd ever seen. And you've been a stubborn one—twistin' and turnin' like a wild pony. Taken me a lotta work to get close to you. Ya tested me and pushed me back, but I couldn't be pushed away.

"It's true, I've never been afraid of your strength ... or your beauty. They only made me chase you harder. I knew a heart like yours would come to trust me ... if I just didn't quit. So, this is it. I'm tellin' ya everything. I want you to be my woman and no other man's. I'm tellin' you straight. You make my heart sing. Bein' apart from ya makes it bleed ..."

His heart was hammering. He'd just bared his throat, and she could crush it. He struggled to look at her. She hesitated for only a moment. "Months ago, we began breaking the ice together, you and me. I swung the axe hard to drive you away, but you seemed to not fear it. It only made you smile, and that made me angry. I tried hard not to like you ... but you'd not let me.

"All the older women in the village saw what was happening—that you'd not let me alone. They counseled me to consider you, that you were a special man. And the young were jealous and told me to run. But I sought the counsel of Black Otter and my mother. They told me it was time to stop running. Black Otter said you were a strange man who needed a strange woman. I knew his counsel was good, but I did not want to hear it. And then I tested you with the ball and you just laughed and played the clown ... and that made me angry again.

"Tonight, I've only a few more words to say. My eye has been on you from the first day you arrived in our village. I saw you when they pulled you out from under the robes, and I said in my heart, 'I would like to marry that man.' My heart's ached to make these words to you, Ezra. My heart beats with yours. It is yours."

They kissed and then, keenly aware of the growing cold, dressed and soon sat around the fire, wrapped ever more tightly in their robes and talking of what might happen next, now that they had disclosed themselves.

He drew her near, but the rigor of the day and their spent conversations relaxed both so quickly they spooned tightly and fell asleep, the happiest either had ever been. And that night they slept as carefree children, each convinced they had discovered the most perfect of treasures.

17

ON THE THIRD DAY, they broke camp and left for home. Ezra counseled Moon to wear her bow case openly, and she beamed like a woman who, having discovered herself with child, wants everyone to know. The thought of being different no longer bothered her, and so they rode into the village that day astride their ponies, dragging their meat and hides proudly behind them. The people took note, pointing at the large cache of fresh meat. Women smiled at Moon and she straightened her spine and returned the favor.

They soon stopped at the lodges of the elderly, distributing their hunt. Black Otter invited them into his lodge for a chat, where he hung the doe haunch high over the smoke of his fire. He lit his pipe and passed it to Ezra.

"I see you had a good hunt, my son," his eyes twinkling. "You must be tired from pulling the string so very many times," he said, grinning at Moon. She arose and sat down beside her old friend, embracing him, leaning her head on the old man's chest. Black Otter spoke just above a whisper, "Aaah ... I have seen this coming for some time. A time when two strange ones face each other with true words and make talk plain. Did you speak of the mystery between you?"

"Yes, grandfather," Ezra said. "We did."

"I knew you had. It's clear to all who've seen you. Your faces shine and it makes me ..." He daubed his eyes. "You have both made this gray hair very happy today. But listen ... you've things to do. Deal with your meat and return your ponies, and then walk together through the village so all may see your faces. The people will know what has happened. Most will be happy, for they have seen this day coming. And several will be confused, for they've never understood the path of Moon. But it does not matter. Today is a day I have waited for. Today, the sun has risen in this gray hair's soul."

When he'd finished, they stood and Moon embraced her old friend. They exited the lodge and made for hers. Ezra hoisted the thick haunch of the bull over his shoulder as they stepped inside. Black Bull motioned for them to sit, pointing to the stew pot. They ate until Black Bull asked, "The bow was to your liking, daughter?"

"Yes, Father. I killed two elk. It shoots like lightning. I'm so happy with it."

"Did the White man treat you well?" he asked.

"Yes. He's a good man and makes me happy. We made talk."

"That is gooood," he said. "He's shown much courage in chasing you. Do you know that? You're not easy to hunt … but he chases like the wolf. I'm glad he has made the words. Soon, he'll talk with me, and we'll arrive at a price.

"The Lord of Life has brought a man strong enough for you. He's become like our son. Today … today you will walk through this village and make clear what has happened. Tell no one, but watch their faces. They will know!"

Several days passed, and the news of the two spread like prairie fire in dry grass. Most thought it the best of pairings. They were deeply in love, and all could see it.

Ezra yearned to tell the captain himself and dropped by his lodge. But the captain was away, and in his absence Ezra took a brutal ribbing from the men. He promised to return later that day, when one of the men blurted out, "Did ya hear 'bout Cap'n? He got hisself a Hidatsa woman. Was married to one of the White traders here, but she turned him out last year. Burnt his clothes and his pistol. She's a 'shiner,' all right. Ten years younger'n him—full a piss and vinegar.

"Cap'n's head's in the clouds, Ezra. I swear … ya gotta drop by and see her. She's a punkin'! All the men's jealous. And bring Moon with ya, 'cause they could be sisters. Left to get shed of us. We been givin' him shit for sure."

Ezra left the lodge and turned aside to see Black Otter, and he came right to the point: "Don't understand how to make Moon my wife. People tell me different things. What do you say, grandfather? Moon and I are growin' fevered. I've no family here to arrange this thing, and I'm short a' horses. How do Whites marry your women, old friend?"

Black Otter's face calmed and his eyes closed in thought. "Well … this thing is not as hard as you think. Do you still have the horse and mule that trailed you here? And what of the weapons of Crow-Killer? These are more than enough for Black Bull. He knows you're young and have not many things. And he's a fine man who cares little for property or how others do things. He needs only what you can afford. No more. He may look stern but means little of it. Go see him, young man!"

Ezra hugged Moon hard and whispered, "I'm talking with your father. This whole thing's 'bout to happen. My ears are ringin'."

"Me, too. I feel like too much coffee. Do this now, my brave man!"

Ezra turned to see the captain strolling leisurely between the lodges, arm-in-arm with a striking petite native woman. He cried out, and McKay spun around, his hand shelved above his brow, squinting against the sun. "We're 'bout to get married, Cap'n," said Ezra. "Real soon. Talkin' with Moon's papa today. She's fine, ain't she?! Had to tell ya, sir. Truthfully, I wanna tell everybody!"

Moon's face flushed. "Yep, son. She's berries and cream alright," Cap'n said. "The men placed bets on whether you'd catch her. Won me a bottle of whiskey 'cause a' your grit! And I got news for you. I—"

"I heard. Your men were bustin' to tell me."

"Sure ... they ... have," Cap'n groaned. "Damn gossips! Anyhow, this lady'll be my bride in two days. This is Miss Red Calf. Reminds me some a' your woman—plain spoken, big heart. I'm all gimpy inside." He leaned in and whispered, "Took my legs clean out from 'neath me. I feel on fire!

Cap'n's eyes pooled. "We're droppin' the hammer on this thing, son. But you ... you go get yours done. Be right behind ya. And let me know if you need anything. Black Bull and I get along well. Plays tough ... but he's a good man—a very good man, and a fair trader for sure."

Within the hour Ezra sat beside Black Bull. The women left and he made clear his intentions. He asked of the bride price. "I'm a prosperous man," said Black Bull. "I've no need of your gifts, but you have two pistols and I have none. I want your best pistol and nothing more. If I were a Sioux or a Crow, and you came to buy my daughter, I'd demand ten horses and three fine guns, for she's like three women. Do you understand?"

"I do. She'll be my only woman. I want no other."

Black Bull smiled. "If you like, you're free to live with us. That is our way. But you are White and if you choose another way, then so be it. Her mother has a dress for her. Let it be a surprise."

"Of course."

Ezra rushed out of the lodge to find Moon and tell her the news, and he spent the rest of the afternoon cleaning the weapon and gathering together its accoutrements. It was a far more modest gift than originally intended, and he was grateful to tears. So, ransom in hand, and squashing the urge to run, he made for Black Bull's lodge—a stallion straining at the bit.

Moon exited the lodge. He grabbed her about the waist and, pulling her behind it, kissed her hard 'til they broke for air. Both smoldered inside.

"I'm 'bout ta step into your lodge and give your father this pistol. We're nearly married!" he groaned. "My heart burns to be your husband!"

She stood, tears flowing, and squeezed him again and again. "I feel like you. My heart's bursting, like we were at the camp before. Oh, Ezra, let's return to our camp soon and begin our life together there. Can we?"

"Of course! But I hafta do this now. We'll be together under a robe … soon! I can hardly wait!"

"Me too!"

Again they kissed, only to find a small crowd of children and old ones gathering. The old women laughed as they trotted to the front entrance and entered the lodge. The warrior motioned them to sit. Ezra mustered every fragment of restraint, slowing himself. The pipe was passed as usual, but this time Black Bull moved even more slowly than before. Ezra willed the man to hurry, but it changed nothing. His pace was maddening.

Black Bull said, "You look impatient, my son. Why is that? Do you have the pistol?"

Ezra, now sensing the joke, sprang his own: "No, father. I haven't brought the pistol. You should pay me for taking your daughter. She's wild, ya know. I need lots a horses … and your best trade gun. Then I'll consider her." Both locked eyes, waiting for the other to break. Moon's face went pale. She looked about to cry and Ezra felt her terror. "Forgive me, sir. I'd give ten times whatever you'd ask. I thought you were playing with me."

"Then you have come to understand much of my way in your time here. Give me the gift, and we'll be done with all of this." Black Bull opened the leather bag. It was a heavy caliber smoothbore that Abe had owned, and it had been well cared for. He ran his hands over it and worked the lock. He fingered the muzzle, sighted down the breech, and smiled.

Moon's mother opened a rawhide container. Inside was a beautiful, lightly smoked antelope-hide dress covered in dyed quill work with a gorgeously painted hem. Both women wiped tears.

"Moon and I are leavin' for the camp where we stayed several days ago," Ezra said. "Good cover and water. She'll wear her weddin' dress, and we'll ride through the middle of the village. I'll be back soon with two horses saddled and provisions for the week."

In an hour, he returned, leading the two horses. Moon mounted and looked about them as they proceeded out the west gate. Yellow Elk and Little Dove, her belly large with child, hailed them. Ezra winked at them both and gazed on his bride, resplendent in her dress, and thought of his parents, and for a moment his heart sank. How proud they'd be, he thought. They would've loved Moon— especially his mother. But neither of them was here. And for a moment, a brief moment, he tasted self-pity. The damnable stuff seemed to drain the strength from him almost immediately, like a poison of sorts. But he caught himself. Today he'd permit no self-pity. Today was a day of pride and joy. And when he thought about it, in some measure he was gaining a new family. Cap'n was becoming like a father, and Black Bull held promise of the same. No ... today was a day to show his new family how pleased he was with one of their own, for Creator was good and had matched the two flawlessly. His new wife was a most extraordinary woman.

Nearing the gate, Ezra heard someone calling his name. It was McKay. "We just done it, boy. She's mine! And we're heading out. We'll stay clear of ya, though. Sure you don't want us too close!" He grinned like a little boy stealing pies.

"Not really, Cap'n! But I got more important things to care for now." And with that, they trotted through the gate out onto the plain.

In a few hours, they'd found their old camp, unpacked their things, and began roasting meat they'd recently dressed. Ezra made his way to the creek and gathered water for them both. When he returned, Moon sat wrapped in a blanket and huddled by the fire. The sun had begun setting, and it was growing cold. He noticed her clothes piled neatly by the edge of the fire and grinned mischievously.

"Moon ... I was hopin' to take your dress off myself, but I sh—" She began to tear up. "Moonie, don't cry. I just had it all worked out in my head and I never told ya any of it. Sooooo ... I think we dip in the creek and come back here and howl like wolves. Watcha think?"

"Black Otter would say it's good," she said.

He ran into the trees, stripped his clothes, and returned draped in his blanket. Her face was scrunched, puzzled. "Why didn't you undress before me? I've seen naked men bathe in the river many times. It's the way of my people."

"But I've never seen you naked, Moon. I want us to see each other naked at the same time. Let's drop our blankets and run to the creek, and when we get back ... we'll figure it out. Let's go play and come back here all red and on fire!"

Soon they were under the water, hugging and fondling each other wildly. They kissed and played, and when they were stiff from cold, ran as furiously toward the fire as their leaden legs could carry them. They squealed and jumped, and Ezra howled like the wolf. And then she danced before him, and his breath caught. He gazed at her ... and wept. "What's wrong, husband? Aren't you pleased with—?"

"Of course, I am. You're just the prettiest thing I ever seen ... but I don't know the way of a woman. Ain't never been with one before. I mean ... I know what to do, but I don't know *what* to do. I fear I might bruise you. I don't want to hurt you, Moonie."

"Among my people," she said, "it's common that young people learn these things with each other before they're given to one other. But that has not happened to me. The young men who hunted me never stayed long enough for these things to happen. So ... I'm like you. I've no experience with a man but I've watched horses and caught young people in the tall grass. Horses bite each other's necks and do wonderful things with their bodies. They know what to do. Maybe we can play like horses—like young lovers in the grass ... and bite each other's necks. I long for it. Do you?"

"More than I can say."

They stood naked by the roaring fire 'til it had stilled their chattering teeth, and he wrapped his corded arm about her and cupped her bottom. She stroked his muscled back and rubbed his belly, the two giggling like children. And then they slipped naked beneath their robes, explored the other, and played like horses all night long.

In the morning, both arose and dipped in the stream once again. Moon watched him. He was handsome. Broad and thick shoulders and lean, powerful hips and thighs, longer legs and a shorter trunk—a belly like quarter-sawn hickory and powerful wrists and forearms, veins rippling under thin skin. He walked catlike with little effort, and she pictured him exploding from the balls of his feet to strike down an enemy with ease. And she felt safe.

And playful. She bit his neck, and they spent the remainder of the morning doing what young lovers do. Eventually, hearing voices in the distance, Ezra peered westward and saw two riders nearly a half mile distant. They dressed quickly and waited.

In time the two specks grew close and turned to people. The captain and his bride greeted the two youngsters. McKay looked playfully at them both and grinned. "Well now. Don't you two look like young ones who stole their mama's sugar? For God's sake … somethin' happen out here we should know about?"

Ezra's face flushed as Cap'n's composure broke. McKay laughed, coughing, hands on knees and bent at the waist, choking for air. Red Calf pinched his wrist and he righted himself. "Sorry, son. Meant no disrespect. We're headed to a stand of trees like this one but saw your smoke and thought … thought we'd say our particulars. I 'member a grove not far from here that we'll find soon."

"Don't go no further, Cap'n," said Ezra. "This grove's a mile long. Lots of cover. Pick yourself a spot. Won't bother ya none 'less you invite us."

McKay glanced at his own bride, and his eyes grew glassy. "Look at her. Ever see anything so pretty in your life? There must be a God. And look at that dress on her. Ain't she a peach! For God's sake, even her feet's pretty … an' I just wanna eat her up!" She blushed, sidled closer to the captain, and pulled herself in close. She whispered in his ear and his face burned red. "We need to set up camp. We'll take you up on your offer, Ezra … Moon. Good day." And they were gone.

Ezra looked forward to evening talks around the fire, talks about his own and Moon's future with the trappers. He apologized to Moon for having allowed the captain and his bride to move so close. "The grove is large and these two people are good," she said quickly, "and the captain makes me laugh, and I like him. And Red Calf … she'll be my friend. She's strong. I've heard stories about her. She throws the axe like a man and burned her man's clothes and his pistol when she put him out.

"Some of our women did not like her, but she didn't care. She'll treat McKay well. I'll walk to their camp and invite them to the fire tonight after we eat, and you drink your black water."

"What'd they say, Moon?"
"I didn't talk to them."
"Why?"

"Their clothes were by the fire, and I heard them playing in the creek. Ezra, they sounded like us, and I couldn't bear to stop them. I'll try again later!"

Later, when the sun grew small, Red Calf and Cap'n walked into camp. As the night passed, Ezra questioned McKay about his plans for the upcoming months. He said he and most of the men planned on visiting Crow country and trapping there in the fall. They'd leave in June, arrive and trade with the Crow, and trap until the beaver had disappeared beneath the ice in mid-November. Then they'd overwinter with them and trap again in the early spring, and when the spring trapping had played out, they'd pack out their pelts and make for the summer rendezvous.

McKay's face lit up like a child describing a carnival. "Rendezvous's a dangerous and magical place, son. Men who've survived the last eight months make their way to the valley to trade their beaver for supplies and pocket the balance."

"Sounds wild," said Ezra.

"Oh, it is! More than wild! Problem is, most don't pocket much. They spend it all on whiskey and gamblin' and women and overpriced supplies—goods maybe ten times what they be in St. Louis. And whiskey, maybe fifty times or more. Some leave there poorer 'an when they came the year before, if ya can believe that!"

"You tellin' me that men piss away all their hard work in a couple weeks?" asked Ezra.

"Sure the hell am. But it ain't all a shit-show. Lonely men come for company and some find Indian wives. And men bankrupt themselves on foofaraw and pretty bangles for their women, 'cause Injun women want fine things and mountain men's known for spoilin' 'em.

"And then there's the horse races and shootin' contests and the occasional duel. And if a man dies, grievin' don't last long, 'cause most a these men growed callous to loss. Watched men shoot plums off'n each other's heads … on a bet. It can get ugly. I—"

"You jokin' me, sir?"

"Not at all. These are the most colorful, foul, and darin'est creatures the Almighty ever made, son. And when they all come together to celebrate, they're celebratin' not being scalped or killed by a grizzer bear."

"My Lord. Sounds wonderful!"

"It is!" Cap'n said. "Rendezvous, son … is a way a' seein' the mountain man not so much for what he does but who he is, 'cause he's the highest of free men and asks permission of none. Them that survive knows he owes his life to his partner and his company, 'cause no man lives long going out on his lonesome. Sooner or later, he'll lose his hair to some young buck lookin' for a scalp to hang on his lance, or he'll break a leg and can't no one find him."

"Anyways, most of us'll be heading west soon, and you and Moon are welcome to come with. We're a big family. You two talk it over for a spell."

"We will," Ezra said.

Cap'n grew pensive, his eyes kind. He paused and sighed. "What you wantin' outa all this, boy? I mean … why're ya here? I know you and your papa came out here to get shed a what happened back East and all, but what's this about for you?" Ezra fidgeted and looked at Moon.

"Not thought much about it, Cap'n. But I know I love all this. Get up ever' day and pinch myself just makin' sure it's real." Cap'n closed his eyes and sighed again.

"A decent answer, son. But you need more 'an that."

"I ain't followin', sir."

"Listen … I don't mean ya ain't the balls or the scrap for it out here. And I don't mean a man can't come out here for the glory."

"Then what, sir?"

"I mean … ya need to know why ya come … 'cause when the shit falls like rain—when the Blackfoot steals your horses … or scalps your wife … ya need to know why. They's a high price to pay for loving this life, son. And sometimes … you ain't never gettin' it back. You gotta be able to live with that."

Ezra smiled awkwardly and went mute. But his heart was anything but quiet. *Why am I here? Have I got the makin's for this? Maybe Cap'n's 'bout to sniff me out and send me packin'.* He felt sick, like he did when his papa used to shame him. But Cap'n wasn't Papa and had never shown him anything but support. "Maybe I do know why I'm here, sir, if I search it out," he said, gathering his nerve. "I got no family, but I feel kin to the Mandan and the Crow … and the men in the camp. They make me feel like I belong … like I'm wanted, and I ain't known that for a long time. Truth is … I feel like a man among these men, sir—like them and this country is pulling somethin' outta me I didn't know was there. And I suppose … I suppose I wanna be part of something that makes me shit myself at times …"

"Now that's an answer, son. I'll give ya the sum of it."

"Yeah?"

"Adventure and danger … and living by no other's permission," said Cap'n. "Moon fears little … and you even less. And that's why I need ya with us. And the men respect you two. Still talk a your tussle with Crow-Killer. Damndest thing they ever saw, they tell me. Wish I coulda seen it.

"Now I know you know nothin' 'bout trapping beaver as yet, but you'll learn quick. And your Moon'll fit right in. You'll spin tall tales to your grandchildren, and the hell of it is, they'll all be true. So, study on it, son. Real hard. Someday ... and you can quote me on this: men'll read of what we done out here."

18

THE FOLLOWING WEEKS were good ones. Ezra and his bride moved in with Moon's parents and settled into the rhythms of her family. There the two spoke of their future together and of McKay's offer, and Moon's mother, grieved at the thought of their leaving, tried hard to conceal it. But, in time, they all judged it the next step to be taken, and McKay and Red Calf embraced the young couple eagerly, throwing open their lodge and sharing food with them.

The spring thaw came on hard, and those who had already vacated their winter camps were glad they'd done so. The muddy Missouri roiled with massive uprooted trees and clusters of dead and rotting buffalo sweeping by the village. The sheer volume of water and debris was stunning to Ezra, and he was thankful he'd no need to be on the river. It smelled of dank destruction and death. And then the rains came.

The Mandan and Hidatsa paid the river very little heed, except to occasionally fish a foul-smelling carcass from the water for food. The Whites called the retrieved meat "bison floats," and it was a delicacy to the Indians. Ezra queried his new bride on the practice and found it to be a common thing.

Moon also told him that sometimes her people drank from water sources where hides were seasoned to slip the hair for tanning. He'd heard of the rotten water before and thought both practices revolting, but said nothing. He could only conclude that his new people were hardy to a fault. The same practices would kill a White man.

He redoubled his language lessons with Black Otter, especially on the Crow tongue, and often probed the old man for wisdom about women. This quest amused the old man no end, and he teased his student mercilessly.

Ezra sought out the hide painter he'd visited months earlier, and the two worked jointly on the robe he'd been given by White Wolf, chronicling his fight with Crow-Killer in bold images. It was a supple, gorgeous piece, and the two were justifiably proud of themselves.

He offered the young man Crow-Killer's knife, but he refused it. Rather, he counseled Ezra to wear it prominently, saying it was his duty to do so; that a warrior must show off his victories to stiffen the spines of his friends and the weak. Ezra smiled, placed the knife in his belt, and embraced Red Paint in His Hair—the man who'd nearly offered him his woman. He was sorry he'd have too little time to know him better.

One day at Black Otter's lodge, Ezra asked the old man to identify the best archer in the village. He paused and cupped his chin in his wrinkled hands. "Son ... you're living in his lodge. No man talks to the arrow like Black Bull. It's why his daughter shoots as she does. He can teach you whatever you need. Why do you wish to know?"

"I'm not sure. I feel a need to learn the bow. I don't know how or why, like a vision or a dream I can't cypher out, but it never leaves me. I'd no thought of the bow 'til I came, but now I can't think of much more than Moon and the wood ... and the string."

The old man's eyes closed in thought; then he burst into laughter, sputtering. "Well, young friend ... you had better master the bow, for you will never master the other. But then ... that's why you chose her, I think. She's a mystery, isn't she? So, talk to your father. There's no better teacher."

"Why'd you not tell me this before?"

"You have not asked." And then the old man grew tickled and could not speak. "So, act the student ... and humble yourself. You'll gain standing with him, though I do not think you need it."

The next two months found Black Bull and Ezra spending long hours together. Ezra pored over the technique and style of his father-in-law. His accuracy and speed were astounding and Ezra soon came to understand much of Moon's skill. He determined quietly to best his mentor. *I'm gonna beat you some day, father.*

On their fourth foray out to the grove, Black Bull stopped his horse to dismount. He pointed to a burial platform a bowshot away and grew quiet, as though he were about to say something of great importance. "That is the body of my father. He has been raised into the sun for several years. Every moon or so I come to check on him. Some ask why we place our family on poles. It's because we cannot bear to see them. It makes our heart sad, so we place them high in the air. When the platform falls and the bones are clean ... we bury them down by the river and place their skulls with the skulls of others so that we can visit them there.

"My father was a great man and our people loved him. He'd be glad I am teaching you the bow. He was taught by the Comanche, the finest horse-archers among all the tribes ... and he taught me."

They remounted their horses, crested a gently elevated plateau, and dismounted. Black Bull pulled his bow from the case, strung it, and ran his hands along its length. "Today, we will work on speed, for a true arrow means little when your enemies are more numerous or quicker. You must shoot faster than them, and today I'll teach you how. You must become better than me, for your path will be hard. You must be ready."

The rest of the day was spent teaching Ezra to grasp several arrows at once in his bow hand, nocking them on the string without looking, all the while pulling and releasing in one fluid movement. Ezra counted Black Bull's rate of fire and was astonished. His teacher released four arrows in less than ten seconds, and all struck where he'd aimed!

But his own efforts were far less noteworthy. He counted the release of four arrows in about twenty seconds, with the accuracy not nearly as good. But he set his jaw and by the end of the day had begun to slowly improve. The instruction had moved from speed to fluid movement, and then back to speed, until the awkwardness began to fade a bit, enough to encourage him, and he came to laugh at himself as Black Bull teased him. They sat under a massive willow in the grove resting, dressing their bleeding fingers in bear fat and soft doeskin.

The next day both were up early and ate a small breakfast. Black Bull bridled his horse and bid his son-in-law do the same. He was oddly quiet.

"Today," he said, "we'll rest our arms and test our horses. And we'll see if your horse is trained to hunt the buffalo ... and how he reacts to the bow. May I ride him?"

"Yes, father. Take him."

"A good buffalo horse is guided by the rider's knees," Black Bull said, "while the hands handle the bow. Today we'll see what this horse knows. I'll run him and press my knees and we'll know. I suspect his last owner taught him well." And then he dug in his heels, and the two were off. Ezra watched them race across the prairie, horse and rider moving as one, tracing a figure-eight about him until Black Bull loosened the reins and leaned from side to side. His mount followed the pressure and veered left to right as the rider nocked several arrows and fired them beyond the horse, all without effect. He exerted more pressure, and the appaloosa responded instantly to the level of force with acute and precise movements. Again, the arrows flew, some directly past the eyes, and the results were still the same. Not a flinch.

Then he sprinted right at Ezra, until the horse slid to a stop before him, his powerful rump scraping the sod, his front legs locked before him as bits of dirt spitted against the young man's face. The rider slid deftly to the ground and handed him the reins. "I would call him 'Antelope.' He's nimble and quick ... and is like no horse I've ever known. The Crow gave you a strange horse. You two will ride as brothers."

Ezra spent the rest of his time at the village with purpose, readying himself for the trip to the Crow. He slipped out onto the prairie regularly with Moon, and there both shot their bows until they were able to feel the arrows to their mark. Ezra slowly approached the skill of his woman, but it was never an easy contest.

He also grew more skilled at discharging arrows from horseback with ever-increasing speed while his horse, nostrils flared and form flattened to the earth, cut jetties across the prairie like molten lightning. He fantasized of hunting buffalo soon from the back of a horse and told Moon so. "I don't doubt it," she said.

The day before the trappers and their women were to leave the village, the war chief, Four Bears, honored them all with games and a feast. The people turned out for footraces, gambling, and great mounds of food. And that day they laughed, gambled, and ate into the early morning hours—their bellies as full as their hearts.

The next day Four Bears pronounced them all "good friends and brothers," and he was right. A few Mandan women would be traveling with their new White husbands, and some might never return home. Moon told Ezra that sometimes a White man tired of his woman and traded her to another man, that that woman might never see her people again, and the thought incensed him. "I would never do that to you!" he said.

Ezra and the people rose slowly in the late morning, confident in the devotion of their sentries. Trappers and their women moved with purpose, packing parfleche with clothes and moccasins. Others checked traps and weapons and saddles and horses.

By noon, a party of nearly sixty people, including the women and a few of the Crow who had overwintered with the tribe, walked out the gate of the village palisade, heading northwest toward Crow country. The whole village had turned out. Many mourned the impending loss of their White friends and their women. Ezra watched as one mounted Mandan pulled a flute from his bag, played a mournful tune, and followed their train for ten miles. Others followed the party for the first two, waving fiercely at the company and shouting farewells, until finally the grieving played itself out. At long last the trappers and their party were alone. And then the caravan was oddly mute, the silence broken only by the squeaking of saddles, the soft padding of hooves, and the clearing of throats.

Ezra cast a backward, longing look at his new friends, and for a time felt deep sadness. God, how he'd miss these people. They'd shown him marvelous kindness and treated him as blood. And now he had family there. He knew Four Bears to be a valiant man who'd care well for the people, though they were not a large force and had suffered from their enemies in recent days. But he consoled himself that they were hardy people who'd always found a way to survive.

It'd be some weeks before the band had firmly entered Crow country. The company would travel at a leisurely pace of about eighteen miles per day. They immediately swung north to the Knife River, rendezvousing with several other trappers and their wives. One was quite notable. Toussaint Charbonneau would be coming with his two squaws. He'd journeyed up the Missouri and across the Rockies with the Corps of Discovery several decades earlier. Nearly seventy now but still quite spry, he packed two women half his age. He'd lived with the Hidatsa for some time, assuming a role as resident trader among them. The story circulated that his favorite wife was Crow and that she longed for a visit to her people, and so he'd relented and packed goods to trade with them. Ezra desired to talk with the older man—to hear stories of when the Missouri and its people had been even more mysterious and wild. Unfortunately, the older man took sick and turned back to the Two Villages to recover.

The early days of their journey were uneventful, consisting largely of stopping occasionally to rest and water their mounts. There was no structured afternoon meal. Many chewed on jerked meat as they rode, or when the animals were being watered. In the evenings, fresh game was roasted over campfires. Some nights they slept in the open and, when things went well, stopped for the evenings in creek bottoms under the willow and ubiquitous cottonwoods. It was a great treat for the weary and sweaty travelers, who were quick to bathe in the creeks and ponds.

He and Moon sometimes waited until the sun had set, and while others were distracted with supper they slid themselves into the cold waters. One night they encountered Red Calf and McKay exiting a pond, naked as jaybirds. Ezra reasoned that life could not excel the present, surrounded by people on a shared mission, eating good food, and swimming naked with a beautiful woman in stunning country.

One evening, a trapper brought out a carefully wrapped fiddle and played a Kentucky mountain jig. "Play us a Virginia waltz!" someone else shouted, and at least a dozen White men grabbed their Indian wives and attempted to school them on the fine art of the dance. Ezra watched the captain and Red Calf, who patiently taught her his foreign steps—she leaning into his lead and trying her best.

Ezra coaxed his own love into the affair. "C'mon, Moonie. I'll show ya." And so, they gave it a go. It was a terribly vulnerable time for the Indian women, and when the fiddle stopped their men cheered and whistled, and the women beamed like triumphant warriors returning with scalps and stories of coup counted.

And then, it was the single men's turn. This time the bachelors cut in for dances, as the husbands obliged them, of course. Moon was flooded by requests from moonstruck trappers and danced until Ezra came to her rescue. He was glad he was strong, for it was clear that some single men were more than jealous of him. But then, of course they were. Moon turned heads wherever she went and "a man'd be a fool or blind not to notice her," he whispered to Cap'n, because he sure had, and was damn thankful he'd not let her get away.

The next day, the two headed out onto the prairie looking for game for the rest. They found a small group of buffalo, and, unsheathing their bows, made their way closer. Ezra cautioned Moon to not engage. He thought it too dangerous, for she lacked both the trained horse and the experience, and he couldn't bear to lose her. And the thought of Old Tom's death was still a lightly-scabbed wound.

Moon listened, pouted for a bit, and pointed toward the prey. And then he swept down on the unwary herd with the force of prairie thunder, the big stud responding to the slightest press of his knees as he maneuvered in close to the running cows and calves.

Clutching a bundle of arrows in his bow hand and leaning his body into the memory of practice, he sent shaft after shaft behind the short ribs of the running cows, puncturing their diaphragms and collapsing their lungs, until three mothers and as many calves lay dead within the span of nearly a thousand yards. Ezra ran to meet his wife, a grin of unspeakable delight stretched tightly across his face. The two scanned the field with pride.

"You've learned well, husband. You ride and shoot like Crow. I wish father could have seen this. I miss him!" Her face grew sad and water pooled in the corners of her eyes. "Go for help. We need more help and horses," she said.

That night the camp feasted and Moon proclaimed the skill of her husband to all who cared to listen. But despite the glory of it all, inside a restlessness troubled him. Why me? Why's all this come so easily? His thoughts chased the inside of his skull like an unbridled colt, annoyed that he cared so much to find answers. Why was he obsessed with questions that others seemed untroubled by? And how might he tame his thoughts?

Days passed into weeks, the company grew more and more clan-like, and evenings became the high point of each day. Close friendships formed, and men talked of the rich beaver country, of the fortunes they would make. Crow spoke wistfully of their homes and children.

The smell of roasting game and sweet smoke wafted nightly as men challenged each other with games of practical skills and strength like shooting, knife and 'hawk, and wrestling. An unassuming Crow wrestled all comers into the ground. He was a good-natured man of average build, and his power surprised them all. His name was Two Horns.

On another occasion the Crow challenged all men to compete with the bow. Several Crow and Hidatsa and a few courageous trappers answered the challenge, along with Ezra. Rudimentary instructions were given to the Whites, and they released their shafts to the amusement of all. Next were the Hidatsa, and they gave a credible performance. But after them came the Crow, who ran parallel to the target and released their arrows at great speed, nearly all striking their mark.

The camp cheered loudly and the Crow strutted, for they were great buffalo hunters and mounted warriors, and all had just witnessed their craft. They motioned for Ezra to try his hand. So he strung his bow and sent the first shaft, which struck its mark nearly dead center. He loaded his bow hand with four more arrows and let all go so rapidly that even the Crow shouted as they clustered in a spot the size of a fist.

He'd not run as they had and shoot—he'd not steal their glory, though he believed himself to be nearly their equal. I'll let 'em have this one, he thought quietly.

He motioned for Moon and whispered in her ear. He spoke low to Cap'n. "Watch this. She's gonna stretch the Crow a mite." She ran to her bedroll and soon stood beside him, bow in hand. They each shot fresh targets, and he discharged four arrows into a smaller ring than the last. Then she matched him, but it was too close to call. Red Calf was called to judge.

After some deliberation, and the frenzied whispering into each other's ears, the call was made. Moon had bested her husband. Some didn't know what to think and mulled it over as they ate, but most concluded simply that the two carried between them very mysterious medicine.

Ezra cared little what they thought. He'd acted with prudence but would boast of his woman whenever he could, for he knew she was meant to be seen and applauded, and he'd never steal her thunder. And he knew she'd afford him the same. It seemed to some a good trade they had going, but in fact it was no trade at all. No smell of contract. It was more an unconditional covenant, the kind where two people look after each other, deserved—or not.

19

Days later, they entered the Yellowstone. Early on, they began to see signs of life, and some Crow galloped on ahead. Those behind followed their trail easily through the lush valley floor. Soon, they spotted large herds of horses, as young boys herding them waved, riding ever closer to see the newcomers. The youths loped easily up and down the line, their horses an extension of their bodies, touching the strangers' mounts with their hands and jabbering excitedly. Many couldn't understand them, but Ezra listened carefully and spoke back.

The boys were surprised and delighted by the White man with the pretty wife who spoke their tongue. A few asked Ezra whether Moon had a sister, and he laughed and replied playfully, "Yes, but she's too strong for you." This they found highly amusing, and spurred their horses on to engage other hapless victims, most of whom didn't understand them either. They seemed not to care.

The village unfolded before them, pulsating with life. Women pegged buffalo skins to sod, their knees and feet coated with blood and fat. And the horses, their coats shiny from rich summer grass, stood picketed outside high, ample skin lodges, the tall poles topped with fluttering red woolen ribbons jutting from narrow upper, smoke-stained openings.

Cooking fires and the smoking of hides cast a cloak of thin blue haze the length of the camp, the smoke only partly masking the overpowering smell of food. Crow ran to greet their guests and embrace returning loved ones. Women and children rushed to meet their men, little ones were plucked from the ground, and wives cried. These were not the savages some ignorant Whites in the settlements believed them to be.

Ezra spied a tall Crow striding toward him a bowshot away, clad in only a breechcloth, leggings, and moccasins and with long black hair that hung to his knees. White Wolf was delighted that Ezra now spoke his tongue and asked whether he'd tried his bow. Ezra nodded and swore he'd talk soon but that he must first find a place to camp with his new wife.

"Find your place, but tonight stay in my lodge," said White Wolf. "We have plenty of room. And my woman is lonely from the death of our son. Perhaps the company of your woman might be good for her."

"I'd be honored. My woman ... she'll be good for yours," Ezra said.

The rest of the day was spent watering horses and settling in. Many erected canvas tents and pegged them into the soft earth, and soon the encampment assumed a foreign cobbled shape, the White tents juxtaposed amongst the cone-shaped dwellings, some of the lodges emblazoned with animal totems and ponies picketed outside.

Visitors strolled through tall grass. Still others walked along the river, removing their boots and moccasins and wading onto the gravel shoals. Ezra and Moon did the same, followed by a playful chase into the tall grass. There they lay in each other's arms, gazing up at the soft clouds drifting lazily to the south, the sun warm on their faces.

Ezra drew her near, his strong arm cradling the curve of her back, she relaxing as his hand traced the sinews of her spine, corded and strong, sweeping gracefully upward, as perfectly formed as his horse. And the more he studied them, the more he understood the reluctance of her earlier suitors. She was elegant and sleek and very powerful, and many had misunderstood her. But he hadn't and now she was his, and he was grateful beyond measure. He groaned with pleasure. He brushed her ear and kissed her neck, whispering all the while, "I love you, Moonie." He pulled her close and soon yawned as contentment swept him, and in minutes both fell asleep to the tinkling soft clatter of water and the wispy whir of dragonfly wings.

The days at the encampment stretched into weeks. Ezra and Moon never set up their own camp. White Wolf proved the consummate host, and his ample lodge became their home. He toured the valley with Ezra, proudly pointing out the vast number of ponies that dotted the landscape and watered at the river.

Ezra learned that the Crow and their brothers, the Hidatsa, were breeders and traders of fine horses and were considered wealthy by reason of their abundant herds. The Hidatsa, while sharing much in common with their Mandan neighbors, had actually split off from the Crow tribe many winters back. But both tribes still shared their expertise with horseflesh.

"Our horses have made us an inviting place for raids from our enemies," said the man. "Two moons ago we caught a Cree about to steal horses tied outside my lodge. On his way to my lodge, he lifted one of our old women who had fallen under a load of firewood. It was dark, and he seemed one of our own, but he did not know that our sentries had seen him much earlier and watched as he moved closer to my lodge.

"When he grabbed my horses, my sentries grabbed him. I would've killed him until the gray hair spoke. He had honored our old woman, and we honored him with his freedom. He was a brave man.

"This is a fine story, but I speak these things for a reason. My scouts say they see horses and men in the hills. I think they've not attacked for fear of the Whites … but I don't know. I'll tell the rest. We must all act cleverly."

In the weeks since their arrival, Moon had shown herself to be a welcome support to Pretty Dog, the wife of White Wolf. The women worked together drying buffalo flesh and tanning and breaking skins. Pretty Dog was a highly skilled quill-worker and schooled Moon in her craft. She embroidered moccasins and shirts and made Ezra a set of handsome leggings. In time the grieving woman began to laugh again as Moon shared her pleasure playing naked with her husband in cold water. The two giggled as their men passed by, and after a while Pretty Dog began to flirt with her husband again. He was elated to see his wife's spirit return.

As the summer progressed, Moon's big heart became apparent, and she gave herself to the craft of bone-setting, apprenticing with an old woman. But the woman was more than a bone-setter. She was a healer of sorts and taught Moon to gather herbs and roots and plants for teas and extracts. Moon preferred this to the bone-setting, for she was tenderhearted and working with children hurt her more than her patients. In time, though, she grew a thick shell and learned to look past the cries, knowing that on the other side was healing.

One day, a young boy had fallen from his horse and broken his arm. His mother had brought him to her, and she ordered him to lie down. He shut his eyes and she stroked his forehead, whispering so quietly that only he could hear. And then, with one deft jerk, it was all over, and the boy lay unconscious. She spoke quietly to the mother: "Splint his arm with stiff rawhide so that he cannot use it for one moon. If you do, he will heal, and all will be well. If you do not … his arm will grow crooked, and he'll not be a good hunter or find a pretty woman. Do it quickly before he begins to move."

20

EZRA AND MOON MOUNTED UP and headed out to explore, their bows and quivers draped over their shoulders. She was still a curiosity to some of the Crow, though they were not wholly unfamiliar with the occasional warrior woman in their midst. One of their own, Pine Leaf, had vowed to keep warring until she'd scalped one hundred of the enemy, but her village was some miles distant.

Ezra sat his own splendid horse, Crow-Killer's beaver-tail dagger tucked in his soft belt. He rode a new Crow saddle that had appeared outside his tent one morning. He asked of its owner, but no one would claim it. "It's yours, silly man," said an old woman with a face like parched earth. "The maker gave it as a gift to a 'great man' … but I am waiting to see." She never cracked a smile.

They followed the river for hours, occasionally pausing to rest and water the horses. This land was far different from that of the Mandan. The green grasses, the frequent valleys fed by mountain melt, and the jutting rocky foothills and mountains overshadowing the valley were mesmerizing. They spoke in low, awed tones, words sometimes failing them. They'd look for a site to camp soon.

Ezra searched for a place that would block the sight of a fire, in light of his recent conversation with White Wolf. Eventually, he found a good site, and when they had picketed their mounts, he smeared the white of his horse with black mud he'd gathered from the creek. He shared White Wolf's concern to Moon, who'd noticed that he'd been quiet and distant. "Does White Wolf know who these strangers are?" Her voice was low and grave.

"He's not certain, but Cree have been in the area recently. Maybe it's the Piegans or the Bloods. I hope not. Heard bad stories 'bout 'em. Cap'n said they got a real grudge against the Americans."

Moon's coppery face blanched pale. "He speaks the truth," she said. "Blackfoot do no harm to the Canadian and the English, but they show no mercy to your kind. They've done my people harm from time to time. Many hate them. We must never fall into their hands, husband. Never!"

That night the two went without fire, eating only pemmican. And they skipped their cold swim and huddled tightly together beneath woolen blankets. Ezra primed his pistol and lent his dagger to Moon, who hugged it to her breast as they slept. He drew her close and pondered the wisdom of their trip. *But we're in it now, and rescue's nearly a day away.* They'd act prudently, watch carefully for sign, and be ready to defend themselves or flee. His horse was as fleet as they came, but Moon's mount was untested. *What the hell was I thinking?* When time permitted, he'd test him or trade for a proven horse from the Crow. But they had what they had, and for one who prided himself on diligent study, he'd missed this one. *It'll not happen again.*

Morning came soon enough. The two ate pemmican, washed down with cold creek water. Each guarded the other as they relieved themselves and saddled their horses. Ezra smeared more mud on his horse and chose a path to a ridgeline overlooking the valley. From there they could see both game and humans below, and they relaxed a bit. They rode high, but not so high as to silhouette against the skyline.

Occasionally, Ezra brought out his spyglass and perused the valley below. He passed the glass to Moon, who stretched high in her rawhide stirrups, scanning back and forth. She stopped abruptly and pointed below. Ezra grabbed the glass, his heart hammering. A thousand yards distant, a naked White man sprinted furiously from six Indians bent on catching him. The pursuers bore lances and ran hard, but the man seemed to be maintaining his lead—barely. Before he'd had time to lower the glass, Moon had already drawn her bow from its case. They swerved their horses and raced hard down the sloping ridge, hoping to ride down the aggressors—he yelling strategy in the confusion, "Let me lead!" and "Stay on my shoulder!" And then closing hard, they shouted, attempting to stop the pursuit, but four of the pursuers turned and loosed arrows at them. All missed, but one arrow struck Moon's horse in the neck and another grazed her upper arm. Immediately, both riders unleashed their first salvo.

Ezra struck his man squarely in the chest. Mortally wounded, he struggled to return fire, but a second arrow struck him in the face, just below the eye, and he fell, writhing, to the ground. Moon's first arrow severed her man's spine, and he fell where he lay. The other two attempted a frantic re-nocking of their bows but were pitifully late. Both soon lay in their own blood, their breasts bristling with feathers. The two remaining Blackfoot loaded their bow hands with arrows, stood their ground, and began their death song.

Ezra waved off Moon. And pondering his next move, he watched the naked White man taking advantage of the distraction. He closed the distance on the two from behind. He grabbed one and snapped his neck in a single savage twist. The other turned his lance on the man, but before he could connect the White giant parried the lance and battered his aggressor's face with a massive right hand. He fell immediately and was bludgeoned with a rock to the head that the naked man swung over and over again.

Then the man, crying and cursing, pulled a knife from the body of one of the dead and quickly scalped them all, sobbing and groaning as he moved—like a bear robbed of cubs. Finished, he limped to a stream only yards distant, moaning as he went, and lay in it for some time—rising finally when his bloody body had washed a bright pink in the snow-melt creek.

Legs quivering, he staggered back to shore. They tossed him a blanket, but he seemed not to notice, and then his giant frame shook and his legs buckled. He fell on his buttocks, shuddering, mute and dazed, tears streaming down a sun-blistered face. *God, he's huge,* Ezra thought. Perhaps six-feet four and two-hundred-sixty pounds. A bull buffalo of a man. He'd literally beaten the last two braves to death. It was no wonder six men had chased him. Maybe it'd been good odds.

Moon slid from her mount and wrapped the blanket about his quivering body. She sat beside him, stroking his arm and singing softly under her breath until his shaking eventually stopped. Ezra offered the man food, but he waved it away, rolled to his side, and quickly fell asleep in the sun.

They surveyed the carnage—six dead and scalped Blackfoot. And it'd all happened within minutes. Ezra was supremely grateful they'd skirted the valley and ridden the ridge, for they'd never have seen the man or been able to effect his rescue otherwise. He felt good about his decisions of the last sixteen hours, and his stiff shoulders softened. They had acted wisely, and Moon had proven herself. He'd been loathe to expose her to danger, but it was good to know she'd not shrink or lose her head in the middle of it. Today had told him much. "Ya did good, Moonie," he said as he stroked her shoulder, "real good."

The big man lay for hours until he came to, and when he finally did he had quite the story to tell. He was French-Canadian and had trapped with the Americans for the last several years. This new alliance had angered the Blackfoot, and two days earlier they'd found and captured him while he trapped in the valley. He cunningly had bet them he was swifter than they, and they had stripped him and told him to run. That, they said, was his only chance.

They hadn't believed a man his size could outrun them, but he was convinced he could. He said he had bested them before, and they hated him for it. So, they had sent the swiftest to run him down and kill him. But they'd not counted on two fierce deliverers watching on, and he was powerfully grateful.

His name was Enrí Joubert. He was thirty-three years old and was "at their service," he told them. He'd lead them back to his camp, and there they'd claim his clothes, some fine horses, and the enemy's property. He noted the wounding of Moon's horse and spoke excitedly of a splendid paint that'd fit her perfectly and had been highly trained. It'd be hers when they found it, he promised them. "Wait'll you see her, little lady. She's pretty as you. A bit small for me, anyhow."

Moon rubbed Enrí's bruised and bloodied feet with grease and wrapped them in soft leather. He'd run over prickly pear and rocky ground for nearly six miles, and one of his toes was broken badly. They placed him on Ezra's horse and traced their way to the temporary Blackfoot camp, now deserted. There they found all as he had described it, including the paint mare—and what a beauty she was—a red sorrel with white patches and the coveted medicine hat markings, with an exquisitely proportioned body. Her quality made her a fine mate to Ezra's stud.

Enrí dressed as quickly as his battered body allowed, and while they gathered the horses and started a fire Ezra questioned the wisdom of building it, but Enrí calmed him. His captors had made it plain they were a scouting party probing the Crow defenses and searching out the sizes of their herds, and the rest of the nation was conducting war on the Cree and hunting buffalo, so the valley, at least for the time being, was relatively safe.

They spent the next several days at the abandoned Blackfoot camp, as Enrí recovered the use of his feet. There they learned the story behind the paint horse. "Traded from the Snakes for the horse. Was going to trade her for a wife, but hell ... She's just gotta be yours, little woman. I'll find another way." He said the Shoshone had been hesitant to sell her but finally did, at a very high price. She came from their very best stock—superbly trained to hunt buffalo and engage the enemy. "She'll not flinch in battle or run from a mad buffalo," he assured them, "and she's ghost fast." They were curious why he'd given Moon such a prize, and they asked him.

"I gave this horse out of gratitude for my life," he said, "and I gave it to this woman to honor her. What happened yesterday was rare, like watching eagles mate, dropping to their deaths. A woman who rides and fights like a wolf needs a horse that's like her. Now she has the horse. Never ride a lesser one!" His eyes danced playfully, but there was a sternness to his tone.

Later, the three engaged the serious business of hunting and scouting for trap lines, and Enrí schooled them as they worked west. They re-engaged the ridgeline, witnessing large herds of elk and some buffalo. They made their way discreetly down the hills, always engaging from downwind, and descended to lower ground as the heat rose and their scent rose past them, away from their prey.

The grass was deep and tall at times, partially obscuring their approach. They hobbled their horses on the edge of a deeply grassed bottom and made for a stand of elk nearly four hundred yards distant. Stalking and moving slowly, with bows poised and Enrí's rifle primed, they crept carefully until they were within bow range, and within minutes their luck held; they were dressing three fat cows, and Enrí had reloaded his rifle.

Then it happened, a primal, hair-raising "waugh … waugh … waugh" sounded to their left, followed by the dreaded snapping of teeth. Immediately, the grizzly sow was on them, and before the others could react Enrí drove a ball through the ribs of the furious mother. Then she turned her fury on him, grabbing him by the shoulder and swinging him doll-like from side to side—he cursing at the top of his lungs. In seconds, both archers filled the sow with arrows, each dart eliciting a scream of rage 'til she dropped the big Frenchman and concentrated her fury on them.

In seconds, Moon was jammed face down into the grass, the bear grabbing her buttocks vice-like in her teeth and lifting her like a toy. And then came the sickening ripping of flesh like the sound of linen tearing. Furious, Ezra leapt from behind onto her back and, channeling his rage, plunged his dagger through the monster's upper spine—the crazed sow collapsing upon his wife. Its life force spent, it sighed and sank into the tall grass, completely covering the little Mandan.

Time slowed as, incredibly, the broken Frenchman, moaning, began the tug, and both men rolled the four-hundred pounder off its hapless victim.

"Moon! You alive?" Ezra cried. "Moon! … Talk to me!" She turned her head slowly and coughed.

"Yes. I'm still here. The bear has not taken me."

"Don't move! Can you move your arms and legs?"

"Yes," she moaned softly.

"Rest while we look at your wound," Ezra said. She lay still as they lifted her dress and found her badly torn left buttock bleeding profusely. "Enrí, there's a small bottle of whiskey in my pack back with the horses. Get it for me," said Ezra. "We'll wash both your wounds with it. They's a small leather bag of goose down. Bring that with ya, too."

The big man left immediately, moaning, his right hand covering the gaping wound in his shoulder, his left arm dangling. Within minutes he had returned with the down and the whiskey, and together they stood Moon up while Enrí lifted her dress.

They surveyed the damage. She'd lost a chunk of meat the size of a goose egg. He grabbed her about the waist and steadied her as Ezra poured. She grimaced. He gently packed the wound with down, and the bleeding slowed. It was a serious wound, so shocking that Ezra could not speak, but Enrí did. He told her the Crow were skilled at wound dressing, that he'd seen more severe wounds they'd cared for, that the flesh had filled in and the scars were nearly invisible. "I've seen wounds like this before, little lady. They'll fix it ... I tell you. You'll see." He patted her bottom, and lowered her dress.

She lay on her side as Ezra tended Enrí's shoulder. It was badly lacerated and deeply punctured, and he winced as whiskey flowed over it. Ezra offered him a drink, but he waved it away, saying, "Whiskey's unkind to me."

Then there was the matter of his shoulder, which hung oddly. When Moon came to herself, she examined it. "It's out of joint, husband. Put it back. I'll show you."

In minutes the shoulder had been relocated, and the Frenchman lay unconscious. As he lay sleeping, Ezra fashioned a tight leather band over his wife's wound, and, at her stubborn insistence, they began to skin the big bear and the elk. *Her ass is bit ... and she's skinnin' a bear. Mama, ain't she somethin'?*

When Enrí awoke, he joined the other two and helped with the dressing, and late that day they arrived back at the camp with their booty. There the two wounded ones bathed in the stream and washed blood and the smell of bear from them, and Ezra redressed their wounds. He pulled the arrow from the wounded horse, but the head remained lodged in the animal's neck and he finally gave up its pursuit. He proceeded to slicing meat and hanging it to dry.

Over the next several hours, fading shock and adrenalin heightened the woundeds' misery. Ezra retrieved a small bottle of rum that had belonged to his father and insisted Moon drink some. She drank slowly 'til the pain muted and her speech slurred. Again, he offered it to the big Canadian. This time he said yes but warned, "You might not like me ..."

In time, the two drifted off to sleep and Ezra continued cutting and hanging meat. There'd be little time or energy to dress much of the bear, but he'd retrieved what meat he could, along with slabs of rich fat. He pondered the events of the last several days and how it had overtaken them all like a storm across the prairie from which there was no refuge, of how violent and brutal it had all been, of how close Moon had been to death, and of how he had acted a man and killed the bear and saved his wife. And how incredibly grateful he was that she was still alive. He thought of Enrí and what he might learn from that good man, and of the generosity that oozed from him, as if he lived to give things away. And then he thought of the favor that seemed to follow him even into the fire, and he had very little answer to any of it other than this: there was an unseen world, and he seemed to traffic in it somehow. And he was beginning to believe more and more that it had something to do with the prophecies of his mother and the dreams of the Mandan.

After a while fresh bear meat spitted over the fire, and the smoke and smell awoke the other two, now in somewhat better spirits but sorer than ever. They moaned as he tore off chunks of bear and passed them around. Moon lay on her side, and the big man lay out flat, a saddle for a pillow propping his head. "Aaaah. This is good bear. She almost killed us, eh? I don't usually hunt my bear with a knife. Seems a little too personal." And then he shook 'til he could barely breathe, and the other two joined in until both of the wounded had to stop. It just hurt too much.

Ezra finished slicing and hanging by firelight into the early hours of the morning, and when the sun raked the camp Enrí arose, sent Ezra to bed, and continued until all of the meat had been hung. He made coffee that morning and offered it to Moon. It was then that she told her story of her previous encounter with coffee. He smiled and offered her more.
"I've learned my lesson from buzzing water and want no more!" she said. Again, he laughed and she laughed at him, and both woke up Ezra. It was quickly becoming clear to both that Enrí loved a good joke, and it was equally clear that he was a powerful asset in a scrape and generous to a fault. It seemed that the three were well on their way to becoming fast friends.
They stayed in the camp for two more days as the sun dried the meat, and the two wounded began to recover. Ezra rendered down bear grease, blended it with salt, and dressed both their wounds until they packed up and left for the Crow.

Moon sat awkwardly on her saddle, her battered butt to the side, sometimes standing in the stirrups to ameliorate her misery, and her odd form and tattered, blood-stained dress made them all laugh. They brought five trophies home with them: Blackfoot horses, a giant Canadian, a splendid new horse for Moon, and six-hundred pounds of jerked elk and bear. And then, of course, there was the sow grizzly skin—the hide of the one that'd nearly sent them all under.

21

TWO DAYS LATER, the three entered the trappers' camp. The two took note that Enrí was known by nearly everyone. Little children hung onto his legs as he swung others, one-handed, above his head—their mothers plainly unconcerned.

Villagers asked why Moon walked strangely and no longer rode her old horse, and some inquired why two of the party were covered with yellow-purplish bruises. Others stroked the bloody neck of Moon's wounded horse and asked about the hunt. One nut-brown old man fiddled relentlessly until he'd extracted the arrowhead and dressed the wound. He grinned broadly, whispered for long moments into the horse's ear, and seemed inordinately proud of himself.

Ezra gave him the horse.

Others gathered around 'til White Wolf intervened and told his people to be patient—that their questions would be answered soon. He ushered the three into his lodge, and there they sat for the next hour as he queried Enrí intensely. The Frenchman repeated what the Blackfoot captors had told him, and White Wolf smiled slightly and seemed satisfied. But he was concerned that it had been the Blackfoot who'd been scouting the herds. They were the most ruthless of the Crow enemies, and the most numerous. And to defend against them was difficult and required constant vigilance.

"Many Crow women are now slaves among the Blackfoot," he told them. "It's hard to restrain the young men, but wisdom is called for. The Cree and the Assiniboine have allied themselves against the Blackfoot but are not strong enough to drive them back. For the time being, we must content ourselves with being clever and fiercer than our adversary. When my people fight them, we show no mercy and make them too afraid to return here." This, he told them, was his hope.

He ended the talk with the passing of the pipe and shook hands with the big Canadian, embracing him like family. He ushered the three out and told them to speak freely of their trip to the villagers. He'd only wanted to hear them first.

Ezra and Moon set up for the evening. McKay greeted Enrí, and the big man displayed a telling, unspoken awkwardness—a near child-like shame. Moon sat down carefully as the tale of the last week unfolded, and the trappers questioned them until they were satisfied.

"It's good to have ya back," said Cap'n. "See you've met my old friend. He's more often our rescuer out here. Enrí and I got a interestin' past. Don't we ... old friend?" Enrí's eyes fell. "May I tell the story, Enrí?'

"Yes ... They'll hear of it soon enough."

McKay paused, a kindness to his tone. "Enrí Joubert's the friend of all good people. Loved by everyone here. Crow'd die for him. But he has weakness for strong drink, and when he drinks he becomes ... not himself.

"Two years ago at rendezvous, he bullied my men. This scar on my face? His doin'. I broke his arm with a war club ... 'cause when he gets drunk, the men who love him nearly kill him to save him. Got no tolerance for spirits. Don't give him none. Never."

Ezra's eyes grew large, and he locked eyes with the big man. "That why ya tried to warn us?" The big man grinned sheepishly.

"I fell asleep before I went wild," he said, "and I swore I wouldn't embarrass myself before your woman. She deserved better. So did you. You both saved my life. Don't apologize. Ever."

The next day Ezra took Moon to the village healer and the old woman lifted her dress, inspecting her wound. She praised Ezra for his treatment and gave him an ointment to rub into the depression every day. "Her rump will grow pretty again, young man. I promise. You'll be pleased. And you must do this every day." She looked at them both and giggled. Her eyes twinkled as she patted his hand.

He spent the rest of the morning with Moon distributing elk to the elderly and the poor, but they kept a bit, and nearly all of the bear meat, for themselves. *Ain't nobody getting this bear but us. We paid for it. Us three'll eat this bear and remember the day we all become family.*

In the weeks that followed, Ezra dressed Moon's wound regularly. In truth, he seemed to enjoy it immensely, and the thing became a point of amusement in the camp. "Dressin' her wound" became a euphemism for other things, or so many suspected. The ribbing at times was brutal, but whatever the exact truth, the result was effectual, and the cavity in her butt began to fill with new flesh. Enrí and the old woman had spoken truthfully. Her bottom was becoming pretty again.

22

It was mid-August and Ezra would be nineteen soon, but he'd never asked Moon her age and grew curious. He made plans.

There was excitement among them all as they anticipated trapping soon. Ezra would stick close to McKay and lean heavily on both Enrí and the captain to learn the new trade. McKay had been leading men on these ventures for the last four years and knew the land and the country well, and Enrí had trapped in Crow country for the last three years and would be a savvy mentor as well. Both wondered where the captain would lead them, and the camp buzzed with anticipation, but not for long. Cap'n made a decision quickly. They'd press deep into Crow country.

They'd leave the village in three days, so preparations began to be made. Saddles, tack, and equipment were cleaned and mended. Drying meat was ground into powder, mixed with fat and berries, and stuffed into greased leather bags. Trappers traded for new winter clothes and buffalo wool to stuff into leggings and winter moccasins.

On the second day of preparation, a stir occurred on the east end of the camp. A group of Iroquois and Shawnee trappers had arrived in camp, hoping to join up. When Ezra inquired how they'd been found, Cap'n grinned and said. "Them Injuns could track us across rock. Ain't nothin' they don't see." He was more than pleased and worked hard at concealing his excitement, for the Indians were hardened veterans and would bolster the camp's defenses as well.

The camp started out midmorning on the third day. The night before had been a time of celebration and dance, and, as in months earlier, the Crow men led the affair around the fire. They were the people of the Sparrow Hawk, and their fluid movements, their paint and their feathers and the jingling of buffalo hoof bells tied to their ankles spelled Ezra. They seemed more creatures than men in their regalia, and he wondered if they knew how handsome they were. They slipped effortlessly between the worlds of men and spirits and animals—mythical centaurs of old with paint on their faces and hair to their knees.

The captain rode his way up and down the line, relaying to Ezra his intended route: "Gonna follow the Yellowstone west 'til she divides. We'll trail the Northwest fork toward the divide deep in the mountains. Drop traps high up there and make camp. Men'll trap in teams and support each other. If trouble happens a man's got hisself a partner ... and if a rifle barks ... we all run to cover 'em." He grew solemn. "Most dangerous out here is the Piegans and the Bloods. They's Blackfoot, boy. Hate us. Got no sour blood, though, with the Canadians and the British. Hell, they trade with 'em and carry English guns. But as far as they're concerned, we're trespassers. Say we've armed their enemies and stolen their beaver. And beaver to them's a sacred animal. You can imagine they don't cotton to our takin' 'em."

"This all worth it then, sir? I mean ... shouldn't we just trap somewhere where they ain't, given the risk and all?" Ezra asked.

"Well now," McKay paused, sighing, cradling his chin and scratching his whiskers. "'Given the risk and all' ... is part of the glory. I say there's beaver enough for all, and I say their enemy's got a right to defend themselves. Blackfoot ain't pure in all this, boy. They're without mercy—black painted devils they are ... and don't you give 'em none!

"But they ain't the ugliest dog in this fight. I'd fight ten Blackfoot to one mountain grizz—"

"How's that, Cap'n? I mean ... Jesus, how's anythin' worse than a Blackfoot?"

"'Cause the sow you and your missus and 'ole Enrí tied into is a taste a what a big boar'll do to ya. Take off your head for pleasure."

"What? You really mean—?"

"You're damn right I do! Lost a boy from out East last year to one of 'em. None of us saw it a comin' 'til we turned, and the kid's head rolled down the trail at us. Damn bear just lifted it off ... clean-like. Left him laying there. We chased that bastard into the brush and killed him, and we ate that shit head. So do yourself and your partners a favor. Treat bear like Blackfoot."

"And how's that ... exactly?"

"Well, ya back up when you can ... and never let 'em behind ya. That's all there is to say! I'd kill 'em just to burn 'em! But I like me the meat. Tastes like good hog."

As Cap'n rode away, Ezra and Moon considered his sobering counsel, and they were quiet for some time. Ezra calculated the entire rest of the day whether the dangers of the trip outweighed its rewards. *We doin' the right thing? Maybe I can't save Moon next time, or maybe there's no one to save me. Don't have much luck keeping people alive that I care about ... do I? And there's more at stake now. I couldn't live without her ... or wouldn't wanna.* But as the day drew on, he reached a resolution of sorts. He was not a timid soul, though he doubted himself sometimes. But he'd been raised to be hard. He'd killed Crow-Killer and slaughtered the sow grizzly with the dead man's dagger. And he'd survived Mama's beatings, and that had to mean something. So, he came to this conclusion:

I'll back down from danger, I suppose ... when I'm old and white-haired and sit on a bench with Moon, with a warm blanket coverin' us both.

But for now, scary stories seemed to only make his blood race. *Now's a time to get wisdom and scars ... and experience,* he thought. Heavy on the wisdom. He reminded himself of the holy man's prophecy. It seemed that he was in league with some Unseen Force guiding his way, and he could not take the easy path and perhaps miss the marrow of it all.

23

THE PATH ALONG THE YELLOWSTONE was pleasant, with no omen of what was about to come. But one afternoon the clouds grew leaden, and lightning forked in the distance. Captain called all to shelter up, "'Cause hell is coming." And well he did, for within minutes perdition arrived and rocked them all.

Rain fell thick and heavy, like wild plums falling in sheets, and bruised the skin. One could not see beyond twenty yards, and the ground and the river seethed and belched beneath them. Others cupped their hands over their noses, fearing they might choke. Men clung to bridles of horses as women and children sheltered beneath white canvas tents they'd had no time to erect. And the open heavens raged on as all moved further from the banks of the river and braced for its inevitable swell. And it did. Within minutes the river had risen four feet, racing by them all, and swept two terrified horses away. And then the rain stopped, as though a great window had suddenly slammed shut. The silence was absolute.

In minutes a fantastic scene swept by them—a large grizzly stood atop a dead bull elk that the victor was desperately attempting to wrench to shore in the strong current. Someone shouted out, "My God … look at that!" And they all watched, stunned, as the two swept swiftly by them, grateful that the winner had been unable to ground himself, for their pans and powder were all wet—their firearms useless.

And then as quickly as it had gone, the sun appeared beacon-like as the sky cleared itself, and they gave themselves to drying their gear and food and gathering up their things. A few traced the course of the river for nearly two miles, looking for the horses, but found nothing but a battered saddle stuck in the fork of a sycamore.

Ezra had grown used to relying on meat as a primary source of nutrition, but it had to be kept dry. It was promptly laid out in the sun and hung over branches.

It'd been much different in Kentucky and among the Mandan, where produce was gathered from the fields and stored for the winter months.

Directly, goods were spread out, and wet tents and hide lodges were erected to dry. And then the sun did the rest. And so, they departed by noon of the third day, the saddles squeaking a bit from the sun's drying, as glue and pegs and rawhide expanded and shrank, but in time they tightened back up, settled back in place, and grew quiet again.

The captain said they would be coming into more rugged territory soon and that all should be caring regularly for the feet of their animals. Some of the enterprising Crow had made their own hoof files by embedding flint shards in hide-glue on small carved boards, and when the edge had degraded the Crow ran water over the glue and exposed fresh, razor-sharp shards. The crude tools were remarkably effective, and some Whites copied their design.

One evening when most had finished supper, the captain called for a meeting in the center of the encampment. The men and their wives gathered, and McKay began: "Many a ya been with me and my men before, but some are new to all this. As you know, we're on a great adventure … and it'll require courage and prudence of us all. Some of ya seen what happens when a man confuses rashness with courage. The rash man gets dragged back all scalped or bear-kilt. If we're lucky we may find his body, or—"

"Or not at all," said Gunny Hanson.

"Gunny's right," said Cap'n. "Ain't no honor given in this company to the foolhardy man, for that man'll get others killed … and I'll not abide him. If you are that man, then you best go back to the Crow … now. Ain't no welcome for ya here. I'll turn that man over to Enrí for a public whippin'." The Cap'n cleared his throat and winked, and his somber tone lifted a notch.

"But you gotta know this country deceives us with its beauty. Hell, it waits for you to turn your backside to it so it can take your hair or maul ya … or drown ya. Maybe bust your spine. And if you're foolish, ya ain't gonna see it comin.'

"So, this is it, boys. Nobody … and I mean nobody—traps by hisself on my watch. Ain't none of ya here gonna be a George Drouillard in this company … not whilst I got anything to say about it. Ole' George got hisself killed some years back 'cause he got too proud trapping all by hisself. His men found him … gut like a deer and missin' his head. Well, that ain't happening here. I ain't presidin' o'er your suicide. We're all free trappers here, but you've asked me to lead and that's ... that's damn well what I aim to do.

"I'm intendin' to bring ya all alive to rendezvous with bales a beaver plew. You, in turn, agreed to give me four plew apiece for my trouble saving your sorry asses." He grew quiet and looked them up and down. "Ya got somethin' to say, best say it now." There was silence. The captain spoke once more, this time in such low tones that all strained to hear: "Watch your hair. Ever' last one of ya."

The company drove high into the mountains, with Ezra and the rest feeling their lungs straining to adapt. Directly, they came into a meadow, covered with good grass and signs of abundant game. They camped for the night, and the captain tightened the perimeters and placed two sentries on duty. Horses were hobbled and picketed inside, close to their owners. That night, many slept more lightly than usual, as bodies adjusted to the altitude and imaginations ran unfettered. The virgins among them dreamt of adventures and painted savages and fat fierce bears tearing through camp and slaughtering them all.

But morning came early enough, and soon the smell of coffee hung over campfires. Men spoke low but excitedly and ate sparingly of jerked buffalo and small handfuls of pemmican. Fresh game would be coming soon, and all wished to conserve their dried foods for emergencies.

Captain rode his roan trailed by nearly forty others on horseback. Most packed six to ten traps and the means to anchor and bait them all. They were a motley group, mostly White but with several Crow, Hidatsa, a few free Blacks, two Mexicans, and some Iroquois and Shawnee thrown into the mix.

The Indians had agreed readily to the rules of the camp as well. They too knew the value of the brigade and the protection it afforded them, and the captain's small fee and his proven skills were worth far more than he charged—and they knew it. The company would become their family for the next months, and they aimed not to shit where they ate. They were good men—tough as they came—and read sign better than all the rest.

Heading on, men began to peel off onto the streams in groups of six to eight. They scouted the creeks, looking for runways and finding magnificent dams loaded with entire colonies of the marvelous buck-toothed rodents, and by the time the final group had settled onto its stream the trappers stretched over the span of nearly six miles.

McKay shouted to Ezra, "Where do ya mean to set up, son? If I was you, I'd go with the Shawnee. Know this trade as well as anyone, and they'll treat ya right. Hell, you sorta look like 'em ... 'cept for the green eyes."

"I suppose I do, Cap'n. Consider that a compliment. Mama's doin'."

"And well you should," said Cap'n. "An' if it comes down to a scrape, they're in for a fight. Tough as any man here. See enemy sign 'fore most White man back yonder. Keep ya from goin' under 'fore your time, I suppose." He grinned. "Watcha think?"

"Sounds good, Cap'n. I need me some Shawnee tongue anyways."

Ezra spent the rest of the day meeting his new partners and scouting the streams. Some of the Crow had told them of the "young man with big medicine," and they treated him with the respect due an experienced hand. They promised to show him the craft, and he liked them rather quickly.

The leader of the group was short and wiry, heavily tattooed, with a buffalo hide cap, print cotton shirt, and blue woolen leggings. His men called him Crooked Nose, and he carried himself with such quiet confidence that Ezra found him instantly likeable. He seemed to be in command, though his words were sparse and carefully uttered.

His brigade spent the rest of the day finding beaver runs and setting traps. They showed him the art of spreading the jaws and setting the trigger for the contraption—applying the pungent castoreum scent to the trap and anchoring the whole affair in the muddy bottom. But the most difficult part was staying immersed in snow-fed streams, sometimes up to the chest. His partner would watch as he set his trap, covering him with his rifle, and then they'd switch positions. They spent hours exposed to the cold that first day, with Ezra soon determining to wear only a breechcloth and moccasins until the weather grew very cold. He saw no way to remain dry and warm, particularly not in wet clothing.

That night they all returned to the main camp, only to rise again at first light, chug hot coffee, and re-enter the streams by midmorning.

The second day offered up a bonanza of traps filled with drowned, heavy beaver, and by early afternoon Ezra had completed his trapline, extracted his catch, and rebaited the traps. He'd had a good morning. Seven of the eight traps were sprung and full, and his entire group had done well. Spirits were high.

Soon all were commuting back to camp, their horses laden with skinned animals tied together at the tails and laid over the pommels of their saddles. A site several hundred yards south of the main camp was their objective. There they dropped the animals, and the Indian women began the arduous task of fleshing them free of fat and muscle. Afterward would come the tedious process of stretching the skins on willow-branch frames to air dry.

In short order the processing area took on the sights and smells of a slaughterhouse, and humans and earth grew slippery with blood and fat. The veterans understood the wisdom of ample distance between the camp and the fleshing site. "Watch yourselves taking a shit in the mornin', boys," one cried out. "Wolves and bear gonna smell this place for sure. Let's take meat and pelts from them sons-of-bitches! And for God's sake ... wait 'til it's light."

Ezra jumped in with Moon as she fleshed his catch. She took to it quickly, as though she'd had experience with the animal, and by his fourth beaver, and under her eye, he began to develop a rhythm for the affair, but was surprised at the thickness of the fleshed skin.

Soon, she hummed and sang under her breath in a language he didn't understand. *That Hidatsa?* He looked at her, sleeves rolled to the elbow, fingers covered in blood, a few spatters on the side of her face, and he was suddenly captivated by this exquisite, earthy creature and the remarkable fact that she loved him. "God, you're ..." he whispered, spooning in tightly behind her. She was no delicate flower, to be sure, but there was a powerful femininity to her that sometimes drove him crazy. "Moonie ... How many winters are ya? You've never told me."

She paused for a moment, cocking her head flirtatiously. "What would be given to the woman who answered such a question as this?"

"I'd let her swim naked with me ... Maybe share a robe with me tonight. Quite an offer, don't ya think?" She pressed back into him, bloodied hands on hips, thrusting out her chin.

"Husband?"

"Yes."

"It's missing something."

"And what's that?"

"When we lie under the robe tonight, you must bite my neck until I tell you to stop. Can you do this?" He paused.

"Hmmm. I suppose."

"Then I'll be eighteen winters when the geese fly south. I thought you'd think me too young. But I never thought you too young. Was I right?"

"Yes. You're perfect. Tonight we'll lie under the robe and I'll kiss your neck 'til your veins pop." He pinched her rump—she slapped his hand, squealing.

"Moon ... We oughta dress that wound again soon."

"Yes. Wounds need constant tending."

The days passed into weeks, and Moon's heart became more and more a thing of wonder to him. She seemed drawn to the lonely or sad, often asking if they might host a lonely single trapper for an evening meal. So she set the bones of the broken and seemed to try her best mending souls as well. And while the camp had known of her unusual skills, she soon shone as the one Ezra had always felt her to be—a splendid soul. And he reveled in the spectacle of it all, proud he'd had the good sense to pursue her 'til he'd finally worn her down.

One late fall day, southbound geese went honking overhead. Ezra checked on his mates, bound his catch quickly on his horse, and made straight away for the main camp. Stopping by Moon's station and dropping the beaver at her feet, he whispered in her ear, "Today you're eighteen, and I aim to tell everyone of it!"

"Husband …? I don't understand."

"Don't need ta. Just trust me. Wash up and put on a clean dress. I'll care for the beaver. It'll all be plain soon!"

That evening was filled with feasting, dancing, and fine Kentucky fiddle music, for the entire camp had been in on the surprise, and the lone baker among them had made a fine berry pie for Moon. Most had never heard of celebrating such a thing—nor had he ever done so—but many stood and told stories of Moon's kindness and skill, and she seemed terribly embarrassed by it all.

Men asked to dance with her, and she obliged nearly all, until Ezra mercifully cut in. She was done in, her face glistening with sweat. She moved little as they danced, clinging to her man like a spent beaver on a floating log. McKay interrupted the last dance for an announcement: "We got somethin' special for ya, Moon. Red Calf has somethin' to say."

Red Calf stepped forward and began, a bit nervously at first. "Hunters brought in some fine sheep recently. The other women and I tanned them up and sewed you this shirt. It's uncommon for a woman to wear such a thing, but we think it suits you." She handed the shirt to Moon. She examined it carefully and raised her head to speak, but only tears talked. Red Calf pulled her close.

"You needn't talk, sister."

And then the fiddle player, noticeably uncomfortable, struck up another tune, as many streamed by to fondle the shirt and embrace the one the big

Frenchman had christened as "little sister." Enrí waited in line and was the last to greet her. He grabbed her about the waist, sweeping her high into the air and gently lowering her again, all the while asking how she liked her new horse.

"I'm so pleased with her, big brother. She's swift and powerful. I'll never find one better. I'll treat her as the great honor she is."

"Well, she's no swifter or more powerful than her master. I gave her to you because she … she fits you. Strange people need strange horses." He paused affectionately. "Good night, mademoiselle."

"Sleep well, big brother."

24

THE FORWARD CAMPS CONTINUED to yield beaver, and bales of plews multiplied. Ezra'd done so well at his location that he took a day off to hunt. Moon saddled her horse, and they packed both of his big-bore St. Louis rifles, along with their bows, for they were in thick bear country. He'd use the trip to teach Moon the art of the rifle, and he'd little doubt she'd take to it quickly, as she seemed to nearly everything. From nowhere, a strange thought nearly stopped him: What might our children be like?

They cantered slowly west, looking for game trails and a plateau from which they could scan for more. In time the plateau failed them, 'til they spied a high, rocky ridge and rode it for several miles paralleling the river.

Afterward, they rode for another hour and set up targets at the base of a small pine, and soon the little knoll reeked of sulfur and stung their eyes. It quickly became clear that Moon fit the shorter rifle perfectly. He remembered the day he and Papa had bought those rifles and how Papa had ordered the one cut for a smaller frame. And then he'd acted all coy and refused to give the reason for it all, all the while grinning and knowing somehow it would fit this day—this woman. *If only he were here now!*

Moon had little fear of the flashing pan or the recoil. "I want to shoot heavy powder like you do, Ezra. I want to be ready for bear."

"Ain't a good idea, Moon. Not yet." Her nostrils flared, her voice pinching—annoyed.

"Why not? I'm strong."

"I know it. But a bear load is best handled by someone with more experience. We'll get you there. I promise," he said.

"But what if my rifle is needed today to kill a bear? What would we do then? I want to learn now. Please!"

"Alright. But I don't feel good about it. I'll load ya up. Watch me ... This measure is one-hundred-fifty grains. Ya top it off and pour it down your barrel just like we've been a-doin.' And do everything else just the same. Alright? Tell me when you're ready."

"I will." She finished her loading. "I'm ready."

"I hope you are," he said. "Pull the butt tight against your shoulder. Get your nose off the cheekpiece. It'll catch you good if you let—"

Phht-boooom!

"Dammit ... Moonie." Blood gushed from her nose and soaked her shirt. "Ya broke it ... I think! I was trying to—"

"I know! ... I know! Please don't scold me." Tears welled. "Will you set my nose, Ezra? Please. I want to be pretty. Please don't leave me. Ple—"

"Leave you? ... How could you say that, Moon? You think I could ever leave you? You—"

"But I'm stubborn," she sobbed, "and you're the only one that's ever stayed with me ... and I—"

"And you think that someday ... I'll leave, like all the rest?" She was quiet. His voice raised but his eyes grew kind. "I said ... is that it?"

"Yes," she sobbed.

"Moon, listen to me now ... real good. I am never ... ever ... leavin'. Never! Now let's see 'bout settin' that nose."

When she'd come to, she said, "Someday I'll shoot like you, if you'll teach me. I can't let this rifle teach me to fear it. I'll listen this time. I promise." Her lip quivered.

"Alright," he said. "Ya know ... both of us got the same affliction."

"What do you mean?" she asked.

"I mean ... we're not that different, you and me. Hear me out."

"Yes."

"You and me ... we sometime get ourselves, like Cap'n says, 'out on the skinny branches.'"

"What does that mean?" she said.

"It means we get ahead of ourselves sometimes. That our bodies outrun our heads 'cause we're pretty damn good at figuring out the mess we're creatin'. You understand?"

"Yes," she said, and began to giggle. "I think he's right."

"I know he's right," Ezra said. "You know what he told me? He said, 'Get 'round folks that think 'fore you do something that can't be fixed.' Cap'n read me like a book—both of us, I think. So, 'fore this day is over, you'll master your fear of your rifle. Go ahead, load it again. Keep your finger out of the trigger guard 'til I tell ya. And keep that nose off the stock. You can't stand breakin' it twice today." He paused long seconds, scanning her wounded face, wonder on his own—his voice nearly a whisper, meant only for him to hear. "Lordy, you're ..."

They reloaded and primed their rifles and turned back toward where they had seen elk and buffalo earlier in the day. Moon'd shown promise, but it would take time before she and the rifle were one. At least now she could fire it in an emergency. They needed to be prepared for danger, and Ezra vowed to avoid another Old Tom moment. He pondered her wounding and how she refused to run from it all and how proud he was of her.

They tied their horses to a cluster of scrub pines and approached downwind of a small herd of elk headed for water; and skirting a tree line, they beat the animals there and waited. Ezra slung both rifles across his shoulders and carried his bow in his hands. They'd create as little stir as possible and take meat with the bow if they could. But the presence of the rifles gave them greater range and protection from the most dangerous of all predators, "Old Ephraim," as the veterans called the big male grizzlies.

So they sat for some time on the edge of a thicket, continuing their vigil 'til they heard the snapping of twigs and smelled the musk of rutting bulls. And then they sat some more. But in time, another strong smell drifted over them. They glanced to their left, and not more than thirty yards away lay a massive blond grizzly male. He too, was observing the elk assembling by the water, totally unaware of them. But they had the advantage of the wind for the present and froze, motionless. Moon pinched Ezra's thigh hard and mouthed, "Rifles."

They sat stone-like, observing the bear watching the elk accumulate at the stream's edge; it sat motionless on a slight spit of earth projecting in front of them by nearly twenty yards. Ezra inched the rifles off his back, and soon both had them in their laps with fresh powder in the pans. He counted the cost. Both guns had large-caliber, thick-walled barrels with heavy powder charges. But Moon was green and less than confident with her new weapon. If things went badly, his only option would be to stop the monster quickly with a perfectly placed head shot, low in the skull. A shot to the forehead would glance off and merely enrage the killer.

Ezra calculated. He'd killed many a black bear back in Kentucky, some with head shots, but those smaller species were almost a different animal entirely, incapable of absorbing the punishment these male grizzlies could endure. If it came to it, his shot would have to be perfect. Both their lives would depend on it. His heart began to hammer so wildly he swore the bear might hear it.

Eventually, the wind began to swirl and both held their breath. The bear, once attentive to his hunt, grew restless and sniffed the breeze. Ezra motioned Moon to stay put, his eyes saying it all. She squeezed his fingers and nodded, and he began closing the distance directly behind the bear. Soon he was inside ten yards and shouldering his weapon. Then a twig snapped under his foot. The bear swung cat-like, rising to full height, opening his massive mouth to roar, and gathered himself to launch his charge. Ezra squeezed off the big fifty-three —it hanging-fire for a terrifying split second. Phhhht ... boooom, and then the ball tore through those cavernous jaws, a crimson puff behind them, the shrapnel of clattering teeth and skull ripping through branches like clustered rifle fire, and the bear collapsing at his feet, a stately old pine—his falling claws grazing his knee, shredding his leggings and slapping his foot ham-like— a soft groan escaping from what had been a mouth, like air from a tired old bellows.

In seconds, adrenalin failed them, and their senses as well, and they collapsed on the thicket floor, their legs little more than soft mush. They were mute 'til Moon broke the spell. "Ezra ... I think I know how you killed Crow-Killer. You kill to save life. You're like Mato Tope. You are like him. I see it now." She lay and laughed for some time, then wept. "You are like him!" Neither spoke for a while.

"Never felt fear like that," he said. He went silent, his body bone-cold, shivering—teeth chattering—gooseflesh prickling his arms. "Noooo?" he said. "Oh, Lord ... could I really be like that man?!" He stretched out, leaning back on his elbows, tears in his eyes. "This really happenin', Moonie? God, it's ... it's like you and me's caught up in some dream a sorts." He began to laugh, crazily, convulsively, seizure-like—the deep toe-curling kind that began in his belly and fanned outward 'til his lungs couldn't fuel it all—racing past his brain, leaving him spent on his back choking for wind, his face blood-red—a mortal strangling on angel-wine.

She sat beside him mutely, words failing both 'til slowly a gentle breeze blew over them. The air grew sweet and thick, and he smelled honeysuckle—his mother's favorite. He glanced about but saw nothing. Only hardwoods and a smattering of pine.

"Do you smell it, Moon—that sweet flower smell?"

"Yes. Yes, I do. Something's happened here. We've been ..." Her brow pinched, straining for something.

"Visited?" he asked.

"I don't know. But I smell it too. It's sweet and heavy and steals my breath. It follows you and me somehow like a …"

"Like what?... Finish it!"

"A prayer."

They sat for some time 'til their strength returned, rising and surveying the giant bear. He was mammoth, nearly ten feet in length and nine-hundred pounds. She insisted they skin him and save as much meat as possible.

In three hours, they had nearly two hundred pounds of meat and another hundred pounds of fat to render. But a decision loomed. What of the magnificent hide? For Moon there was only one path. They'd not allow it to go to waste. She decided for them both. "The hide will be a memorial to you, husband, and you'll wear it on special occasions," she said, "or we'll make a fine robe of it." He thought it over and judged it best to not argue. He'd already fought one bear.

It took another four hours to flesh the big skin and another to pack the whole affair onto the horses. Judging fresh meat and blood dangerous bait, they purposed to ride straight through and not arrive back at camp until nearly nightfall. So they skirted the valley as much as possible, until at last they spotted smoke rising in the distance and the flickering of campfires. They descended quickly, shouting their arrival a quarter mile out. Soon, the news spread throughout the camp of their adventure, and Moon proudly babbled the tale of her husband's courage to all who gave her time.

Two Crow women took the hide, and arrangements were made to pay them for their best work. The meat was roasted throughout the camp that evening, and fat sizzled on spits and made people glad that Creator had made such a delicious animal for his humans to enjoy.

Some asked why Moon looked like she'd fought the bear with her fists, but the two just grinned with Ezra quipping matter-of-factly, "Yep. Had ourselves a time, we did." But the people talked among themselves and said things like, "He don't see it yet, does he?" And though he was embarrassed by their talk, he found a measure of pride and comfort in it all. Maybe he wasn't what his father had called him all those years—"a pants pissin' no-good who couldn't take care of those he loved." The death-grip of that shame seemed to be slipping some as he entered into this wild life. And that—well, that felt better than good to him.

25

THE PLUNDERING OF THE RIVERS and dams continued unabated. The fall air grew bitter and the streams began to freeze as the trappers began their descent back down the mountain to warmer parts, trapping as they went, the main camp staying just beneath them.

The beaver haul had been a bonanza for all the cold and wet stream-warriors, and the women stayed busy and fatigued from the arduous processing of skins. Bears and wolves frequented the fleshing areas and frightened many in the early morning hours, as heavily armed men and not a few women drove the beasts away. Those who would not leave or thought themselves the better of the foreign two-leggeds were shot, butchered, and skinned just like the beaver. The irony was not lost on the camp, and bear meat, along with even the occasional lion, was enjoyed heartily, making hearts glad and bellies tight.

By mid-November all of the beaver plews had been fleshed, dried, and baled. The camp moved further down the mountain into an ample meadow with sufficient game, water, and cottonwood bark for the horses. It'd be their home for the next four months until spring came. There, some built sod enclosures for the winter and roofed them with buffalo hides. Others would bear up in their tents or hide lodges, and when the winter broke they'd mount their ascent once again, trapping as they went, and finish in time to carry their plews to the summer rendezvous.

There they'd exchange them for fresh supplies and cash money. Young and lusty single men would find plenty of opportunity to debauch themselves, because Indian women abounded. Some would contract diseases from their dalliances. Some serious. Their faces would rot off in a couple years and they'd go crazy. Or they'd beg a friend to put a ball through their brain or run their horses over a cliff. Still others would gamble and drink away an entire year's pay.

Some might even risk life and limb in horse races and shooting matches, and a few would not show up for the rendezvous at all. They would've been seduced and "kilt" over the long winter by disease, bear, or Indian, or drowned, or have fallen to their deaths. These were the ones who would have "gone under," in the parlance of the mountain, and they weren't grieved long. Life became cheap under the hardships. "Mountain's got its way," many would say, "and it needs to be respected."

When they'd made their final settlement, Ezra and Moon erected their tent. It was spacious enough for the two and tall enough to allow them to stand. They made beds of pine boughs covered with robes, and it quickly became their winter home. But the mercury fell in December and the interior was covered with hoarfrost in the mornings, and they were glad for each other's warmth. It was, to their chagrin, too late to erect a sod and timber place so they packed their belongings around the edges of the tent to block the draft, but soon found the measure woefully inadequate. Even packed snow could not fully stop the violent winds.

After one especially windy night, they awoke to a tent full of snow. After coffee, Ezra announced he'd "had enough" and proposed a solution. He and Moon would hunt for the day, as much for hides as for meat. They'd return with fresh buffalo skins and wrap the outer edges of their tent with the still damp hides. These would freeze into place and chink the holes—or so he hoped.

Moon's eyes brightened. She'd lived in earthen lodges and skin affairs that were quite comfortable, but last night had been miserable, and Ezra's plan smelled of hope. The present lodgings would just not do. So, after a small breakfast they left, trailing another horse behind them. They headed west, hoping to find signs of buffalo. By noon, their plan began to pay.

They forded a small stream following a sizeable herd of shaggies, large enough to pack the snow in a swath nearly one-hundred yards wide. They trailed them until they crested a rise, and there they paused on the lip. Below them in a plain near a river lay an ambling herd of nearly two-thousand animals. A few lay, but most pawed the snow to uncover the rich grass beneath.

So they plotted their strike. They'd circle downwind and approach from the south, supremely confident of their mounts to pursue skillfully. They'd need at least five animals to secure their tent and had sufficient arrows and ball if it came to it. And Ezra possessed a fine horse and a woman who was every bit his equal as a hunter. This day, he told himself, we're ready. "Let's do this,

Moonie." She nodded and said playfully, "And when we're done, we'll play horses ... if you'd like?"

He rode close and raked her ear with his teeth. She groaned low and kissed him. They were powerfully agreed. The hunt for hides would be foreplay, a means to a glorious end. And they burned for all of it.

They closed from the south and, inside of three-hundred yards, covered themselves with their robes, hair out, and leaned forward, hoping to look like the wooly ones they sought. They closed slowly, walking just a bit faster than their prey. Most of the animals had their backs to them, and in time they were in their midst undetected, an ample wind blowing their scent behind them. They filled their bow hands with as many arrows as they could hold and picked their targets. Ezra uncovered himself, loosing a shaft into a sleek cow at only four yards. She groaned, trotted away, and collapsed in sixty. He scanned for bulls, the closest being only a bowshot away and unaware. It was Moon's turn, and she let go two shafts. The young bull ran confusedly, stopped, wobbled, and dropped. The two "buffalo people" continued their ruse for the next quarter-hour, 'til six plump animals lay dead.

Moon galloped for help, and in her absence Ezra continued to fell another three. Within two hours, eleven riders and eighteen horses appeared, descending on a trot toward him. He told the men to set aside six intact skins for his home, and she dragged them back to camp at a feverish pace, before they froze hard.

Within hours, travois were built and animals rendered, and the party made their way back to camp. They'd deliver thousands of pounds of fresh fat buffalo. Cap'n met them. "Dammit, you two!" he said, a fatherly grin on his broad freckled face.

The men noted that all of the animals had been taken without noise or the spending of powder and ball, and those who'd given little respect to the bow had their minds bent a bit, some talking of trading for bows at rendezvous and enlisting Moon as teacher. She'd "kilt five buffalo in one hunt, after all," some said.

But the pair cared little for the accolades. They had what they had planned for—six fresh hides wrapped around the base of their tent, and the inside swept clean of the morning's snow. It was no cabin, but it was no longer drafty, and Moon grinned contentedly as she pulled him under her robes. *He's a good man, and makes me happy.* "Ezra!" she said, "do you still want to play horses?"

"Yep ... been wantin' ta all day."

26

THE WINTER BECAME FIERCE in January and temperatures plummeted. Horses retreated to the cottonwoods and girthed the trees for bark and twigs, for the snow had grown too deep to paw for grass. Daily, the men broke icy streams with axes, watered horses, and brought water back to camp. The buzzing of saws and the cracking of axes in pursuit of fuel became a daily staccato ringing through the trees.

Men hunted the valley and beyond for bison, elk, and whatever other game might present itself. Often, Ezra and Moon headed out with the others. One day they returned to camp with four horses burdened down with buffalo and a sow grizzly that Moon had taken with her rifle, minus the paws she'd saved for herself.

Shortly thereafter, McKay called the two into his tent and began to speak. His face was crimson and his hands trembled. "Ya need to know there's trouble brewin'. Crooked Nose is talking crazy 'bout Moon. Says she's a witch. You believe that? No one's listenin' to him, but he's aimin' to leave soon and take his men with him. Says a curse is coming on all a us on account of her."

"Does he hate me? I don't understand," she asked, tears welling in her dark eyes.

"I don't know, young lady, but he aims to hunt tomorrow and lay by some meat … and then light out. Need to see him now 'fore this goes any further. I suggest the meetin' be just the men. He's afraid a you, Moon. Let's go stop this bullshit, Ezra!"

Within minutes, the two men stood before Crooked Nose and shared their minds, but he was sullen and unmoved, an unbending piece of ugly iron. He'd been a lieutenant years earlier to the Shawnee prophet Tenskwatawa, he said. And there he'd prosecuted Shawnee accused of witchcraft and burned some of them. He claimed he saw signs on the young woman—signs of arrogance and too much success. And this was proof of her crime. The captain spoke sharply in her defense, "Ya stupid son-of-a-bitch!" but his words fell on deaf ears. Crooked Nose's mind was set and his knees locked. He'd leave before disaster befell them all.

The two men left, angry, heartsick. Ezra was enraged. "What the hell's wrong with him, Cap'n? I wanna thrash him somethin' awful!"

"Well, son," Cap'n sighed, "in my judgment gotta let this play out. Some things ain't solved with fists or knives. Trick's knowin' when to let a man hang hisself. Pride got a way a turnin' on a man like that."

And they were all grieved. Crooked Nose and his brigade were fine trappers and a great early warning crew, and the captain had relied on them heavily. But in their present state, they were no longer trusted. And they'd shit on Moon, and that had alienated nearly everyone. Crooked Nose had been a favorite of Ezra and had taught the young man well. And Ezra had looked up to him like an uncle. But this foolishness disappointed him beyond words. And then there was the camp. The men would not abide the lies about Moon much longer, for she'd become everyone's daughter. Only a miracle of the first order could repair the breach.

The next morning found Crooked Nose and his troop headed out for an early hunt, their faces stoic as they rode east, chasing news of the last game sighting in a creek bed to the north. But when the sun reached high overhead, two riders from their party approached the camp, riding hard. They slid to a stop before the captain and spilled their story. Crooked Nose had been ambushed by a sow grizzly. He'd killed the bear but was barely hanging onto life himself. He'd several broken bones and suffered a sucking chest wound and untold cuts and bruises.

They begged for help, but few had the skills required, and by a strange twist of fate the only ones with much experience with wounds and broken bones were Moon, Ezra, and Enrí. And Enrí was gone from camp, having left for several days to hunt and scout.

When the two offered their services, the Shawnee reluctantly accepted, and all four mounted up and left. Ezra packed whiskey, goose down, bear grease, and some of the mysterious ointment the old woman had used to pack Moon's wound, as well as four thick winter kill robes.

In two hours, they were at the site of the fallen hunter. There they found the snow spattered with his blood and the big sow lying lifeless beside him. Ezra shouted directions to his brigade mates to carefully skin the bear. "And keep the claws!" Moon shouted. They nodded dutifully.

They inspected the broken form. He'd been savaged, for sure. His clothes were soaked with blood, and half of his nose hung from a thin ribbon of flesh resting across his cheek. His left ear was gone, a sick gurgling sound came from his perforated right lung, and both arms were broken. His legs were badly battered, and his shoulder had been dislocated. The man was fortunately unconscious.

Ezra tore open his shirt, flushed the deep puncture wound with whiskey, and kneaded the down into the holes. The gurgling stopped almost immediately, and the men stopped their skinning to watch. He glared back at them icily and bellowed out, "Get on with it! … you heard me." They looked away and resumed their work.

Moon asked Ezra for help to set the bones of both arms, and when she relocated the shoulder the man woke screaming, before immediately losing consciousness once again. She flushed the ravaged nose and ear, nearly waking him a second time. She pulled a small sewing box from her capote and, while Ezra held the nose in place, sewed and checked the stitches. She checked them again, and they seemed firm. They slathered all his wounds with bear grease and wrapped him in robes.

They built a travois for transport and soon headed back to camp. Rearward glances at Crooked Nose's men found them all shame faced and unwilling to make eye contact.

Two hours later, they entered the camp, but few wanted to house the broken man, his own crude accommodations inadequate for recuperation. The camp was angry at him and jealous for Moon. "She ain't deserved a lick of this," they muttered angrily. But finally, the soft heart of Red Calf prevailed. She opened their large white canvas tent to the three, and Crooked Nose was carried in. There they laid him on robes and covered him with two more. His breathing was ragged, his color gray.

Throughout the night, Moon slept beside her enemy and checked his breathing frequently. In the morning, he was no better. In fact, his condition had worsened, and fever wracked him. Then came the chills that clattered his teeth so loudly that Red Calf tied a band about his head to bind his jaws together. It stopped the noise, but the shaking seemed to spread to the rest of him with even greater violence, so much so that Moon feared he might dislodge the splints on his arms or separate the two halves of his nose.

Ezra came by to see her, and she whispered in his ear. His nostrils flared angrily 'til finally he nodded. They uncovered the man and disrobed him as she stripped, rolled Crooked Nose onto his side, and pulled herself tightly in behind him. Red Calf and the captain covered them both with three thick robes, and the wait began. The irony was thick. The only one in the camp with sufficient skill and grace to save the plaintiff was the unjustly accused, and she aimed to give it her best effort. "I won't be like him!" she told Ezra. She'd follow the path of Red Calf and show mercy, even if Crooked Nose were to spit on her when he came to. But she hoped for better.

Late that evening, by the light of tallow candles, Ezra slowly pulled back the top of the robe. Crooked Nose had stopped shaking, his fever broken. Moon glistened with sweat. He dragged her free and wrapped her in a woolen blanket until she cooled, and pulled her dress over her shoulders. She'd done all that was humanly possible. Tomorrow she'd dress her accuser's wounds again, check his stitches, and make certain he'd begun to drink and eat.

She and Ezra went to the creek, and there he stripped her and bathed the blood and smell of bear and the sweat of the Shawnee from her exhausted body. She was utterly spent. The bracing water enlivened her a bit, and Ezra helped her dry and dress, but the strength didn't last long. He lifted her, sack-like, tossing her over his shoulder. He lay with her for the rest of the night and she lay stone-like—but she did snore. Loudly.

The next morning Crooked Nose awoke, so sore and weak his proud soul couldn't fight those he'd offended. McKay told him how Moon and her husband had saved his life—that he owed them everything. And then Cap'n's eyes darkened, his face forming a scowl. "Listen to me, ya sorry son-of-a-bitch," Cap'n said—jaws flexed tight like a terrier clamped on a rat. "You got what's comin' to ya! Ain't no one here on your side!"

The broken man tried to rise but quickly toppled over. Red Calf informed him that the only healer left was the "witch" and that without her he'd die among those who did not care. He cursed loudly in Shawnee, collapsed, and passed out. The captain swore, "Damn him!" under his breath and then chuckled with his wife. Old Crooked Nose had the "pride-wolf" by the ears and was loathe to let it go. "Bastard's gonna ride this colt over the cliff. You watch," he said.

In the early morning, Enrí arrived at the camp, horseless and nearly frozen.

Some unknown natives—though he suspected they were Cree—had stolen his horse and all that he had while he lay sleeping. And when Ezra told him of the crazy words spoken by the broken Shawnee, his face grew dark and animated—fierce. "That bastard! If he were younger and strong, I'd teach him a lesson he'd never forget, eh? He'll kiss my French ass 'fore I forgive what he's done to little sister!"

"No need talkin' to him," Ezra said. "Whole camp feels like us. He'll pay for it. If Red Calf hadn't won out, he'd be layin' stiff in the snow by now."

Ezra dropped by to see Crooked Nose in the late morning, just as he awoke. He dropped to his knees and whispered low in the man's ear, "The only one who'll doctor ya is my woman. So ... if you ever wanna leave the camp where the witch lives, you better treat her right, 'cause if you don't, I'll treat ya, and I'll be as rough as the grizz that put ya here! You'll beg to have her back. You savvy? Do ya?" The Shawnee was mute.

"Won't have her disrespected by one who's disappointed me, and everyone here. Even your men been 'shamed by ya! Won't even look at the rest of us. And now ... now you gotta decide whether to live or die or hurt more. Maybe the bear beat ya to teach you about your pride. You're full a pride, Crooked Nose! Makes me sick!"

The man was visibly shaken, his hard expression softening slightly. Ezra turned to leave as Moon entered the tent, sank to her knees, and inspected the wounds of her patient. His face was blank, inscrutable. She applied warm bear grease to his chest wound and inspected his nose. The stitches had held and there were no signs of infection. "I've sewn your nose to your face," she told him, "and you mustn't touch it for seven suns or it might fall off, and you'll have no nose at all." He remained silent, but his scowl had left. She also warned him not to use his arms for at least a month, or they might grow crooked and render him unfit to trap again. Still, he said nothing. She drew water for him and fed him elk stew. "I'll be by later," she said. He turned away and instantly fell asleep.

Later in the day she returned and asked Crooked Nose if he needed to relieve himself. He nodded. "I'll get my husband," she said, but his face fell and he shook his head no. "Would you like me to take you?" she asked. He nodded yes. She slipped a long woolen shirt over his bruised body and wrapped a blanket about him, and with his arm over her shoulder and hers about his waist, they made for a group of trees nearby. His battered legs carried him feebly into the trees, and when he'd finished he wiped his backside and hands with snow, and they limped back into the tent. She helped him back under his robe, and he was gone.

This routine continued for eight days, each day the patient growing a bit stronger. On the ninth day, she heated bear grease in a brass pot until it was warm to the touch. She pulled up his shirt and began to knead his deeply bruised legs with the slippery mixture. He stifled a cry but finally relaxed, and she continued 'til the pot was empty, pulled down his shirt, and left.

On the tenth day, Moon opened the tent and sat by his side. She squeezed his arm firmly below the splint and held on. This time, he looked at her as tears welled in her eyes. She handed him a soft leather bag and gestured that he open it, saying, "This is my gift. Only one strong enough to kill the bear should wear it."

As he pulled the object from the bag, his hand began to shake and his eyes widened in disbelief. It was a magnificent bear-claw necklace. "This is from the bear that you killed, father. I made it for you," she choked out.

Crooked Nose clutched the necklace between his trembling hands, inspecting its craftsmanship. It was fine in every way. And in moments his eyes grew glassy, and his chest heaved as great tears formed and dripped from his chin. He placed the necklace in his lap and spoke to her for the first time. His voice was kind, but trembled. "I have played the fool. And you ... you've shown me nothing but kindness." His voice broke. Finally, he quavered out, "My pride has blinded me. Your man saw it in me right off, and told me so. I was angry, but I knew he was right.

"Oh, my child ... I've fed the black dog, and I must make amends for what I have done. And I've offended you above all others. One who loves like you could never be a witch. I beg your forgiveness. I'll confess my pride before all those I've wronged. Tenskwatawa was a fool, and I was a fool for believing him. I'll do so no longer."

When he'd finished, he motioned for her to lean in. He embraced her clumsily and shortly grew faint and fell asleep, his beautiful necklace draped across his chest, his shamed face now peaceful. She gently pulled his robe over him and left to tell Ezra the good news. She had chosen the high path, the one her mother had taught her, and she was proud she had done so. And strangely, she felt a growing bond to the broken little Shawnee as if she had won a war to gain a friend. But today the battle was over—finally over, and they had both won.

She exited the lodge and made for her own, but it seemed her moccasined feet floated above the cold, frozen ground.

Deep in the shadows of the captain's tent, McKay and his woman whispered in the darkness of what they had just seen. "My God ..."

27

J ANUARY WAS A BITTER MONTH for Ezra and the camp, and the snow, even at the lower elevations, grew deep. Crooked Nose grew stronger, and when he was able he limped about the camp and confessed his foolishness. It crushed him to see the face he'd lost, especially among his own men, but he bore up and handled it manfully. It would require some months to recover what he'd pissed away.

Moon continued her doctoring, and by mid-month he'd regained the use of his arms, and his nose had healed. He wore his hair low to mask the missing ear, and his legs were slow to recover from the bone-deep bruises. She mixed some of her mysterious ointment into the bear grease and continued the massages, until he walked with barely a limp. Time would complete the rest, she hoped.

The snow had restricted hunting for a week, and some women began crafting snowshoes from buffalo sinew. The buffalo wallowed like pigs in deep snow, becoming easy prey for men on snowshoes, and within days shoes and crude toboggans had been fashioned for dragging out the meat once it had been found.

Almost immediately, Ezra and a party of sixteen hunters left in search of food. They hadn't worn the rigs before, and the going was slow and ungainly. Some of the strongest slogged up a ridge to scout. They were gone for nearly two hours, eventually returning breathless and excited as they clambered back down.

A mile to the west, in a deep ravine, were a thousand animals pushing against snow nearly four feet deep. "They can barely move," the scouts gushed. So they trekked ponderously forward, unconcerned that the prey might outdistance them. In three hours, they were on them. They made no attempt at stealth, for it wouldn't have mattered. The big bulls bawled and groaned and threatened but were impotent to stop the slaughter. Some even used lances to run the buffalo through.

Within minutes, thirty-eight cows and many calves lay dead as Ezra and Moon deftly demonstrated to all the efficiency of the arrow. They had slaughtered fifteen in the time the others had killed the rest. There were nearly five tons of fresh kill.

Several with rifles stayed behind to guard all that could not be loaded on the first round. The youngest and strongest would drag the first load and return with fresh draggers. Those left behind watched the exertions of those leaving and were inwardly glad. It'd be a brutal three miles to camp, and one man whispered to his friend, "Thank God it ain't us!"

Late that night, by the light of torches, the last toboggan pulled into camp. There, meat was divided among the sites, and exhausted workers pulled off their sweaty, blood-stained clothes. On a bet, the hardiest of them plunged into the nearby creek and washed away the grime and fatigue.

The men screamed and laughed like schoolboys, and some secretly hoped Moon might join in the communal bath, but it was only a fevered dream. Ezra had a different plan. The couple waited in the trees 'til all the others had left and then scrubbed themselves until they were so numb from cold they barely dragged their purple bodies from the water. They screamed and shook so fiercely they couldn't talk, and laughed like crazy ice-people. Finally, someone threw blankets from the darkness and shouted, "We seen enough. Cover up, for God's sake!" It was Cap'n and Red Calf. Loud, crude laughter erupted from all along the bank, for they had been watched—the brunt of a well-executed joke.

In time all had replaced their clothing, dragged their weary bodies back to their lodging, and fell asleep like those who'd plowed all day uphill with mules in the sun. And the next day, the hunters and draggers slept late, their bodies tender and spent from the extraordinary exertions of the previous one, but happy and proud they'd stretched every sinew and lived to tell it all.

In late March, the lower streams began their melt, and beaver emerged again. Traps went in water, and men braved icy streams. It was testament to strong constitutions that none took sick or needed doctoring.

Moon spent long hours hooping beaver, and her skills with the rifle sharpened from nearly daily hunting forays as she sallied out on her paint, her rifle cracking in the distance, dragging multiple loads of freshly harvested game and distributing them to those who lacked the skill or were otherwise occupied. She had found her stride and became the undisputed camp darling. Ezra jokingly told his friends, "I'm 'bout to be known as 'Moon's man.'"

He re-engaged his old brigade and partnered again with Crooked Nose, now nearly recovered. The man's face and nose had healed well. In fact, his nose was no longer his namesake. The attack and Moon's treatment had straightened it somewhat, and he traded for a mirror to look at himself from time to time. He'd also reconciled with his men. And though he had not requested his leadership role be restored, his repentance had been so complete the others looked to him once again. He walked now with an almost imperceptible limp and a humility that framed his scars. He hunted for those who could not and scouted for enemy sign as the days grew warmer. And Ezra—well, Ezra slowly and finally ... forgave him.

Soon the camp followed the melting streams back up the mountain. The beaver were less numerous this season, requiring them to press even higher than last fall. At the higher elevations, the scent of pine in thin air was so pure that even the melancholy smiled, open-mouthed, at the snowy teats. Here, even the atheist rethought his most deeply held beliefs, for this was the cathedral of the mountain man, and "By Gawd, there could not be a finer!" he would say.

The brigades trapped the icy streams until early June, dried and baled their plews, and packed for the summer rendezvous on the headwaters of the Wind River. Cap'n estimated the distance to be about three-hundred miles and the meeting nearly six weeks out. He said they'd make it easily in four but wouldn't hurry. It had been a long winter, and the spring trapping had been arduous. The camp needed leisure, and they'd live lightly from the land as they moved. They were a living, breathing organism, and as Cap'n said, "Even a tough mule needs rest and green grass or he'll just give out somewhere, and can't no one use him."

The traveling weeks were times of recuperation and repair. Bodies chilled and stiffened in cold mountain creeks lounged and lay in deep grass under cobalt skies, the warm breezes regenerating them all. Indian wives lay by their men's sides, the sun warming their copper faces and reminding them of their status as wives of free trappers. Some made love and conceived children by the gurgling brooks.

Their lives were not easy by White standards, but they were doted upon by their husbands and spared some of the backbreaking labor of regular tribal life, and a few would not be wives for long. Their fickle husbands would tire of them and turn them out, or trade them, and they might return to their people. Others would live long, happy lives with their husbands and birth many children. Their men would shower them with fine clothes, saddles, horses, and bangles, so much so that they would come to expect such pampering. This was the lot of the mountain men's squaws. And for most, the benefits seemed to outweigh the risks.

The single men hunted and fished rivers and streams. Trout spitted over fires or fried in beaver fat in iron skillets. And those tired of large game relished the new fare. Others ventured from the camp and returned with berries, wild turnips, and duck and geese. The fat birds became a coveted item, and the Indian women seemed especially proficient at killing them. Each night became a kind of contest among the women as to who might kill the most for the day. Eventually wagers were made, and men bet on the skills of their women. Moon sat out and quietly cheered on her friends. Ezra placed bets of his own—a beaver plew here and there—but with little success.

One night he watched as Red Calf was narrowly beaten by a woman married to one of the Iroquois. The woman had killed four large geese that day with snare and her husband's trade gun. The camp lionized her, and her man strutted like a tom turkey in early spring. She jumped on his back, and he ran her the length of the camp as the men whooped and hollered and cried her name. She was a remarkably plain woman with a large birthmark on the side of her face, but on that day she fancied herself a queen—and the camp obliged her. "Ti ... lee ... Ti ... lee ... Ti ... lee," they cried, as she waved a hand full of goose feathers and grinned proudly back through two missing teeth.

These became days the people would long remember, days that prefigured the excesses and glories of the rendezvous on the headwaters of the Wind. The young among them had seen similar games and feasting in the villages, but these times seemed especially sweet, for they were purchased high in the mountains with sweat and cold and long hours spent fleshing and hooping beaver, marked by constant struggle against bear and hunger and horse-thieving Indians. And now all the tension and struggle of the past months came leaking out in laughter and silliness and games. And they all relished it.

Days from the rendezvous site, Cap'n placed his fingers in his mouth and blew a piercing whistle, calling all to "listen up" again as he stood on a large rock. "In two days, we'll be at the Wind to trade our beaver. Now some of ya never been to rendezvous before, while others have, and have little need for my words. But I feel a word a caution is a good thing, even for the veterans among us.

"You're all about to see wondrous and wild things. Men ... the lucky an' the wise, lived another year to trade their pelts. And ya all know that breeds a certain kind a man—a man that judges hisself worthy of great celebration, a man who prides hisself on living another year havin' beaten bear and cold and hunger and fearsome Injuns, 'cause the mountain man's a proud man who lives by no other's leave. He's a shinin' creature for sure, and that spirit serves him well in the mountains, but he can get hisself killed at rendezvous.

"Many of ya know how years back, old Tom Mink got hisself killed dead quarrelin' over a Flathead woman. I think old Tom was a damn fool who deserved what he got. But ain't no one here a Tom Mink, ya hear me? This's the finest group a men I ever seen, with some of the prettiest wives. So, ya men that's been here before ... watch out for the youngins, 'cause they're full a' piss and stupid, and when they're full a whiskey they're dumber than a green colt.

"I'm done buryin' men who broke their neck racin' horses, or who got gut-shot dead over a woman ... or lost a nose in a knife fight ... and got no way to get it back. And worse yet is spendin' all the money you made gamblin' and drinkin' like profligates, and left with nothing to show for a year a hard, dangerous work.

"So, ya'll go ahead and wear your finest clothes, and bargain hard for the highest prices on your plews. Enjoy yourselves, and don't embarrass yourselves too much. And ya single men, watch the women that's there. Some'll be worth keepin'... but others'll leave ya with more than you bargained for, if ya get my meanin.'

"Look 'em over good, boys. Ain't no time to be in an all-fired hurry. Sometimes, a pretty woman ain't the best. Rather have me a plain woman full a fire—one that'll stick with me no matter how stupid I get. As for me and mine ... we intend to trade like all a you. But if prices are good, we aim to save some. You might well consider.

"This ain't the sort of speechifying you expected from me ... is it? 'Cause you're all free trappers and wild bulls, and hell ... I know that. I just don't hanker burying any more a ya, and I'd like to see some of ya prosper, is all."

He paused awkwardly, staring at his feet, the camp tomb-silent. Finally, a man's voice broke the stillness with a deep French accent. "I'll watch over the young men, Cap'n!"

The men roared! It was Enrí who had just rescued the captain—the very man the captain had fought grievously at the last rendezvous. Some would later come to say he had a growing fancy with words.

28

IN TWO DAYS, the camp rode onto the wide plain beside the Wind. The night before, Indian women could be seen with their husbands, heads in their leather laps, combing through their men's hair and crunching lice they'd found between their teeth. Ezra was repulsed but found it hard to look away, incredulous that any one might do that for another human, no matter how treasured they might be.

Men wore their finest, brightly colored shirts and gaudy bandanas, and Ezra broke out a borrowed shirt and vowed to trade for his own when he could. Others, not given to razors, had shaved themselves and combed fresh bear-grease into their hair. Squaws had donned dress saddles with brass and copper bells and adorned their foreheads and the parts of their hair with red trade paints.

Others had gone so far as to wash their horses in the river the day before their arrival. Still more had boiled pine needles and smeared the fragrant mixture on their bodies and hair, made clean in the river just hours earlier.

Eventually the young single men, proud of their winter's survival and their generous caches of plews, rode stiff-spined down into the center of it all, hoping to attract some pretty Crow, Shoshone, Flathead, or Nez Perce girl.

From the vantage of the eagle, the growing chaos expanded until nearly two hundred-fifty souls, plus wives and children and hundreds of friendly Indians, traders, and horses, stretched along the river for miles. The native horse herds were separated to themselves. The Snakes and the Flathead, the Crow and the Nez Perce, all were well represented and brought excellent horses to trade. They'd trade some to the Whites, who, in turn, would trade them for wives or replenish those stolen by horse thieves or eaten during starving times. These entrepreneurs had every reason to believe they'd do a fine business.

The captain and Red Calf led the parade down onto the site, followed by the men and their wives. Cap'n sat the same fine roan he had ridden out of St.

Louis nearly two years earlier, his rifle rocking once again on the pommel of his saddle, confident and relaxed, his face and heavily veined forearms a mass of freckles, looking every bit the lion.

Red Calf rode at his one-o'clock. She wore a blue-print tunic and elk-skin leggings embroidered with quills, seated astride a magnificent Crow saddle. She wore no moccasins—her small, tanned feet dangling prettily over the stirrups—a freshly burnished copper gorget about her neck. She shone for certain, and the men stared long and hard. But their stares didn't anger the captain in the slightest. *She's a fine woman in every way, and made to be looked at,* he mused. He was enamored with her and counted himself the most fortunate of them all.

Crooked Nose and his brigade were next. The shame of Crooked Nose had been behind him for some time, but he reckoned this a season of forgetting. Moon had asked that he wear his bear-claw necklace for her sake, that it was time to show proudly he was a bear-killer and feared nothing. But few knew he wore it as much to honor his "daughter" as himself. He rode easily on his rangy little gruella, his stunning necklace draped about his neck.

Ezra, Moon, and the big Frenchman brought up the rear of the entire procession, riding three abreast. Enrí sported a fresh haircut and well-combed, flowing beard, his massive frame draped over a powerful chestnut stud. But it was the two younger ones that caught the eyes of those watching. Moon wore a yellow print shirt that hung to her knees, belted with an elk-skin, quilled sash paired with tall Comanche-style moccasins, and around her neck hung a necklace of bear claws from the sow that had bitten her ass. She sat her mare like a Blackfoot—her gaze fixed straight ahead—a proud, curious smile on her lips as if she carried a secret worth prying free.

Ezra sat his stud like a Crow. He felt more at home than he'd ever been—that his presence here was no accident. He felt an odd, inexplicable peace about it all. *This is school and I'm learnin' all I can.* Only those who knew him understood that the dagger on his belt had once belonged to the infamous Crow-Killer and that he had taken it from that dark man. But what thrilled them most, especially the younger two, was the promise of it all. Ezra vowed to suck life from it all. "You'd a loved this, Papa," he whispered under his breath. "You watchin', ain't ya?"

McKay's group quickly claimed space on the east end of the affair and set up their lodges. Those packing hide lodges and poles had them up within the hour. Ezra never ceased to marvel at how rapidly the Indian women could erect their lodges, and they needed very little, if any, help.

In the middle of the camp the trappers jostled for place to redeem their beaver plews and haggle for the best prices, and those coming early felt the advantage. Ezra and Moon traded and received nearly seven dollars per plew, for a total of almost fourteen-hundred dollars for the year. "Moonie ... even after we trade for goods, we just got rich!" Ezra cried.

As the day wore on, more trappers arrived. They were a colorful lot. Some dressed so much like the Indians that they were nearly indistinguishable from them, while others wore their best "White clothes" and led the horses of their finely outfitted women. But all them had one thing in common: a pride in who and what they were. And when the sun set on that first day, campfires pricked the darkness like flickering constellations, and the smell of freshly roasted game, mingled with tobacco smoke, wafted the length of the river, hanging in pungent clouds. Freshly purchased over-priced whiskey flowed everywhere, and candlelight silhouetted figures in lodges and canvas tents like great bloated giants.

Single men who'd borne the privations of winter celebrated with whiskey in one hand and Indian women on their laps. And more than a few would awaken the next morning to discover some of their possessions to be not only missing but worn or used by another. But that would concern them little for the moment. They'd deal with that in the morning.

Ezra and Moon strolled the length of the river in the waning light, soon finding themselves in the Indian quarter, walking among hide lodges and admiring the fine horse flesh at its edges. Young warriors cast bone dice in gambling games, and a few, drunk from cheap fire-water, lay where they had fallen, their limbs cast at odd angles.

Ezra felt eyes on them. "Reckon we made too big a show, Moonie?" He swore some stared holes into the dagger hanging from his belt. And that others seemed mildly amused by his wife, and he wondered what they thought. He couldn't stop his speculations, and his mind whirled.

The owner of one lodge called the two to halt and share some roasting elk. They soon discovered he was Nez Perce but spoke English passably, and a little Mandan. His name was Yellow Snake, an enterprising Pierced Nose businessman. "I brought one-hundred horses. Whites need horses to replace those stolen, and others need horses to trade for wives. I bred and trained the horse you own. I knew him as soon as you rode in. You should race him here. No one can beat him."

"Really?" Ezra asked.

"I don't lie about horses." He smiled and pointed at Ezra's dagger. "How'd you come by that knife?"

"I took it from a man named Crow-Killer." Ezra said. "He killed my friends, and I counted coup on 'im and took it. It killed the bear that tried to kill my wife. I paid dearly for it. Twice."

"Well, you do well to wear such a piece," said the man. "Now I know why you have your woman. She has bear medicine, too. I see it in her. She has amused my friends, but I think they've … not understood her."

"She's a curious sort," said Ezra, "and rides and hunts like a man, but … she's no man." Moon listened, saying nothing, smiling faintly. The three stood quietly by the fire, feasting on fatty beavertail, and soon they said their goodbyes and made their way back home.

"Husband, I think he will be a friend." she said.

"I think so."

The next day saw a slow arousal among the camp. Many had stayed up late around the fires, sharing stories and tobacco and too much whiskey. They groaned, stretched, and wiped swollen eyes with dirty hands. Ezra noticed many a lone trapper walking about wearing his finest and looking for a young, pretty Indian woman. Others could be seen in the dark recesses of trader tents or in the high grass down by the river, fondling and debauching the willing for money or trade.

The real action, however, began to spark outside the tents and lodges in games of skill and strength. There, a flathead man wrestled all comers into submission and won a string of six ponies, while a trapper lost an eye in a fight over a Snake woman, and a hapless White drunk got bitten badly by a rogue stud that nearly crushed his windpipe. And the day was just getting started.

In time, the Nez Perce and Flathead challenged all comers to race their finest mounts over a two-mile stretch parallel to the river. Some who drew up to compete were still well liquored from the night before. They stumbled about, but miraculously seemed to regain their focus and vigor once mounted.

"Ezra … you need to race. Remember what Yellow Snake said? Do this for me, handsome man!" Moon whispered in his ear, and bit it. He initially had no thought of racing his mount, for his riding skills were not at the level of these red men, or at least he didn't think so. *I might get myself killed today.* But he had little option now. She'd put him on notice, called him out, and implied a reward for his risk. *You're a fox,* he thought. And now he'd need to concentrate or get his spine broken. The other would come in time.

He listened carefully to the instructions shouted out over the valley floor.

The broadcaster was drunk and repeated himself four times, and the riders milled about, annoyed and anxious, kicking up dust. The winner would be given a plew from every rider, and it tallied nearly forty overall. At seven dollars a plew, the purse was a rich one, and the riders risked little but their lives.

Soon, a tall, drunken Flathead with a runny nose and watery eyes stumbled to the starting line. With much fanfare he primed his pistol, weaving from side to side, spilling powder on his feet. After two aborted attempts, and the annoyed swears of the riders, he adjusted the flint on his hammer and touched the battered piece off. Pphht-boom … and the riders sprinted off in a cloud of white, acrid smoke. Ezra's mount got a poor start, but he cared little about his present position. Somewhere in the melee his thoughts formed. Let 'em all burn out, and trust Yellow Snake. So that's what he did. He hung back for the first mile as the front riders drove their ponies mercilessly, hoping to open up insurmountable leads. At the mile mark they arched wide around a large willow and began hurtling back to camp, churning up sod and screaming war cries, some so confident in their horses that they hung low on the side of them, as though engaged in combat, and discharged arrows from beneath the foaming necks in mock battle.

But then, Ezra let the big stud go—his powerful frame lengthening and lowering and gobbling up earth like a saddled greyhound. He could feel the stride change, the wind whistle through his hair, the watering of his eyes and the clods of dirt striking his face from the horses before him as he began to reel them in. It all happened so quickly and with such ease that he felt a tinge of remorse for the rest. But that did not last long. The riders in front, hearing the roar of the crowd, craned behind them to see the predator closing hard on their heels. Some swung wide from side to side, hoping to block the leopard-like charge, but it was all in vain.

Two horses caromed off the path of the appaloosa, and one rider was unseated in spectacular fashion. Ezra and his horse beat the second rider by nearly twenty lengths. And then the crowd, stunned by the feat of horse and rider, hushed eerily for the span of nearly ten seconds, as if they'd just witnessed a miracle of sorts. And then a fulmination of whoops and cheers filled the valley floor. Grown men slapped each other's backs and threw hats in the air with whiskey-fueled wonder and exclaimed things like, "God Almighty, ain't never seen such as this!"

Ezra punched his fist triumphantly skyward and scanned the crowd, looking for Moon, but soon returned to the fallen rider. Dismounting, he knelt beside the bruised man and carefully helped him to his feet, placed his own arm about his waist, and walked him and his horse to the finish line. And then the crowd cheered again as if Lazarus had been raised the second time.

Ezra whistled for Moon, "Whoooweee." She appeared quickly with a bag, and a crowd gathered. Gathering her supplies, she went about setting the man's arm. He promptly fainted, and by the time he came to she was forming his splints. She leaned into him, whispered instructions for his recovery, and he nodded.

As the crowd milled about, Yellow Snake shouted to Ezra. "I told you, White man! He'll grow old before he's beaten. Enjoy him, my friend!"

Later, that night about their fires, nursing a whiskey or engaged in a game of chance, many trappers and Indians spoke among themselves of the strange young couple who cared for those who little deserved it. McKay took note of the two yet again and marveled. They'd made him proud as though he were an older brother—so proud he vowed to return to his tent, eat a fine buffalo steak, and make love to his wife. This day he'd seen marvelous things.

On the afternoon of the third day, more contests ensued. Ezra nearly outraced the entire lot of the Indian contingent in a footrace but tripped on a stick in the final few yards. All took note that he had been in firm command until the very end when fate had seemed to rise up out of the earth and oppose him.

Later, the Snakes organized an archery event, and forty-seven men lined up. First came a shooting-for-distance match, and Ezra was narrowly eclipsed by a big Nez Perce. Their arrows soared upward and stuck in the sod at nearly two hundred-twenty paces. Men ran to the site to judge, but it was a toss-up. And then Ezra grabbed his rival's arm and thrust it skyward, and the crowd, having witnessed his magnanimity earlier, cheered him again.

After the cheers had faded Moon whispered something to Ezra, and straightaway he handed her his powerful Crow bow. And then he grabbed her about the shoulder and whispered, "Ya sure?" She nodded. She slowly drew an arrow from his quiver, inspecting it carefully, sighting down its length. The crowd went quiet. One said, "What's she doin'?" And then she nocked the same on the string, set her jaw hard like a predator on a prey's spine, drew the string as far as her shoulders could pinch together—drawing the string clear across her chest and nestling it into her shoulder, wringing every fraction she could from her shorter arms, and then—let it go. The shaft rocketed forward, comet-like, arching high and long as the watchers let out a collective sigh 'til it reappeared again and buried like a lance into the sod.

It landed only yards shy of Ezra's, and Moon finished in third place. But she was the happiest of all, for, unknown to all the rest, she hadn't known she could pull the great bow but had risked the humiliation. Afterward, many of the Indian men began to acknowledge that she carried big medicine, and secretly wished she had no husband. But the wiser among them reckoned she needed a special man and that Ezra seemed a good fit. And the news of Ezra's coup on Crow-Killer and his lancing of that mortal enemy made for big stories. It was not long before most perceived that the Lord of Life watched over the couple and that only a fool would ever consider their molestation.

Ezra whispered to Moon later that night as they lay under their robes with him spooning her, "I thought you were gonna break it."

That evening, a drunken brawl broke out, and Ezra and Moon entered the tent just as it unfolded. A young, lean man with too much red hair for his scalp and hairy arms like a wolf spider had head-locked a trader, squeezing the life from him. He was furious and accused his victim of cheating at cards. Soon several stepped forward to intervene, but the aggrieved drew a knife and held it at the other's throat, threatening its use if they drew any closer. Its raspy edge nicked his neck, and blood seeped onto the man's collar. The trader had little time left if the strangle were to continue. Quickly, a deep voice with a heavy French accent broke over the whispers.

"Let the man go, my friend. He's not worth your life. I, too, think he's a cheat. We'll find a way to make him pay. I swear it." When Enrí had finished, he knelt beside the accused and whispered in his ear. The man's purple face drained white as the other man released his grasp and the cheat fled the tent. Later, around the captain's fire, Ezra asked Enrí what he'd said to the trader that had scared him so.

"I told him some of the Flathead have a taste for human flesh. That if he did not return the man's money, one night I'd knock him unconscious and deliver him to them myself so they could cut off the top of his skull and eat his brain while he still lived. I said he must act honestly from now on, and that … that I will be watching him."

Moon's eyes grew huge. "Are these things so, big brother?"

"No," he laughed, "but he doesn't know, and that gives me great power over him. It's a good joke, eh!?" The big man's eyes watered, and he laughed so hard all caught the same malady. When they'd recovered, the Cap'n and Red

Calf emerged from their tent, their faces flushed, and sat by the fire with their friends. Enrí recounted his "private" conversation with the trader, and again the laughter came and spent them.

"I have a story to tell," said Red Calf, "and I've never told it to anyone." Cap'n's eyes grew wide.

"Not me?" Cap'n asked.

"Not even you, my fine man. Can I tell it?" His eyes widened even more, his left brow arching high.

"Of course. Not like I could stop you, anyhow."

"When I was a little girl," she said, "an uncle forced himself on me." They leaned in and their smiles fled them. "This went on 'til he was killed raiding horses against the Arikara, and I was glad he was dead. But I felt shame. I was only ten winters and I told no one ... and I became hard inside.

"One day, I met a White trader who came to live in my village. He was handsome and kind and courted me. My father reminded him that I was 'very pretty,'" she laughed, "and that he would need six good horses and a fine trade gun. I was sixteen winters, and I became his wife.

"That man treated me like a fine rifle and my heart grew soft again. He gave me a wonderful horse and a beautiful saddle ... and everything my eyes wanted. We had big hearts for each other for some time. But in time something happened. He grew cold and tired of me. He married a second, and she came to live with us, but it was not long before he began to mistreat us both. She left ... but I did not. I made a plan." She paused, a finger to her lips, teasing the moment.

"And what was that?" Moon asked.

"Well, I was very clever. I traded some dressed leather for a hand axe and a fine knife. And every day for two winters, I rode my stud to the cottonwoods, away from everyone ... so no one might know what I was up to." She paused again, this time even longer.

"And ...?" Ezra asked.

"I found a tree."

"A tree?" Enrí asked.

"Yes, my friend. A tree. But not just any tree. It would be the tree that would save my life."

"And how was that?" Moon asked.

"Well ... I found just the tree to throw my knife and axe at. And every day the weather was good, I threw my weapons at that tree until I could throw like a man—better than most men, and in the second spring the tree bore no leaves. It was dying and I had killed it. I knew I was ready—"

"For what?" Cap'n asked.

"To spring my plan. I—"

"Yes ... You told us about the 'plan.' Please!" he begged.

"A good story takes time, husband. Would you not grant me the time you gave Enrí to tell his?" She stared coolly at him, a chord of anger in her voice, her face flushed, hands on hips.

"Of course. I'm sorry."

"Sooo..." she began again, "When I went to bed that night, I slid in behind my husband under the robes and pulled myself in tight behind him. I bit his neck and spoke playfully to him—he had been drinking and was easy to talk to—and I told him what I had been doing for a year. I told him I had become as dangerous as most men. That if he touched me again, I would cut off his manhood while he slept and slit his throat. I told him he would leave me the next day. That if he did not, I would kill him ... or my kinsman would. He laughed, but I smelled his fear.

"The next morning when he arose, I had burnt his best pistol ... his best clothes ... his finest trade goods in our lodge fire. I was ready to die, and he knew it. I had a knife in one hand and my axe in the other. He laughed, but his voice trembled. He left and was gone the same day. I left him only one horse. And today, when I think of that man, I have no hate for him any longer ... for he taught me to be strong." Her eyes danced, "But I no longer wish to see him ... ever!" She threw her head back and laughed and laughed.

Her story seemed to have pulled some frayed thread, especially for Cap'n. He stared across the circle at the big Canadian and spoke bluntly, but with a kind tone. "Ever get lonely for a woman?" asked Cap'n. Enrí paused, a wince in his eyes. He looked about him, a man searching for a door to escape a dangerous room. He took a deep breath and groaned.

"I'm so lonely for a good woman that the pain of it all seems sometimes too much to bear. Sought one here, but I'm finding none. I need a shining woman the likes of Red Calf or Moon. Kinda wish, and I mean no disrespect ... but kinda wish I'd never met 'em. I'd give all I own for a woman like them."

Red Calf's face grew troubled, and she whispered to the captain. He nodded. "My husband has been teaching me to read from the White man's books," she said. "I'm reading the stories of this strange God, and He's begun to speak to me. Last night I had a dream about you, Enrí. Listen to me ... now. I mean this with all kindness.

"A powerful and frightening man with yellow hair told me to give you a message. He said soon a fine woman will come to you. That she will be yours if you give up the whiskey and allow Him to bring her to you. He said you are not to search for her—that He will bring her; that 'you will recognize her when the time is right.'

"And He says all this will happen very soon, and you must trust Creator to do this. It will happen in the most unusual way."

The talking circle went mute as a corpse. Finally, McKay spoke. "My dear wife, I think, speaks truthfully. She's seein' things, and she tells me of 'em ... and they're all coming to pass. She reminds me of your father, Ezra, and we do well to heed her. Enrí, I think Creator has felt the pain of your loneliness and is bringin' you a good one, soon. Take hope, friend."

Ezra listened carefully to the Cap'n. He kept running into this "strangeness," first from his mother, and then his papa, and now even Cap'n. It was as if some divine pursuit were in process, set in motion some months—perhaps even years—back, and he kept colliding with it. It scared him a bit and he tried to explain it away, but it just kept coming. He halted his reverie and stared at the big man.

Enrí's eyes pooled, and tears flanked his nose and soaked his beard. He seemed undone and embarrassed, but stood as each friend squeezed a shoulder or a hand, and he did not push them away. The pride of the mountain man had been laid bare for the last little bit, and it had struck him like blessed relief. So, he walked to his tent, pulled his robe about him, and slept soundly—more soundly than he had for a long time. He finally was known by those who were closer than blood and for the first time in a long, long time, no longer felt alone.

When Ezra and Moon retired, Ezra found himself unable to fall off to sleep. Enrí's disclosure and Red Calf's pronouncement had stirred something deep. Enrí had humbled himself, and while it had seemed risky, it had bled the man of pain. A simple, honest, ugly answer to a question, and all had felt it seep away. In truth, a deep admiration for Enrí was brewing in him. He had felt Enrí's fear, but the big man had spoken anyway, and the result had been good for them all. Here was a man to learn from, he thought, and, as with the Cap'n, he would observe him and seek his counsel from time to time.

29

THE NEXT MORNING came early enough. Ezra had not fallen asleep 'til the early morning hours, but Moon had risen before him and made coffee. She had come to love its smell and, though she rarely drank any, enjoyed its making. Even her dog seldom rose before its strong scent wafted through their tent.

She roused Ezra with a pinch to his rump, and soon he sat beside them both, a tin of coffee in one hand and a packed clay pipe in the other. The tobacco, the scent of the dark liquid, and the poor night put him in a hazy trance. He stared into the small fire, wordless, trusting the coffee to work its magic and, snaking his arm around Moon's waist, content in his lot.

And then commotion arose on the west end of the camp, with all the delicacy of a cannon, and Ezra and Moon pulled on their moccasins and sprinted toward the sound of howling women. There they forced their way through the crowd, only to burst upon a heartrending scene—Red Calf kneeling beside the Cap'n, his face smashed and purple, his body lifeless. She lay grotesquely upon him, his bloody face smearing her own. Ezra attempted to pull her off, but she shrieked, pounded her fist into his chest, and fainted.

Ezra moved reflexively, his body numb and his mind slowing, suddenly standing in Kentucky again, his mother dead and ugly before him, and no more time to speak. *My God, you can't be gone, Cap'n. No ... Noooo.* His head swam and he fell to his knees, too numb to cry.

A crowd gathered round. They carried Red Calf into her tent and laid her on her robe. Ezra regained his feet and, returning to the Cap'n, found Enrí kneeling beside him. Enrí picked up the body, carried it to his tent, and laid him gently beside the entrance. There he sat beside him, clutched the dead man's hand for the next hour, and bawled like a child abandoned by his father.

When the pandemonium had faded a bit, the story became clear. A trapper had been leading a young, green colt by the captain's tent at exactly the moment he was exiting it. The colt, sensing some sort of phantom threat, delivered a deadly, twisting kick in his direction, instantly snapping his neck and crushing the side of his face. Poor Cap'n had never seen any of it coming.

Within two days, preparations had been made for Cap'n's burial. It was a dark time. His troop had respected him greatly, and most had loved him. All knew he had treated them fairly. The few who'd been tardy on their plew payments dropped them off at the tent entrance, where Ezra dutifully saw to their collection.

When Red Calf came to herself, she gave special directions for the burial of her man. She said the captain had spoken several times of his desire to be buried like a Viking, in a boat of some sort. He would talk of it and laugh. But in time he'd grown more serious about it—that he saw no sense in being buried in the dirt or on a scaffold in the air. "A dugout canoe on a funeral fire sounded good to him," she said.

So, men were dispatched to fell a pine and to carve out a space big enough for his body. The summer was hot, and seven men worked continuously with axes and chisels throughout the night and the next day. They sank his body in the freezing river for nearly two days, and on the third day the preparations were complete.

They laid him in the canoe on a platform of tinder and dried deadfall logs nearly nine feet thick. Red Calf had seen to it that her man was arrayed in his finest. His entire face had been painted blue, overlayed with white lightning bolts—crafted by a Crow holy man—and his finest rifle lay across his chest. He looked magnificent.

The entire camp turned out for the event, and a large contingent of red men drew up as well, for he'd always treated them fairly. Ezra asked his widow if he might light the logs—that the Cap'n felt like a father to him. He put on a bold front though he was sick to his stomach, his heart broken and fearful—fearful he'd never have another Papa-like figure after Cap'n. But he bit his lip and exercised more courage than he ever had. Matters of the heart frightened him more than conflict ever did.

He strode manfully forward, lit the pyre, and watched it roar to life. The logs were so dry and resinous that the mess burnt like coal oil and soon drove them all from the flames. So they watched from a distance as first the body and then the canoe were consumed, thousands of fiery embers belching skyward like a great crackling furnace. When it was done, the only evidence remaining was the still-smoldering barrel and lock of his rifle in the ashes.

Red Calf bore the whole affair stoically, Moon by her side, her arm about her shoulder as hardened men wept openly. Others stamped out small fires with moccasined and booted feet. None had ever seen such a thing.

The death of the captain had blunted the carnival-like atmosphere of his band, but the hardened resilience of the people pulled them from their grief enough that most re-engaged the festivities, albeit with less passion. Ezra was stunned how people got on with it. More whiskey flowed, and games and gambling and shooting matches resumed. A few squirreled away their winnings, and some of the single men bought or traded for wives and their gaudy trappings.

And for some, life went on in much the same way it had before. This was, after all, the way of the mountain, and those who lived by its code knew that extended, incapacitating grief was a luxury they could ill afford. It could get a man killed as surely as the one being grieved, or at the very least, diminish the joy of a short, brutish life. But a new question arose. Who'd lead the troop back into the mountains, and what would become of Red Calf? Enrí visited the widow one night and sat beside her for some time. "Would you like me to take you back to your people?" he asked.

"I am going nowhere, Enrí. These are my people and this ... this is my family."

"But how will you care for yourself? You're strong, but you're not Moon."

"It's true. I'm not, but I've dried a lot of meat and I can manage my lodging well enough. And I can learn to hunt if someone will teach me. She'll teach me if I ask ... and I'm no ordinary woman. You should know that by now."

"I do," he said, "but in the mountains a woman needs a man as much as a man needs a woman. It'll be deadly by yourself. Don't you see?"

"I see the Lord of Life will care for me. He'll send me a man when I'm done grieving. I'm sure of it. Go home and think on what I have said. I'm too weary to talk more. Please ... please go. My tongue is weary."

He rose slowly, his heart heavy, for he had no words to offer that would do any immediate good. But he had determined to find ways to help her heal or to exhaust himself trying. He owed that much to the captain.

The rendezvous began its inevitable wind-down, and Ezra and his mates had done well. They'd arrived early, wrangled good prices on their plews, and he and Moon had cashed in his race winnings and traded for a hide lodge. But many had worn out their purses, having drunk and gambled away their year's earnings.

The captain's company had fared better than most. Some had followed the counsel of that good man and laid back some of their plew money. Others had drunk and gambled a little less this year than in the past. Even in death, McKay had blunted the tendencies of the rowdies, and the men in the company with wives treasured their women a bit more. The recognition that life was a slender thread had played out tragically before them all. And if the Cap'n could be taken, then all were vulnerable. It was a gritty reminder of harsh reality—of the snake that might strike the strongest of them.

The campers began their tear-down, and by late morning questions began to percolate about their future, with no leader yet apparent. By noon, all the baggage had been packed onto the animals. Some chewed jerked meat, waiting for directions—their faces a mirror of anxiety and confusion. It soon became apparent that smaller groups might break off and go their separate ways unless something was done quickly. People mumbled and whispered. Others seemed just plain irritated by the uncertainty of it all, and grumbling began.

At last, Enrí rode his horse into the center of the confusion, stretched high in his stirrups, and let out a piercing whistle. "So, you're all asking many questions, eh? Who'll be our leader, and where do we trap this fall? Do we go through the south pass and over the mountains?

"We must make decisions today, or some of you'll leave and go elsewhere. And to lessen our numbers is a dangerous thing, and you all know that. Today ... today we'll determine what we'll do. You've earned the right to speak, haven't you? You're free trappers, by Gawd. Speak up!"

One veteran on the edge of the crowd mounted his horse and spoke boldly. "Enrí, as I see it, you should lead these folks. Ain't no one here got more beaver sense ... and no one's got more grit. I seen ya deal with all kinds, and you always find the best path. I say you lead us, that we have a council of sorts from among us that gives advice and help and such. Like to hear the rest of the people, though."

Crooked Nose stood on a log and spoke his piece. "I think what's been said is good. The big man is good and strong, and he's humble. He does not seek power. He'd do well."

Red Calf replaced Crooked Nose. "My husband once spoke to me of these things. He said that, if he were taken, Enrí would make a fitting replacement—that he saw greatness in the man he did not yet see in himself. Cap'n also said that, even though he is young, Ezra must have a place of training under him, that he would be a great help to Enrí. I believe he would be happy you consider this."

Ezra stood beside her then, his arm about her waist, and his voice cracked. "As for me," he said, "I believe the words about Enrí are all good, but you must decide about me. I'm humbled ... but I don't know." His face looked heavy. "I fear it may take me under. I'd need support from the veterans. I'd need that council. Won't accept without it."

"So, how do we decide about Enrí?" Ezra asked. "If he's the one, then shout your approval. If not, shout no. Won't be held against any of ya ... one way or the other. What do you say?"

The crowd erupted in shouts of "Yes! Yes! Yes!" and then the plea was called for "No's." There were none. Enrí stretched high in his stirrups again, towering over the assembly and asking them all, "What about Ezra?"

A veteran spoke up quickly: "Ain't no need for a vote on the boy, Enrí. He's a natural. Picks up things right quick. And he'll listen ta us. We'll school him what he's green on. Anyone disagreeing's a damn fool. I'll kick his ass right here!" And then the camp broke into shouts and whistles and laughter and rushed on the two. Moon stood in the shadows and wept—her heart swollen with pride. Red Calf listened to the crowd, knowing the choice to be the right one, and it eased her pain a little. She sobbed quietly.

That first night the trappers, Enrí, and Ezra made some decisions about the fall. They'd head west through the south pass and press deep into Snake country and trap the streams there. The Snakes were friendly and would ally with them against the Blackfoot and the people of the White Clay, sometimes called the Gros Ventre or Atsina.

All knew the Blackfoot were a fearsome and populous nation, and the Snakes had been horribly reduced by disease. The trappers believed they'd be welcomed as fellow beleaguereds and allies. At least they hoped so.

Ezra and the rest watched over Red Calf as an orphaned child. Some dropped food by the entrance to her tent and made gifts. She acknowledged their kindness, but her smiles came hard. Enrí dropped by every other day or so, sometimes just sitting beside her and saying nothing. When he left, he often squeezed the top of her shoulder or tousled her hair. She sat mute, deep within herself, a hollow look in her dark eyes as if she had left home and could not remember the way back.

One night, nearly three weeks after the death of her man, Enrí rose to leave as usual and walked past her. She grabbed his leg, startling him, and mouthed words. He bent low to listen.

"I see you, Red Bear. Keep coming back. I need you. You give me hope." And then, as abruptly as she had stopped his course, she released him and motioned him away. Leaving, he padded into the darkness, his chest heavy.

The company moved leisurely to their new territory, for it was still late summer and the beaver not yet prime. They hunted and lived off the land as they traveled, enjoying the time before trapping and fleshing, before constant vigilance and hard toil sapped their strength.

It had been six weeks since the death of McKay, and Red Calf slowly grew more animated. Enrí continued to come by, and in time she began to open up. One night she told him of a joke that she and the captain had shared. She suddenly stopped and teared up and then laughed aloud as though she were remembering it all afresh. She was so overcome by the humor that Enrí found himself laughing at her, thrilled that she had forded some unseen river. Laughed out, she stared blankly into the fire, and the two spoke nothing until Enrí broke the silence:

"It's good to hear you laugh again. I've sat here for weeks but not seen you 'til tonight. I miss the captain more than words can say. He believed in me when I didn't. I can barely ... talk about him."

In time, Ezra and Moon sat beside the two somber figures. Something was different. Red Calf's face seemed softer—her eyes less sad. Moon wrapped her arm around her waist and drew her close. Red Calf's form softened into hers, and the two held each other while the men sat awkwardly by, fidgeting, looking past the other. Ezra said to Red Calf, "We're goin' huntin' tomorrow. Wanna come with us? Moon's a good teacher. I think it's time for you ... you know, to learn how."

"I'll go soon, but not tomorrow. I'm waiting for a man to show up—the man who'll be my new husband." Her eyes twinkled playfully. Enrí looked stunned.

No one spoke. He gathered himself.

"Is he here in this village gathering his courage to speak with you?... I'll fight him."

"Why?" Red Calf asked. "Oooh, Enrí ..." She paused and gazed at him—her face a sweet blend of sadness and mirth. "Can you fight yourself? Do you ... do you not yet understand? Does your heart beat hard for me, Enrí? I know it does. I nearly hear it at times. When I'm done grieving, I'll let you ask me to be your woman, if that pleases you."

He struggled, his tongue thick. "Are you saying you'd become my woman if I asked you. Tell me plainly. It sounded as—"

"Of course, I would. I want no other man. Do you remember my dream, Enrí?"

"Yes. Like it was yesterday."

"The yellow-haired man said that the Lord of Life would bring you a woman if you gave up the fire-water, and He's done what He promised. You've not sought a woman, and today ... today I am here," she said. He looked faint.

"I knew on the day that Cap'n died," she said, "that you would be my husband, but I couldn't tell you then. My heart was broken. But today I can. What do you say?"

His heart thumped. Words caught in his throat as he wondered for the briefest of moments whether the three figures before him were real—or if he was dreaming. *Is this real?* He reached out to touch the hand of Red Calf, and her flesh was warm and smooth. He touched her wrist and fingered her pulse. *This is not a dream. Oh, God! This is not a dream!*

30

THE NEXT WEEKS AT CAMP oozed with amusement. Ezra and Moon whispered nightly of what everyone saw in the light. Shortly after Red Calf's revelation to Enrí, most perceived the shift that had occurred. Red Calf's sadness began to lift, and light returned to her face. And Enrí often dropped by to give her freshly killed game in exchange for the mending of moccasins or clothing. But it was all a ruse, a thinly veiled means to see each other.

Both worked tirelessly at keeping their feelings hidden, out of respect for the dead, until one day the facade collapsed entirely. They mounted their horses for a ride and, as they departed, heard whispers and felt the looks. Enrí, annoyed and feeling especially bold, stopped his horse in the midst of them all and glared. "What are ya looking at? Haven't you seen a man ride with a woman before? Mind your own business!"

A grizzled veteran with a lean, leathery face growled back, "I'll tell you what we're lookin' at. We're wonderin' why she ain't wearin' a weddin' dress and you two ain't headin' out for some time away ... 'cause it's time. Hell ... even Cap'n'd think so! We seen the way you pine for each other. Ain't foolin' nobody. And we're tired of actin' like we don't see it.

"So, ya better ask her soon, big man ... 'fore I do. She's fine, Enrí, so what the hell ya waitin' on? Dammit, man! Ya needn't worry 'bout honorin' the Cap'n no longer. If our mind means anything to you two, we say get on with it. God knows you're both about to pop."

When he'd finished, Enrí's face had softened, and a grin curled his lips. He turned to Red Calf and said, "Will you be my woman?"

"Yes! Yes. I will!"

And so, the camp exploded with laughter and tears and rushed hard on them. They dragged them from their mounts and threw them both into the cold creek.

The concern all had felt for them had broken into violent affection. But it could have been no other way. They were hardy, rough people, and they celebrated the way they lived—with all their might.

Several Indian women worked furiously over the next days, fitting and sewing and embroidering a wedding dress with beautifully dyed quills. Finally, on the fourth day, it was ready.

Moon smoothed Red Calf's hair and wove it with fresh wildflowers. She straightened and pulled her new dress down over her, fussing out each wrinkle and meticulously brushing it clean. Her long, straight hair hung to her midback. The hem of her dress burst with yellow ocher paint.

One woman gave her some fine, quilled, high-topped Comanche-style moccasins like Moon sometimes wore, brushed with green pigment on the uppers. A copper bracelet adorned her left wrist, and a string of yellow trade beads hung about her neck and draped across her breast. She was resplendent.

Enrí arrived at her lodge midmorning and slid stiffly off his chestnut stud, a bouquet of fresh flowers in his left hand. A crowd had gathered round. Ezra and Moon, dressed in their finest, stood outside their lodge. Enrí looked ill at ease. Ezra touched his shoulder and whispered, "Turn around, my friend." Enrí spun quickly, awkwardly. He stood nervously, his eyes darting, 'til Ezra spoke low, "Turn around again." And then he stopped dead in his tracks, his gazed fixed on his love, unable to speak, tears welling in his big blue eyes. Ironically, the big man, afraid of nothing, was suddenly frozen—unable to move. Finally, one of the young men broke the awkward silence with, "Well, kiss her, for God's sake, or I'm gonna!"

It was the perfect word. Enrí, relaxed now, stepped forward and swept his bride off her feet like a small child, kissing her hard, years of pent-up loneliness on full display. Then men cheered as some tore their hats from their heads, throwing them high into the air. Others shot rifles and pistols, and soon a thick cloak of white, acrid smoke draped over the camp. Enrí, playing his part and spreading his feathers, pulled his lips from Red Calf, tilted his head, and crowed at the top of his lungs, "How's that?! Sweeter than Four Bears' wild honey. And all mine!"

Red Calf, her face crimson and feeling the eyes, playfully thumped his thick chest in front of the gathering crowd. Enrí lifted her onto her horse, mounted his own, and motioned patiently for quiet. It was some time in coming. "We'll be gone for days," he said. Some of the men smiled and poked their wives. "And while I'm gone, Ezra's in command, as much as anyone can command this den a sow grizzlies. Now you all be good to him, for I'm coming back!

"I suppose we should tell you we look forward to returning. But, eh ... not true. You'll be the last thing on our minds!" And at that, their well-wishers shouted and slapped the rumps of their horses, and they trotted east out of camp. Some single men were broken hearted that day, for one of the finest women they'd ever seen had just left with one of the best men they'd ever known. But when their hearts had settled enough that their heads could reason, they concluded this: Enrí and Red Calf were a fine fit. Perhaps the finest they'd ever seen. Nearly as fine as Ezra and Moon. And that—well, that was saying something.

31

FOR FIVE DAYS, Ezra and the camp continued west and over South Pass, hunting and making a leisurely twelve to fifteen miles per day. On the evening of the third day, nearly fifty miles from Enrí and Red Calf, a near tragedy occurred. There a mother lion attacked a trapper's child from behind but was heroically beaten off by the enraged mother.

The child's life hung in the balance as Moon sat vigil by him. But then he grew fevered—so hot she feared the fever might kill him. Growing desperate, she whispered to his mother, "I'm taking him!" She threw the youngster over her shoulder and ran into the river. She stood chest deep as the bitter cold stole her breath and covered them both, standing there some minutes 'til her speech slurred; then she waded back to shore and laid the young boy on the grassy bank.

By this time a crowd had gathered, some with blankets. Ezra stripped her and wrapped her in blankets and instructed they do the same for the boy. She, Ezra, and others repeated this process all night long, 'til the sun rose. By midmorning the boy awoke in his right mind, his fever gone, wondering why he slept by the river. He had no memory of the cat attack at all.

Enrí and Red Calf had spent three days together before they gave the first thought to their friends. They filled themselves with love, playing like children, naked in the river, their guns leaning on logs by the bank. Enrí left a belt and knife comically lashed to his naked loins, dutifully prepared to defend his love.

Red Calf marveled that a man so ferocious could be so gentle. He made her feel alive again, and she found herself in awe of him. He was ecstatic, humbled that he'd been given such a gift, for he'd admired her since he'd met her, but she'd belonged to another.

One night, under the blankets, he brushed her cheek and accidentally wakened her. She stared curiously at him. "Is everything all right, Red Bear?"

"Yes. I touched you to prove I'm not dreaming. I fear I'll close my eyes and you'll be gone."

"I'm going nowhere, husband." She grew quiet, her face troubled. "There's something I must tell you. But I fear to say it. You'll be angry with me and … and I couldn't bear if you hated me."

"I'd never hate you. I swear it," he said.

"Enrí, when the captain was still alive, we were trying to have a baby. Days after he passed, my belly felt strange. His child may be inside me. Will you forgive me?"

"Forgive what?" He slid his hand onto her belly, a smile forming, feeling for a kick. "I'd consider it an honor to raise the child of that good man. It'd be as my own."

"Are you teasing me?" she asked.

"Not at all. The whole thing makes me laugh. What a great joke! Cap'n would find it funny, wouldn't he? It'll be a surprise then."

"Enrí … you're a wonder," she said.

"I know," he said. She squealed and pulled him under the robes. But he'd proven himself to her, and her disclosure had bound them ever more tightly.

The next morning, the two took a cold swim, packed up their camp, and headed back the way they had come. They'd not gone far when they saw human sign and the prints of at least a dozen unshod horses heading west. They headed up higher for a better view of the valley floor.

"Gotta be careful," Enrí told her. If they hugged the heights, they could see for miles. It'd be slower going but far less dangerous. He counted on the party being out for horses and not scalps. It seemed too small for war. But then again, his was a coveted scalp among the Blackfoot and their allies. A White Clay warrior could draw a very pretty woman with Enrí's red scalp on his lance, and he would do all he could to not let that happen. And no Blackfoot warrior would ever take his wife. If they knew who she was, they'd treat her badly as long as she lived—and that might not be long at all.

So, they rode the heights and made no fires, living off pemmican and wild onions, and on the fourth day they spied a party traveling single file along the valley floor, stopping occasionally to water their horses and scan upward into the hills. Nearly a mile away, the two froze, hoping they'd not been seen. In moments, still hoping against hope, they knew better.

The party below divided, and six men on horses came racing toward them, flanking them from both sides. They had only minutes to prepare, but Enrí had wisely armored heavily for their trip. He had two good rifles and two belted pistols. And he still reckoned these Indians were not a war party. If he were to drop two of them early, the rest would lose stomach for the fight, and the chase would cease. The leader of the party would lose face if he lost men while out raiding, and might never regain it.

He looked for a place from which to mount his defense and fortunately found it quickly—a large boulder leaning against a rock face. Big enough to shield the horses as well. He primed the pans on all of the pieces and waited behind its bulk. In minutes, they heard the thudding of hooves and the crashing of brush. Seconds later, the first rider passed the rock, and Enrí dropped him promptly with heavy ball from the first rifle before handing it to Red Calf to reload.

Quickly, the movement in the underbrush ceased, and all went quiet. He peered around the rock to find two braves slithering to recover the first. He ended both with his pistols. They thrashed, then lay still. Seconds later, Red Calf screamed, and Enrí spun in her direction. She was pointing his rifle at the chest of a young Big Belly two paces away. Enrí instantly grabbed the man's war club, broke his arm with it, and signed a ghastly message for his comrades to consider.

The man fled to his horse and rode for his life. Enrí had sent his message and the Big Bellies would all be gone soon. They had violated their own mission by going after humans instead of horses, and their leader would be disgraced.

The two rode hard that day and made camp late. Enrí didn't fear retaliation, for he'd taught them a costly lesson. But they would tell their Blackfoot friends, and that would only fire more hatred. He'd become an American trapper, and they detested the Americans, and when they had tried to kill him he'd made them pay dearly—a blood feud of the highest order.

They were up early and rode nearly forty miles the next day and caught up with the camp by late afternoon. The brush with the White Clay people had given him fresh feeling for those with families, and it had personalized it all. Privately, Enrí shared the encounter of the Big Bellies with Ezra and sought the counsel of the advisors, who agreed to keep the matter secret for a time, unless further intrusions were noted. Most comforted themselves that the Americans had garnered a storied reputation for furious warfare and deadly accuracy with their rifles. They'd keep their eyes peeled for sign, report it immediately, and avoid conflict when necessary, but never back down when challenged. They couldn't. Any perception of weakness could get them all killed.

32

THE WARM DAYS GREW SHORTER, and Ezra and the camp pursued the streams up into the mountains once again, settling into routine and stockpiling fresh pelts. The streams were loaded with more beaver than the previous season, and some believed a location this rich might never be found again. Even the flesh and tails were cooked and roasted with gusto, and the women sometimes fried game in their fat in iron skillets.

Ezra reluctantly ate the great rodent. He enjoyed its flavor but had never completely forgotten the near deadly feast two years earlier, when his father's counsel to hungry men had gone mostly unheeded. The memories pricked him. *God ... I miss him.* If only his parents could see him now, growing up and hardening into manhood—respected by those older and more seasoned. He was leading men and married to a fine woman—one others coveted and loved almost as much as he. He'd been shown exceeding favor, and it humbled him—made him pinch himself sometimes—and yet he couldn't share it with blood. It all seemed so unfair. Some of the men spoke of their fathers, and it saddened him; he missed Papa's practical sayings and his love of life and was sad that Cap'n was gone so quickly and that he'd no time to say goodbye. *I can't even find Papa's grave.*

The mornings grew crisp and trappers donned capotes and fur hats. The geese flew south, honking loudly overhead in their majestic floating phalanxes, "ark ...ark ... ark," their wings lacerating thin mountain air like an arrow shot in secret gliding past one's ear. Ezra gazed often after the winged creatures, pulling his capote over his head, tracing their fading flight paths, and pondering how this life had changed him. The raw grandeur of it all sometimes made him wince.

The days shortened, and soon the high streams began to freeze, forcing the migration of the trappers and the main camp lower. They stayed just beyond the forming ice as they retreated, plucking every fat beaver they could from the cold waters. And they finally came to the end of the season and settled at the base of a mountain, sheltered by pines close to the river. Game trails were abundant, and they began to lay up meat.

There were camps of Snake Indians in the area—some called them Shoshone, who welcomed their presence as a safeguard against their enemies. Winter shelters were erected, tents were pitched, and the few Crow among them erected their fine tall, white, skin-covered lodges. The first snows had yet to arrive.

They had not been more than three days in their new location when they received a most unanticipated surprise. On the third day, it began to snow, lightly at first, and then big heavy flakes until it was impossible to see past the furthest tent.

The sun had begun to set when a commotion erupted on the far end of the camp. A party of four Snake riders had entered the camp at a walk, carrying torches to make sure they were seen. It was an eerie sight, their illumined figures nearly hidden by the thick, driving flakes—like a candle flickering beneath filmy cloth. They stopped in the middle of the camp as their leader slid from his mount and signed for help. Ezra spoke to him. Instantly a cry rang out from one of the riders, and Ezra recognized the voice. It was his father-in-law, Black Bull.

In the next hour, Black Bull's story tumbled free. Moon's mother had fallen ill once again and this time had failed to recover. She had passed three months earlier, and her remaining two daughters had both married shortly thereafter. Black Bull had less to anchor him in the great village and, homesick for family and desperate for diversion, had set out to find his daughter and new son.

His face was sad and drawn by the loss and the journey but brightened as the two told of their experiences of the last year. He was especially moved at the news of McKay's death. They had been fast friends, "almost brothers," he told them both.

He grew quiet, staring pensively through the smoke and erupting with the most pitiful cry Ezra had ever heard. "Aaaaaaaaaaaaawwwww!" Moon sidled closer to her father and wept on his chest. The news of her mother, and the deep pain of her father, had broken her.

The three Snakes stayed with the Crow that night, and Black Bull found lodging in the spacious tent of Enrí and Red Calf. Ezra comforted his disconsolate wife, and the two consumed the last bit of rum that had belonged to his father. He massaged her temples until she fell asleep in his arms and, his own energy spent, collapsed beside her.

That night he dreamed strange things—that he and his woman would fight and love and live and have babies. They were wonderful and terrifying dreams, but in the morning, though he could not say why, he sensed it best not to share them. At least not yet. He would know when the proper time arrived.

In the days following Black Bull's arrival, the camp worked hard preparing for the rigors of winter. Hunting parties scavenged for game and found it in abundance. Black Bull's face grew full as food began to taste good again, and Moon relished the times hunting with her father, just as in the old days. They spent many a day away from camp together, arrowing elk and bison and all sorts of game. They butchered and laughed, wiped blood from their knives, and talked of old times and Moon's mother. "Tell me of my mother and the eagle," she said. "You've not told me since I was little." He nodded.

"Well ..." he said, "when you were a little girl I sa—"

"How old was I again, Father?"

"You were only two winters. We believed you would not see three."

"And why not, father?"

"Because you were always running from us. We thought you would get yourself into trouble and no one might find you. We worried much about you."

"And what of the eagle, father? Please."

"Why do you wish to hear this story again, child?"

"Because I want to tell Ezra, and I think I've forgotten parts of it," she said. "He doesn't yet know why I'm called 'Moon.'"

"And why must you tell him?" he asked. She dropped her head and her eyes began to pool. "What is wrong?" he asked.

"It's Ezra. He has bad dreams sometimes ... and will not tell me why. He holds a secret, Father, and I cannot help him. I thought if I tell him about me ... then perhaps ... then perhaps he will tell me what troubles him so. There seems to be a rock between us neither can lift alone."

"Alright," he said, pausing, a glint in his eyes. "One day ... as the moon began to rise ... your mother took you with her to the river to water the horses. She had done this with you many a time. But on that day she had turned her back on you for only a moment ... and you were soon the length of a lodge away. And then ...." His eyes flickered.

"And then what, Father? Don't tease me."

"And then ... then a great eagle saw that you were by yourself and swept down on you. He fastened his talons and tried to lift you ... but you were too heavy and your mother ran you both down and gra—"

"And how did she save me, Father?"

"Well ... she clenched that powerful one's neck in her teeth and bit like the wolf ... 'til he made no more sound." He began to cry. "And that is why you are here today, my child. A brave woman bore a brave daughter who now carries a scar on her face. Finger the scar when you feel fear, my child. Let it remind you that your life with that one you call Ezra ... is no mere accident. You fit him.

"That day your mother became 'Woman Who Bites the Eagle,' and the village named you 'Moon' ... for all this took place under a full moon. Now you may tell your man. And tell him ... you tell him he is stronger than he knows."

After they had finished reminiscing, they resumed their hunt that very afternoon. Black Bull treed a cougar, hoping to kill and skin it for a fine quiver. But the attempt nearly got him killed when his bow shattered in the bitter cold. Despite a misfire from her flintlock, she rescued her father with a well-placed rifle ball through the ribs of the big tom, but not before her father had been slightly mauled. The daughter had become the protector, and Black Bull's pride at his daughter's rescue overcame his own. He boasted of her prowess in the camp to any who might listen.

Few were surprised.

By December it was clear to all. Red Calf was pregnant and growing huge. She and Enrí were ecstatic, though he proudly told all that the two were uncertain of the child's father. "It might be the Cap'n's!" he bragged. Red Calf was less enthusiastic of his candor but soon came around and joined her husband.

"Either way," she stated matter-of-factly, "the father is the finest of men." And that was the end of the matter. Enrí's joy in the odd declaration caused his few detractors to re-evaluate him. Undeniably, he carried a large soul.

33

IN MID-JANUARY, the temperatures plummeted, and game became scarce. It seemed as though even the animals had wandered far, looking for relief from the cold. Ezra joined hunting parties that ranged further as well, desperately seeking anything to shoot. They treed cougar and shot wolves and found the occasional buffalo wallowing in deep drifts. Some even looked for bear dens to plunder, but with little success. The families and single men reluctantly tapped their stores of jerked meat and pemmican and rationed it carefully, calculating their own supply against the breaking of the weather.

Those with families grew deeply concerned. Even the wolves, usually shy to reveal themselves, began harassing horses and mules. Guards were set to protect them, and those headed out beyond the perimeter of the camp were given strict orders to leave at least in pairs. The predators had grown as unpredictable and desperate as the two-leggeds, and in time a quiet, unspoken dread crept into the camp and began to choke hope.

An ever-swelling Red Calf, preparing for bed, was torn by the anguish on her husband's face. She needn't ask the reason. Food was growing scarce, and faces were thin. Children were crying at night and begging for food, and some had begun to slaughter their horses and dogs, with no end in sight.

So, Red Calf did what she did so well. She prayed to her God, who'd spoken to her many times. She prayed boldly and loudly, and when she had finished a look of utter peace swept over her, enough to calm even her distraught husband. Often he'd wished to disabuse her of her strange practices, but felt restrained. That night a thick, sweet, heavy Presence cocooned them, and they both fell deeply asleep. Enrí was quickly gone, but Red Calf dreamed and dreamed.

They awoke the next morning feeling more alive than they had in two months. Red Calf asked Enrí whether she might address the camp—she had a message of hope for them.

"Will you trust me, husband?"

"I know you hear from God, crazy woman. I don't understand, but I trust you. And our people need courage, eh?"

Enrí called for a meeting. Ezra and the men and families poured out of their dwellings, pulling thick robes about them. Cold stung gaunt faces and teared hollow eyes as Enrí lifted his wife onto a log before them all, her big belly swelling the thick robe he had twisted about her, her long black hair fluttering behind her in the bitter thin air.

"Friends ... I have good news I must tell you all. All here are hungry ... Our faces have grown pinched. Our bellies growl like hungry bears, and our children cry at night and ask for food, and we have little to feed them. We eat our spare moccasins and boil them for soup.

"Last night, my husband's face broke my heart. So, I prayed to Creator whom I have come to know. I told him we have need of food, that our children cry ... that we have begun to kill our horses and dogs. And I must tell you this. He spoke to me last night in our tent.

"Last evening, a Magnificent Being with hair like the white buffalo and a face like lightning came to me. His voice was like the rushing of powerful waters, but then ... then it grew quiet, and He whispered to me. He said He is about to answer my cry in a way that will make us swallow our breath, that the weather will break and we will soon have so much food we can give it away to our Snake friends, and that they will replace our horses and dogs. He says He will do all these things to prove that He loves us. And, my friends, He has holes in his hands. This is too much for ..." Her voice broke. "I can speak no more."

Worn out as she was by the prophecy, and wobbling and faint, Enrí swept her off the log and carried her back to their tent, and there she slept for hours. Many in the camp who knew her well took great hope in her words. Others, of a more cynical nature, would wait and see. They would not have long to wait.

The camp conducted its daily affairs as usual that day. Ezra and Moon foraged for game, and men broke ice in the stream to water their animals. But no one slaughtered their animals that day. That day, they lived on the faith of their prophet.

By midmorning of the following day, the sky grew oddly dark, and the wind ceased. The air became strangely still, like heavy snow dropping through deep forest. Some peered out of their lodges and sniffed the air, waiting anxiously, and within the hour the temperature rose nearly twenty degrees. Camp dogs quit yapping and scrounging for food and lay on their bellies. Others slithered on skinny haunches into lodges and huddled close to their masters.

And then it began, slowly at first, an almost imperceptible shaking of the ground. "Did ya feel that?" Ezra asked. Moon nodded and stroked her frightened dog. In minutes, cooking pots shivered and collapsed into fires, the shaking so fierce that most sat down, feeling as though they could not stand. Horses and mules jerked free of picket lines and bolted through the camp, wild-eyed, knocking down all in their path. And then, as quickly as it had come, the shaking stopped. Most continued to sit, and a few grabbed panicked animals. Some prayed. And then, it happened. Again, a faint rumbling. But this was different from the first. It began with a distant crack, like a double-charged rifle shot or the firing of a small cannon, followed by a rumbling and building roar, until someone cried out. A massive shelf of snow had separated itself from the nearest peak and was hurtling toward them at incredible speed.

There was little time to react. Those who could grabbed their wives and children and ran for their lives. Women screamed and all was terrified panic. But not Red Calf. She would not be hurried despite Enrí's protests. Finally, he grabbed her roughly under his bullish arm like a rolled-up robe, shouted, "Dammit woman!" and ran like a man possessed, while she laughed—a serene, child-like look of wonder on her face. He would later conjecture that the shock had driven her mad.

Long moments later, the avalanche slowed and stopped just shy of the camp, less than a hundred yards away. Not a lodge or tent had been touched, nor an animal or human injured. A thick, crystalline curtain hung in the air for minutes, the fine particles settling and covering them all in white, shimmering dust.

And when the air had cleared, the sight in their midst, given what had just happened, left all speechless. A large eagle with a massive white head stood in the center of the camp. He'd been wounded in the cataclysm. His right talon lay useless—the side of his head shorn of feathers. He clamped a fat white winter hare in his left talon and stared about him, seemingly more concerned about his watchers than his prey. Not a soul moved or spoke. The sight, layered on the events of the previous moments, had undone them all.

Oddly, the great bird did not tear his prey but continued his bold stare, and then, as if he had planned it all along, he pumped his massive wings and was gone, leaving the lifeless hare in the center of them all.

In the hour following the avalanche, some ventured beyond the camp, curious of the path of the great snow train. Soon loud shouts and whoops pierced the winter air, and in minutes rifles and smoothbores cracked. Ezra and many others ran toward the noise. What they found was nothing short of biblical.

A very large herd of elk had somehow gotten entwined in the path of the snow, along with at least eighty buffalo with calves and several large bulls. Nearly all were mired up to their chests, encased in the concrete-like snowpack. Some, only their heads protruding from the surface, cried pitifully.

Ezra and Moon grabbed a mule and their knives and ran toward it all, and then the slaughter began in earnest. Even the tough old bulls did not escape. Ezra's mind whirred. *Are we all dreaming?... Oh, Papa ... you woulda loved this! Are you and Mama watchin'? My God ... this is life!* Near-starving people shot their gifts and ate raw heart and liver on the spot. Parents cut slivers and fed their children raw meat as though feeding the camp dogs. Others, more restrained, butchered and loaded the still-steaming treasure onto their horses and dragged the fresh protein back to camp.

There, men and women sliced meat into thin strips and hung them from sapling frames to dry. Others built corrals to secure the meat temporarily from predators until it could be processed, while sentries were posted that night to kill the starving wolves.

Ezra and Enrí thought it good to share their plunder with their Snake friends, and messengers were dispatched. The Snakes returned toward evening and butchered by torchlight, but they were in bad shape and many pitched in to help them. Their meat was laid aside in the far corner of the corral, and at nearly twelve tons worth it would feed them 'til the weather broke. They'd stay the night in the Crow lodges and return to their villages in the morning to bring help to retrieve their meat. But that night, they and all the rest would cook and eat fat buffalo and roast elk steak. And they'd waste nothing.

That evening, the exhausted fell asleep under thick robes and woolen blankets, too spent to consider the surreal events of the day. It had all seemed like a great dream. A prophetess had given them hope of deliverance, and some had believed, but one had never doubted that Creator would vindicate His word to her. She had laughed at the avalanche. Her name was Red Calf.

In the days that followed, the prophecy continued to play out. The grateful Shoshone brought fresh horses to replace those eaten during the starving times. Oddly, some of the camp dogs that had trailed their party seemed reluctant to leave, and their owners bid them adieu. Trappers winked at each other as the Snakes left for their own lodges, leaving their dogs behind them.

Within days, Red Calf left the camp for the shelter of the pines, accompanied by Moon. That afternoon she gave birth to a healthy boy and returned to camp within hours. She'd wanted to go alone, but Enrí insisted that Moon accompany her, armed with two of Ezra's heavy rifles, for wolves were frequent visitors now that the camp was laden with fresh meat. Moon thought her role as escort and midwife a great honor.

Enrí was elated at the sight of his son. His eyes watered as he held the boy aloft in the center of the camp and shouted, his voice breaking, "Has anyone seen a woman and child as handsome as these, eh?" No one countered him. Not a soul dare blunt his joy.

"Hold my boy, Ezra. Feel his strength," Enrí said.

"Ya sure? I might bust him."

"Not so. My little brother needs to hold my boy, doesn't he? He's a bull. You can't break him."

"Your brother?"

"Yeah," he paused. "I couldn't have a finer one." Ezra turned away, wiping his eyes, his mind a steaming pot of feelings. He couldn't speak for long moments, for a man the caliber of Cap'n and Papa had just called him "brother," and it was too much to take in. He would need time.

"Then I'm honored to be your brother," Ezra said. "Give him to me."

Ezra and Moon visited Enrí's tent frequently as the winter returned with fresh vigor. Snow fell deeply, and again temperatures plunged. But while food was no longer a concern, feeding the animals was. Ezra and the others were kept busy breaking ice on the streams for the horses and searching for cottonwood bark for them, now that the snow was too deep for them to scrape clean for grass. But the nights were free of care, and much visiting took place by candlelight. Many made love to their wives, mended clothes, or built new powder horns from the recent buffalo kills.

Moon was captured by the new arrival and held him as much as she could. Ezra could not help but notice her obvious fascination with the child. She calmed him easily, made him smile, and seemed a natural-born mother. The boy, still unnamed, would be soon, the parents promised. They were waiting for just the right name and were in no hurry, assuring all that they would recognize it when it came. And the name did come. One night Ezra asked to hold the child, who fussed mercilessly. At his wit's end, he finally slid the big knife sheath from his belt—the one he had taken from Crow-Killer. He hoped the brightly-dyed quill embroidery would pacify the lad, and it did—immediately.

From that night on, the robust infant stared and mewed and fondled the implement of war whenever he could, so the parents took note and christened their boy War Knife. "It is a good, strong name," they said. "Perfect for a man of distinction," Enrí exclaimed. "He'll be a great one, and needs a good name. This one will do!" The child's mother smiled and nodded.

"Yes. It is a very fitting name."

34

THE MONTHS OF FEBRUARY AND MARCH passed without incident, and Ezra and the men slowly made their way back up the streams in early April. Beaver flowed into camp, and blood and fat stained the snows once more.

Men came home in the evenings soaked and shivering. Some carried a dry set of clothes with them and changed before they arrived back at main camp. Still others led their horses on foot, jogging beside them to warm themselves, desperate to generate heat. Some dreamt of lying with their naked women under warm robes and rising afterward to feast on fat game.

Single men passed the evenings with a smoke and the occasional game of chance. Some told off-color stories and speculated on the chances of finding a fine woman, the likes of Moon or Red Calf, or seeing their new women nude and making babies and growing their own families. The rest, their character less formed and visions less noble, craved riches and encounters with wild women at rendezvous, and very little more.

The camp was home to a mixture of adventurers, exploiters, and explorers, Indians, Whites, some free Blacks, and a few Mexicans. But it had been touched and shaped a bit more than most by strong and just leadership. Ezra thought their camp must surely have a more familial nature than others he had heard of. And while other parties may have had their Jim Bridgers and Smiths and Fitzpatricks, they lacked a prophet who could call down the mountain and flood their camp with meat, or a young man, for that matter, who'd slain the likes of Crow-Killer, or a Mandan woman of eighteen winters who rode down her enemy with the bow—or an act of great kindness.

Yes, Ezra thought. They were a mixed lot, rough as they came. But he'd go to war with any of them.

35

RED CALF WAS TROUBLED, and it grieved Enrí. "What's wrong? Your heart seems clouded."

"I've much I must tell, Enrí, but the words come hard."

"Then say it. Can't abide your silence."

"I had another dream, husband. I ... "

"Yes ... I'm listening."

"I've dreamed things. Things I could not share."

"And?"

"Hard things, Enrí. I'm ... I am going away."

"What?" he quavered. She paused, searching.

"I only know I must leave for a while, and—"

"And what?!"

"And that you must not follow me. The Great One says you must not pursue me. That if you do, you will die and our family'll be destroyed."

"You cannot ask this." He hesitated, tasting vomit. "How're ya to leave then ... and when?" His voice was rough.

"I don't know. I only know I'll return. And husband ... you must do as I say. I think I'll not be gone long, but you must stay here."

"But what about our son? Who'll care for him? He needs a woman's tit!"

"Then put him in the care of Moon. She'll find women to share their breasts. Our son'll be treated like a prized pony."

"But how? ... I'll send men. Ezra'll protect you." Her eyes grew large and fierce. Her voice rose, a bit cool.

"I'll not need an escort, Enrí! Somehow, we'll not choose this thing. The way has been chosen for us. Do not doubt this, husband. If you cannot trust me, then trust Him."

His face hardened and he sulked for the rest of the evening, and when they retired he failed to spoon her, as was his custom. Finally, she backed into him, gently at first, and then with force. "Don't pout. You know I need you!" And then she spun, locked her legs about him, and licked his face like a puppy 'til he broke, laughing.

He confessed that he could not imagine a life without her for even a brief time—that the very thought sickened him but that he had endured many tough times in the past and would bear up again. He vowed to obey her warnings, even if it broke bone.

His confession uncoiled him, and they played lovers.

36

BY EARLY JUNE the streams had cleared. Ezra and the men wore dry clothes again, and the last of the pelts were hung to season before baling them. The privations of winter and the rigor of the cold waters had become a distant memory. War Knife was growing quickly and continued to exhaust his parents. Ezra and Moon visited them almost nightly, and "Uncle" Ezra bounced him on his knee and told him how strong he was.

It also appeared that the identity of his father might never be known. He had a sizeable frame, but his face and temperament were dead ringers for Red Calf. Enri assumed paternity since they had been robbed of a more certain template, eventually consoling himself that he was not meant to know. Some said Red Calf's comfort with mystery was rubbing off on him.

The camp experienced tragedy in mid-June. Four men had left to hunt and were gone for nearly a week, but only two returned—with a heartrending story. All four men had been bitten by a rabid skunk as they slept. Two had fallen ill on the way home. One of them had grown disoriented, despondent, and aggressive. He'd put a pistol to his temple and ended his suffering. The other, equally confused, had waded into the river and drowned. The two remaining men fled home to Red Calf, burning with fever and frantic. There they halted outside the camp and signaled for help with their rifles. Within minutes, Ezra and Moon had arrived and assessed their plight. Half of the group wrote them off as doomed, but not Red Calf.

Ezra asserted before all the rest that the prophet must pray, and this she proceeded to do, but differently than in the past. She was far bolder than any had ever seen. Laying hands on the men, she uttered nine words in her Hidatsa tongue, and then, following a series of odd shudders, both fell to the ground like dead men. Small, yet strong, she grabbed one by the hand and dragged him to his tent, and after some cajoling and scolding from her most concluded that they were safe to touch. Within minutes, both were fast asleep and covered with blankets.

In the morning, the men arose, stiff but sound, their fevers broken, their appetites voracious. They had become walking witnesses to the power of Creator. The Unseen had come down once again and visited their camp.

The long-anticipated rendezvous that summer was a bust. The traders were delayed in arriving, and the crowds eventually dispersed, going their separate ways. But the trappers would be pursued by the traders, who would eventually track them down. Pelts would again be exchanged and goods purchased for the next year, but the carnival-like fair would have to wait until 1832 at Pierre's Hole, as had been arranged. Ezra was disappointed that there would be no horse race for him this year.

The younger, unattached men were especially distraught, some angry as hell and threatening violence for the blunder. Ezra, after hearing of their threatenings, calmly finished his meal and walked boldly to their tent. For an hour they discussed the debacle of the missed rendezvous and who was truly responsible for its absence. He allowed them to flex their anger for a while but never backed down. And the few who had thought him a poor choice for second-in-command had their minds bent a bit. He had come to them, had come alone, and must be carrying some big stones, they reasoned. Little did they know that it took everything in him to pull it off. He had felt the same fear he'd experienced when he performed for the Cap'n's men in the tavern two years back. It was not the fear of physical conflict that spun him, but rather that he might not have the right words and would look a fool. But he had overcome his reticence and felt good that he had.

A few still blamed Enrí and Ezra for the miscue, though they had obviously no culpability for any of it. Their chances of finding a pretty Flathead or Nez Perce woman would have to wait 'til next year.

On a hot summer night, Moon returned to the tent, her face dripping with sweat, her eyes blood-red, clouded with grief. She clutched Ezra and sobbed, and he let her cry it out 'til she could talk. She had just come from Red Calf's tent. There her dear friend had apprised her of the prophecy that only Enrí had known of, that soon she would be "gone" for a time and that she desired Moon to look after her child.

The news gut-punched her. They'd become like sisters, and the thought of losing her friend for even a brief time seemed unbearable. Her only consolation would be in caring for her boy, but she feared that great harm—or worse—might come to Red Calf.

Ezra searched his mind for some consolation for Moon. This seeing her distraught was new to him. He felt sick, helpless. What could he possibly say that would make a bit of difference? He sank into himself, searching, probing. "Aren't you going to say anything?" she pleaded. Again, he said nothing but went for a walk through the trees, desperately seeking relief for the shame that racked him. *Moon needs help ... and I'm no good to her—none at all.* So he stayed away the entire afternoon, racking his brain for answers 'til finally, exhausted and hungry, he headed back to camp, dejected. *I'm leadin' men ... but I got no word for my wife.* And then, like a gentle squeeze of the hand, a tiny stirring of the breeze, it came to him—a canoe paddling up to a drowning man. He picked up his pace.

"She's got a mark on her, Moon. Can't no one touch her 'fore her time," he said. When Moon protested, Ezra spoke strongly. "Stop it! That woman calls down thunder! When has she ever failed us? ... Trust the word of the One who speaks to her, or grief'll send you under. She's comin' back. I'm sure of it! Red Calf'd be grieved, knowing you're so broke up. Moonie, ya know what I'm sayin' is true."

Her chest heaved and she leaned into him, wiping her cheeks. "I want to swim with my husband. Now."

And they did.

37

IN EARLY SEPTEMBER, Ezra and the rest moved higher and set traps. One morning a group of nine Snakes on lathered and stumbling ponies skidded into camp, and they bore unsettling news. A war party of at least forty Blackfoot had burned their camp and stolen their horses. Their men had been out hunting and returned to find everything they loved, gone.

At least twenty men, women, and children had been murdered and scalped, the rest taken captive. The Snakes were delirious with grief and rage and begged for help to recover their people. An immediate meeting was called to decide what should happen, for there was not a moment to spare.

Enrí, Ezra, and the council determined that only a third of the able-bodied and willing could be spared, for the present good weather might encourage raids all along the Snake territory, and their own camp might come under fire soon. But Enrí owed the Snakes their help. They had opened their land and streams to the Whites and were good neighbors, and some men were courting Snake women. It was a simple decision, but not an easy one.

Ezra would lead the party, along with ten of the best White riflemen, a few free Blacks especially handy with smoothbores, and two Mexicans. At least another eight Indians would ride with them, including Crow and a few Iroquois trappers. The Snakes were anxious for revenge. They'd lost friends and family to the fierce northern tribe before and lusted to coat scalping knives with Blackfoot blood.

It was quickly determined that Ezra would be supported by two members of the council, Robert Johns and Ian Davies, both scarred and gristly characters, hard as antler and wise in the ways of battle. Enrí would stay back to protect the remainder of the camp. Having a family had tempered his ardor somewhat, but the thought of leaving the punishment to others still galled him. He longed to rush like Samson into their midst and "pull down their temple around them," he said. But this would be Ezra's call. "Kill those bastards!" Enrí muttered.

The Snakes were outfitted with fresh horses and food, and twenty-two men departed the camp in less than an hour. They stopped along the way by the smoldering ruins of decimated Shoshone lodges, the smoke only partly masking the smell of death and chaos. The gruesome images only refueled the grief and rage of the warriors, and some of the young trappers retched at the sight of the scalped children and women. The few who might have questioned the fight now set their jaws and clutched their own scalping knives. One White snarled like a cornered wolf, "I'm killin ever' one I can!"

Ezra knew the task ahead would be a delicate one and conferred with the veterans. "Forty well-armed Blackfoot ain't surrenderin' their captives without a fight. They got no backin' up in 'em," said Davies. But Ezra owed it to all to act wisely. The Snakes' anger could make them unruly and careless, so he pled with them on the basis of first principles. They'd secure the captives first and only then vent their fury.

He understood the Indians' anger and their predicament. If they didn't administer harsh and swift justice, they'd be thought weak, and this would only encourage further attacks. The Snakes needed to bite their enemy. Hard. Brutally. They had to instill fear. But they needed the trappers. They had few men, and the Blackfoot contingent bristled with them. He pleaded with them for nearly an hour until they finally accepted his plan with great reluctance.

His heart raced at the thought of war. His scalped tingled as he ran his tongue over his rough tooth. *I'm made for this.* And though he didn't enjoy blood, he did relish the contest and the risk of it all, strange mix that it was. So he sharpened his blades, primed his pieces, and met with the council. *Thank God for them,* he thought.

In two days of hard tracking, with the scouts riding the forward flanks, the group found the enemy encampment, just over the next rise and nestled in a stand of pines on the edge of a small creek. The Blackfoot had chosen a good defensive position, surrounded on all sides by open ground and water on the north.

A stalk during daylight was impossible. They'd need to scout the perimeter under cover of darkness, kill the sentries, and quietly lead the horses away. But there were simply too many challenges to surmount without getting the captives killed. No, they would instead follow the camp at some distance, determine its forward trajectory, and wait for the perfect ambush opportunity.

Two days later, their patience paid off. The Blackfoot, thinking they'd given their pursuers the dodge, had grown sloppy. Skirting a tangled deadfall, they rode single file through a deep and narrow creek bed, surrounded by high banks. Davies and Johns flanked them and waited. The Snakes, Crow, and Iroquois were next in line, just forward of the rifles and smoothbores. The riflemen would direct their fire at those leading captives, and while they were reloading the Snakes would rescue any who remained—and only then vent their rage on the rest. Ezra spoke to his council and then strongly to the Snakes. "If ya hope to remain friends and allies," he told them, "ya gotta wait your turn or the captives'll be cut up!" They protested again but finally and reluctantly agreed.

Within a quarter hour, the Blackfoot had fully entered the gauntlet-like creek bottom, and the riflemen had secreted themselves high on the banks behind the trees. And when both ends of the creek were irreparably blocked, Johns let out the gutteral cry of an angry crow—"Caww ca caw caaw!"—and instantly the first shots rang out. Boom ... boom boom b-b-b boom ... boom ba ba boom. The riflemen and free blacks picked their targets and let go nearly all at once. Only one man missed. At once, nearly sixteen men fell from their horses, most mortally wounded or already dead. The rest, about twenty-five, plunged forward at a furious pace, only to find their way blocked by a curtain of arrows and lead.

In desperation, they attempted climbing the banks but found them too steep and fell, plunging backward into the creek, some pinned and crushed beneath their horses. Time stood still for the executed and their executioners. Screams and groans sang the length of the creek bed, and the air grew white with bitter sulpher smoke.

And then the slaughter intensified. The riflemen, having reloaded, again let go a deadly fusillade, mowing down men in machine-like fashion. With murderous efficiency Snakes and a few Crow moved like men possessed, wielding 'hawks and clubs with such force that skulls split and were scalped immediately thereafter, some of the victims still breathing.

One of the captives, a pretty young squaw of the Snakes, was brutally struck down by her captor in sight of her enraged husband. It would be the last blood that Blackfoot ever spilled. For within moments the captor's body had been mutilated by the maddened Snake, running his horse over it repeatedly, 'til the corpse no longer resembled a man—a pulpy mess of feathers, paint, and broken shield.

Within minutes, all of the Blackfoot were dead and scalped, and many were dismembered and mutilated, their bodies plucked clean of weapons and treasure. The Snakes had sent their message. Not a single Blackfoot survived the melee. The corpses would be found eventually by scouting parties, the story pieced together, and the ghastly message delivered. The Snakes had recovered all but one of the captives alive. They had bitten the heel of the great Blackfoot nation, and she would limp for a time, wondering what had happened to her men.

Ezra's mission had been an unqualified success. Only a few Whites had been slightly wounded, and a young, free Black man and the two Mexicans had played the lion and slain several in brutal hand-to-hand combat.

One young man, Skinny Martinez, went nearly mad with grief over a missing woman. She was the White widow of one of the Snake warriors who'd been killed by the Atsina, and she'd remained with the Snakes, alone, for the last six months. Skinny had taken a shine to the auburn-haired beauty, dropping off fresh game and paying her to mend his clothes.

His fellow trappers teased him relentlessly, often chiding him with words like, "Pretty woman like that ain't never gonna care 'bout your skinny ass!" For a while, he partly believed them but continued to care for Mattie, until eventually the most remarkable thing happened. He wore her down, and she began to have feelings for him. However, this only intensified the teasing, for now it was born of jealousy, the most powerful and deadly of all drivers.

On the day of the ambush, Skinny saw a big Blackfoot brave, painted up like Satan himself, sporting one of Mattie's ribbons tied about his neck. Skinny flew at him like a deranged lion and dragged the heavily-muscled man from his horse while playing woodpecker with his 'hawk. He screamed and cried and swung with such force that, long after the man was dead, Ezra ordered someone to drag him off. But Skinny wasn't having it. He growled so fiercely that no one dared touch him, and when his arms locked up and his eyes crossed he fell unconscious onto his victim.

The men pulled him off and laid him on his back, hoping he might revive. But he didn't. Ezra checked for a pulse but, finding finding none, feverishly searched his mind and quickly landed on a distant memory from his father. So, sitting astride Skinny's belly, Ezra delivered three brutal strikes to his chest. And then Skinny gasped, his eyes bursting open, crazed with grief and confusion. Someone shouted, "We ain't found her body yet, Skinny! Don't give up. We ain't!"

Two days later, as the men returned to the Snake camp, they found Mattie. She was very much alive, though suffering badly from exposure and hunger. She had escaped from the Blackfoot after a day on the trail with them and had been wandering ever since. Mattie and Skinny's reunion was poignant in the extreme. Hard men wept.

Enrí never again scolded the men about Skinny and their teasing. He'd earned Mattie's love and displayed his fierceness on the Blackfoot, and he would never again be called Skinny, for the men feared him now. He would be known by his given name, Tomas.

Today Ezra's role had been different. He'd killed only one warrior with his rifle but had strategized the rescue with the help of Davies and Johns. He'd asked for advice, they'd given it, and he'd used it well. And he was proud of himself. *Didn't get out on them skinny branches, Cap'n. Lord, I miss you.* Today, the glory had been shared, the aggrieved satisfied, and the innocent plucked from death. He'd fought little but learned much, especially how to plan and execute the wisdom of his peers.

Ironically the party had plucked over ninety pairs of "raiding moccasins," each loaded with dried meat, from the Blackfoot ponies. Those who had boiled their moccasins for food not many days earlier had just been resupplied in the most unexpected manner. Red Calf's esteem grew.

38

SEVERAL HOURS AFTER THE BATTLE with the Blackfoot, the skies grew dark and the cold rain fell so hard it battered the face. By the third day, Ezra and his troop arrived back at the Snake camp and helped their friends care for the bodies.

The scene was grievous. Wolves had found the camp in their absence and ravaged it, so that the bodies had been picked clean of flesh. The grieving began anew as the rescued attempted to identify the dead. Grown men cried and sat with their friends in silence, until, finally, they left reluctantly. Those departing wished they could kill the Blackfoot again … and again. The satisfaction Ezra had felt over the victory over their enemies, for the time being, anyway, seemed ripped from them all.

On the fifth day, in the early evening, the exhausted men arrived back in camp. Immediately, Ezra sensed something amiss. Few welcomed them, a strange silence hung over the tents, and no one laughed or shouted their greeting. Even the dogs refused to bark as Enrí weakly exited his tent to meet them, a near stagger to his gait.

"What's happened here, Enrí?" Ezra asked. "Somethin' has. I feel it."

"She's gone, Ezra. Red Calf's gone… and so is Crooked Nose. His horse and clothes and weapons are all here. Somehow, his fate's tied to hers."

In the next hour, the story became clear. The day after Ezra's men had left to apprehend the Blackfoot, a hunting party had seen signs of strangers in the area. Crooked Nose had scouted large arcs about the camp for the next two days, until he reported back that he'd detected a sizeable party of Gros Ventre nearly twelve miles to the west. He judged the group to be about sixty men strong and moving in their direction. The Snakes were warned of the intruders, and the camp doubled the number of sentries. And then the rains had come and continued without relief.

One evening, Red Calf had stepped outside her tent to relieve herself in the driving rain and never returned. When the morning came, the storm continued unceasingly. Enrí and others mounted their horses and vainly searched for a trail, but to no end. And then, when the rain had stopped, any sign that might have been, was gone—wiped clean like the inside of a freshly scoured pot.

"What's wrong with these people, Enrí? They act as though someone's died. Don't they know a' Red Calf's dream?"

"I suppose they don't. Not unless she told some before she was taken."

"Well, I mean no disrespect," said Ezra, anger rising, "but you've robbed 'em of hope by not tellin' 'em. They think she's not returnin' and you gotta tell 'em—now! Wake up, my friend! She's comin' back to us. For God's sake, lead us. This ain't you!"

Enrí's face flushed crimson for a moment, and he caught himself. "Only one man ever talked to me like that, little brother. Of course, you're right. I'll tell the camp of her dream within the hour."

Enrí's voice gained strength with his disclosure, and many believed him that Red Calf would return. A few were angry he hadn't shared with them earlier, but most concluded that grief had seriously clouded his judgment.

After morale had been restored, Ezra and his fighters shared the story of the Blackfoot ambush and the rescue of the Snake captives. The camp had lost not a life, except for a single horse so sorely wounded he had to be put down.

Ezra praised the men publicly and said nothing of his own contribution, though it had been indispensable. But the men knew, and they respected him for it. Even the older men recognized his growth. And the younger men, sometimes jealous of him, thought it best to keep their mouths shut, for he was fast becoming a man of power, and someone not to be trifled with.

Moon was heartbroken, nearly as much over the absence of Crooked Nose as for her "sister." She'd come to love her second "father" and feared he would never be found, that some unspeakable violence had overtaken him and his bones lay bleaching in a creek bed somewhere. But Ezra would hear none of it. He believed that Crooked Nose and Red Calf were together, perhaps abducted by an enemy band and moving north up into Canada, away from the wrath of her husband. Moon pressed hard to scout and pursue, but Ezra urged caution. He soon came to believe that the only constraint tethering his wife to the camp was the care of War Knife.

As a half-measure to pacify her, the two met with Enrí and formulated a plan. They mutually concluded that, while Enrí could not be permitted to pursue, they had been given no such prohibitions. Timelines were discussed and strategies considered. They were certain of this: the Big Bellies had been seen in the area just prior to the rains, and they had no love for Enrí. He'd killed three of their number and wounded a fourth, and to take his woman would be for them a powerful act of retaliation. But they might trade her to the Blackfoot out of spite, and God only knew how they might treat her, given Enrí's history with them. Then again, perhaps none of the Big Bellies had recognized her. If that were the case, she might be safer overall until she could work her way back home on her own or with Crooked Nose's help.

Considering possible stratagems exhausted the three. If they chose pursuit, they'd need to leave quickly, before the snows cut off the high passes and turned the whole affair deadly, if not impossible. So, they mulled over ideas for three days until, on the fourth, the decision was made for them. Crooked Nose walked into camp naked, beaten, and limping badly, but very much alive.

Ezra led Crooked Nose through the camp to Enrí's lodge and placed a wool blanket over him. Once there, the grieving giant modeled calm restraint, ordering Crooked Nose to be cared for and fed before even hearing his story. When the man had recovered sufficiently, he gave his account. He had stepped into the darkness on that fateful night, regaining consciousness several hours later, tied wrist-to-ankles over the back of a green filly.

The raiding party were Atsina or Gros Ventre, or Big Bellies, as some called them. He believed them to be from the same party he had detected earlier, roughly sixty strong and painted for war. They had chosen not to attack the camp because of the White marksmen.

One of the Atsina warriors with a splinted arm had recognized Red Calf, and that had sealed her fate. They had captured the wife of the big Frenchman and considered it a great coup. They'd broker her to the Blackfoot.

Crooked Nose had been taken to gain intelligence but told only what he felt would prove of little value, feigning memory loss from the blow to his skull. And when his mind did not "recover," they chose to execute him. But it was at that point that Red Calf had intervened, making an impassioned plea for Crooked Nose's life. "He's beloved among the White trappers," she had asserted, "and they'll avenge his death many times over if he does not return to them." But that would be the least of their worries. The real danger, she skillfully argued, would be from the adopted daughter of Crooked Nose. "She's very big medicine and kills from the shadows with her bow like a witch. You'll never see her coming," she whispered coolly.

She went on to report that the husband of the witch was none other than the slayer of Crow-Killer. She paused and smiled curiously at this last assertion, scanning the faces of her captors. Some of the Big Bellies seemed unnerved by her words and her carefully crafted calm smile. But Crooked Nose had taken hope.

The next morning a course of action had been decided. Crooked Nose would be released, but not before they had beaten him, stripped him naked, and stomped on his foot. They even robbed him of the eagle feather woven into his hair and urinated on him—laughing as they hosed him down. And then he'd begun his hobbling, humbling walk east and south back to camp, at one point driving two wolves, weaponless, from an elk carcass to assuage his gnawing belly.

He had proved himself once again to be the man Moon knew him to be. Within nine days, he had returned, confident that Red Calf was very much up to her "mission." Enrí's desolate spirit rose.

39

IT WAS NEARLY OCTOBER now, and decisions had to be made. The camp was plenty riled up and galled by the abductions. Enrí, of all people, calmed them, assuring them that Red Calf's return would be a matter of waiting it out. Privately, Ezra and the council knew the Big Bellies must pay a price for their arrogance. Failure to retaliate would send a message of weakness the camp could ill afford. Their allies, the Blackfoot, would also learn of the reprisal, and that might purchase a bit of grudging respect as well.

Ezra and nine others, including Crooked Nose and one very angry Mandan she-bear, set out on an early October morning to pursue and punish the Atsina and perhaps retrieve Red Calf if she remained among them. In truth, the punishment was given higher ranking than the rescue.

For none were clear on how Red Calf was to be returned, or whether they should be the instrument. The only certainty was that Enrí was forbidden to participate. And few wished to intervene too early on what seemed to be some sort of sacred mission. They'd find the arrogant Atsina and deal with them, and if Red Calf were not among them most would return home, work their traplines, and wait for it all to play out.

But that was not the mind of Ezra and Moon. They would shadow Red Calf, monitor her progress, and make the fateful decision whether to affect the rescue themselves. Moon longed to humiliate those who had abused and shamed Crooked Nose and stolen her friend. And while Ezra warned her that blood seldom pacified rage, though shedding it might be unavoidable, she was having none of it.

"I'll stick Mandan arrows in Atsina bellies and be the better for it!" she muttered. "I might even take some scalps." She was impervious to his words.

They traveled north for nearly a week, moving quickly and scouting wide on their flanks, cutting sweeping arcs looking for sign. In time, they were deep into Blackfoot country and on high alert, and by the eighth day their pursuit paid off. They found the trail and picked up the pace.

The Atsina were nearly two days distant, and moving quickly as well, despite the rain having made their trail nearly impossible to follow. Their fear of the big Frenchman had not completely abated, and they posted sentries at night and scouts during the day. But then a break came. An Atsina scout was captured as he attempted to flee, his horse brought down by arrows from two Crow pursuers, sparing the report of a rifle. Almost immediately the frightened man began his death song, but he was quickly knocked unconscious and returned to the temporary camp for interrogation.

Red Calf had been traded to the Blackfoot two days earlier, and they knew who she was. They were taking her farther north, perhaps into Canada—"Where she might never be found," the scout insisted. His eyes grew large as he finished his story. The look of courage on Red Calf's face "had been a wonder to us," he said, even when she had been handed over. It had rattled the confidence of the Big Bellies, and they had been glad to see her go.

The need to make decisions pressed hard on them all now. After deliberation, it was decided that only two would continue on—Ezra and his woman. The rest would return home, they said, and wait for their return. But what of the scout they had captured? Some were for killing him—especially the young Mandan. But she was overruled by Crooked Nose, who suggested that they send him back to his people with a message: that the slayer of Crow-Killer and his witch wife were close at hand, ready to kill and scalp those who had stolen their friends, that only the restraining counsel of the Shawnee they had abused was keeping them alive, that any disruption of their mission would bring death to the troublemakers, that many would lose their scalps, and that all who had ever opposed these two were dead.

Crooked Nose made clear the message to the young man, who bravely masked his fear and nodded his understanding. They offered him a horse, and he was gone.

The entire party waited for several hours before they split up, anticipating a retaliation, but it never came. In point of fact, quite the opposite. Three hours after releasing their captive, a delegation of four warriors approached the camp under a flag of truce.

They led a string of nine horses and a splendid, dun-hued stallion. And they made themselves clear. The horses were a peace offering for the abduction of Crooked Nose and of the "crazy" woman. She was "marked," they said, and taking her had been a great blunder. And they hoped the horses would show their contrition. But when they asked to see Ezra and his "witch woman," Moon stepped forward immediately, black pupils dilated with rage, her necklace hanging ominously about her neck. She stared defiantly as they extended their hands and instead grabbed the leads of the horses. Immediately, she handed the dun stallion to Crooked Nose. "Small payment for such contempt," she hissed out in broken Blackfoot.

Ezra conferred with the veterans and then stepped forward and willed himself to shake the hand of their leader. He'd let the Atsina save at least some face. They had humbled themselves, but they were warlike people, and his party was small. Best let 'em feel like men, Ezra reasoned to himself. He shook their hands, nodding his head. He supposed this was enough for the Atsina, who'd seen the scowls of Moon and some of the Whites. They'd been duly warned and chastised.

There'd be no further trouble, he thought, for it had been a wise and solid piece of negotiation. It had been good to allow the veterans to give their counsel. They were his eyes and ears when his experience fell short. *I need 'em, for sure.*

The main party stayed back, though most wanted to continue the pursuit. Ezra and Moon pressed on alone 'til dark, stopping by a tiny stream. There'd be no campfires from now on. They ate pemmican and jerked buffalo, picketed their horses, and fell exhausted under their robes. In the morning, they slept longer than expected. The pace of the last ten days had taken its toll on both them and their horses. "Not movin' today, Moon. Us and the horses ... too damn tired! We'll find a campsite and let the animals rest." It'd be a day to sharpen knives and 'hawks and arrow points and regain their strength.

He told her of his concern for her that she'd grown hard with anger, that her big heart seemed small. "I miss you, Moonie. Not seen your teeth for weeks. We may hafta kill soon ... but don't need to like it. And Lord ... I miss our dance! I need you! She'll be found. Don't know our place in it all, but we'll see her again, and so will Enrí."

She was expressionless, pondering. Her lip quivered. He stepped closer, embracing her tightly. She groaned, her stiff frame buttering into his, tears streaming down her cheeks.

"I've been a fool," she sniffed. "I've been so angry. I've burned to kill those who took her and shamed Crooked Nose. And you know how I feel about him. Yesterday, when the Atsina traded the horses for peace, I was ... angry with you. I wanted to kill them all!"

She sobbed and sobbed. Ezra wiped the tears and kissed her soft cheeks. She leaned in and kissed him back, deeply. He thought about how good and strong it felt to have some answers for her. And how terrible it was to not. He groaned with gratitude that she was back; he had missed her so, and life had been difficult without her. *But she's back ... and I can never... ever lose her like that again.* The hot wash of relief flooded over him strong, whiskey-like.

Within moments, they lay under their robes, their bodies glistening and pistols at the ready. In minutes they lay spent, more content than they had been in weeks. Moon had returned to her man, and to herself.

The morning arrived too soon, and they agreed that the horses needed one more day to recoup themselves. They needed to plan their course of action when they encountered the Blackfoot. What if Red Calf had been taken to Canada, or if she were already nearly home, and they had missed her? And given the object of their pursuit being so unusual, perhaps they might encounter the unexpected, and so they spent the rest of the day mending tack and weapons, making love, and planning multiple scenarios.

But the next morning found a man, woman, and ponies chomping to pursue. They were gone at first light and pressed harder than they were comfortable with. And though they knew that too much haste made detection more likely, the mornings were growing ever more chill, and the prospect of an early winter, coupled with a stalled pursuit, he thought, might be too much for Moon to bear. However, they had the finest of mounts and took a measure of hope in them. "Less'n they surround, don't reckon they'll catch us," Ezra told her, forcing a grin. But in truth, he spoke to console them both, for there was no template for their mission. And they didn't know the country, or what lay ahead—just that it would stretch them both, perhaps rupture the sinews that held them to life itself. They'd be heroes or martyrs. And he saw no other possible outcome. He wished the Cap'n were here. He'd say something wise, like when he gave his counsel before the Hidatsa rescue, "Let wisdom and fury lead ya." Lord, he wished he could hear him now.

Late that afternoon, a break came in the form of the discovery of a trail only several days old, heading deeper into Blackfoot country. They were especially cautious and rode nearly a thousand yards apart, always within sight of each other, each providing an early warning for the other. But the country grew more rugged and cover thicker, forcing them closer together, until they rode as a unit once again, following a group of riders seemingly unconcerned about anyone pursuing them.

Ezra suddenly halted his horse and stood high in his stirrups, sniffing the air, and Moon did the same. They were close now—so close they could scent man and the musk of horses and food. They dismounted their own horses and led them nearly a half-mile away. Hobbling and picketing them, they strung their bows and quickly set out. They could ill afford the report of rifle or pistol, so the bows would have to do. They stuffed spare strings into pockets and knives into their belts.

Within two hours, they had worked their way within earshot of the camp. And hiding themselves in a deadfall, they studied their enemy by spyglass. The party was nearly forty braves strong with one woman. Ezra's heart raced as he handed the glass to Moon. She looked a moment, squeezed his hand, and groaned softly. It was Red Calf!

They glassed for some time and found the security perimeter quite relaxed. Red Calf walked about freely, her captors handing her food, appearing to give her leave. The benign treatment puzzled them as they retreated back to their horses to plan their next moves. They'd come this far and would not ruin a rescue through haste. They owed Enrí as much.

Both slept fitfully that night, keenly aware that the morrow might entail blood. 'Til now, Ezra had seldom worried about battle—or Moon's safety. But this was different. They were deep in enemy country, and thoughts flooded over him that this whole chase might have been reckless and poorly conceived. His mind galloped wildly. If he got Moonie killed, he'd never forgive himself. And all those he loved seemed to die—his parents, Cap'n, Old Thomas ... and then there was Abbie. Poor little Abbie. He hadn't protected them well. How had he been so foolish? His doubts swirled dangerously like a sack full of scalping knives, threatening to bleed him from a thousand different cuts. Perhaps he had not yet learned wisdom well at all. And he, by all accounts, was risking all that he had ... or ever would have.

That night Moon dreamt of coming battle. In her dream, Ezra fell in the thick of a great fight, attempting to save two women, and she was powerless to save him. She woke and sat bolt upright, soaked, her heart pounding hard, struggling for breath. Immediately, they were both awake, words coming fast—a final accounting of what they meant to each other before a possible day of bloody reckoning—a termination of everything, without their ever having had a child. "Moon ... I must tell you somethin'," he choked. "Somethin' no one livin's ever heard. I can't go to my grave keepin' this inside—not tellin' ... my best friend ..."

"What is it, husband?"

"I fear if I tell you ... you will not see me the sa—"

"I know who you are, husband. Nothing could change that."

"Well, this might. I'm about to tell ya what made my papa ... hate me."

"I'm not your father, Ezra," she said.

"I know that."

"Do you?" she asked. He paused, shifting uncomfortably. "Do you really?" Again, Ezra said nothing. "Do you remember when you taught me the rifle, and I listened poorly?" she queried.

"I do."

"And I broke my nose?"

"I'll never forget it," he said.

"Remember what you told me?" He paused.

"But this is diff—"

"No, husband. This is not different. I'll tell you what you said. You said, 'I am never ever leaving.' You do remember, don't you?"

"Yes."

"Well ..." she said, "I'm going nowhere. I have plans to grow old and die with you, so ... tell me what troubles you so." He stared beyond her, eyes opaque. He grabbed her hand and squeezed it hard—a man about to drown clinging fiercely to life.

"Alright...." He swallowed hard. "When I was a little boy ... my father taught me to shoot. He cut down Mama's rifle for me and we hunted together. I was seven years old and killin' game—deer and bear and turkey—and Papa was so proud of me. I suppose we was close as a papa and a boy could be. But then somethin'..." His voice broke. Moon stroked his cheek and he soon started again, faltering, his voice low and moaning, a wounded animal deep in a burrow.

"One day, Papa told me to watch over my little sister. That he was going to visit our neighbor, Reuben—that he'd be back 'fore dark. He said, 'If you two go in the woods, take your rifle with you, boy, and watch over your sister. She'll be safe with you.'" Ezra laid his head in Moon's lap, and she began to stroke his brow. In time, he recovered enough to begin again.

"Abbie begged me to go fishin,' so I said, 'Yeah, little Sis. Let's get us some fish so's when they get home we got a surprise for 'em. Won't that be somethin,' Ab?,' I said. Ab squealed and got the pole, and I picked up my rifle. We headed over the ridge and through the woods ... and then on the way there we stumbled on some blackberries ... and that's—"his voice broke—"when it all went to hell." He stopped and she whispered, gently rubbing his arm,

"Go on."

"So we forgot about fishin' for awhile and startin eatin' berries like starvin' bears, and we were laughin' and spreadin' out ... and she disappeared over a ridge. And then in a little bit I heard her scream my name ... like somethin' was terrible wrong. So I ran at her hard carryin' that damn rifle like her life depended on it ... and when I topped the ridge I saw her being drug off by a young bear. And ..."

"What, husband?" He waved off her question, groaning, his face contorted. She pulled him tight 'til he spoke.

"My rifle misfired. Been in such a fever to fish that my rifle couldn't fire ... 'cause I'd forgot to prime it, and I couldn't save her. That bear drug her into the woods and killed her 'cause I got in a hurry. I got her killed, Moon, and my Papa never forgave me for years ... and he was right not ta, and I've never told nobody 'bout this but you, Moon. And I'm so sorry ya haven't known 'til now. I fear I'll get you killed tomorrow ... just like my sister."

And then he told Moon how her little body had never been found, except for bits of her bloody dress and a shoe. He sobbed again and Moon cradled his head in her lap, and she sobbed along with him.

When morning finally came, they remained just beyond detection, glassing once again. The camp seemed about to move, and the two had little choice but to follow some distance behind, waiting for just the right moment to snatch their prey from them—best done under cover of darkness. So, they followed the camp for three days, waiting patiently for their fortunes to turn.

40

ARLY ON THE FOURTH MORNING, a twig snapped just beyond them in the darkness. Ezra cocked his pistols as Moon gripped her knife. Soon a calm voice called out, "Put down your weapons. They'll not harm you." It was the clear, unmistakable voice of their friend, Red Calf.

So they slowly stood, dropped their robes and lay down their weapons as the first rays of dawn raked through the trees. Surrounding them stood nearly forty fierce-looking men.

"Pack your camp, my friends. We'll join the Blackfoot. I'll make plain what is happening here … soon. Don't be afraid. Trust me." She grinned, her eyes a-twinkle. "I knew you were coming!" She pressed them for patience, for all would be explained soon, she assured them, insisting that it was too fine a story to tell quickly. Rather, she babbled on excitedly about the fine elk and bear stew that awaited them for breakfast, that the Blackfoot used some unknown herbs to season their stew that made it especially tasty. She seemed totally unconcerned about her "plight."

After they had eaten, the warriors returned their weapons and property and retrieved their horses. It was only then that Red Calf told her unusual tale. The three went for a walk beside a narrow river and sat down on its graveled bank. There she told of being sold by the Atsina to her captors for six horses and a smoothbore, for the Blackfoot thought her an "especially pretty woman," she laughed, and felt she could be bartered for even more in Canada. But then the "dream came," she said. And after that, the "broken legs."

She'd had a dream shortly after her trade to the Blackfoot, making clear the reason for her abduction. She was here, she shared, to barter a truce with the Blackfoot on behalf of Enrí and his camp—for him and his camp only. The Splendid Being with hair like the white buffalo and holes in his hands had told her that this was what "she had been born for," that she must tell the elders of the Blackfoot that it was time to stop the bloodshed with Enrí and his people. She was to tell them that Creator had sent her, that their refusal to listen would only bring more death, and that more Blackfoot children would live without fathers.

She had shared this message with her captors, but they had received her report badly. They had mocked her and struck her hard across the face. On the morning after her abuse—she carrying a black eye—a young warrior had been carried into camp, more dead than alive. His horse had fallen on him while descending a steep grade. Both his legs had bones protruding from the thighs, and his chest had been nearly flattened. When he arrived, they laid him out and all watched his life force leak away.

They had stood by helpless, except for Red Calf. She had hesitated for a moment and then strode defiantly toward the young man, tears in her eyes. Kneeling down, she placed her hands on the lifeless form and prayed most passionately to the Being of her dreams. For several minutes her fevered words had stung the air, and then without notice she had leapt to her feet, hands on hips, and snarled, "No!"

And then, she recalled, it had happened. As though pulled by unseen hands, both legs had straightened, the bones had slid back into his thighs, and the wounds had filled with fresh flesh as the stunned gawkers looked on. And then came the flattened chest ballooning back to full form as the young man coughed twice, opened his eyes, and lapsed into an exhausted sleep. And when he awakened, all evidence of trauma had left him. "Oh my, you two!" Red Calf enthused, "it was something to see. The air was filled with the smell of lightning and sweet flowers. The Blackfoot men shook and I laughed … and cried. None of us could speak at all!"

Her fortunes had pivoted that morning, and now Red Calf's relationship with her hosts was one of much standing. She had "very big medicine," they whispered among themselves, and they feared her. Though she was not much older than most of them, they quickly christened her "mother," treated her bruised face, and gave her the choicest pieces of venison.

But she was quick to remind them of her purpose with them. They were to transport her to the Blackfoot elders so she might deliver her message, and they must do it quickly so she could be escorted back to her people before the snows came. They seemed shame-faced over her mistreatment, and gave her a stunning chestnut mare to keep as her own. And they would see to her mission, they pledged.

Ezra and Moon noted that they too, were treated with great deference. He caught the men several times staring at his knife and Moon's bear-claw necklace.

Red Calf had made certain their reputation preceded them, and he was glad, for he couldn't help but see the admiring, lustful glances at his wife. "See how they're looking at you, Moonie?" He poked her, chuckling. But he couldn't blame them. She was something, alright. His life had come a long way in the last several years. He'd encountered battle successfully and acquired the most fetching she-bear of a wife. It seemed to him as though his life were charmed—a most excellent roasted buffalo hump of sorts, drizzled in Four Bears' fresh honey. *God, how I love this, and nearly everything about it—even here!*

They decamped later that morning and continued north. The mountains and the rivers were growing ever more jagged and swift, and the beauty caught in his throat. Ezra whispered to Moon, however, "I think we're being watched."

By morning of the fourth day, the riders began to hear a faint roar in the distance, like a heavy wind in the tops of the trees. Two hours later, the mystery was solved. They were approaching a massive cataract, a waterfall of such height and mass that it roared like some prairie storm, the kind that'd sweep a bull off his feet. They maintained a distance of nearly half a mile and established camp. The Blackfoot sent out messengers to four local chiefs, who would arrive within not more than three days. When they did, Red Calf was to deliver her message.

Within three days, three big men arrived, followed by a fourth on the following day. On the evening of the fourth day, women arrived with hide lodges and erected an especially large one in the center of the camp. Red Calf and her friends were invited to attend a meeting that evening in that same lodge.

Two prominent braves, the four war chiefs in their upswept eagle bonnets, and the three friends sat around a cooking fire over which hung a brass pot of elk stew. For some time no one spoke as horns dipped into the steaming mess. The food seemed to soften the awkwardness, and finally one grizzled chief broke the silence in remarkably fluent English.

"I am Pounds-Like-A-Fist," he said, and proceeded to introduce the others in turn. He grew silent, sliding the most beautiful of pipes from an ornately quilled otter-skin bag. Shortly after, the ritual of the passed pipe began in earnest, finally reaching Red Calf.

She paused, but Pounds-Like-A-Fist beckoned her to smoke. "We have heard of you," he explained, "and believe you're a great medicine woman." She nodded and put the pipe to her lips. Ezra's breath caught, remembering his first smoke with the captain. But he need not have worried. She handled the pipe expertly. The old chief, had he hoped for some amusement, was disappointed, and Ezra smiled at her performance. It was no wonder Enrí was so taken with her.

And now Pounds-Like-A-Fist gave Red Calf the lodge floor, as it were, and she commanded it for nearly an hour, forcefully pleading her cause, padding down the grass floor with her tiny feet, flitting back and forth, fiercely animated. And when she had finished, she sat down and stared straight into the coals, sweat on her upper lip, her face serene as a mountain pool. No one spoke.

Finally, several inquired as to the identities of Ezra and Moon and why they were there.

Ezra extended his hand and began his introductions: "My name is Ezra ... and this is my woman, Moon. I've been living with the Mandan and later in the camp of the red-hair you hate. I've become close friends to him and his woman. That's what brung us here. We came to steal her away ... but it seems ... it seems you have stolen us first." The chief smiled wryly.

"We trust you will be kind," Ezra said, "and let us keep our hair."

This last thing amused the chief no end. He grabbed his belly and laughed, and after translating to the rest the other Blackfoot joined him. Finally he spoke. "You've nothing to fear from us, though we could kill you all if we wished ... but we do not wish. We have heard much of you two and think it wise to leave you ... untouched."

"I think that's a good plan, sir," Ezra said, grinning, extending his hand.

"Yes," said the chief, smiling back. "I see how you would."

The Blackfoot were obviously captivated by them, and one chief of nearly forty years asked Ezra, "Would you trade your wife? She's a sturdy and pretty woman and will make fine babies."

Ezra, acting the diplomat and acknowledging the man's report, fired back, grinning, "I've reserved this pretty one for myself and have plans to make my own fine babies." The man nodded and Pounds-Like-A-Fist grinned. Ezra's quick wit had been duly noted.

After the pipe had passed again and the stew pot wiped clean, all retired for the night in the big lodge. And while nothing had been determined with regard to Red Calf's plea, she seemed not the least disappointed by the lack of resolution. Her spirits were high. She had done all that had been asked of her, and she was properly satisfied. And coming had not been her idea in the first place.

41

IN THE MORNING, the chiefs asked for privacy, and the three "guests" vacated the lodge. In less than an hour, they were called back in and given the chiefs' verdict. They unanimously believed Red Calf's words to be sound and confessed that they were weary of war with Enrí and the burial of their children in an endless blood feud. But they were even more moved by the strong mystery of Enrí's wife, believing that her words deserved far more consideration because of who she was. "We fear to let your counsel drop to the ground," they said. And they promised to return to their villages and plead her cause to their people. "We'll tell of the strong words of the woman who stops death with her prayers."

The chiefs departed within the hour, but the rest of the camp lingered for some time, although by noon half of them had packed and were gone. Two proud-looking warriors were chosen to escort Red Calf back home, and as they readied her new horse Ezra unpacked a small clay pipe and crammed it with tobacco. The two women sat beside him, and his tiny pipe passed among them as his powerful arms drew them both close.

For a while—a good long while—not a word was spoken as they savored the moment as the best of friends, celebrating the end of the most unusual of missions. They chortled like children, drafted deeply, and re-filled the little pipe several times, smoking again and again until they were all light-headed. He embraced the two women once more. But this time his voice lowered and he tightened his jaws. "Listen up … and hear me," he whispered. "We're bein' watched. I feel it. And it don't feel right. I'll saddle the rest of the horses while you both sit here and pretend all's good. Red Calf's escape must not be stopped. It's why we came!"

Within minutes, all of the horses had been saddled and packed, and the two escorts informed them that they were ready to leave. Immediately, Red Calf was in the saddle and following her escorts, when the first shots rang out from the perimeters. Five Blackfoot fell dead or wounded at the first blast.

Ezra screamed at Red Calf, "Run! ... run!!!" and then they were gone, battering through the perimeter of those left reloading their guns. The remaining Blackfoot were heard shouting "Cree, Cree!" as the Blackfoot ran for their weapons, returning fire frantically—fighting for their lives and their scalps.

Ezra and Moon strung their bows in the chaos as the whistle of balls and the zip of feathers flashed about their heads. Ezra's mind slowed and his hearing dampened from the shock. Instantly he was all feeling and reflexes, which, like the friends of all who fight for their lives, gripped his hands and his feet, and now he was one with the ebb and flow of the slaughter, running toward the booms and the belching smoke blanketing the enemy. He fired both pistols at close range, dropping one attacker and disabling a second.

They shot and ducked and weaved until their quivers were nearly empty, and it quickly became clear that the Blackfoot were outnumbered. Ezra had not the time to think in those first few moments, but now hard reality flashed before him clearly. *Are we dyin' today? Is this the way it's gonna happen? I can't let 'em scalp Moon ... Grab her and run!*

And then the two, left with little option, sprinted furiously toward the mist and the noise of the great waters. But they hadn't run more than a quarter mile when their escape was noted by the Cree, and a vicious chase ensued. So, they raced toward the falls and hid behind a rock on the very edge. Ezra peered into the chasm but couldn't see through the swirling mist, noting only that the river in the distance cut deeply into the valley floor. And a jump would likely kill them both.

They checked their quivers and discovered only eight arrows between them; using them quickly, they poured their fury downrange into the soft flesh of their enemies. The Cree suffered much in their rush. They swarmed their position, and soon the two were taking wounds, the rock too agonizingly small to conceal them both. A ball struck Moon in the shoulder, leaving her left arm dangling. She groaned as a second creased her skull, plowing scalp and bone. A third took the last joint of her little finger, and she cried out in rage, "Aaaaawww!" Ezra's mind slowed enough for his own rage to surface. He could take a wounding, but they could not have her. *They will not have her.* "This will not happen," he moaned. "We ain't missing all the special words spoken over me. If I ever needed You, Lord ... it's now or nothin'."

He drew Moon to him. Blood gushed down her neck, and her eyes began curling upward. A fourth heavy ball pounded his forearm, spinning him partly around, and an arrow buried itself deep in his upper thigh. "Not like this," he screamed. "Not now!"

He grabbed Moon tightly about the waist and leapt into the mist.

Epilogue

In early December, a small party of three riders rode into camp, past the sentries in the driving snow. It was Red Calf and the two Blackfoot. They were immediately ushered into Enrí's tent. He was so overcome by her arrival that the presence of his implacable enemies went almost unnoticed. It was cold, and the last half of their journey had been a running battle against the weather, staying "just ahead of the worst of it," she reported. But they were here now, weak and ravenous, and very much alive.

Red Calf's admirers brought their best victuals for them to eat, and she doted on the Blackfoot escort with mounds of hot food. They understandably were alarmed by the presence of Enrí, but upon hearing the story of Red Calf play out, the big man uncoiled, and they sensed it. "Bring these men more food!" he bellowed. Then he asked of the whereabouts of Ezra, Moon, Crooked Nose, Black Bull, and the White trappers. Had she seen any of them?

Her face grew puzzled. It was then that she told of Ezra and Moon's escort to meet with the Blackfoot chieftains and of how she'd escaped from the Cree encirclement with her bodyguard. "I saw no one, husband, other than our two friends. But Ezra thought we were being watched."

Enrí was excited to hear that the Blackfoot were pondering peace but seemed more enchanted by the return of his woman than the story of her rescue. She was back, a little lighter from her journey, but as compelling as ever. Speech failed him. He gazed at her as if she were a ghost, and tears welled in his blue eyes, forcing him from the tent twice to regain his composure. "Oh, my God! ... Jesus in heaven! ... Oh, my God!" he cried, over and over again.

Red Calf was as excited to see her man as he her. She rose from her seat and rushed on him, wrapping her lean legs about his waist and kissing him fiercely. He held her aloft like a child. The Blackfoot, unperturbed and calm as trout, ate on like ravenous wolves.

And then War Knife was brought by one of his wet nurses from an adjacent lodge and handed to his mother. The joy on her face was otherworldly.

Eight days after Red Calf's arrival, the trappers arrived back at camp. They were haggard and spent from the journey and the struggle of the snows. They had shadowed Ezra and Moon, they reported, "clean up to the battle of the Cree and the Blackfoot," and had come upon the melee just as the Cree had driven the couple to the great waterfall, shot them, and driven them over the edge. "No one could have survived that fall." On that point, most agreed. "Not even those two." The dead, though, had wrought havoc among the Cree. The trappers had found their painted arrows in many of the slain and dying.

The trappers and the two fathers had killed many Cree after that, and all were heartbroken that they had not arrived in time to save the beloved couple. Crooked Nose and Black Bull refused to leave until they had found and buried their bodies and retrieved their horses. The returned trappers had little doubt the Blackfoot would care for the two grieving fathers for the winter, for the duo had helped rescue their own people and would otherwise have been trapped in the winter snows by now. A small number of them could be heard, arguing amongst themselves, "Not them two. Don't care what we seen. I ain't believin it 'til we find 'em."

For her part, Red Calf was deeply troubled by the absence of Ezra and Moon, sensing more than most the pall of grief, like a smoky black robe, that hung over the camp. The laughter seemed to have left them all. Their two shinin' ones were gone.

She was tortured for weeks. The two missing—she could not say "dead"—were not only dear friends but had walked in a deep mystery of sorts that even those who knew them for a short time, envied. They had burned brightly in their brief lives—shooting stars that lit up the sky and then tragically fell, consumed by their own heat and the friction that grabs all things that oppose it.

So yes, she was troubled—troubled that she hadn't seen it coming when she'd seen so much before and warned others of danger, troubled that perhaps she could have warned them but failed, and troubled that they had been taken trying to save her. For weeks she slept poorly, tearing her bed with moans and fits and night sweats, praying for answers and finding nothing but a great hollow space deserted by her Maker, feeling abandoned to the dark night of the soul and waking her poor, helpless Enrí every night in anguish, nearly as deep as her own.

But then one morning …

— End of Book One —

www.ingramcontent.com/pod-product-compliance
Lightning Source LLC
LaVergne TN
LVHW012012060526
838201LV00061B/4275